The train had picked up speed. She released her grip on the open door, closed her eyes, and hurled herself toward the rushing ground. She waited for the shock and the impact. There was none.

She was being held in a steely grip. Someone was speaking in her ear. The tears she had fought down rose again, and she was suddenly weeping.

"If you must cry, you know, it's best not to do it alone."

She turned and looked up, and through her shock and anguish she was aware of another sensation. It jolted her and she caught her breath. She collapsed against his shoulder.

"It's true, we don't know one another. But you can do me a service."

She raised her head, tears still wet on her cheeks, and was startled again by the stern masculine beauty of his face. This new feeling running through her was powerful and frightening: the tug of her own womanhood, aroused by this strange and beautiful man.

But she couldn't quite believe what he was saying.

"Yes . . . I find it difficult to cry myself. You can do it for both of us."

THE FAR SIDE OF DESTINY

Dore Mullen

A DELL BOOK

Published by
Dell Publishing Co., Inc.
1 Dag Hammarskjold Plaza
New York, New York 10017

Dell ® TM 681510, Dell Publishing Co., Inc.

ISBN: 0-440-12645-2

Printed in the United States of America

First printing—January 1979

For Don, who wrote the music

Chapter 1

Daria Petrovna, wrapped in her sheepskin and wearing her fur hat and gloves, stepped out onto the log porch of the *izba*. The shocking cold struck her face like a blow, and automatically, from long habit, she took shallow breaths to keep it from stabbing her lungs. Thank God there was no wind. It was the only thing that kept the cold bearable in this part of eastern Siberia, this still, dry air, with no wind. The village of Saravenko stretched before her: a lonely icy road, lit by starlight, and two rows of log huts like her own izba, and straggling wooden fences, and beyond them, snow-covered fields rolling away into the distance. Above the village, cold white stars looked down from a black velvet sky onto the cottages dwarfed against the snow.

In her mind she was saying good-bye. Her small vivid face beneath the fur hat was set with determination; her huge dark eyes were clouded with fear and excitement. Daria, at twenty, was a slender dark flame of a girl, with the tzigane heritage of her gypsy grandmother showing clearly in her vivid beauty, her tumbling black curls and enormous dark eyes, her slim waist and high full breasts. In years and in body she was a woman, but she had yet to explore the meaning of her own womanhood. Perhaps that lay before her, she thought. But destiny was always veiled in darkness. Like this dark, starlit night in Saravenko.

It was strange, she thought, to realize you might never see your home again. All those familiar fragrances of the cottage you knew so well—scrubbed pinewood and clean cotton sheets . . . hot tea bubbling and hissing in the samovar on the wooden table . . . the smell of burning logs from the great tile stove in the corner of the room. Good-bye, Saravenko.

She and her grandfather had to leave. It wasn't safe to remain. In this revolutionary year of 1918 tempers were high and passions were aroused in the village. Old grudges had come to life. The Bolshevik Revolution had taken place in November. Now it was March, but the word had just arrived from the Council of People's Commissars in Petrograd that the land now belonged to the peasants. And the *muzhiks* were calling for bloody vengeance. Destroy the landlords' houses! Fly The Red Rooster of Flames! Seize the land!

Her grandfather, Alexey Alexeyevitch, was pleading for moderation. *It's time to build, not destroy. Don't burn down the houses. We can use them for schools, meeting halls . . .*

But her grandfather wasn't trusted in Saravenko. The peasants had taken his advice thirteen years ago, in 1905. *Subscribe to the socialist newspaper. Write a petition, present it to the landlord, ask for justice . . .* Thirteen years ago the revolution had failed, and Mikhail Efimovitch's son had been shot to death in front of the church. There had been floggings and reprisals. Now Alexey Alexeyevitch was being called an enemy of the people, reawakening the old bitterness.

We're still outsiders, Daria thought, waiting for Alexey to join her on the porch. Dedushka and I have never really been accepted.

She herself had been born in Moscow, although she'd been brought to Saravenko as an infant, just before her mother's death. Her grandfather was a political exile. He was an intellectual, an alien, a man who read books and thought strange thoughts. Even after years in Siberia, he was regarded with suspicion.

These were dangerous, uncertain times.

And tonight there was a train at Chita Station. They had to board it. Safety lay in Harbin, in Manchuria. Chita was only twelve versts away, a two-hour journey by horse-drawn carriage. If they were in time to board the train, they would cross the border tonight to Manchuli, and from there the

Chinese Eastern Railway would take them to Harbin. It was the only choice.

Alexey Alexeyevitch stepped onto the porch. "Come, Daria, we mustn't keep Lev Omansky waiting. It's my fault, I know. I'm old, and I'm slow, and I make people wait . . ."

"No, Dedushka, that's not true!"

He smiled gently, looking into her face. "Yes, it's true. Just an old village schoolmaster with one comfort to his name: his beautiful granddaughter."

"Oh, what nonsense!" With a rush of love and affection, she took hold of his arm. "But you're right, we'd better hurry."

There were no longer any schedules on the Trans-Siberian Railway. This train would be the first one in nine days. If Lev Omansky was right, and it was truly on its way to Chita Station . . .

Lev himself was waiting for them in the *tarantas*, a boat-shaped carriage without springs, lined with straw, hitched with wooden poles to a horse that stood patiently shaking its head from side to side, its breath steaming white against the darkness.

Daria looked up and met Lev's troubled gaze. "Are you all ready?" he asked.

"Yes, Lev, we're ready."

Lev Aronovitch Omansky had come to Saravenko five weeks ago from Kiev with his comrade Yuri, to organize the peasants' soviet. Since then Daria had come to know him well. Each of them was lonely, in a different way, and perhaps it was natural, she thought, that they had become friends. She studied his face in the shadowy starlight, thin and serious, with a lock of straight brown hair escaped from his cap and falling over his forehead, and worried blue eyes. He looked very young, and she wondered suddenly what she felt for him. Friendship? Love? What was it like to fall in love? She'd never known anyone like Lev. So intense, so committed to his beliefs. All his words vibrated with the passion of his commitment.

Except for the night they'd met. That night his voice had been taut with the urgency of fear.

Lev hadn't been with Yuri that night. He'd been alone. He'd been hunted and desperate as he stood on the wooden porch of the izba, shivering and grim-faced, his lips white with cold, ice crystals glinting along his eyebrows.

She remembered it vividly. She and Alexey had been sitting at the table. Alexey had been reading a book of poetry, and she was mending socks. The izba was quiet; the only sounds were the hiss of the samovar, the rustle of pages, and the snapping of logs in the big tile stove.

Then the pounding started at the door.

Bang. Bang. Bang.

She put the mending down in her lap. "Dedushka," she said quietly, "are you expecting someone?"

Bang. Bangbang.

Ivan the Simple came twice a week for a reading lesson, sitting with a puzzled frown on his face as he traced the letters in a child's primer with his big fingers and shuffled his long legs under the table. But this was past the hour for Ivan the Simple. And there was a desperate sound to the pounding at the door.

"No," Alexey answered, closing his book. "But perhaps we'd better see who it is."

She nodded and stood up, controlling a sudden tremor of anxiety. In these days, in these times, a pounding at the door could be ominous. Even here, in a remote Siberian village. Daria knew that. Civil war was coming; everyone said so; and if it came, what would happen to villages like Saravenko? You tried not to think about it, but you couldn't help it. You heard predictions of horror; of savage fighting to come between Cossacks and partisans, with peasants and villagers trapped in the middle, and flaming izbas, screams of terror, and blood on the snow.

You tried not to listen. Still, when someone pounded at your door, in that desperate way—

She went to the door and pulled it open.

Lev Omansky stood staring at her with hunted eyes.

But he wasn't Lev Omansky, then. He was only a strange young man in a sheepskin jacket and fur hat, half-frozen, his eyes begging for help.

"What's wrong?" she asked gently. "Are you in trouble?"

He didn't answer, only stared. She brushed self-consciously at her hair. It was unnerving to be stared at that way. "Come in, please," she said. "You're very cold."

Blasts of frigid air were sweeping in through the open door.

He spoke finally.

"I think I'd better tell you that I'm being followed." His voice was low and taut. "I was seen leaving the train. It's probably dangerous to invite me in."

"Tell us about it over a glass of tea."

It was Alexey's voice. The old man had come to the door, the book still in his hand, and was gazing curiously at the stranger.

After a moment the young man nodded and stepped inside. His eyes widened as the warmth of the izba wrapped itself around him, and the pinched look began to soften from his face. Daria closed the door.

"I don't understand," she said. "How could you leave the train? We're twelve versts from Chita—that's the nearest station."

"Jumped."

"At the bend in the track," Alexey said. "When the train slowed down."

The young man nodded again. "I was planning to leave at Chita. There's a friend waiting to meet me at Chita Station. But I couldn't take the chance. They were questioning all the passengers on the train. Somebody told the Cossacks a revolutionary spy was on board. They would have found me pretty damn quick."

"Ah. Cossacks."

The feeling was bitter these days between Bolshevik commissars and Cossack counterrevolutionaries. Already civil war was breaking out all over Russia, like brushfires. Soon the country would be in flames.

The young man sighed and sat down at the table. His boots were dripping, making a puddle of water on the floor, and melted ice was running from his eyebrows. "My name is Lev Omansky," he said. "I've been traveling east from Kiev on the Trans-Siberian line. But at Novocherkassk they added boxcars for Cossacks and their mounts. And after that—well, it was only a matter of time. I was lucky to get this far."

"Are you sure you were followed?"

"Almost certain."

Daria stepped forward. "Do they know what you look like?"

"No, I don't think so."

She bit her lip. "You'd better take off your jacket and hat and dry your face. I'll mop the floor. You mustn't look as though you've just come in from outdoors."

"We must hide him, Daria," Alexey murmured.

"Where, Dedushka? We have no hiding place."

Lev Omansky gazed around the izba, with its benches flanking the glowing stove and its row of bookcases bright with color along one wall. "You have so many books. I wouldn't expect . . ."

"I'm the schoolmaster."

Lev stood up and stripped off his jacket, and then wiped a hand down his dripping face. Daria frowned.

"City clothes," she said, half to herself. "Around here people don't wear that sort of jacket and shirt. You'll have to change into something of my grandfather's." She turned to Alexey. "An embroidered blouse, a pair of homemade trousers. A rope belt. And an axe to swing from it, so he looks like a villager. But we'll have to move quickly."

"What are you thinking of, Daria?"

"Ivan the Simple, Dedushka! He can pretend to be Ivan! Let him sit at the table and read the primer with you. If he can convince the Cossacks he's simpleminded, perhaps they'll go away. The train won't wait forever while they search for a spy. They'll have to give up after a while!"

"Yes. Perhaps . . . it might work." The light of agreement dawned in Alexey's eyes. "That is, if he can be convincing."

They both stared at Lev Omansky.

The young man from Kiev suddenly laughed. "You don't even know me, but you're willing to help me. All right, I'll do my best!"

Daria saw intelligence and humor written across Lev's thin face. Now that his cap was off and rumpled brown hair was tumbling over his forehead and he was relaxing in the warmth of the stove, it was clear that he was quick-witted. His voice disclosed a good education. His blue eyes were direct and honest. And there was a curious softness in his expression as he looked at her.

Could he impersonate a simpleminded Siberian village boy?

Yes, as it turned out, he could.

She still remembered the sweating, fearful tension of the moment when the two Cossack officers arrived in the izba, stamping their boots on the wooden floor and filling the room with their frowning broad-shouldered menace. Oh, God. It had seemed like forever. Lev sat at the table beside Alexey, just as Ivan the Simple would do, puzzling over the words in the child's schoolbook spread out before him. When he raised his head to look at the new arrivals, he wore a foolish, expectant smile. His blue eyes were hopeful as he struggled to understand the questions being asked.

"We're looking for a Bolshevik traitor! Have you seen him?"

"No, Your Honor. I'm only a schoolmaster. This is my pupil, Ivan Ivanovitch. And my granddaughter, Daria Petrovna."

"Your pupil?"

"Yes, Your Honor. As you see, he understands little of what goes on." Alexey patted Lev's shoulder fondly. "But we are making progress."

The Cossack narrowed his eyes.

Daria felt perspiration trickling down her sides, but she kept her face calm as she stepped forward.

"May I offer you some tea?" she asked politely. "It's very good tea—sweet, and steaming hot—"

"Keep your stinking tea!"

They had other cottages to search and no time to waste. They made up their minds quickly. They wheeled around and left.

Tension melted as the door slammed. It had worked.

Later, after he'd eaten, Lev himself stood at the door, looking down into Daria's face. He would borrow a horse from the stable behind Vladimir Ilyich's blacksmith shop.

"I have to meet Yuri in Chita. But I'll be back, Daria."

She nodded.

"Tomorrow."

She nodded again. She was growing uncomfortably aware of the tenderness in his eyes, and she wondered if it was only gratitude he felt. But they'd only just met! It couldn't be anything else. Could it?

And what of herself? There had never been anyone like Lev in Saravenko.

Five weeks later the situation had changed, terrifyingly, and Alexey Alexeyevitch himself was in danger. She still didn't understand her feeling for Lev Omansky, but time had run out. Lev had sat at her table, as he'd done so often in the past weeks, cradling a glass of hot tea in his hands. His face was miserable. "Daria, you know I'm here for a purpose: to struggle against the counterrevolution. Do you know how long it takes to win the muzhiks to our side in a remote village like Saravenko?"

"I know, Lev."

"I'd do anything to help you and Alexey. Anything in my power. But I can't stop revolutionary action! No matter what the spark is, the revolutionary flame mustn't be extinguished. Do you understand that?"

"Yes. I think so."

And Alexey is the spark, she thought. In Lev's mind politics came first. Perhaps it always would.

But he was torn. He looked down unhappily at the table. "You know I can't come with you across the border. My work is here, in Siberia. But some day, Daria—if you go—I'll meet you in Harbin. I promise you that."

Now, standing by the *tarantas* in the cold starry night, she wondered if he was thinking of that promise.

It was time to start. Alexey climbed up front next to Lev. Daria settled herself in the straw in the back and wrapped herself in the bearskin blanket she found there. She knew the road to Chita was rutted and icy. You would feel every rut, every bump, but she was used to it, she'd ridden in the tarantas many times before. There would be no conversation. They would need all their energy just to keep warm.

They set off in the direction of Chita, jolting, bumping, creaking. They were traveling east, toward the hills that loomed in the distance, crowned with the spiky shapes of pine trees black against the black sky. Chita was beyond the hills. As they left the village behind, balls of ice formed beneath the horse's hooves and rolled away across the snow with a noise like crackling glass.

Daria looked up at the sky, very clear and black and far away, with ice-white stars. No clouds. There were never

14

any clouds on a cold still night like this. It hadn't snowed for a week. Was she really leaving? How often had she dreamed of going away from Saravenko on the train? She had dreamed of it. But not like this, not in fear and haste . . . and not to Manchuria. She had dreamed of Petrograd or Moscow.

It was always in the summer that she would daydream, the short, hot Siberian summer, lying in the fragrant grass of the meadow by the railroad track. She would hear the world calling to her from somewhere west of the Urals, somewhere beyond the endless rolling steppes. She would gaze along the tracks, waiting for the train to arrive, seeing the telegraph poles stretching off into the distance and vanishing over the horizon, until she heard the faint, faraway rumble of the train, coming closer and closer, then speeding out of the east to thunder by with a roar and a hissing of steam until it disappeared over the edge of the world, leaving her alone in the tall waving grass, wondering when she would leave Saravenko.

Now. Tonight.

They were passing between ridges of hills that rose on either side of the road, thickly covered with birch and pine trees. The hills loomed overhead in a gentle upward slope, blotting out part of the sky.

Aaaooowww . . .

Daria started. That was a wolf howl, she thought. It came from the trees. Why were the wolves howling? Maybe one of the pack had gotten lost, and the others were calling it home. Maybe they sensed the tarantas passing and felt restless.

With a whinny, the horse came to an abrupt halt and the tarantas jolted to a stop. Daria stood up, brushing straw from her jacket. A thick tree branch lay across the road, toppled by a heavy load of ice and snow. Icicles gleamed in the starlight. Lev was already jumping down from the carriage to pull the branch away. Daria leaped to the ground. It was better when you kept moving, she thought. She shivered, running around and getting a grip on the top of the branch with her stiffly cold, gloved fingers, and hoped the wolves wouldn't howl again. It was a romantic, eerie sound, heard from within the izba, when you were cozy and safe with the stove going and the samovar bubbling, but not when you were out here in the open, unprotected, beneath those looming, forested hills. The branch was moving. She heard Lev grunt with effort. Suddenly she felt it give way; Alexey had come down to join them, adding the strength of his corded, ropy muscles to their effort, and the branch was heaved aside onto the edge of the road.

"Dedushka, you shouldn't have done that," she said. "We could have moved it."

"Never mind, never mind."

It pleased him to have helped. He grinned, and she saw the flash of his teeth against his white beard. He was seventy-five, but not so old that he had to sit by and watch while other people worked. She understood that.

She began to climb into the tarantas again, but Lev's arm held her back. "Daria, I know we have to hurry, but I never had a chance to speak to you at the izba. I wanted to say—"

"It's all right, Lev. I understand. I think I know what you want to tell me. But there's no time now. We'll meet in Harbin. In Manchuria . . ."

"Will we?"

"You said so yourself. You promised."

Lev's thin young face looked somber in the darkness by the roadside. "Yes, I promised. But I wonder—when we meet again, will we be the same two people?"

She was silent for a moment. "There's no answer to that—"

Alexey called out from the tarantas. "Look, the snow fence! Over there, between the hills—it's the railroad track!"

Daria's heart thumped in her chest. Would the train be there, waiting? Or would the track be empty?

She climbed back into the carriage. *Don't think about saying good-bye to Lev. It's not forever . . .*

They continued. She listened to the clopclop of hooves against the snow, heard the hiss of her own breath between her teeth, saw the dense white mist it formed in front of her mouth. Suddenly she saw yellow light shining on the snow and glimpsed the tall silhouette of a water tower against the sky and made out the square, blocky shape of the railroad depot with its pointed gabled roof. *Chita*

Station. She peered into the shadows, looking for the train. Anything? Yes. It was there. Still there. A long string of boxcars . . . *teplushkas* . . . forty-and-eights, boxcars meant to hold forty men or eight horses . . . and up ahead, the locomotive, its headlights striking silver along the track. The locomotive was pointing the way east. I never thought I'd go east, she thought wonderingly.

The tarantas stopped and she leaped out. "We'd better go inside and arrange for tickets!" She felt in her skirt pocket. Alexey had given her the purse with all their savings, saying he didn't trust himself to look after it. Yes, it was there.

"If we have time," Alexey was saying, "and if we can find the stationmaster . . ."

"Look there." Lev was pointing ahead, along the tracks. Daria saw the smoky red glow of a lantern waving from side to side. *The stationmaster.* A head appeared out of the window of the locomotive, wearing an engineer's cap, and shouting echoed back and forth. Then, unexpectedly, steam hissed, and she started. She heard a low rumble. Clouds of white steam boiled up from beneath the train.

"It's leaving!" She whirled and stared at the nearest boxcar. The door was closed. Lev ran up to it and banged on the door with the flat of his hand. The locomotive began to inch forward. Lev banged harder. Slowly the door creaked open, but all Daria could see was the red glare of a stove in the darkness. Alexey came up beside her and took her by the arm. "Hurry, Daria!" He was holding her suitcase in his other hand. The boxcar was beginning to move, and she ran forward. She was lifted up from below by two pairs of hands and propelled inside. Her suitcase followed. She regained her balance, leaned out of the door and stretched out her hand. "Lev—good-bye! We'll meet in Harbin! Come, Dedushka! Quickly! We're moving!"

But instead of taking her hand, Alexey took two steps backward on the platform and shook his head. She saw him smile, a sad wistful smile, and he raised his hand, standing beside Lev. She stared in horror. There was a chugging sound, faster and faster, and suddenly Chita Station was sliding away in front of her eyes.

"No!"

17

Who had screamed? Whose was that anguished voice? Her own. Alexey couldn't mean to stay behind and send her away!

But she knew him so well. She understood, in a panicky flash of agonized insight, what he was thinking. He believed he was too old. He believed he would be a burden and a worry to her on this long, cold journey. He meant to stay behind in Saravenko. He'd meant to do that all along. She saw that now.

No. She bowed her head and gritted her teeth. *No.* She wouldn't let him. Whatever his fate was in Saravenko, she would share it!

The train had picked up speed. Steam was boiling up, and she couldn't see the station any longer; the pistons were moving quickly, back-and-forth, back-and-forth, and the snowy landscape was beginning to rush past her eyes. She heard a roaring sound in her ears. She released her grip on the door, closed her eyes and hurled herself forward, toward the rushing ground. She waited for the shock and the impact. But there was none.

She was being held in a steely grip. Someone was speaking in her ear. She heard a low masculine voice, taut with anger. "You little fool, are you insane? You'll break your neck."

She turned and looked up, and through her shock and anguish she was aware of another sensation: startled surprise. It jolted her and she caught her breath. She was imagining this. None of it was happening. She wasn't alone on this moving, speeding train. And no one—surely, no one—could have eyes that blue. Or dark eyebrows so perfectly arched above them.

But someone did: the man whose strong arm was still holding her back from the open door. He was angry. She was dimly aware of a curved mouth set firm and hard beneath a dark mustache, a strong cleft chin, and a jaw clenched in annoyance. It was the handsomest, most forbidding face she had ever seen.

But tears were beginning to blur her sight. "You don't understand!" she cried. "My grandfather—"

"And how do you suppose your suicide will help him?"

"I—"

The train was rocking back and forth with its speeding

motion, and she almost lost her balance. She fell against him, and his arms enclosed her. She caught the faint fragrance of pine cologne and tobacco; another strange sensation washed over her. "When will we stop?" she said in a whisper.

"My dear girl, speak up. I can't hear you." He reached out and rolled the door shut. She heard a metallic click as the latch caught. The cold, blowing wind was shut out. She was suddenly warm.

"When will we stop?"

"Not for ninety kilometers."

"But that will be too late!" She drew back. When would there be a westbound train? These days there were no more schedules. It would be too late . . .

"I'm sorry," he said coolly, "but I don't have the faintest idea what you're talking about."

"No, of course not, how could you? But it doesn't matter." She turned her face away. "Please let go of my arm."

"If you'll assure me that you don't intend to throw yourself onto the tracks."

"No, I won't do that."

"Very well." He released her arm. She stepped back. "I'm sorry if I was abrupt with you," he said, "but you gave me a scare."

"It's all right."

"How far do you intend to travel?"

"As far as Harbin, in Manchuria."

"Then I'm afraid I have unhappy news."

"What do you mean?"

He shrugged and looked down at her. His gaze swept her up and down. "Are you alone?"

She flushed. "Yes."

"That's not a very wise idea. For a young woman like yourself."

"It has nothing to do with you."

"Perhaps not. But——" He stopped. "Are you crying?"

"No."

But she was. The word "alone" had begun to echo in her mind, and the full realization of her aloneness was flooding through her. The tears she had fought down had risen again, and she was suddenly weeping. She covered her face with her hands.

"Don't be absurd. Of course you are." He reached out for her again and drew her forward.

"Don't," she muttered.

"If you must cry, you know, it's best not to do it alone."

It was hopeless to resist. She collapsed against his shoulder, letting the tears flow.

"We don't know one another. But you can do me a service."

"Do you a service?" She raised her head, the tears still wet on her cheeks, and was startled again by the stern masculine beauty of his face. He wasn't angry any longer. She saw now that the curve of his mouth was tender and sensitive beneath the dark mustache. She suddenly knew that what she felt for Lev Omansky was only girlish friendship. This new feeling running through her was much more powerful and much more frightening: the tug of her own womanhood, aroused by this strange and beautiful man who was holding her against him.

But she couldn't quite believe what he was saying.

"Yes . . . I find it difficult to cry myself. You can do it for both of us."

Chapter 2

Nicholas Federovsky looked down at the girl in his arms, wondering how long she would weep. Her body was soft and slender against him, and he felt a rising stir of emotion he thought he'd buried the day he left Kharkov, the day he'd left a woman with copper hair. But this girl was very young and very lovely, with huge dark eyes now brimming with tears, a slim curving body, and a cloud of dark hair smelling faintly of woodsmoke and violets. He was suddenly, poignantly reminded of another fragrance, more sophisticated and less subtle, a haunting and expensive perfume tipped out drop by drop from a crystal bottle. The fragrance of Céline.

But he preferred not to think about that. There were a great many things he preferred to forget.

Yes, weep for us both, he thought, as the girl's sobs continued to shake her body, muffled against his shoulder.

It would be dangerous to let this go on very long, he told himself. She was too young. She was alone and vulnerable, and it would be all too easy to console himself with those scented curves and melting dark eyes.

But she was stepping back, in shaky control of herself, brushing at her wet cheeks. "I'm sorry. I'm terribly sorry."

"There's no need to apologize."

She took a deep breath. "When you said before that you had unhappy news—what did you mean?"

"Ah yes." He rested one hand against the closed door, which was vibrating with the movement of the train, and stared into space. His expression hardened. "We should be on our way to Manchuria, right now. We should be crossing the border south to Manchuli. But that's not the case. Instead we're going east, to the Pacific. To Vladivostok."

He glanced over and met her gaze. She looked confused, almost shocked. Did she know what that meant? Traveling to Vladivostok? To the Pacific? He was still swallowing his own bitterness. He'd only learned about it himself at Chita.

"I'm not sure I understand," she whispered. "I thought that by tomorrow we'd be across the border."

"Yes, I thought so too." He stared at the floor. They'd been delayed at Chita Station, and he'd felt a twinge of superstitious apprehension. Chita was three thousand miles from Kharkov, where he'd started his journey, and it was a milestone in his mind. From here, he thought, they would cross the Manchurian border to the town of Manchuli. It meant the last leg of the journey, and the end of commissars and soviets and the danger of arrest that had threatened him since his last days in Kharkov. He was carrying a set of identity papers that described him as a civil engineer, but the papers had been issued by a friendly official who'd been willing to overlook the fact that Nicholas hadn't practiced his profession for years. He'd been a capitalist exploiter, as a matter of fact. If you cared to use the current jargon.

He'd decided to find out for himself what was going on. He'd opened the boxcar door and jumped to the ground, onto the snowy slush by the railroad track. Cold. My God, it was cold. He forced himself to take short breaths, wondering if you ever got used to it. How cold would it be in Harbin? He would find out soon enough. If he was lucky.

He'd entered the terminal building and felt himself relaxing in the sudden warmth. He unbuttoned his jacket and gazed around him. The terminal building was like dozens of others he'd seen across the continent, smelling vaguely of damp leather and unswept floors, burning logs and stale sweat. But this one was empty of people. They weren't expecting a train tonight at Chita, he thought. And it was too soon for these Siberian towns to panic. In a few months —maybe sooner—there would be a civil war, and then the exodus would begin. Unless something prevented a war.

But the revolution had happened; it could no longer be reversed without bloodshed.

Facing him across the room was a closed door marked FIRST-CLASS WAITING ROOM. Beyond it the engineer was undoubtedly negotiating with the commissar of the station. Next to the door stood the usual log-burning stove, with a clock on the wall above it. Ten-thirty, he noted. To his right, benches stood beneath a window that looked out on the road to the town, but there was nothing to see, for it was dark now. To his left, a glass door led to the platform and railroad tracks. Beside the entrance where he stood was another closed door. PASSENGERS KEEP OUT. Light was seeping from beneath it, and he heard a clacking noise. The telegraph room. Fine, the best place for information. You starved for news, shut up in that boxcar, depending on rumor and gossip. He pulled off his black sealskin cap, shoved it into his pocket, pulled open the door, and went in.

It was a long narrow room with a desk at the far end and a scattering of wooden chairs. The telegraph operator, a heavyset, balding man, seated at his keyboard, turned in his chair at the sound of Nicholas's footsteps. He started to say something, then changed his mind and frowned. "You can't come in here."

"Why not?"

"It says so on the door. Passengers aren't allowed in the telegraph room."

Nicholas stared grimly at the floor. He knew what he looked like, wearing the rough clothes of a refugee: the sheepskin jacket, the sashed woolen tunic buttoned high at the throat, the shabby trousers tucked into knee-high leather boots. But this was no time for humility, he told himself. He raised his head and surveyed the room very thoroughly, with his hands in his pockets. Then he did the same to the telegraph operator, looking him over from top to bottom. Finally he stared directly into the man's face with a level regard. It was a deliberate challenge, an unspoken declaration of authority: tell me to leave. Say it again. But be very sure of yourself, *gospodin*. Otherwise, take it on faith that I'm perfectly entitled to walk anywhere I choose.

The man cleared his throat. Then he flushed, dropping

23

his eyes. "Well, well, take a seat." He waved at one of the chairs. "I suppose it can't hurt if you stay for a while."

"I believe I will." Nicholas sat down. The old habits of obedience and deference were hard to erase, he thought wryly. It would take quite a while before the citizens of Russia unlearned them.

The telegraph operator gestured at the papers on his desk. "Latest news from Moscow," he said with an apologetic laugh. Now that Nicholas was seated, he seemed to feel the need to be hospitable.

Nicholas nodded pleasantly. "Moscow? Is that where the news comes from these days?"

"Yes, didn't you know? The Council of People's Commissars has moved its headquarters from Petrograd to Moscow. They're afraid of Kaiser Willy's troops moving north."

"The Germans have taken Kharkov, I understand."

"Kharkov, Kiev, the entire Ukraine."

"But for how long, I wonder?" Nicholas reached absently into his breast pocket for his gold cigarette case. It was not there. He had no breast pocket. He had no vest or watch pocket, either, and no diamond watch. No rings. No jewelry at all. Only this rough sheepskin jacket, and this high-necked woolen tunic scratchy against his throat. No more monogrammed silk shirts. No fur-lined topcoats or pigskin gloves. All part of the past . . . the very recent past. He reminded himself grimly to forget the leather pouch clipped to his belt under the tunic, and not to think of its contents if he could possibly help it. *If you don't think about it, you won't call attention to it.*

The telegraph key began to clack, and the man swiveled back to his desk, suddenly absorbed in his task. When the key was silent again, he sat back, ready to talk. "Listen," he remarked, "last month the Bolsheviks held Kiev for three weeks against the Kaiser's army. But in three weeks, they executed five thousand counterrevolutionaries. What do you think of that?"

"Remarkable," Nicholas said drily. "Thanks to Djerzinsky, no doubt. Has he moved his headquarters to Moscow too?" Felix Djerzinsky was the head of the secret police. They called it the Cheka, in this government. The Extraordinary Committee for the Suppression of the Counterrevolution. But it was the Czar's dread Okhrana in another guise.

"Yes, a new address. Twenty-two Lubianka Street. Formerly the Russia Insurance Company."

"I believe that will be a good place to stay away from."

"Indeed, *gospodin!*" the man agreed.

Nicholas had located his cigarettes in his trouser pocket, and offered the box. The man helped himself. Nicholas struck a match on his thumbnail, and they both lit up. Blue smoke drifted in the air. The conversation wandered, interrupted occasionally by the chatter of the telegraph key.

"What do you hear of the Czeska Druzina?" Nicholas asked casually.

The Czech Brigade had been fighting in Kiev on the side of the Bolsheviks, against the Germans, but rumor had it that the Czechoslovakian troops, who had originally been prisoners of war, were ready to move east along the Trans-Siberian Railway, to Vladivostok. It was their only route back to Europe, to rejoin the World War. They couldn't cross the lines of the Eastern front, they had to travel to the Pacific, the long way around, and hope to board a ship bound for Europe. Going east had been Nicholas's only choice, too, leaving Kharkov. But his destination was Harbin, in Manchuria, not Europe. That was a much shorter journey. Or was it?

"I hear Comrade Trotsky's given the Czech Brigade permission to leave for Vladivostok. They should be on their way by now."

"That means they're behind us, on the Trans-Siberian tracks." Nicholas drew deeply on his cigarette. It was fortunate, he thought, that the train was crossing the Manchurian border tonight. To be followed by the Czech Brigade along the railway line could only mean delays, holdups, commandeered trains, all kinds of frustrations and problems. Why did he have this uneasy feeling that something would go wrong? He'd never been superstitious when he was young. But as you got older, he thought, you saw the workings of fate and destiny, and you changed your ideas.

At thirty-five, Nicholas sensed the past receding farther with every moment. There was nothing now but the damned cold, filthy boxcar, and this struggle to reach Harbin. But why? For what? For the future? It might not even exist. Did he care? Yes. God only knew why, but he kept wanting to live. Even here, even now, cold and dirty and half-starved and fighting all the bitter memories, still he went on. There was nothing heroic or admirable about it, just this primitive will to survive. That was all he had left.

He stood up, suddenly restless. "I wonder what's taking so long. We've been here over two hours."

The telegraph operator shrugged. "You should be used to delays by now."

"I'm anxious to cross the border." Nicholas spoke, half to himself. They were so close. So very close. Manchuli by tomorrow morning. But somehow . . . The door opened and they both turned to face it. The engineer of the train stood in the doorway, still wearing his official cap. He pulled it off. "Do you have another cigarette, *barin*?" he asked politely, looking at Nicholas. The smile on his broad face was a nervous one.

"Yes, of course." Nicholas held out the box of cigarettes.

"Thank you." The engineer bobbed his head.

The telegraph operator sat back in his chair and laughed, as though the memory of his own quick surrender to authority still rankled, and he was glad of an opportunity to jeer at someone else. "Such respect, Comrade Engineer! Courtesy titles and humble thanks—why? This comrade is just a poor refugee. A citizen of the new Russia, like ourselves. Nothing special. Isn't that right?" He directed the question to Nicholas.

Nicholas smiled. "It would seem that way," he agreed pleasantly.

The engineer blushed and sat down in one of the chairs, searching in his pocket for a match. "Sometimes, you know, you forget . . . it hasn't been very long."

The telegraph operator was emboldened by company. He glanced up at Nicholas and cleared his throat. "Listen, comrade," he said. "Why are you running away on the train? Why don't you stay and help us build the new society? We could use men like you. Clever, well-educated . . . why not stay?"

"The new society doesn't seem to want me." Nicholas sat

down again and crossed one ankle on his knee. He leaned back and folded his arms. Even in his sheepskin jacket and shabby boots, he made a picture of unconscious elegance. "There are decisions you make in the past that narrow your choices. After that, it becomes a matter of survival."

The other two men nodded in agreement, only half understanding.

"Is everything cleared with the commissar?" Nicholas asked the engineer.

He nodded.

"Good. Fine. Then by tomorrow we should be in Manchuria."

The engineer stared at his hands, one of which still held the cigarette, still unlit. "Not Manchuria."

"Oh?" Nicholas felt his muscles tensing and deliberately kept his voice calm. "Why not?"

"Listen, my friend," the engineer said in a low voice. "My life isn't much, but it's all I have. You understand? I protect it however I can."

"What do you mean?"

"We can't go to Manchuli."

"For what reason?"

"It's not safe."

"Good heavens, man, what's safe?" Nicholas tried to keep his anger out of his voice.

"You don't understand. Semenov's men are holding Manchuli . . . the Savage Division."

"Semenov!"

"Yes, Manchuli, and the railway station, and a whole section of tracks. Next they'll be in Chita. You know what they'll do. They'll stop the train and search everybody, and if they don't like your face, or the angle of your hat, they'll hang you from a telegraph pole, and then let your body dangle in the air while the crows pick out your eyes." It was a long speech for the engineer. He stared miserably at the floor. "And the women, you know what they'll do to them . . ."

Nicholas sprang to his feet, trying to control the surge of fury running through him, the wave of hopeless, frustrated anger. He turned aside. Semenov, he thought. Like Orlov. Like Kalmikov. Like Dmitri Chernov. A wild-eyed

Cossack adventurer roaming through eastern Siberia in these times of violence, raping and looting and flogging, yes, and hanging people from telegraph poles . . . Semenov's Savage Division. They were proud of that name; they'd chosen it themselves. And lived up to it. *Damn. Something. I knew it would be something.* His hand went to his mouth, stroking his mustache. The bleak conviction came over him that fate was against him on this attempt to reach Manchuria. You can never win, he thought, when you struggle against fate. Sooner or later, you run up against disaster. Somewhere. Somehow. This was a warning. He took a deep breath and brought himself under control. He dropped his hand. All right. He must face facts. The engineer was right, Manchuli was too dangerous. A trainload of refugees would be irresistible to Grigor Semenov. And they had no weapons. He had made the decision himself in Kharkov not to carry a pistol, and it had proved to be a wise choice. The passengers were searched for weapons at almost every station stop. Anyone discovered with a sidearm was detained as a spy, and usually not seen again. So you took your chances unarmed.

"What will it be, then?" he asked finally, turning back to the engineer. "Vladivostok?"

The man raised his head. "Yes, the Trans-Amur line. I have clearance to keep going east, along the river."

The Trans-Amur. From here on they would follow the Amur River. In China it was called Hei Lung Ho, the River of the Black Dragon. He would be able to see Manchuria from the train window, on the other side of the river. But he would still be in Siberia.

"Are you aware," he said, seating himself again, "that the Czech Brigade will be breathing down our necks? They've already left the Ukraine."

The man nodded. "What can we do?"

Nothing, Nicholas thought. Nothing at all. Just hope to reach Vladivostok before the Czechs did. Or before Siberia went up in flames. Or before the train was stopped by Semenov or someone like him.

"How long do you suppose it will take?"

"If all goes well . . . if there are no delays—"

The telegraph operator burst out laughing. "If there are no delays! You have a good sense of humor, comrade.

From here to Vladivostok, expect one long delay. Just hope you reach the Pacific before spring."

From Vladivostok, Nicholas thought, in order to reach Manchuria, he would have to backtrack along the Chinese Eastern Railway. Now he could foresee endless opportunities for something to go wrong. According to rumor the Japanese were landing troops in Vladivostok, preparing for an invasion of Siberia on the side of the counterrevolution. Czechs, Japanese, Cossacks, partisans, who else? At least there weren't any Germans in that part of the world.

"We'll be leaving soon," the engineer said. "The track is cleared for the next ninety kilometers, so we'll be ready to leave in fifteen minutes."

"I'd better go back to the car." Nicholas stood up and stretched. "Well, thank you for the conversation, my friend. I don't suppose we'll meet again."

The telegraph operator grinned up at him. "Good luck. You'll need it."

Once he was back in the boxcar, with its familiar odor of dirty straw and unwashed bodies, he paused by the open door for a moment to look out at the landscape. Only darkness, and the gleam of starlight on the snow. Rolling meadows, and off in the distance, the spiky shapes of a stand of pines on a hilltop. Vast open spaces and cold still air. Hidden beyond the hills lay the town of Chita. Someone called irritably, "Close the door, we're freezing to death," and he rolled it shut. It was only the end of March. It was still winter, Siberian winter. It would be a long time until spring.

Then had come that pounding on the boxcar door. He'd rolled it open again. And here, suddenly, staring at him with dark gypsy eyes, still shocked and confused, was the girl destiny had flung into his arms at Chita Station.

He saw that she badly needed to wash her face. It was smudged and grimy with soot stains and tears. Her bosom was still rising and falling with the aftermath of her sobs. In the shadowy light, as she looked down, her eyelashes made curving little fans of shadow against her cheeks.

Traveling alone? As far as Harbin?

She would need someone to look after her.

Ah, no. He glanced away. Don't appoint yourself her guardian, Nicholas Sergeievitch. How foolish that would

29

Chapter 3

Daria stepped back, away from the somberly handsome man who confronted her with an unreadable expression on his face. What was he thinking about? She wondered again who he was. His clothes were those of a refugee, rough and shabby, but his figure was lean and elegant, broad-shouldered and slim-hipped, and he stood leaning against the door with an air of unconscious grace. She couldn't help noticing his hands, which were long and well shaped, with prominent veins and tapered fingers.

She felt an inward flush of embarrassment. Stop staring, she told herself. She thought of what he had just said: Vladivostok. "Is it possible to get to Harbin through Vladivostok?" she whispered.

"I don't know. Anything is possible." He shrugged. "If you can board the Chinese Eastern Railroad going west, then certainly you can reach Manchuria."

"But it's the long way around, isn't it?"

He laughed. It was the first time he'd laughed, and she was amazed at how wonderfully attractive it made him look. "Why yes, I would say it's the long way around."

She felt young and foolish. "I haven't traveled very much, you'll have to forgive me if I ask obvious questions."

"How much is not very much?"

"I—" She set her chin. *Don't apologize. Tell the truth.* "Not at all, as a matter of fact. I've never been away from Saravenko."

"Where is Saravenko?"

"Twelve versts from Chita."

"Of course. Why didn't I know that?"

She flushed again. "Because it's just a little Siberian village that nobody ever heard of. You couldn't be expected to know where it is."

"Ah. You're angry. You think I'm patronizing you."

"I didn't say that."

"No, but that's because you're much too polite." He smiled. "Very well. Now that I've made you cry, and then insulted you, I suppose it's time to introduce myself. My name is Nicholas Federovsky."

"My name is Daria Petrovna."

"How do you do." He turned and gestured at the interior of the car. "And this is your home, for the next few weeks. Or however long it may take to get where we're going."

She looked around the car. Three tiers of wooden shelves lined the walls, mounting to the ceiling, fading into the shadows. A sheet-iron stove in the center of the floor was glowing dull red. Straw was scattered on the floor. She heard the sounds of people coughing, muttering in their sleep, clearing their throats, and the faint whimper of a baby crying. A stale, musty odor was in the air, mingled with sawdust and burning wood.

"Those shelves on the wall are to sleep on," she heard Nicholas saying. "So perhaps you'd better choose one for yourself."

"Yes, I will . . ."

Her gaze swept the interior once more. *Your home. For weeks. Or however long it takes to get where you're going.*

She wondered what lay ahead. In the morning. And the morning after that. How many nights and how many mornings till Manchuria?

And as for this man who had held her back from the open door and the rushing ground—who had asked her to weep for him—would they speak again? Or was this meeting only a bend in the road of fate, not to be repeated? She knew, with a strange ache in her chest, that she wanted to hear him laugh again. She'd seen a look of pain in those blue eyes, fleeting and evanescent, but it was there; she'd seen it, she knew.

"Good night," she said. "Thank you for . . . for . . ."

He'd grown serious again. He looked down at her with a grave expression, reflecting about something, but what? "Good night."

Nothing about tomorrow.

Nicholas turned aside. Stay away, he told himself. It had been a long time since he'd left Kharkov. A long time since he'd boarded this wretched train. And there'd been no one . . . no one . . . since Céline.

And this girl, with her dark eyes and lovely face and sensuous body, would trouble his dreams.

There were enough troubles ahead, he thought grimly, without adding the torments of the flesh. But it seemed destiny had placed that too in his path.

Stay away.

Three days later, Daria found herself bathed by a flood of new impressions. The anguish of saying good-bye to Alexey had faded a little. The rocking, jolting motion of the train was insinuating itself into the rhythm of her body, and she hardly noticed it any longer.

Now she sat on a bottom shelf of the boxcar, swaying back and forth, deep in conversation with a young woman named Ludmilla, who was traveling with her husband and two-year-old baby. As they spoke, Daria held the baby on her lap. Irresistibly she found herself asking about Nicholas.

Ludmilla's eyes widened. "The man with the blue eyes? Everyone calls him the Man of Ice."

"Why do they call him that?"

"Because he won't speak to anyone. Not really. He'll just say something very polite and impersonal about the weather, or the journey. He's very mysterious."

He spoke to me, Daria thought. That first night.

"It's easy to have romantic daydreams," Ludmilla added softly.

Daria didn't answer. She bent her head to the baby in her lap and nuzzled his neck. The child's skin was as soft as a rose petal; he'd just been crying, and the creases of his neck tasted of salt tears.

"We have black bread and cheese," she whispered in the baby's ear. "Fresh bread. Think of that." "Bread," he echoed tearfully. Ludmilla was cutting up the bread with a small kitchen knife, hacking off a slice for the baby. He reached out for it with his fist and began to squirm in Daria's arms.

"I'll take him," Ludmilla said, holding out her arms. Daria handed him over and he settled down happily on his mother's lap, chewing on his piece of bread. "Take some for yourself," Ludmilla added. "Cut off some cheese." She sighed. "Who would ever believe that plain bread and cheese could be this delicious?"

"But it's fresh." Daria helped herself and tore off a bite of crust with her teeth. The crust was hard and shiny, dotted with poppyseeds; inside it was soft and yielding, rich with the flavor of pumpernickel. Most of the vendors at the stations where they stopped offered day-old bread, and you were glad to get that. But this woman had been kinder. The loaves had just been pulled from the oven, she'd told them, offering the basket, her face softened with pity beneath her woolen headscarf. "Take a loaf, they're still warm. Maybe someday I'll have to run away myself. Who knows? The rumors you hear are terrible. Anything can happen in these times."

Ludmilla held out a piece of cheese on the tip of her knife. "Thank you for helping me with the baby."

"Don't thank me. I like to do it."

Some of the other passengers were frightening, she thought. There were the gypsies; not like the gypsies who came and went in Saravenko. These people were cruder and bolder and more boisterous, and according to Ludmilla's husband Boris, were probably escaped convicts from the Siberian prisons. The gypsy woman named Zora, with her grimy neck and coarse tangles of black hair falling around her face, was a prostitute. You tried not to listen at night to the mutters and grunts and low laughter coming from the direction of her shelf; you tried to shut your mind to what was happening. During the day she strutted around with her hands on her hips and a cigarette drooping from her mouth, her eyes half-closed against the smoke.

Then there was the man with the steel teeth who called himself Peter No-Name. He was another ex-convict, who liked to tell gruesome stories about prison life on Sakhalin Island and other notorious Siberian penal institutions. Now he was singing, in a deep resonant voice, as he reclined on his shelf. "Long I carried heavy chains . . . long I roamed the Altai Mountains . . . but an old comrade helped me escape . . . I was born anew . . ."

"Why don't you sing something else for a change?" Zora was standing by his shelf with her feet planted wide apart to balance herself against the rocking of the train. "We've heard that song a million times before."

"I'm tired of singing." Peter No-Name grinned, displaying his steel teeth. "Why don't you entertain us, Zora? Get your balalaika, and sing your own song."

"I'm not in the mood."

"Then tell us a story. Tell us what you're running away from."

"Running away? Not me!" Zora tossed back her hair. "I'm running *to* something. To the east, where my lover waits."

"Does he have your price?" Mocking laughter spilled from Peter No-Name.

She made an ugly grimace and jerked her shoulder. "My lover is seven feet tall, with hair the color of wheat and the temper of a mad bull. He's killed fifteen men already, and one day he'll kill me, too." She laughed softly. "The first was in the Urals, where he lived. It was harvest time, and they quarreled, and he chopped his enemy's head off with a scythe—*whop*—" She gestured with the flat of her hand. "And it went rolling in the wheat!" Then she shrugged. "They sent him to prison in Siberia for that."

"What were you doing there?" Peter No-Name asked slyly.

"Ah, things happen. This and that. One gets into trouble with the authorities; you know how it is. But I met my lover there and we escaped together and roamed the prairie, free as two birds. One of them—my lover—was a bird of prey! They called him the Yellow Hawk and trembled at the name. But I left him, like a fool, when he tried to strangle me one night. It was a mistake. I belong with him. We belong together!"

"How do you know you'll find him? Siberia's a big place."

"Oh, I'll find him. He'll love me, the way he did before . . . and then one day he'll kill me." She laughed and glanced around the car.

Daria suppressed a shudder. "Do you suppose she's telling the truth?" she whispered to Ludmilla.

"Who knows?"

Daria's eyes went to another part of the car, to see if Nicholas had been listening. No. He was standing alone by the door, slightly opened to bring in some fresh air. You needed to do that every now and then, cold as it was outside. Daria had learned in just a short time what a constant struggle it was just to satisfy your physical needs. The need for fresh air. The need to keep fed. The need to keep clean, washing in the bucket of melted snow in the corner of the car, and hoarding your soap. Most of the men had given up shaving and were letting their beards grow. The need to use the dirty little water closet in the one passenger car, located behind the engine. You had to make the long trip between cars, buffeted by the icy air outside and balancing against the rocking car, and when you got there, you had to steel yourself to go in. She'd learned to wait for the stations, whenever possible, and use the facilities in the first-class waiting rooms, which were usually clean and decent. But sometimes you had no choice.

"Hey, little girl, shall I tell your fortune?" She looked up. Zora was standing in front of her with a bold smile on her face, smelling of sweat and cheap, strong perfume. Her balalaika was dangling from her hand.

Daria shook her head. "No . . . no thank you."

"It won't cost much. I'll give you a special price."

"Oh no, I don't think so."

"I'll do it for nothing. I'm bored."

Daria hesitated. "Well, perhaps another time."

"Whenever you say." Zora grinned, and held out the balalaika. "Want to amuse us? Join the group."

"What makes you think I can play it?"

"Can't you?"

Daria reached out hesitantly and took the balalaika from Zora. She ran her hands over the triple strings. The soft, sweet resonance of music drifted up like a sigh. She strummed another chord. She had left her own instrument at home, in the izba. She wished now she had taken it with her.

There had been a time, when she'd been young, when she had tried to write poetry, to express her feelings, to put into words the confused and shapeless dreams of youth. But it was so much easier to pour your feelings into a song. That was the most natural thing in the world. It was effortless.

She began to hum softly under her breath.

By the door, Peter No-Name had left his shelf and come up to Nicholas's side. "Look there, my friend." Nicholas started. He'd been daydreaming. He'd almost forgotten where he was. You slipped so easily into the past, once the memories started to come back. The train had slowed down. He saw that they were approaching a prison, a big whitewashed building with plank paths just below the top of the walls. Bearded sentries in tall fur hats were pacing back and forth along the paths, bayoneted rifles slung across their backs.

"Matters can always be worse," Peter No-Name said. His voice was suddenly somber. "Think of the poor wretches inside that prison."

"I suppose it can happen to anyone."

"That's true, *starosta*. Anyone."

"Why call me *starosta*?"

"Because you're the head man around here."

"Nonsense."

Peter No-Name chuckled. "That's right, refuse the title. Positions of authority can be dangerous. Did I ever tell you what happened to the executioner on Sakhalin Island?"

Without waiting for an answer, he began to relate a horrifying tale. It involved axes splitting skulls and charcoal fires on the soles of someone's feet.

"Maybe you'd better save your story for another time," Nicholas said, interrupting the tale. "I'm not a very good listener today."

Peter No-Name wasn't offended. "Perhaps I'll tell it to the little dark one with the big sad eyes," he said musingly. He looked into the car, and Nicholas followed his glance. He was gazing at Daria, whose head was bent over Zora's balalaika.

Nicholas felt unreasonably angry. "Keep away from her," he said. "Don't bother that girl with your bloodthirsty stories."

"Afraid I'll give the little one nightmares?"

Nicholas didn't answer.

37

"What's it to you, starosta?"

"Never mind. Just stay away."

The ex-convict grinned and bent low from the waist in a mocking bow.

What is it to me? Nicholas asked himself, rolling the door shut. The big whitewashed prison had disappeared, and the train was picking up speed again. He wasn't her guardian. He'd already made that decision. He'd decided it the very first night. Keep your distance, he told himself. It was the safest course of action.

But he was still angry at Peter No-Name.

He turned and leaned against the door, reaching into his pocket for a cigarette.

Then he became aware that someone was singing. A low, husky voice, full of feeling, untrained, but throbbing with emotion and strangely moving, was floating into the car. He realized it was Daria. As the words reached his ears, he felt a pang of remembrance. *I Do Not Speak to You.* It was one of Panina's songs, a poignant lament of unrequited love. The great gypsy singer had been before Nicholas's time, but in the gypsy cafés of Petersburg one heard that song over and over . . .

Yes, in those days. Sixteen years ago—no, seventeen. He realized he would be thirty-six next month.

Before his world fell apart.

He remembered a photograph of himself that had stood on his mother's dresser, and felt bitterly amused. What a spoiled and complacent young man had gazed from that tortoiseshell frame. What an arrogant face, clean-shaven and young, self-confident, certain of his place in the world, taking for granted the surroundings of luxury and privilege, the growing-up years of English governesses and German tutors, the closets crammed with expensive clothes and handmade leather boots . . . everything but his parents' love. But he'd gotten used to doing without that. You became accustomed to loneliness as you grew up. After a while you even preferred it, sometimes.

And certainly, in all material ways, he'd been monstrously spoiled. His parents had lived their own selfish and glittering lives, and never worried about their only son. Didn't he have everything a boy could want?

Yes, almost.

Until it all came to an end, he thought. The time of the great shock. The spoiled young man facing reality. He had never forgiven Sergei Nicholaevitch for what he had done. But why should he? What his father had done had been unforgivable. He had died, and left Nicholas poor. Nicholas hadn't been prepared for that.

He had been nineteen. He was studying mathematics at the Institute of Technology in St. Petersburg, although not very seriously. He thought idly that some day, when he was ready to settle down, he would take an advanced degree and teach mathematics at a university. He wouldn't have to worry about a low professor's salary, because he would have a substantial private income. Or so he'd believed.

And then the catastrophe descended. His father died.

"There's no money, Nicholas Sergeievitch. It's gone. All the money is gone."

"You're lying! I don't believe it!"

He was in the family drawing room, behind a closed door. He could still smell the aromatic fragrance of his father's cigars, coming from the open humidor on the desk. It was making him slightly ill. Upstairs in the rose and gold bedroom, his mother lay collapsed across her bed, white-faced and silently hysterical. Here, confronting him across the desk, was the family lawyer, his pudgy face as pale and ugly as an uncooked pudding.

"It can't be true!"

"But it is, Kolya," the lawyer muttered. "It's true."

"It's your fault. It must be!"

The lawyer spread his hands helplessly. It was not his fault. There was nothing to be done.

Nicholas made a fist and pounded it on the desk. Later he found a dark purple bruise on the side of his hand, but at the time he had felt no pain. "No!" he shouted; veins bulged in his neck. The lawyer shook his head.

"It does no good, Kolya. It's all true. You are poor."

What am I going to do?

He went to his father's funeral with a face made of stone, convinced that if he moved a muscle in his face, it would crack and shatter into dust. But at night, when he was alone in bed, he broke down and wept, not with grief, but with rage, hating his father, wishing he could bring him to life again, just to have the pleasure of strangling him with his own two hands. Damn you! Damn you, Sergei Nicholaevitch! Couldn't you have left me the only world I knew? No . . . you died and took it with you. But what about me? What am I to do? Did you think of that?

Nicholas sighed, standing against the door in the jolting boxcar. You realized, finally, that it did no good to hate, or to curse.

You faced the facts.

He remembered an afternoon in St. Petersburg, the winter after his father died. He'd been standing on one of the little stone bridges crossing the Neva. Alone. He couldn't afford his former friendships any longer. The card games, the champagne suppers, the ballet girls, the nights at the Maryinsky Theater, all were part of the past. Now there was only this cold gray winter, and the wind off the Gulf of Finland, and this frozen river, and the dampness seeping through the soles of his shoes. The beautiful hand-made boots were gone; they'd all been sold to a second-hand dealer, one pair at a time, for the price of a meal. Now there were cheap rooming houses and grimy restaurants and constant fatigue, but Nicholas missed what he had lost. He missed sleeping on clean linen sheets, and putting on fresh underwear every morning, and eating well-cooked food, and drinking fine brandy.

He stared down at the gray ice. He was studying civil engineering. It was a profession, it was practical, it would help him earn a living. He made friends only with people who could be of use to him some time in the future, and tried to forget the careless companions of his youth. Because now he had a goal.

He would get it all back, he vowed to himself, shivering with cold, leaning on the cold stone railing of the bridge. Behind him, a troika pulled a gleaming carriage over the icy expanse of the Nevsky Prospekt, and he heard a woman in furs send tinkling laughter back across the snow.

He would get it back. Somehow.

"Hey, what are you thinking about so hard?"

He was on a train, crossing Siberia. The past was gone. He knew without turning around who had spoken. You didn't have to recognize the voice, only sniff the rank animal odor of Zora, to know she was there.

"The little one sings well, doesn't she?"

The gypsy was referring to Daria, who had come to the end of her song.

"Yes, she sings very well," Nicholas replied.

"She's using my balalaika, of course!"

"Congratulations, Zora," he said. "For lending your balalaika."

"Ah, what an elegant gentleman! How cool, how much in command of himself! See that handsome face, how little it shows! But I think . . . I think . . ."

In spite of himself, he was curious. "What is it you think?"

"That you are interested in the pretty little girl with the big dark eyes."

"Do you?" He lit a cigarette, deliberately not offering one to Zora. Her eyes followed the flame hungrily.

"Yes, I've watched you. And Zora always knows." The gypsy laughed slyly. "Shall I get her for you?"

He waved out the match and dropped it onto the floor. "What do you mean by that?" He kept his voice low and controlled, stifling the anger he felt at her words.

"Don't put on airs with me, starosta. I've seen the look in your eyes. Peasants or gentlemen, it doesn't matter, the look is always the same." She moved a little closer. "The girl likes you. I can tell. I'll whisper in her ear. If you have your way with her, then pay a small commission to Zora. That's a small price to pay for so much pleasure, don't you agree?"

He narrowed his eyes but said nothing.

Zora put a hand on his sleeve. She lowered her voice to a whisper. "The girl's a virgin, starosta. Depend on it. Come to me later after you've had her, and tell me if I wasn't right."

Nicholas took a long drag on the cigarette. Then he tossed it to the floor, crushing it out with the toe of his boot. Zora looked down with regret at the shreds of tobacco. Useless. Too bad. He could almost read her mind. He reached out for her tangled greasy hair and twisted it around his hand, forcing her head back. "What about you, Zora?"

41

"Me, starosta?"

"Yes, you, my love. I might prefer someone with more experience. Did you think of that?"

She was repulsive and filthy, and probably worse, but she had one great sexual attraction: she was available. And at night, when he couldn't sleep and lay awake smoking cigarettes in the dark, listening to the grunts and moans coming from Zora's shelf, he asked himself angrily what difference it made what she looked like, or smelled like. She was there, she was available for the taking, and why was he so fastidious, why was he such a fool . . .

During the day it was easier. And right now he felt no desire for her at all. He was too disgusted. But at the same time he was aroused by the picture she had painted of Daria, soft and yielding in his arms, her pink mouth trembling in surrender, her eyes heavy-lidded with passion.

Damn the woman.

"You have an easy time of it, don't you, gypsy?" he said through gritted teeth. His hand tightened in her hair.

"What do you mean?"

"Your customers don't ride you very hard. I've heard them. It's all over very quickly."

She tried to laugh. "Hey, don't pull my hair like that. You're hurting me."

"I think you've been cheating your customers, Zora. You've been saving yourself. You need to be taught a lesson."

Her eyes drooped. "Tonight?" she whispered suddenly.

Nicholas flung her away in disgust. God help me, I'm as bad as she is, he thought abruptly.

No, not tonight. Not any night.

Not with the gypsy.

The train rattled on, toward the east.

Chapter 4

Screeech . . .

Daria lurched forward, clutching at the edge of the shelf. The train was suddenly shrieking to a halt. The agonizing scream of metal-on-metal was sounding in her ears. She heard a long-drawn-out grinding noise. She felt another lurch, another jolt, and heard more metallic screaming. Then there was nothing. Only silence. Stillness. They had stopped. She sat back on the shelf, rubbing her head where she'd struck it on the tier above. What had happened? She heard Ludmilla's baby wailing. All around the car, people were muttering, sitting up and looking toward the door, one man dabbing at his forehead, which was streaming blood. What was it?

She reached for her clothes.

Nicholas swung his legs to the floor. That jerking, lurching halt signaled an emergency. He decided to go outside to see what had happened. They wouldn't be starting again for quite a while, he'd be willing to bet on that.

Pulling on his sheepskin, he strode to the door and wrenched it open. Faces gaped up at him from the side of the tracks; dark, aboriginal faces, with high cheekbones and almond-shaped black eyes, framed by shaggy fur. A horse whinnied. A strong fishy odor swirled in the air. The figures were seated on horseback, muffled in furs.

"What tribe are they?" asked a soft voice at his elbow.

Daria had come up beside him. "Kirghiz," he murmured. "They're still fascinated by the train."

This section of the Trans-Amur line had only been completed three years before, and the train was still an object of wonder to the Kirghiz nomads. They came from miles around to watch it pass, galloping their horses over the steppe in a race with the locomotive. Further east, he knew, they would find other tribes: Kalmucks, Golds and Ostyaks, Ainus from Japan, Dahurs and Buryats from Mongolia, Chukchi and Koryaks, Yakuts and Samoyeds. West of Irkutsk, they'd encountered Black Tartars from the shores of the Yenisei. Few of the aborigines changed their clothes more than once a year; that accounted for the odor.

He jumped to the ground, then turned to help Daria down. "Shall we investigate? There must have been an accident."

On the ground, Daria looked past the Kirghiz tribesmen, who sat in impassive stillness. Beyond them, the snowy landscape rolled away to the horizon. Off in the distance stood a birch forest; to the left she saw a frozen pond, with the tiny black shapes of crows flapping above it. Alongside the tracks straggled the snow fence and a ridged icy ribbon of road. The windless, biting cold enveloped her body. She shaded her eyes against the light, diffused gray light that came pouring down from the limitless sky of the tundra. Was there another sky in the world like this one, she wondered? It was so vast and empty, you could almost see the curve of the earth disappearing below the edge.

Voices floated over to her from the front of the train. The fireman, the engineer, and some passengers were standing in a group near the locomotive.

"We might as well join them," Nicholas said.

She began to walk with him over the snowy ground. Now, outside, you could see the river between the cars. There lay the Amur. It was wide and frozen, reflecting the grayness of the sky. The hills of Manchuria rose high in the distance beyond it. The River of the Black Dragon, she thought, the border.

Closer to the locomotive, they both saw what had happened: a near disaster. The train had almost started across a wooden railway bridge spanning a bend in the river, but the engineer had halted just in time. The bridge had been burned. In the center, the tracks twisted and sagged uselessly.

"Partisan activity," Nicholas said, half to himself. "The war is beginning."

"If we'd continued over the bridge——" she whispered.

"Luckily we didn't. Now the problem is how to repair it."

"Very nice," the engineer commented as Nicholas approached. White puffs of breath appeared with each word. "You see, my friend, what a pretty situation we're in."

Nicholas squinted out at the bridge with his hands in his pockets. "Didn't we pass a railway repair shop at the last village?"

"So we did. They'll be able to repair the track. But what about the bridge?"

"It's a simple pier bridge." Nicholas walked out onto the ice, and squatted to inspect the supports. "The piers aren't really damaged, they're reinforced with steel. It's only the span itself that's been burned. You need some heavy timber and beams and a few good carpenters."

"If there's one thing you can find around here, it's a carpenter," someone remarked. "They all carry axes and saws in these villages. No, what you need is an engineer to supervise the job."

Nicholas stood up and shrugged. "I could probably help. I was a civil engineer, at one time. Roads, bridges . . ."

"Good, I'll take your word for it." The engineer hunched his shoulders against the cold. "What choice do we have? I'll send one of those Kirghiz nomads into the village for help. For once they can make themselves useful."

Nicholas walked back to Daria's side. "It's too cold to stand out here. You'd better go back inside."

It was true. For exercise, you paced up and down inside the depots, where a stove was burning. You couldn't stay outside very long.

They began to walk again, boots crunching on the snow. "You'll have to stay outdoors in the cold," she said, troubled, "if you're going to help them fix the bridge."

"It's different when you have a job to do. You can keep moving."

"How long do you think it will take?"

"That's hard to say." He glanced down at her and

smiled. "Perhaps there'll be a way for you to go into the village, while the repairs go on."

"But you won't have a chance to do that."

"No, I don't suppose so."

It was absurd to feel so disappointed, she told herself. She climbed back into the boxcar. Ludmilla was right, she thought. It was impossible to know him. He was a Man of Ice.

By early afternoon the mayor of the village had arrived to look over the damaged bridge. Nicholas was waiting for him by the river.

"Are you the chief engineer?" the mayor asked.

"Yes. Can you do the job?"

"Oh, I think so."

The mayor stroked his beard reflectively. Like almost all the Siberian natives, he carried an axe swinging at his belt. "Around here we like the long rubles from the railroad. Of course," he shrugged, "without the Czar's picture on it, maybe the ruble won't be as good as it used to be."

"You can't tell." Nicholas spoke cautiously. He didn't want to discourage the work, although it was his private opinion that the nation's economy was going straight to hell.

The man nodded. "Well, it doesn't make much difference. The bridge has to be fixed or Chernov will find out and then there'll be the devil to pay."

"Chernov? Is he here?"

"Yes, he and his Cossacks are quartered in the village."

The Mad Major, Nicholas thought, shoving his hands into his pockets. Damn. Chernov was another renegade Cossack, like Grigor Semenov. He had been with his regiment in Chita, when the revolution had broken out. Now he had gathered his men here in the east and was carrying out his own private war against Red partisans. "What is Chernov doing in the village?"

"Preparing a *bronevik*, in the railway repair shop. He needs the tracks, and he needs the bridge. What armored car can run on empty snow?" The man laughed harshly.

The armored cars—the broneviks—would be a key factor in the Siberian war, Nicholas thought, staring at the ground. The broneviks were converted railway cars, with armor plating bolted to the sides and sandbags piled on the roof. Machine guns were installed on top, or if machine guns weren't available, mounted rifles.

Chernov's bronevik would certainly need the railway bridge. The mayor of the village was right, it must be repaired as soon as possible. "How soon will the timber be ready?" he asked.

"Not until tomorrow."

Damn. More delay.

The mayor suddenly laughed with genuine mirth. "Hey, Inspector, I see you've gotten old in the last hour."

"Old?"

"Yes, your hair's turned white." With a chuckle, he pointed to Nicholas's dark eyebrows and mustache. They were frosted with silver. Then he winked. "Don't stay in Siberia too long; it's not good for your health."

"I'll bear that in mind."

"You might as well go into the village. There's nothing else to do today."

"Perhaps I will."

Horse-drawn sledges had already appeared by the side of the tracks, their drivers offering to take the passengers into the village. A market was in progress. All kinds of goods were on sale there—everything you need! Why sit out here in the middle of the wilderness?

"Ludmilla, do you want to come?" Daria asked inside the boxcar.

"Where?"

"To the market in the village. Drivers are outside with sledges. They'll take us back and forth."

"Oh no. I'll stay here, with the baby. It's too cold for him out there."

"Then I'll buy you something. What would you like?"

Ludmilla's face grew wistful. "Do you suppose they have dried apricots? We haven't had fruit for so long . . ."

"I'll look for some," she promised.

She climbed into one of the sledges and huddled in her sheepskin coat for warmth. She told herself to think warm thoughts. What could she think about? She closed her eyes. The smell of hot cabbage soup bubbling on the stove in the izba, the hiss of the samovar on the table. The livery stable: the warm, pungent odors of horseflesh and hay and leather,

47

and the blacksmith's strong male sweat, and kvass, the sour beer he drank with his bread and cheese and onions.

Spring along the meadow. The delicate scent of wild-flowers and spearmint and fresh grass. Lilies, forget-me-nots, damp earth, and a west wind on your face.

Her grandfather's pipe tobacco, and the smoky tobacco fragrance of his beard. Her mother's cheek, dimly remembered, cool and smooth and smelling of violet soap. Then a disturbing and vaguely exciting memory from years ago: the strange new womanly odor of her own body when it began to change; frightening, musky, and thrilling.

They had reached the market. It was being held outdoors in a huge space in the center of the village. There were no buildings, only hundreds of shaggy, ice-covered horses standing each with an ice-covered sledge. Peasants in huge fur hats and coats that swept to the ground, of black-and-white calfskin, black goatskin, black or brown or white bearskin, were selling goods of all kinds: wheat, oats, potatoes, onions, rough leaf tobacco, jars of cream, frozen blocks of milk, frozen freshwater fish, from sturgeon to bream, frozen meats, safety pins.

But Daria stopped short, walking between the sledges, as she caught sight of an animal that had haunted her childhood nightmares: a dancing bear.

The animal was led on chains by his owner, a narrow-faced man with darting eyes, wearing a wolfskin coat with a whip coiled at the belt and carrying a tambourine. The bear was shambling and filthy. His fur was matted, and patches had fallen out, showing scabby bare skin. His little eyes were dulled with apathy, and he snuffled pathetically as he walked. A ring passed through his snout, attached to a chain, and a heavy metal collar was fastened around his neck, rubbing it raw. The owner yanked on the chain, forcing the bear onto its hind legs. Then the animal lumbered clumsily from one paw to the other in a travesty of a dance. Villagers stood by clapping and laughing, enjoying the spectacle.

Daria watched in stormy silence. She'd clapped and laughed too, as a child. Then one day her grandfather had explained how the bears were trained. How vodka was forced down their throats to make them docile. How rings were speared through holes in their tender snouts. How collars were riveted around their necks and muzzles put over their mouths. How the bears reared up and fought in clumsy desperation, cutting their own flesh with their claws, trying to tear off the chains.

Worst of all was the way they learned to dance. A vicious tug on the nose chain was painful enough to make the animal rear. Then heated sheets of metal were placed beneath their forepaws, so that when they landed on all fours, they rose up again at once, lumbering from side to side, bewildered and tortured.

She hated it. She stood clenching her fists, knowing she should walk away.

The bear leader was banging his tambourine, quick eyes scanning the crowd for kopeks. He caught sight of Daria and grinned nastily. "You, there! What's wrong with you? Don't you like the performance?"

Go away. Don't answer.

But she couldn't help herself. "Somebody should put a ring through *your* nose," she said in a low angry voice. "And a collar around *your* neck, and see how you like it. I wonder how well you'd dance."

His face darkened. "What kind of remark is that?"

"You asked me how I liked the performance. So I told you."

The bear leader looked around to see if Daria was accompanied. He fingered the coiled whip at his belt. "Suppose you give me a more courteous answer, my girl. I don't care for your tone of voice."

"I don't care for the way you earn your living." She felt reckless and rebellious. She was a visitor and a stranger in this village, and her comments were unwelcome; she could see the frowns and muttering lips of the onlookers. But she didn't care. The spectacle of the miserable, mistreated animal was too vivid.

"Maybe you could do a better job," the bear leader sneered. "Suppose you come over here and make him dance."

"I certainly won't."

The bear had fallen back on all fours and was moving his massive head from side to side, relieved to be left alone. Some of the villagers began to call out. "Hey, make him dance." "Let's see a show!" "What's going on?"

"The young lady will provide the show," the bear leader yelled back. His mouth twisted meanly. "She doesn't like the way I do it. So she'll do it herself!"

Someone took Daria by the arm and pulled her forward. "Leave me alone," she said angrily, yanking her arm away.

"She doesn't want to." "She's too shy." "She needs to be encouraged."

"I'd rather see a pretty girl with a bear, than *your* ugly face!" somebody yelled. The bear leader laughed heartily with the others. This was turning into an unexpectedly good show. Daria was shoved forward, and she stumbled, then regained her balance. She heard a rattling of chains. The bear was padding back and forth restlessly, very close to her, and she could smell the musky animal odor of his body. The chain was being offered to her by a dirty hand with broken fingernails.

"Come on, take it. Don't be so timid. I'll share the kopeks."

"I don't want your money."

She only wanted to get away now. She hadn't accomplished anything by speaking her mind, except relieving her own feelings, and it was turning into an ugly, unpleasant scene. The crowd now had a human victim to torment for their entertainment. She'd been impulsive, and now she was regretting it. But whatever happened, she told herself, she would not tug on that chain. She curled her hands into fists and put them behind her back. Let someone try to force them open; she'd resist as long as she could.

The bear leader took a step forward, with his hand extended. Daria set her jaw.

"Oh good Lord, what sort of trouble are you in now?" It was a bored, world-weary drawl. Daria looked up to meet the cool blue gaze of Nicholas Federovsky. He was standing with his hands in his pockets, shaking his head. "My dear girl, what a talent you have for creating scenes." He glanced over at the bear leader and raised an eyebrow; one man of the world communicating with another. "You'll have to forgive my niece," he murmured. "She has a wayward tongue. She hasn't caused you any inconvenience, I hope?"

The other man narrowed his eyes. "Inconvenience?"

There was acid in the man's tone. "She ruined the whole performance."

"I did nothing of the kind," Daria said hotly.

Nicholas ignored her. "That's a pity. She has a bad habit of causing trouble." He'd casually taken Daria's arm and was drawing her away. "Perhaps you can make it up next time around."

"Wait a minute. How about *you* making it up?"

"I would if I could, dear fellow. But I'm just a little embarrassed for cash right now. Next time we meet, though, I'll do better, I promise you."

They were moving through the crowd, which was parting to let them by. Some of the villagers were snickering behind their hands at the expression on the bear leader's face. He stood holding the bear's chain, scowling in baffled frustration. In the next moment, Nicholas and Daria had moved away.

Daria took a breath. Cold, hard little knives of air moved in her lungs. They were standing among the sledges, far away from the dancing bear. "I was afraid there'd be violence!"

Nicholas laughed. "Well, that's the last resort, isn't it? Usually there's a better way." He paused, and she could feel the warmth of his fingers through her sheepskin jacket. "Of course, it isn't always possible to avoid it. Perhaps you would have been wiser to walk away."

His voice was gentle, but she sensed a subtle warning underneath the low tones. "I know that," she said, dropping her eyes. "Thank you."

"Not at all."

"I keep having to thank you."

"Fortunately for me, I keep finding opportunities to be of service."

She laughed in embarrassment. "You probably think I'm a nuisance."

"On the contrary. You might be surprised to know what I'm thinking."

She felt a tiny shock in the pit of her stomach. She tried to think of something to say that would be casual and light. As she searched her mind, Nicholas spoke again, and she caught a fleeting scent of pine cologne. "Do you know the meaning of 'avos'?" he asked softly.

She felt another lurch of surprise. Her eyes widened. "Avos?"

"Yes, it's a peasant belief—"

"Yes, I know what it means." In Saravenko they spoke often of avos. "Fate."

"Yes. Fate."

Why did he say that? Did he mean it? The sky overhead was a sullen gray; tonight it would snow. She seemed to hear the word *avos* sounding between the calls of the vendors and the whinnying of the horses, and she thought, I'll remember this market . . . this village . . . this day . . .

"Do you believe in fate?" she whispered.

"I don't know. I used to think not. But now . . ." He shrugged. "Well, it's hard to deny the Goddess of Destiny, isn't it?"

She stopped and gazed up into his face. How beautiful he was. There was silver frost along his eyebrows.

She felt overcome by confusion. Be careful not to drown in blue eyes, she whispered to herself. Then she realized he was changing the subject.

"I wanted to tell you how much I liked your song yesterday," he was saying casually as they continued to walk. "Where did you learn it?"

Daria flushed with pleasure. "I heard it for the first time in Chita when I was fourteen. My grandfather took me to Samsonovitch's Hotel, as a special treat. I was so impressed, because Samsonovitch's is the tallest building east of Irkutsk—it's four stories high. Well, that probably sounds silly to you—"

"No, it doesn't sound silly."

She had a sudden, violent wish, glancing up at him, that he would betray boredom or impatience. Instead he was gravely interested as he waited for her to continue. Oh, Nicholas, why aren't you ugly? she thought desperately. Why don't you have bad manners? Why aren't you pompous, or boring? Instead of being charming and interested in me, and listening so politely to my schoolgirl stories . . .

"Please go on, Daria," he said. "I would like to hear about it."

"I'm afraid I'm boring you."

He stopped. "My dear girl," he said quietly, "will you stop these foolish apologies? If I'm bored, I'll tell you."

52

She looked up uncertainly, wondering whether to believe him.

"I'll explain something now," he went on, "and then we'll drop the subject. Will you listen?"

"Yes."

"We're here together, at this moment, because we choose to be. That means both of us. You and I. If either one of us is bored, or wishes to be somewhere else, that person will make his or her feelings known very plainly, and the association will be ended. Until then, you'll have to assume that I like being with you, and enjoy your company. And I'll have to assume the same for you." He smiled. "Do you agree?"

"Yes."

"Good. Then after I buy you some dried sunflower seeds, you'll tell me more about Samsonovitch's Hotel."

After that, somehow, it was easy. As they walked between the sledges and she ate dried sunflower seeds and bought dried apricots for Ludmilla, she told Nicholas about the theater-restaurant at Samsonovitch's Hotel, on the Damskaya. About the performance she'd seen of scenes from *The Inspector General*. And afterwards, the gypsy singer, and how Daria had learned the words and hummed the melodies of her songs at home in the izba long after she'd forgotten the play.

When it was time for them to return to the train, she blushed guiltily. They were waiting for the sledge to take them back. "You know, I've talked about me all this time, and you haven't said a word about yourself."

"Haven't I?"

"You know you haven't."

"What would you like to know?"

Everything, she thought. "What did you do before the revolution? Before the train?"

"I lived in Kharkov. I owned an iron foundry."

"But you said at the train that you were a civil engineer."

"So I was. Until I bought the foundry."

Daria looked puzzled and Nicholas smiled. "You find that hard to understand, I see. How does a civil servant, working for the government on a small fixed salary, accumulate enough capital to go into business for himself?"

She nodded.

"Suppose," Nicholas said, "that the civil servant is an engineer in charge of a road-building project in the Ukraine. Suppose he has important decisions to make. For instance, shall he run the road here or there? Shall he buy this bit of property or that? Shall he build the highway through this little town or that one? Think of how important it could be to the officials of a town—to the merchants and property owners—to influence the engineer's decision." Nicholas raised an eyebrow. "They might even offer him money. Bribes, in fact."

"I can understand that."

"But would you be shocked to hear that the engineer accepted?"

Daria had to laugh at the ironic expression on his face. "No, I don't think so."

"Well, I'm glad of that. Not that I'm admitting anything, of course. Ah, the sledge is here."

It was easy, Nicholas thought, handing her up into the sledge, to tell it in a few words. But living it—that was not so easy.

It had taken him five years, after graduation from the Institute. Five years of waiting. Of cultivating the right friendships. Learning to know the proper people. Gracefully giving up credit to your supervisor when he expected you to do so. Flattering people at certain times, speaking up bravely at others: yes, Inspector General, no, Inspector General. That rotten game you hated, but had to play, knowing your time would come, forcing yourself to wait.

And then the road-building project had come along. It was the opportunity he'd been hoping for. He asked himself if he would balk at this hurdle. Was he too scrupulous? That would be fatal. His father had lived his life according to the code of a gentleman. But Nicholas didn't have that luxury. His father had died a pauper; he didn't intend to do the same.

The engineer of a road had great power, he knew that, all out of proportion to his title. So he would have to take the fullest advantage of that power. And he did.

Three years after the road-building project came along, Nicholas had accumulated enough money to hand in his notice and take the next step on his path. Now he had enough capital to borrow at a good rate of interest, and now he could strike out on his own.

He was living in the industrial city of Kharkov, near the coal-mining region of the Don Basin. If you wanted to make money, it was a good place to begin. He knew he had the most important personal qualification for making money: he was willing to devote all of his time and attention to it. His personal life didn't exist. His emotional life was barren. He was thirty years old, and he had no family, no wife or children, no brothers or sisters, only himself, and his goal. And if he was still lonely, well, he had grown so used to it he didn't even notice anymore.

He remembered the day he went to see the iron foundry. It had been the first week in April. It was still cold in Kharkov, still snowing, that time of year when energies ebbed and spirits drooped and spring seemed only a fantasy conceived by a winter-weary dreamer.

He'd been wearing his fur-lined overcoat and karakul hat as he stood within the gate, looking at the foundry. He was excited and happy, in spite of the weather, in spite of the dreary surroundings. Facing him was a small building of dirty red brick. Tiny windows in the brick wall were sealed shut and so coated with grime and dirt that only a bit of watery daylight could penetrate inside. Heaps of grayish snow covered the ground and the rutted road in front of the building. Next door to it was an empty lot filled with more dirty snow, with a few patches of bare brown earth showing through.

Overhead the sky was the color of steel. A few tired snowflakes drifted down one at a time, reminding him that spring was still in the future. Still a dream.

But it didn't matter, because his own personal dream was on the verge of coming true.

It was lunchtime. Workmen were pouring out of the main entrance, filling the yard, lighting cigarettes and unwrapping greasy bundles of food. Standing by the door, defiantly handing out leaflets to the men as they emerged, was a young man wearing steel-rimmed spectacles, hunched in a shabby jacket.

A socialist agitator, Nicholas thought. What damned audacity. Handing out his propaganda papers in the open, in the foundry yard.

The leaflets were printed on secret presses all over the city. It was impossible for the government to stamp them out. When the gendarmes smashed one press and arrested the agitators, another sprang up somewhere else, behind a dilapidated storefront with black-painted windows.

Even the young man with his leaflets didn't bother Nicholas. He felt only mild irritation. He dismissed the trouble-making agitator from his mind, strolled into the yard, and mingled with the workmen. They eyed him suspiciously. Too well dressed, too polished, too obviously upper-class; what the hell was he doing here? Nicholas ignored that too. He selected one of the men for conversation, an old worker with a grizzled beard and watery blue eyes.

"Tell me, Grandfather, how does it go?"

"What the hell do you care?"

Nicholas laughed. "I have a special interest."

After a moment the man hawked and spat on the ground. "Rotten."

"Oh?"

"The owner's a pig-faced bastard. He's a drunken pig." The man stared at Nicholas with hard little eyes. "Now go and tell him I said so."

"What's your name?"

"Ivan Grigorovitch."

Nicholas gazed reflectively at the old man. "I don't think I'll tell him," he said after a moment. "But I may do something else about it."

"Such as what?"

Nicholas only laughed and turned aside. Such as buy him out, he thought. This confirmed what he'd heard himself: the owner was more interested in his vodka than his profits.

But he, Nicholas, could make it pay. He was sure of it. The Trans-Siberian Railway was still not completed after all these years. With good friends in the government—and contracts to cast lengths of railway track—you might be able to do very well.

He did. Amazingly well, in an amazingly short time. He found that you didn't have to confine yourself to an iron foundry, although it began to thrive and expand and he hired more men. But there was real estate, there were stock market investments, there were influential friends to advise you, and there were various ways to get rich . . .

And then one day there was Céline.

Nicholas took a breath. He remembered where he was. Siberia.

The sledge had reached the boxcar, standing on the tracks in the icy wilderness. Céline was only an aching memory, and the only reality was here, now, this train, this burned-out bridge, this eye-hurting white tundra.

And this girl, whom he was now helping down from the sledge, and whose soft breasts were suddenly crushed against him, as she leaped to the ground.

Oh, Lord. A fiery pang of desire shot through his loins, taking him by surprise. He clenched his teeth. This wasn't the time or the place.

He held Daria away from him with his hands on her shoulders. "Are you frozen?"

She nodded, clasping her packages.

"We'll warm up inside."

Daria stepped back. She couldn't speak. Words were suspended at the back of her throat. She could still feel the warmth on her arms where Nicholas's hands had been. For no reason at all, she thought of Lev.

When Lev brushed my hand with his, she thought, back in Saravenko, did I feel this electric tingle? This deep shiver somewhere inside myself?

No.

What did it mean? Perhaps she would never know. *But if I could choose my destiny . . .*

Chapter 5

Four hundred miles to the north of the Trans-Siberian Railroad and the Amur River, a sleigh was approaching a small Siberian village. It was the end of March. Lev Omansky sat in the sleigh behind the driver. His friend Yuri sat muffled beside him. Lev felt the cold wind blowing against his face as they climbed uphill over a snowy road to the top of a rise. Another meeting ahead of us, he thought, feeling half-weary and half-excited. There'd been so many meetings. So many gatherings, so many speeches.

He knew what it would be like. He and Yuri had done it so often. The meeting would be held in the schoolhouse, a one-room log building. Inside they would find a group of scowling, bearded peasants with their arms folded across their chests and axes swinging from their belts. The women would be there too, with their broad faces and work-roughened hands and strong round arms. The place would be hot, thanks to the stove with its roaring logs in the corner of the room, and it would smell of onions, perspiration, and rotting leather. He would stand on one of the desks to make his speech.

But maybe not, he told himself tensely. Maybe things were changing. Maybe the time for speeches was coming to an end, and the time for fighting beginning. Skirmishes were breaking out along the railroad line to the south. Bridges were being burned, battles were being fought, a civil war was starting. What about this village? Would the peasants join the fight? On which side?

He shivered uncontrollably as he suddenly thought of another village: Saravenko.

You'd thank God, he told himself, if you believed in God, which you don't, that Daria got away on that train. Because a bloodbath was coming to Saravenko sooner or later.

He felt a strange ache in his chest as he thought of Daria, and remembered her dark eyes looking down at him from the open boxcar door. Why had he let her go? He had wanted her. So much. Why hadn't he taken her with him?

He knew why. It wasn't safe. Should he have put her life in danger too?

Was it safe on the Trans-Siberian Railway?

No. But it was better than here.

He should have done something, he thought unhappily. Something. Perhaps they could have been married. Yes, he should have insisted on that. Before Daria left. Then he would have a claim. Then she would have to wait for him in Harbin. She'd be his wife.

But he had a job to do in Siberia. He might never live to reach Harbin. Face facts, damn it, he told himself. Grow up. Stop thinking like a schoolboy.

Determinedly he turned his mind to the village that lay ahead.

"I think this time it'll be different," he muttered aloud.

"What will be different?"

"The muzhiks in this village, Yuri. They'll be different. I have a feeling."

"Don't you ever think about anything else?"

"What else is there to think about?"

"Some day," Yuri said patiently, "you're going to answer a question with a statement, instead of another question. Some day."

Lev grinned to himself. "All right, here's a statement. I know what you were thinking about."

"What?"

"Girls."

"You're a mind reader. How could you tell?"

"Because you were just too damned quiet." Lev put his hands into his pockets. "Christ, it's cold. You'd think we were in Siberia."

"Very funny."

"How far away are we from the village, do you suppose?"

"Not far. It's in the valley, at the bottom of the hill."

"It will be different when we get there. You'll see." Lev looked up at the vast gray sky. He was a long way from Kiev, he thought. Thousands of miles away. What was happening in Kiev? In Saravenko? "I was thinking about a girl myself."

They had topped the rise. The village came into view, nestled at the bottom of the hill. Two rows of log izbas lined the road, looking tiny and neat against the snow, with sheds and a lacing of fences behind them. The schoolhouse was a square log building with a porch. The church was painted white, with its onion dome making a deep blue curve against the gray-white sky. A long way from Kiev, Lev thought again. He remembered his mother, the worry and suspicion in her eyes, as she'd looked at him across the dining room table of their home in Kiev. Seven years ago, he thought. He remembered his father's house, with the white pillars standing by the front door, and the tea-rose bushes clustering by the porch, and the linden trees growing in the yard. He'd been sixteen, and already deeply involved in the revolutionary movement. But he hadn't told his parents. His mother suspected, though he hadn't told her. Dr. Omansky, his father, had no suspicion at all. Dr. Omansky's oldest son, a socialist revolutionary? Nonsense. Lev would become a physician, like his father. Anything else was adolescent foolishness.

Sorry, Papa.

Was it that night that Aaron Omansky's complacency had been shaken? Lev remembered the soup tureen steaming in the middle of the table, in the warm, fragrant dining room. It was schav, spinach soup. Dr. Omansky had come in late, as usual, after the meal had started, and he'd been furious. He held a printed leaflet in his hand, and he flung it angrily onto the table. "Look at this, Ida," he said to his wife. "Look what the fools are doing."

"What do you mean, Aaron?"

"Illegal printing presses all over the city are putting out this miserable rubbish."

Lev picked up the leaflet curiously.

"Let me see it, Lev." He handed it silently to his mother. "Aaron," she murmured, "sit down and have your soup." She began to read aloud. " 'Down with the Czar-murderer. Down with autocracy. Long live social democracy. Long live the constituent assembly. Long live the revolution!' " She put it down and shrugged. "This is nothing new."

Aaron glared at her. "Did you read what they said in the *Kievlanin* yesterday?"

"I read the paper every day."

"Papa," Lev remarked quietly, "there's some truth in what the leaflet says. The Czar *is* a murderer. He authorizes the pogroms, doesn't he?"

Dr. Omansky flushed. "Lev, that's enough. I won't be contradicted in my own house." He put down his soup spoon. "This revolutionary movement is foolish and dangerous," he said heavily, "and that's the end of the discussion. Now eat your dinner."

It wasn't the end, Lev thought rebelliously, staring down at the tablecloth. He picked up the fork. It was heavy silver, intricately carved with a pattern of grapes and grape leaves, and made a solid weight in his hand. It wasn't the end. It was the beginning. When he looked up, he met his mother's eyes; they were filled with dawning suspicion.

Was it that night, after dinner, or another night, that he'd told her the truth? He'd tried to explain, sitting beside her at the table, smelling her delicate French cologne.

"Mama, *you* taught me to care. To look around and see injustice. To read, to think, to take action. Not to sit by and watch while other people suffer. To do something about it. I learned it from you!"

"God help me, Lev." She'd gripped the edge of the table, and he saw her knuckles whiten. "What about your schooling? Your plans? Your medical studies? Have you given that up?"

"No, I'll go on with it, as long as I can."

"Lev, you're just a boy!" she cried. "Stop going to these meetings. Concentrate on yourself, on your goal. Sympathize if you like, but—"

"That's not enough, Mama." He shook his head. "It's not enough. You taught me that."

Her eyes grew dark with apprehension. She bowed her head. "My oldest son . . . my first born . . . what have I done to you?"

Two months ago in Kiev . . . seven years later . . . all Ida's fears had been realized. Those three days in Kiev, Lev thought as the sleigh began to move downhill toward the village, over the snow. Would anyone who lived through them ever forget those three days?

He'd been waiting with the rest of the Red Guard in the Lukianivka district, by the railroad station. There was no more thought of medical school in his mind. That was over. Now there was only the fight, and the battle to be won, and he'd felt frightened and happy at the same time. There would be action, at last. Right here in Kiev. After all the meetings, the leaflets, all the shouting and quarreling and confusion, and Piatakov rushing to the telephone every hour to consult with Stalin in Petrograd, and watching events in the north, in Petrograd and Moscow, the revolution had come to the Ukraine.

By the evening of the next day, the sky above Kiev was fiery red. The city was burning. Artillery shells were exploding, one after the other, boom, boom, boom, without stopping. People were hiding in their cellars, weeping with fear, clinging to their children. And at the intersection of Volodmyrsky and Pidvalna Streets, where the heaviest shells were falling, the pavement was splattered with a hideous pink gruel that had once been human flesh.

Lev finally made his way, grimy and exhausted, through the burning streets to the house beneath the linden trees. The home of his parents.

He found the Omanskys in the cellar. His mother and father. His brother Daniel. His little sister Rhea. All the servants. He descended the stairs in his filthy, sweat-stained clothes, reeking of cordite and blood, and stared at them with red-rimmed eyes. Dampness and the odor of coal dust filled his nose. "I have to leave," he blurted hoarsely. "I came to see if you were safe. But now I have to leave."

"Where? Where are you going?" It was Ida, with her arms around her daughter.

"Siberia."

"Oh my God—"

"Lev," Aaron said. "Lyova—what about your family?"

Oh, God. He was tired. He felt like crying. He turned away to hide the tears in his eyes. He had no more family. You made a choice and you were committed to it. For better or worse. You put your feet on the path and you had to follow it all the way to the end. *Don't you understand that, Mama? Papa, don't you see?*

They had reached the foot of the hill. The sleigh was coming to a halt in front of the schoolhouse. The schoolmaster, a young man with round steel-rimmed spectacles, was standing on the porch.

Yuri grabbed Lev by the arm. "Look at that, comrade," he muttered. "All power to the soviets—I think you were right."

"Yes, I was right!" Lev wanted to laugh out loud. He felt a wave of fierce joy as he stared at the group of people on the porch. Behind the schoolmaster stood a gathering of muzhiks, all armed with scythes and axes. Some were carrying rifles. A few had attached homemade red stars to their caps. They surged down to the side of the sleigh, surrounding it as soon as it halted.

"Where's your partisan camp?" one of them growled.

"Not far from here," Lev replied. "In the pine forest."

"We'll go back with you. Never mind a meeting. We're ready to fight."

"What happened?" Yuri looked up at the schoolmaster.

"Two weeks ago, the White Army asked for volunteers from the village, to fight the Reds. We told them to go to hell, we weren't interested in fighting. So last week they sent a punishment squad. They built a bonfire, down there"—He pointed to the end of the road. "And then they took hostages—"

"All right," Lev interrupted. "You don't have to say any more." He looked around at the peasants, and raised his voice. "You know now what kind of bastards we're up against!"

"We know."

"And you're ready to fight back, with everything you've got!"

"We're ready."

"Very well. We won't have a meeting. We'll go back to camp!"

Committed, he thought passionately, as some of the men climbed into the sleigh. He felt the cold stinging his eyes and tiny beads of ice forming on his eyebrows. He brushed at them impatiently. Committed. No turning back. He remembered another village schoolmaster: Alexey Alexeyevitch, Daria's grandfather. Lev had done his best for him before leaving the village. "You'll need all your people in Saravenko, when the Savage Division comes! You'll need to defend your izbas, and your soviet! You can't afford to lose anyone who can fire a weapon or swing an axe! Let Alexey Alexeyevitch live! Wait for the Savage Division! There'll be enough bloodshed to satisfy everybody then!"

The villagers of Saravenko would probably go down fighting in a welter of blood when Semenov's men rode in, he thought. The civil war would spare no one. The Bolshevik government was established in Petrograd and Moscow, but resistance continued everywhere else. Officers of the Imperial Army were organizing a White Guard. There was fighting in the Ukraine. In the Don Basin. Here in Siberia. Cossack *hetmans* were running wild, desperate to return the Czar to his throne.

But this village would be different, he thought. It would not be like Saravenko. These people were taking to the woods. It would be partisan tactics from now on. And they'd win. He felt fiercely certain. No matter how long it took, they would win.

The driver turned the sleigh around and they started back up the hill.

Chapter 6

Daria stood in the snow by the railroad tracks. Behind her was the stalled locomotive. Ahead were the pewter sheen of the frozen river, the jagged shape of the half-repaired bridge, and the swarming figures of workmen with axes, hammers, saws, and lengths of timber. The work was going well; she'd heard the fireman say so to one of the passengers.

Because of Nicholas, she thought. She wrapped her arms around herself, searching for him among the workmen. Then she found him, standing on the ice, talking to a barrel-chested man who was the head of the village work crew. The man was nodding his head as Nicholas pointed out something on the span.

He was busy. And she couldn't stand still very long, she had to keep moving. She'd come out only to get some exercise, she told herself, not to stand gazing wistfully at Nicholas from a distance like a moonstruck schoolgirl.

She began to walk up and down along the tracks, as she'd been doing, head down, moving briskly, keeping in motion, swinging her arms, trying to stay warm, and taking shallow breaths of the icy air. She became so absorbed in the rhythm of her movement that she barely heard the thud of hooves until it was almost upon her. Then she raised her head in surprise.

Men on horseback?

Yes—eight of them. No, ten.—No, a dozen—galloping all around, wielding whips and calling to each other in deep hoarse voices, circling the train and then pounding toward the river. She could see woolen coats with wide skirts flaring over polished boots, the gleam of silver spurs, the flash of swords, and the glitter of belt buckles on wide leather belts.

Cossacks!

They'd come to inspect the bridge repair, she thought. She knew they were quartered in the village. She'd seen some of them strolling through the market the other day, and people were gossiping on the train that Chernov, their hetman, was making inquiries about the repair. He'd been threatening to come and see for himself how matters were progressing.

Which one of these men was the Mad Major?

She had little time to wonder. Hooves suddenly flew by dangerously close to her cheek, startling and frightening her, and she sprang back to avoid them. A Cossack was wheeling his mount and coming back toward her. He was laughing; she could see the flash of his teeth under his red-blond mustache. He dug his spurs into the animal's flanks, drawing blood, and the horse neighed long and loud, rolling its eyes. Then it was galloping forward, straight at her. She barely had time to think. She dodged at the last minute, jumping to one side, feeling hot animal breath on her face as the horse galloped by.

The Cossack wheeled again, preparing another charge. This was some kind of malicious game, she thought angrily. Her indignation overcame her fright.

"What do you think you're doing?" she shouted.

"Trying to get your attention, my sweet!"

He was charging again, and she backed away, wondering where she could go. There was no way to outrun him, and no shelter. She was too far from the train, and if he intended to run her down . . .

But he reined abruptly, by her side. The heaving flank of the animal was almost brushing her arm. Quickly, before she could move, he leaned down from the saddle and clasped her under the arms with hard strong hands, yanking her up in front of him. His arms locked around her, one hand fastened firmly over her breast.

She tried to wrench herself away. "Put me down!"

"But you're cold. You need to be warmed up." He

brushed back her hair and spoke directly into her ear.

"Stop that!" He was pinching her nipple through the jacket. He was hurting her, and his touch was revolting to her. So was the heat of his breath against her cheek.

"Stop what?" he whispered, laughter gurgling in his throat.

"You're hurting me. Stop it!"

"Give me a kiss, darling, and I'll stop."

"No!"

"Why so stingy? Pretty girls should be more generous with their kisses."

A strong, cruel hand was suddenly gripping her jaw, forcing her head around, tilting her face up. She was looking straight into his eyes: green, with hazel flecks, glittering with harsh laughter. He brought his mouth down on hers, slowly and deliberately, holding her head perfectly still, demonstrating her helplessness. Then he began to explore her mouth with his, prolonging a hot searching kiss. He forced his tongue between her lips. She kept her teeth clamped, trying to twist away.

Finally he drew back. "You're not very cooperative, darling. Do you always keep your mouth closed like that?"

She drew her sleeve across her mouth, as if to wipe away the taste of his kiss.

"That's not what ladies usually do when I kiss them."

"Put me down!"

"Try another song, sweetheart. I've heard that one before." He leaned close to her ear. "I'll tell you what. Suppose you come back with me to the village, and we'll try again. Under—shall we say—nicer circumstances. With a warm fire and a soft bed, perhaps you'll thaw out a little and say something else. Such as 'Grisha don't stop, I love what you're doing, it's heaven.'" He laughed softly. He pulled her closer. "Maybe we'll leave right now."

She tried to calm down and collect her thoughts. "Don't you have something to do, like the others? Some business to attend to, other than tormenting a perfect stranger?"

"No. It can wait. Chernov isn't here yet."

He gripped her chin again, and turned her head up. She steeled herself for another ordeal of resistance.

This will be over soon, she thought. It had to be!

67

The hot mouth was on hers again, and the hot tongue was seeking again, more insistently. He sank his teeth into her lower lip, biting sharply, and she cried out in pain.

"Don't fight me, sweetheart," he whispered hoarsely. "Cooperate."

It couldn't last much longer, she thought, fighting panic. He couldn't mean to gallop away with her. But she felt the tension of his body and sensed the horse moving restlessly beneath her, and told herself desperately not to cry.

On the river by the bridge, Nicholas was standing among his workmen. He raised his head and glanced angrily at the circling, galloping Cossacks. "What the hell do they want?" he muttered aloud.

"They're Chernov's men. I warned you." The mayor had come up beside him. "They're anxious to get their armored car moving. There's fighting to the east, and they want to get into it."

"Where's the famous major?"

"I don't see him."

Nicholas suddenly caught sight of a mounted figure on a restlessly moving horse with a small form clasped in the saddle before him. It was Daria, he was sure of it; he'd seen her walking back and forth by the tracks only a few minutes ago. Anger surged over him. Without stopping to think, he picked up an axe and started forward over the ice.

"Hey, where are you going?" called the mayor.

"I want to see what's going on over there. I have a feeling it's something I'm not going to like."

"It's just one of the Cossacks, and a girl."

"Yes, that's what I'm afraid of."

The mayor called after his retreating back, "What are you going to do, threaten him with an axe? He has a rifle and a pistol."

"I'll decide when I get there."

Nicholas came to the edge of the ice and started up the river bank, holding the axe. Then he stopped. A horseman had reined up just in front of him, blocking his way; a new arrival. This man was seated with careless ease on a chestnut stallion. His gloved hand toyed with a riding whip. Like the others, he wore a cartridge belt strapped across his chest over his greatcoat. From the wide leather belt at his waist hung his sword in a black-and-silver scabbard, his pistol in its holster and a leather map case. The skirts of his coat flared to midcalf, meeting the tops of his polished boots. A rifle was slung across his shoulders.

"What seems to be the trouble, Inspector?"

The tone of careless authority was unmistakable.

Beneath his tall karakul hat, the officer's face was hard and handsome. But there was a hint of cruelty in the thin-lipped mouth; a touch of madness in the hot, restless eyes.

Dmitri Pavlovitch Chernov, the Mad Major. His reputation was spreading from Trans-Baikalia to the Golden Horn, like that of his fellow hetmans Semenov and Kalmikov, and he knew it, and enjoyed it, and now he smiled thinly down into Nicholas's eyes. "Are you the chief engineer?"

"Yes."

"Why haven't I seen you before?"

"Perhaps you have. In the village."

"I think not. I would have remembered." Chernov's eyes flickered over Nicholas's face. "I am Dmitri Chernov."

"Nicholas Federovsky."

"If you're the engineer, then where are you headed? The work is in the other direction."

Nicholas nodded shortly toward the figure by the tracks, with Daria still clasped in the saddle. "We seem to have a problem over there."

"Oh? What sort of problem?" Chernov turned his head.

"One of your men, Major. Call off your dog."

"Call off—ah, yes." The Major laughed. "Striabin. As usual, he's found himself a bitch." He turned casually back to Nicholas. "Striabin's a good officer in combat. But he's like a woman, he gets confused about his brains. He thinks they're between his legs, instead of between his ears."

"Call him off, Major."

"Of course, Inspector Engineer. At your service." The major lifted an ironic eyebrow and shifted in the saddle. "Striabin!" he called across the snow.

"Yes, sir." Striabin straightened his shoulders and lifted his head.

"Put the bitch down."

"Yes, sir," came the prompt answer.

Daria felt herself released. She was suddenly sliding to the ground, across the horse's flank. The soles of her boots hit the snow and she staggered before standing upright. Her mouth trembled, and she felt a stinging in her bottom lip where he'd bitten her, until the frigid temperature, like an anesthetic, stopped the hurt. She struggled to keep her face impassive and not betray her revulsion at the coarse handling she'd received. She told herself that nothing had happened. It was nothing. It could have been worse. Much worse. She wasn't a child. She mustn't act like one.

"Striabin," the major called pleasantly.

"Yes, sir?"

"Twenty-five lashes, when we return to quarters."

Striabin's face paled beneath the cold-bitten redness of his skin. But he only repeated tonelessly, "Yes, sir."

"Remind me, Striabin, when we get back. In case I forget."

"Yes, sir."

"You must learn how to behave among civilians, lieutenant. After all, we're not animals, are we?"

"No, sir."

The major chuckled and turned back to Nicholas. Amusement glinted in his eyes. "Satisfied, Inspector Engineer?"

"I asked you to release the girl, and you've done it."

"What about Striabin's punishment?"

"That doesn't interest me."

"No?" The major was mildly astonished. His eyes flicked up and down again over Nicholas's form. "Not interested in twenty-five lashes?"

"No."

"But it's an instructive sight, to see a man stripped and lashed."

"How you discipline your officers is no concern of mine."

Chernov leaned forward across the pommel. "No, perhaps not," he said in a soft voice. He began to study Nicholas's face; his expression changed subtly. When he spoke

70

again, his tone was different, and held a more intimate note. "Tell me something. Were you ever in the east before? Perhaps in 1904 or 1905? During the Russo-Japanese War? I was here myself then."

"No."

"St. Petersburg, then. Were you ever in Petersburg?"

"Yes. Years ago."

"When? What year?"

Nicholas paused. "I was last there in 1903," he said shortly.

"Yes, that would fit. It is possible . . . I entered the Corps of Cadets in 1903. Perhaps I saw you in Petersburg a long time ago. You seem familiar to me after all."

Nicholas narrowed his eyes. "I don't believe we've ever met."

"You'd recall, is that it?" Chernov laughed.

"I'm quite sure of that, Major," Nicholas said coldly.

Chernov laughed again. "Well then, you must remind me of someone." He fell silent for a moment. Then his eyes widened. "Andrey, of course. My good friend Andrey Mikhailovitch. He's dead now, poor fellow. But I remember him very well." He looked off into space, and permitted himself a reminiscent smile. "Exceedingly well," he murmured, half to himself. Then he turned back to Nicholas. "Not that you resemble him particularly. He had rather coarse features and a pitted skin. But still, Andrey had certain natural endowments that were quite . . . remarkable." He leaned forward. "Shall I describe them?" he asked softly.

"No."

"Ah. How quickly you say no." Chernov sat back with an amused look on his face. "But I believe you are like Andrey in those respects. I'm certain of it, in fact." His eyes flicked again, up and down. "In those judgments, my friend, I am never wrong."

There was nothing to say to that. Nicholas clenched his jaw and remained silent.

"Not interested, I see," Chernov remarked. He cleared his throat. His tone of voice changed again and became brisk. "I think you're a stubborn man, Inspector," he said. "I see a stubborn look on your face. That's a pity. Because otherwise it's quite a nice face. But you could use a little discipline." He paused. Then he demanded casually, "Have you ever been whipped?"

Nicholas's eyes hardened, but he continued to keep silent.

Chernov sat back, fingering his whip. "Well, you won't answer, but I would think not. But it is quite amusing. There is a point, you see, when pain becomes the exquisite agony of pleasure." He raised the riding whip in his hand and then lowered it slowly until it was at right angles to his chest. Then he burst into harsh laughter. "Do you take my meaning?"

Nicholas narrowed his eyes. Chernov had made himself quite clear.

The major smoothed his mustache with his hand. "If you were under my command, I think you would be lashed quite often." He suddenly glanced down at Nicholas and the casual amusement died away from his face. His voice hardened. "Do I disgust you, Inspector?"

"Yes, Major, you do."

"You believe in telling the truth, I see."

"I see no reason not to."

"You should lie, and try to please me. Don't you know how to lick boots?"

"When it's necessary."

"But you don't think it's necessary now, is that it?"

Nicholas gave him a steady glance. "I don't think it will make any difference, Major Chernov," he said evenly, "whether I flatter you or insult you. You seem to have come to your own conclusions about my character."

"Quite right. You have an arrogant nature. I can see that clearly. You're in need of punishment; it would be very beneficial to your character."

"No doubt it would."

Nicholas's sarcastic tone was not lost on Major Chernov. But after a moment he chose to ignore it. "Come and have dinner with me tonight," he said pleasantly. "In my quarters. I have a fairly decent bordeaux put away, it will go well with the shashlik. It ought to make an agreeable change from this filthy train." He smiled. "And after dinner, of course, Striabin will provide the entertainment."

"No thank you." Nicholas's voice was curt. "I prefer familiar surroundings."

"Are you sure?"

"Very sure."

"Ah." The major glanced over at the small figure of Daria, standing in the snow beside the train. "You prefer to stay here and ride the mare." His mouth twisted. "That's too bad. You see, I am a dangerous enemy." He gave Nicholas a meaningful stare. "She can only give you a few moments of pleasure," he said with heavy emphasis. "I, on the other hand, can promise you a great deal else."

"I'm afraid I'll have to refuse your offer."

"Suppose, then," the major said slowly, "I take the bitch with me. As a hostage. Along with"—his glance took in the snow-covered steppe, the frozen river, and the burned-out bridge—"five or six passengers. And treat them to some of my famous hospitality." He settled back with a charming, intimate smile. "Will that please you?" he inquired, lifting his eyebrow. "It will be your fault, you know—your choice. Like Striabin's twenty-five lashes."

Nicholas came to a swift decision. He had to gamble now, he thought, he had no choice. He walked up close to the chestnut stallion and put his hand on the saddle. "If you take any hostages," he said steadily, with a level stare at Chernov, "any at all, I will call off my workmen and walk away from this job. At once. The bridge will stay as it is. Useless. You will remain trapped in this village with your armored car until you can find yourself another engineer. And that might take days. Maybe weeks." He paused. "Can you lose the time?"

Chernov stared down angrily. He had undergone another lightning change of mood. "Bolshevik tactics, Inspector?" he demanded coldly. "Are you threatening a strike?"

"Call it whatever you choose."

Nicholas was perspiring lightly under his jacket. He had no idea if the men would obey his command to stop working. They were probably more frightened of Chernov and his Cossacks than they were responsive to his own authority. But he had put the steely ring of conviction into his voice, and he was gambling on Chernov's impatience to be on his way east with the bronevik.

"How soon," Chernov said in a cold tight voice, "will the repair be finished?"

"Day after tomorrow."

"Very well. Finish the job. But I'll come back to inspect it when it's done. And when I do, if I find any flaw—any fault whatsoever, in the smallest detail—I'll hold you personally responsible. Do you understand?"

"Certainly."

"Pray I find nothing to criticize."

Nicholas said nothing.

Chernov threw back his head and laughed. "I'll find something, Inspector! You can depend on that!" He indulged himself in one last lingering glance at Nicholas's face. Then he spurred his horse. "I'll be interested to see," he called as the animal reared on its hind legs and whinnied, "how well you respond to discipline. When the time comes!"

He wheeled the stallion and galloped off across the snow, signaling with his riding whip to the rest of his men, who spurred their mounts and followed in a flare of skirted coats.

Nicholas let out his breath, watching the disappearing figures of the Cossacks, who were rapidly becoming flying black shapes against the skyline. Chernov hadn't even bothered to disguise his intentions, he thought. Or his own nature. He would treat Daria cruelly, if he got the chance, since he obviously hated women, but the true object of his torture would be Nicholas himself.

He couldn't let Chernov have that opportunity.

He shot a worried glance at Daria. She seemed to be unharmed; he didn't think she'd been hurt in any way. But he would have to speak to her later. Right now he had more pressing concerns.

He walked onto the ice and called over the train engineer, the mayor of the village, and the head of the work crew. When they were all standing in a group, he turned to the barrel-chested workman.

"How soon do you think this job can be finished?"

"You know that better than I do, Inspector."

"I want you to tell me."

The man pulled his bottom lip. "Noon tomorrow?"

Too late.

Nicholas looked down at the bumpy ice. After a moment he said slowly, "I told Chernov it would take another two days. Naturally I was lying, and he probably didn't

74

believe me. I expect him back tomorrow, to look over the work. If he does come back, and finds me still here . . ." Nicholas smiled ruefully, "Well, I have a strange itching feeling across my shoulder blades."

The barrel-chested man laughed harshly. "I'm not surprised. I've seen a man's back, when Chernov's finished with him. It looks like raw meat."

"Exactly." Nicholas looked into his eyes. "I'd like you to ask your men to stay, Akim Igorovitch, and finish up tonight. With torches and bonfires, and food and vodka from the village, I think we can have the bridge in good enough condition by midnight for the train to get across. By tomorrow morning we'll have Chernov behind us. And then I think the Red partisans will keep him busy."

Akim Igorovitch considered. He glanced at the mayor of the village. "Who pays for the vodka?"

"I'll pay," Nicholas said.

"Can we trust you?"

"That's up to you." Nicholas gave a wry shrug. "The truth is, Akim Igorovitch, I care more for my skin than a few rubles. I can assure you of that."

After a moment the mayor nodded. He held out his hand. "Done, Inspector. I'll speak to the men. You'd better set the passengers to work building bonfires."

He strode off across the ice to the crew of workers.

Nicholas turned to the train engineer. "How well are we supplied with wood for the engine?"

"Fairly well, I think. I'll talk to the fireman. If we need more, there's a wood station a few versts up ahead. We can put the passengers to work fetching it. They can use the exercise."

"Right. Let's get started, then."

The sun would be setting in about an hour, Nicholas thought, looking up at the sky as the engineer walked away. These days were so short.

But God willing, by midnight they'd be moving again, and out of Chernov's reach.

Chapter 7

The train was moving. The pistons were beginning to pump back and forth, and steam was boiling up in a hissing cloud, white against the darkness. Nicholas heard the engine begin its low chug. He looked back once at the bonfires leaping crimson-orange-black against the dark snow, and raised his hand in farewell to Akim Igorovitch, the mayor of the village, and the other men, who were waving back, just shadowy figures now in the light of the torches, bulky and shapeless in their sheepskins and furs. Then he put both hands on the side of the moving car, hauled himself up in one quick surge of movement, and leaped inside.

He leaned against the door, feeling the train shake beneath his feet. He asked himself tensely if the bridge would hold.

The work had been done quickly and well, but would it hold the weight of the train? He'd checked the time before leaving; it was only half past midnight. They had hours in which to put distance between themselves and Major Chernov. One of the bridge crew, whose brother worked in the railway yard, had assured him that Chernov's bronevik would be delayed for a few days before it was completed.

"We have no love for the Cossacks," he'd muttered to Nicholas. "Or the Czar either, when it comes to that. In fact, the true feeling is—" He dug his elbow into Nicholas's side and spoke in a growl, "all power to the soviets, comrade."

76

Most of the railway workers felt that way, Nicholas knew. In this case it had worked to his advantage.

Suddenly he drew in his breath. Abrupt silence had fallen in the boxcar. The train was starting over the bridge. The vibration of the car was subtly different, and the atmosphere was suddenly charged with tension and fear.

Inch by inch now, the train was dragging itself forward. Groaning, hesitating, like a wounded animal, it was putting more weight on the bridge with every second that passed.

Nicholas closed his eyes and imagined the sensation of falling. The sound of a crash. The blinding pain of broken bones. If something went wrong—if anything went wrong . . .

The locomotive picked up speed. The rhythm changed again. The train was moving faster and faster, with the clacking confidence of solid ground beneath the tracks. Nicholas let out his breath. They were over the bridge.

He sighed. He began to look around the car for Daria. He hadn't spoken to her all day, he'd been too busy; and now that the danger was past, he began to think about the Cossack Striabin, holding her in front of him on the saddle. At this moment, the lieutenant was paying for that playful little bit of business, but it didn't prevent Nicholas from feeling angry at the memory.

Most of the passengers were gathered by one of the shelves, talking excitedly. He saw faces turn to him, and knew they wanted to come over and offer congratulations and thanks.

"Will you join us?" someone called. "We have some Georgian wine. We owe you a drink."

"Later," he said, smiling briefly. "Save it for me. I need a few minutes to rest."

They would leave him alone for a while, he thought, taking out a cigarette. Was Daria with them? No, she was alone on her shelf, looking slightly wistful and lost. He wondered why she wasn't with the rest of the group. Maybe that lieutenant had been more abusive than he'd thought. Damn that son of a bitch. He stared at her, willing her to get up and come over to the door, away from the others.

After a moment, sensing his gaze, she looked over and met his eyes.

"Do you want company?" he said in a low voice.

"I don't mind."

"Come and join me, then. The air is a little fresher over here."

She rose from the shelf and walked over to him, balancing against the rocking motion of the car. When she reached him, Nicholas crushed out his cigarette against the wall, and then took her arm. He looked down carefully into her face. "Tell me, did he hurt you?" Displeasure at the memory of what had happened curled in his mind.

"You mean this afternoon, by the train?"

"Yes, the Cossack lieutenant."

"No, he only—he—" Daria touched her mouth; the stinging had gone away. "He kissed me, that's all."

"I imagine you survived that fairly well."

Nicholas heard the undertone of anger in his voice and disliked himself for it. He wasn't angry with her, but at what had occurred; yet she had no way of knowing that. He told himself to be reasonable, it wasn't her fault. Still, she was here, and the lieutenant was not, and he had no other outlet for his anger. "I'm sure you'll recover."

Daria blinked. Nicholas's gaze was cold and withdrawn, the Man of Ice again. She wanted to rouse him. It was all very well for her to make light of what had happened. But she wanted Nicholas to care, to show some concern. "Actually that wasn't quite all."

"No? What else was there?"

"He put his hand on my breast."

"I see."

It wasn't the answer she'd been hoping for.

"And then he—he did something quite disgusting," she added.

"What was that?"

"He tried to force his tongue into my mouth."

She waited for a reaction. There was none.

"Indeed," was all he said. "And you found that disgusting?"

She looked at him indignantly, "Yes, I did!"

He put his hands on her shoulders and drew her forward. "Oh Daria, what a child you are sometimes."

"I am not!"

It was an absolutely childish answer. She hated herself.

78

But at least Nicholas didn't resemble the Man of Ice anymore. He was almost smiling.

"Come here," he said.

Obediently she moved closer to him.

"Now tip up your head."

She did as he asked. Instinctively she closed her eyes. Her heart was racing. She felt his hand on her chin, tilting up her face. It was what the lieutenant had done, but there was no other similarity. This time she was deeply excited, and she felt a sudden pulsing throb somewhere in the center of herself, in a place she couldn't name. Nicholas bent his head and covered her mouth with his.

She melted. Everything inside her was turning to liquid. She was afraid she would fall. Her arms went up around his neck, and she swayed against him. He held her steady with his hands on her waist.

"Open your mouth."

She parted her lips, knowing what would happen. And it did. Oh, God. Her breasts tautened. She pressed closer. *Go on. Please, go on. Don't stop, don't ever stop, you're making me feel that I want . . . I want . . .*

He drew back and held her away, while she took long steadying breaths. "Were you disgusted?"

"No," she whispered. Her knees were trembling.

"Why not?"

"It—it was different."

"Only your feelings. And mine." He reached out his hand and touched her cheek. "I'm sorry, I shouldn't have done that. But you were teasing, you know."

"I didn't mean to."

He laughed. "Yes you did. But it's all right. I wanted to kiss you. That way."

"Nicholas," she whispered, "this afternoon, by the bridge—when you were talking to the major—I saw him look at me."

"Yes."

"And then he made a remark to you, and you seemed angry. Was it about me?"

"I believe it was."

"Did he say something about you and me?"

"Yes."

"Did he say that I was your mistress?"

.79

"Something of the sort."

She felt herself flushing, and knew her cheeks were red. Nicholas looked down into her eyes. When he spoke, his voice was gentle. "Would that be such a terrible fate?"

She couldn't answer. She felt a thrill of fear and excitement run through her, and knew it was what she dreaded, and longed for, with all of her mind and body.

"I—I'd better say good night," she managed to say.

"Good night, Daria."

She knew she wouldn't sleep. She turned aside to go to her shelf, knowing she would relive in her mind the warm, searching pressure of his mouth and tongue, and the taste of his breath, and the touch of his hands, over and over, and she wished she could turn back time and make it happen again.

Two days later, the train was halted again. This time there was no apparent reason, and the passengers discussed it among themselves in worried voices. Every delay now was a greater threat to their safety.

But the nearby village had a *banya*—a public bath. It was a way to escape the cold and grime of the railroad car, if only for an hour or two, and the passengers grasped eagerly at the chance to go into the village.

At the hour for women, Daria and Ludmilla entered the shabby little entrance room of the banya. The plank walls were lined with wooden shelves that were stacked with coarse cotton sheets and wooden buckets. They both stripped off their clothes and wrapped themselves in the sheets. Then they helped themselves to buckets and entered the steam room.

Daria sighed deeply. Heat and moisture surrounded her. Hot humid clouds of steam were swirling around her face and body. After a moment she could see the row of wooden benches along one wall, and the brick oven in the corner of the room, with steam pouring out of it. A barrel of hot water stood next to the oven, and as she watched, a woman dipped her bucket into the barrel and flung it onto the bricks of the glowing oven. Fresh clouds of steam rushed hissing into the air.

"Come," Ludmilla murmured, "let's not waste our time. We may not get another chance like this."

They went to the barrel and filled their buckets. Daria unwrapped her sheet and soaped herself with her precious bar of soap. Then she splashed the hot water from the bucket over her body. Streams of hot water and soap lather went pouring down her legs, and puddled on the wooden floor, washing away the dirt and grime.

She sighed again. How simple, how commonplace, how incredible. A hot bath.

Finally she wound the sheet around her clean body and climbed to the highest row of the wooden benches where the temperature was hottest. She sat back and let the heat and the steam turn her hair into wispy, curling tendrils around her cheeks, and closed her eyes, perspiring and content.

After a while, lulled and soothed by the heat, she began to think about Nicholas. He hadn't referred to the night he had kissed her, but instead acted as though it had never happened. Deep in her mind, she felt baffled and frustrated by his behavior, although she knew it would be sensible to follow his lead.

But she didn't feel sensible. She wanted to provoke him and make what had happened before happen again. Was that wise?

She wondered if she ought to ask Ludmilla for advice. But Ludmilla had had little experience with men. She'd known only Boris, who'd been her childhood sweetheart, and she might even be shocked at the idea of Daria's willingly becoming the mistress of someone she'd only known since boarding this train.

There was always Zora. Daria shuddered slightly. No, she couldn't approach Zora and face the sly grins and coarse remarks of the gypsy woman. And she knew without question that Nicholas would be very angry if he found out.

She would have to wait for an opportunity, and act on her own.

I will, she resolved, wrapping the sheet more tightly around herself. When the time comes, I'll do something.

In the boxcar, the men had already returned from the banya.

Nicholas, lying on his shelf, was staring at the ceiling

with his arms folded under his head. He looked around at footsteps. Ludmilla's husband Boris was approaching.

"Excuse me, I don't mean to disturb you," Boris began.

"Not at all."

"You know we've been at this stop for a long time . . ."

"Yes, there's obviously a problem." Nicholas frowned.

"I've been making inquiries. The trouble is with the officials. The commissar of the station and the commissar of the traffic service are delaying. They say they need instructions from Moscow before the train can move."

"The usual story."

"I thought if we all contributed a few rubles and offered them an inducement . . . you know . . . maybe that would get us moving." Boris looked troubled. "My baby isn't very well. He's coughing, and my wife thinks he has a fever . . . well, that's not your affair. But I'd like to get to Vladivostok as soon as I can."

Nicholas was silent for a moment. "How many rubles can you afford?" he asked.

Boris flushed. "It doesn't matter. Whatever is required, I'm willing to contribute."

"All right. I'm sure your reasoning is sound." Nicholas stood up. "But before we all put up our cash, let's make even surer."

"How?"

Nicholas looked reflective. "Suppose someone goes and talks to them. That's the simplest way. Then comes back and reports to the others. We'll have a clearer idea of the situation, after that."

Boris nodded. "Shall I go?"

"If you like."

The young man straightened his shoulders. Then he hesitated. After a moment he cleared his throat. "I think you'd better go. You'll know better than I what to say. That is, if you don't mind."

"Very well. If you think it's a good idea."

"I do."

When Boris had gone back to his family, Nicholas stood reflecting. There were other things you could offer, besides money, to the commissar of the station. For instance, that unopened bottle of French brandy he'd carried all the way from Kharkov. What an exercise in self-control it had been, not to break the seal. He thought of all the cold, shivering moments when he'd fought down the impulse to open the bottle. After a while it had become a test of his own willpower. Wait. Save it. There may come a time when you really need it. Was this the time? No, he thought. There were *two* commissars. One bottle of brandy would not go far enough.

Then he had to smile at himself. Was he just making excuses, in order to save the brandy for himself? At any rate, he had two fresh bottles of vodka. He would try that first.

He slipped the bottles into his sheepskin, one in each pocket, where they bulged fatly, then buttoned it up to the throat, left the car, crossed the winding tracks of the siding where the train was shunted, and entered the depot. It was the usual little Hansel-and-Gretel gingerbread-style doll's house, with the usual first class waiting room inside; behind that closed door, he thought, were the people he needed to see. All but one, apparently, because the door to the men's toilet had just banged shut.

He opened the door to the waiting room. On a leather sofa sat the stationmaster and one of the commissars. A low table before them was covered with papers. The train engineer was perched on the window sill. Their faces all turned to him, peering through a haze of cigarette smoke.

"Who are you?" the commissar grunted. "This is a private meeting."

"I beg your pardon, Commissar," Nicholas said politely. "I'm here representing the passengers' committee." The commissar frowned. "Chief delegate," Nicholas added. "I've just been elected."

The man nodded. That sounded like correct procedure. You held a meeting, formed a committee, elected a delegate. "Very well. Close the door and come in."

"Is there a problem?" Nicholas asked. "I've been asked to report back to the committee."

"No problem. You need a permit to continue along this line. We can't issue it yet. That's the whole story."

"I see." That didn't explain anything, of course, but Nicholas nodded his understanding. He walked over to the table, removed the two bottles of vodka from his pockets and set them down. "I've been empowered to offer you a

83

toast on behalf of the passengers' committee. To the success of the revolution, and all power to the soviets."

The commissar had bushy gray eyebrows overhanging his eyes, and he smoothed them back thoughtfully, one at a time. "That shows the proper spirit."

The stationmaster cleared his throat. "I'm afraid we have no drinking glasses."

"We'll just have to share the bottle," Nicholas said. "That is, if you'll join me?"

"All power to the soviets—what the hell is going on here?" The second commissar had entered the room and was standing in the doorway, still adjusting his trousers.

"A small toast, Konstantin Ivanovitch. To the success of the revolution."

"Ah." He stalked over to the table. "And after that, the defeat of all counterrevolutionaries."

"And then the triumph of the peasants and the workers," Nicholas added.

"To say nothing of our gallant Red Guard," the stationmaster put in.

They opened the bottle.

Two hours later, when Nicholas returned to the train, the boxcar was dark. Only the sullen red glare of the stove illuminated the center of the car. All around the walls, the tiers were draped in shadows. Someone was snoring. He put a hand out against the wall to steady himself. Just . . . a little . . . unsteady. But they'd be moving very soon. Permission granted. Clearance issued. Everything correct. All proper, official, and in order. Nothing to worry about. For the time being.

He was just a little drunk. Not very much—there'd only been two bottles, unfortunately—and then some whiskey one of the commissars had produced. He remembered the French brandy with a twinge of pleasure. He had kept it in reserve all this time . . . for what? Stupid thing to do, he thought. What was he saving it for? The return of the Czar?

Daria heard the door roll open, then close again. Then she heard footsteps inside the door. They halted almost at once. A match scraped against the wall. It was Nicholas, she was sure of it. He would be standing by the door, smoking a cigarette before going to bed. This was a perfect time to be alone with him, with everyone else asleep, even Zora, who'd complained that she was exhausted, and would everyone please leave her alone.

Her heart began to thud. She got out of bed and stood up. She was fully dressed. It was senseless to undress for sleeping. No one did, you slept in your clothes; it was just too cold to do anything else. She made her way over to the door, where she saw the tiny red glow of a cigarette twinkling in the shadows beyond the glare of the stove.

"Nicholas, is that you?"

"Yes."

"Can I talk to you?"

"Why aren't you sleeping?"

It wasn't a very promising beginning. His voice had an odd huskiness that she hadn't heard before. But it was too late now to return to her shelf. She went up to him. "What happened in the depot? Is everything all right?"

"Fine." He cleared his throat. "We'll be moving very shortly. All is well."

She recognized the husky quality in his voice now. He'd been drinking. "Did you have to bribe them?"

He made a sweeping gesture with his hand. "The commissars are reasonable and honest men. They wouldn't accept a bribe."

"Oh." She paused. "Are you drunk?"

He laughed. She saw the gleam of white teeth in the shadows. "Oh, a little. Not much. Don't forget, there were only two bottles." He stopped to think for a moment. "Oh yes, and some whiskey. I almost forgot about that."

He *was* drunk, she thought. Good, it would make things easier. It would give her a small advantage. Perhaps he wouldn't be as alert as usual. She thought about Lev Omansky, in Saravenko, and Lev's thin, intense face looking down at her in the starlight. Lev was quick-witted too, but closer to her own age, and easier to handle. And Lev, although bright and clever, was more excitable than Nicholas, and had less control over his emotions. Her experience with Lev wouldn't be very useful, she thought. Anything that put Nicholas slightly off balance was a good thing.

"I don't suppose you feel like going right to sleep," she said.

"No, not right away. Why aren't you sleeping?" He frowned. "Did I ask you that before?"

"Yes, you did."

"What did you say?"

"I didn't say anything." She smiled to herself. "I thought we might talk for a while."

"My dear sweet Daria, I've been talking for hours. I'm tired of talking."

She moved closer to him and turned up her face. "Then what would you like to do?"

She could see his expression in the shadows. He was scowling. He dropped his cigarette and took hold of her shoulders. "You know very well what I'd like to do."

She felt a lurch of excitement.

"Unless," he went on, "you believe that I've been feeling toward you like a kindly uncle. Do you believe that?"

"I—I don't know."

"Surely not." There was a new edge in his voice. "You're not a stupid girl."

She stared at him without answering

"And don't tilt up your face like that. Because I'm not going to kiss you." His scowl grew deeper. "Kisses, my love, are not an end in themselves. You understand that, I'm sure. And right now, in this place, at this time, they are a very subtle form of torture."

She nodded. Disappointment was flooding through her. He was right; he was only a little drunk, not enough to forget where they were, or who they were. She might as well go back to her shelf and try to sleep, try to forget this useless conversation.

"Damn," he muttered suddenly. He pulled her against him, put one arm around her waist, drew her head back with his other hand, and brought his mouth down on hers.

Time stopped. She lost all sense of where she was. Everything disappeared except the one reality of her own body and what was happening to it. She dimly realized that his hand had moved from her waist to her breast, and that the tips had hardened, and that she was clinging to him as tightly as she could. Rivers of honey were flowing between her legs. She moaned, deep back in her throat. This was not like the first time. It was longer and more intimate, and

86

she sensed a reckless abandonment in herself and in Nicholas that she hadn't felt before.

Then it was all over. She felt Nicholas draw away from her even before he set her back with his hands on her arms, and she knew he had reined in his emotions. Frustrated anger swept through her. She stared at him, stormy-eyed, her chest heaving.

"That's enough," he muttered. She realized that the huskiness was gone from his voice. But she didn't care. She hated him, she wished she had the courage to slap his face.

"It's true," she said in a low hard voice, "what people say about you."

"What do they say?"

"That you're a Man of Ice."

"Nonsense."

"No it isn't. It's absolutely true."

"Daria," he said, "I'm not made of ice. Or steel, or iron, or any of those things. Come back here."

She took a step forward again. He pulled her roughly against him, hip to hip. She became aware of something she had ignored in the previous moments: a strange warm pressure against her stomach, pulsing and hard, frightening and thrilling, weakening her knees.

"As you see," he said low into her ear, "I'm not ice. Only flesh and blood, like anyone else. Just a man, like any other. Who wants you very much."

"Then—then—"

She had no more will. She didn't hate him at all. She was afraid to admit what she felt, except that she was aching for something, and she wanted to cry. "If you want me," she began miserably.

"I know. Don't say any more." He brushed back her hair. "I know. But there's nothing we can do."

"There is," she said rebelliously. "You can—"

"I can what? Take you over to the shelf and seduce you, with everyone listening? And have you face the smirks and winks tomorrow?"

"I wouldn't mind."

"I would."

"Is that what's stopping you?" she demanded. "What people will think?"

87

"Oh God." He sighed. "No, that isn't it."

"Then what is?"

"Daria," he said, "tell me something. Have you ever been with a man?"

"I—" She paused. If she told the truth, he would send her away immediately. She would have to lie. "Yes," she said quickly. "In Saravenko, before I left, there was a young man from Kiev who was very persuasive, and he told me we'd be married, and so we—"

"Tell me the truth."

She hid her face against his shoulder, flushing with misery. She'd always been a terrible liar. "No. I haven't."

"That's what I thought."

"If I had, would you make love to me?"

"Yes, I think so."

Damn.

She pulled her head back. "I wish," she said furiously, "I had a whole list of lovers. As many as Zora! I wish I'd had everyone on this train! Including the fireman!"

Nicholas's hand went to his mouth, pretending to stroke his mustache, but she was sure he was hiding a smile. The fireman was a small, bent-over old man with one leg missing and a wooden stump.

"Don't laugh at me!"

"I'm sorry," he said. "I'm not laughing. But I'm going to try to explain something to you, and I hope you'll try to understand." He paused, gazing down into her face. His voice gentled. "The first man who makes love to you, darling, will be a very important person to you. And if it's done in a quick, forced, hurried way, under shabby circumstances, you'll remember him with fear and loathing for the rest of your life. I don't want that person to be me. Not that way."

She nodded.

"If I'm to be your first lover, it will have to be in a way I choose. In a place where there will be cleanliness and privacy, and where we will have time to be alone with each other. Where I can think only about pleasing you and fulfilling you and making you happy. And if I can do that, then it will bring me pleasure, and we'll both be happy. Can you understand that?"

"Yes . . ."

"Do you hate me?"

"No."

"Then kiss me once more, before we say good night."

This time the kiss was gentle, without passion, and she left his arms in quiet resignation, without protest.

Nicholas watched her go regretfully. He wouldn't have an easy time sleeping tonight, he thought. He'd have to try to think about something else.

He walked over to his own shelf and flung himself down. All the effects of the vodka had disappeared, and he was no longer tempted by the thought of the unopened brandy bottle. He would save it for another time, he thought.

He put an arm over his eyes. Unbidden, unwanted, the vision of Céline came into his mind. *No, not now. Don't think about that now.*

It was useless. The memories were returning, and he surrendered and let them flood back.

He'd been very sure of himself, before he'd met Céline.

He'd been having lunch with a friend called Alexander Fyodorovitch. They'd been sitting in a restaurant over coffee and brandy. "But my dear Kolya," Alexander Fyodorovitch had said, "you must come to dinner. Romaskaya will be there . . . the beautiful Céline . . . and she's very eager to meet you."

"Is her husband eager to meet me?"

"Don't worry about him, dear fellow. He's quite elderly and very rich and very tolerant. No, it's Celine you'd better worry about. She's famous for melting a man's heart with a single glance."

Nicholas laughed. "I'm afraid pampered beauties aren't my weakness, Sasha."

How wrong he had been.

Céline was wickedly beautiful, with tilted green eyes, copper hair and the creamy skin that went with it, a full red mouth, and a marvelous lush body. Within a month, Nicholas believed he was in love, for the first time in his life.

She must leave her husband. She must ask for a divorce. This was absurd. It couldn't go on . . .

At last she consented to leave her husband and live with him, although it meant defying society. But now, as he thought back, Nicholas believed she'd enjoyed that, in a way. She liked dramatizing herself, when it didn't involve any real suffering. The only one who truly suffered was her husband, he thought, who'd behaved in a decent way and maintained a dignified silence. He must have loved her in spite of her infidelities. But then, so had Nicholas.

She refused to ask for a divorce. "It would be too cruel, darling," she would say, "I'd be afraid of killing him, I couldn't live with that on my conscience." But that wasn't the real reason, Nicholas thought. No, she was keeping an escape route open, just in case. He knew now he had been too much of a fool to see that. It had taken almost five years.

But in the meantime, he had almost everything he wanted. He bought a large stone house in a residential section of Kharkov and staffed it with servants in order to have a suitable home for Céline, and she assured him that in time the problem of her husband would be solved.

Meaning, of course, that sooner or later her husband would die. It was a ghoulish point of view, and he preferred not to think of it that way. He saw no flaws in Céline. Not then. He settled down to the business of making money.

And then the revolutionary storm had begun to gather.

How quietly it began, Nicholas thought. The war against the Germans was going badly, and there were strikes and shortages and premonitions and rumblings. But it had all happened before, everyone said. It will blow over, if we don't panic . . . and if the Army will pull itself together . . . if Rasputin is removed from the scene . . .

Even after the March Revolution. Even after the November Revolution. Even then, you kept thinking something would happen to reverse the tide.

But the morning came when Nicholas had to face the truth.

He remembered it vividly. A winter morning. He was on his way to the foundry in the back of his chauffeur-driven Daimler. He had left early, as he always did, leaving Céline asleep in her bedroom. She was a late riser, and he preferred to be at work by seven-thirty or eight. Darkness still covered the city. Bonfires were still burning on the street corners, where sentries with rifles slung over their shoulders were warming their hands and stamping their feet in the cold. The Red Guard. The civilian militia. Every now and then an armored car went by, with its siren making a dull whine and a tiny red flag flying from its hood and a machine gun peeping ominously from its turret. Kharkov, like Petrograd, was a revolutionary stronghold.

Every other street was barricaded. Some of the barricades were primitive, made of broken wood, bits of fence, kitchen furniture, old tile stoves. Some were elaborate, enforced with stones and bricks. But they all told the same story: a city under siege. Sporadic bursts of machine gun fire still echoed around the post office, the telegraph office, the railroad station, the police station, the printing presses.

How long could he stay in Kharkov, Nicholas asked himself in the back of the limousine, drawing moodily on a cigarette. How long would it be safe? He wondered if it were true, as his friend Sasha maintained, that one could cooperate with the Bolshevik government. Or was he endangering his own life, and that of Céline, by remaining?

But he couldn't believe that everything he had worked so hard to build up, for so long, was facing ruin. Oh God. He didn't want to believe it. When he looked out again, he was staring at a placard. It was too dark to read it, even in the light of the streetlamp, but he didn't have to see the words.

"Workers, soldiers, peasants! In March you struck down the tyranny of the clique of nobles! Now we must strike down the tyranny of the bourgeois gang! Our task now is to organize the revolutionary power, and assure the realization of the popular program . . ."

It would be something like that, he thought wearily. Signed by Commissar Lenin, or Commissar Trotsky, or Commissar Rykov, or Commissar Uritsky. Every fence, every wall, every siding, was plastered with manifestoes and placards. The streets and gutters were littered with them. After a while you knew them by heart.

They passed a corner with a newspaper kiosk. People were snatching eagerly at the papers just being delivered from a truck. Nicholas leaned forward. "Stop the car, Pavel. I'd like to get a paper."

But when he had the paper—one of the last two available—he folded it without looking at it and tucked it into his coat pocket. There would be time enough to read it when he got to the office, he thought. He had a sick feeling there was bad news in those pages. He was in no hurry to look.

Inside the foundry, he was enveloped by the hot steamy atmosphere, smelling of onions, sweat, and molten iron. He paid no attention to the noise, the grunting and shouting of workmen, the din and clang of metal on metal, as the main work of the foundry went on: casting molds for lengths of railway track. The work had started at seven. In one corner of the enormous dirt-floored room was the molding shop, where the molder, the most experienced craftsman in the foundry, sat at his bench mixing the sand that was the basic material of his craft. Overhead on a clanking conveyor belt came buckets of sand to be poured into the open bin which adjoined his bench. In the center of the room, where the casting took place, molten metal flowed in a white-hot river from great ladles into the sand molds. Because it was used as a final dressing for the molds, coal dust was everywhere, filming everything, men and machinery, with a coat of black.

Nicholas went straight to his office, a small room at the rear of the building. There was a time, he thought, when the men greeted him respectfully as he went by, muttering good morning, a cold day, snow is coming. But now there were only wary glances, speculative frowns, an occasional stare of outright hostility.

As he unbuttoned his fur-collared coat and stripped off his pigskin gloves, he saw the usual sheet of paper neatly centered on his desk. He picked it up and tossed it aside angrily. He didn't have to read it. He knew it contained the usual list of demands, signed by the chief steward of the factory-shop committee, informing him that the workers were now equal partners with him in this enterprise, and he was no longer entitled to profit by the exploitation of their labor.

He was no longer the owner.

It was just as simple as that. Overnight. By proclamation.

He sat down slowly behind the desk and stared into space. After a while he reached for the cigarette case in his breast pocket. Were things really this bad?

He remembered the newspaper and got up and withdrew

it from the pocket of his coat, narrowing his eyes against the rising smoke from the cigarette between his lips, ready to read of the latest disaster, whatever it was.

It was worse than he thought.

He stared down at the smudged newsprint. A new agency had been formed: The Extraordinary Committee for the Suppression of the Counterrevolution. A political police force to be known informally as the Cheka. It would be dedicated to the extermination of enemies of the state. All those suspected of opposing the Soviet government would be vigorously uncovered and eliminated.

This had to come, he thought, feeling a sick apprehension begin to stir at the back of his mind, as he crushed out the cigarette in the ashtray. It was the next, inevitable step. He returned to the article.

Felix Djerzinsky would head the new agency. The great Puritan. The icy fanatic. Perfect, Nicholas thought, the perfect choice.

He read the printed excerpt from Djerzinsky's first speech: "Do not believe that I am concerned with formal justice. We do not need any laws now. What we need is to fight to the end. I request, I demand, the forging of the revolutionary sword that will annihilate all counterrevolutionaries!"

Annihilate with a sword. Terrorism.

He put down the paper. He should have guessed, he should have known. Now the only question was, how soon would Djerzinsky's agents arrive in Kharkov? Or were they already on their way?

By the end of the afternoon, he had his answer.

"May I speak to you, sir?"

The stocky figure in the doorway of the office was a familiar one to Nicholas: Stepan, the molder, still loyal and still respectful, one of the few men he could still depend on. The short winter day had already come to an end, and outside the grimy window of the office there was darkness. Hard little snowflakes were falling now, swirling in the air, illuminated by the yellow light of the streetlamps. The workers were beginning to leave the foundry. Nicholas felt cold and weary. He knew he had to make a decision very soon. Stay or leave?

"Of course, Stepan. Come in."

The man advanced toward the desk and stood before it, holding his cap. Nicholas didn't embarrass him by asking him to sit down. The man would have refused anyway.

"I heard some news today, in the yard, at lunch," Stepan said. "It's about you, sir. I wanted you to know right away."

Even before Stepan spoke, Nicholas knew what the news would be. He felt a coldness settle in the pit of his stomach. Agents of the Cheka were already here, in Kharkov. Taking names. He, Nicholas, had been denounced to the Cheka as an agent of the counterrevolution. By whom? Did it matter? Some incompetent worker, dismissed for cause, or someone with a grievance. What difference did it make? He could be arrested at any moment.

We do not need any laws now.

They might be on their way to his home right now, to make an arrest. And if they found Céline . . .

He had to get home right away. He was suddenly sick with anxiety.

The car was waiting at the curb in the snowy darkness. He was still buttoning his coat as he made his way toward it, half running, and yanked open the door. He had come to the end. The foundry, the real estate, the investments, the years of work, all were for nothing now. Now he had to worry about saving both their lives. He had waited too long. Silently, he urged the chauffeur to hurry.

Even now, with all that was happening, the restaurants and tea shops were still crowded. He stared unseeingly out of the automobile window as they drove through the darkened city. Life went on. People still hoped. Something will save us. Kaiser Wilhelm's troops will come and drive out the Bolsheviks. Kaledin and Kornilov will raise a volunteer army in Novocherkassk. There'll be a counterrevolution. *Something will save us.*

Will it?

Oh God. What was happening at home?

He shoved his hands deep into his pockets. It was taking forever. Barricades, detours, a militiaman advancing through the snow with his hand up. . . . Identity papers? Yes, yes, it's all in order. . . .

He was pale with worry and fear by the time they reached the stone house, imagining every kind of disaster and cursing himself for not acting sooner, not sending her away, not anticipating, not leaving before now. If anything happened to Céline, it would be his fault.

He took the stairs two at a time and burst into Céline's bedroom, dreading what he would find. Tumbled bedclothes, ransacked closets, an empty room?

He stopped and took a deep breath. No, it was all right. Céline was seated calmly in front of her dressing table, brushing her hair, which tumbled in a shining copper mass over her shoulders. She wore an emerald green chiffon robe. How beautiful she looked as she turned and smiled sweetly at the sound of his footsteps.

"Nicholas, darling, what's wrong? You look so pale."

"A great deal is wrong." He walked into the room. "Get dressed, Céline. Right away."

"You know I always dress for dinner."

"Not tonight. There'll be no dressing for dinner. We have to leave Kharkov. Tonight." He strode to the closet, pulled out a stack of dresses, and flung them onto the bed. "Where's Sonya? Where are the rest of the servants?"

"Sonya's gone out on an errand for me. And the others, I suppose—"

"Céline, why are you still sitting there? I asked you to hurry!"

"Calm down, darling, please. I've never seen you so overwrought. It isn't like you."

"Céline," he said, forcing himself to be patient, "I told you to get dressed. I have reason to believe I've been denounced to the Cheka, the secret police. It may not be true, but I think it is. I'll know tomorrow, but in the meantime this house isn't safe. So you see, we don't have much time."

"But Kolya, darling, what has that to do with me?"

He'd been looking on the shelf of her closet for suitcases. But at the tone of her voice, sweet and reasonable and silvery, he stopped and turned around. He felt himself go calm as abruptly as if someone had thrown a bucket of ice water into his face. Suddenly he knew. All at once and completely, he knew the truth. He knew what was going to happen. He knew what had *already* happened. Their life together had come to an end. Just as abruptly as his fortune had been erased, so his relationship with Céline had been severed. Snip. A monstrous celestial hand had wielded a scissors and cut a thread, and everything was over. But he pretended to himself he didn't know.

"We have to leave here, Céline," he repeated quietly. "There's great danger in Kharkov, and we have to leave by whatever means we can."

"Leave? But where will we go?"

"I know you'd like Paris, but with the war still on, I don't see how we can get through the German lines. So for now it will have to be Harbin, in Manchuria."

"Manchuria! Nicholas, that's thousands of miles away, across Siberia—you can't expect me to make a trip like that!"

"Don't you understand, we can't stay here—"

"And I don't particularly want to go to Paris, either." She turned back to the dressing table mirror. She removed an earring and set it on the table. "Why can't I stay here?" she said.

"If I tell you that I've been denounced to the secret police as a counterrevolutionary, do you know what that means?"

"Of course."

"Then how can you ask that question?"

"*I* haven't been denounced to the secret police." She turned again to face him. She was smiling. "And neither has my husband, Kolya. He's always been a little less . . . flamboyant than you, darling, in his business affairs. And I don't believe he has *quite* so many enemies."

He was still refusing to understand. "Are you saying that you'd stay here in Kharkov and return to your husband?"

"Yes, Nicholas, that is what I'm saying." She shrugged her creamy white shoulders and made a face. "Try to see my point of view. Try not to be so selfish. Think of the wonderful years we've had together, and be grateful for that. I know I am."

She wasn't coming with him. She was remaining with her husband. Be grateful. Five years. Be grateful. Oh my God. He felt a hideous choking sensation in his throat, and suddenly he had to swallow in order to control his nausea. He could not look at Céline. He stared at the rug and thought, in a surge of unreason, that he'd paid a great deal of money for that rug. And the furniture. And the furs in the closet. And the dresses that were heaped up on the bed. And as for that lovely, treacherous woman who was sitting at the dressing table and staring at him with sudden fear in her eyes . . . what was she afraid of? He wanted to laugh crazily. The house, the rug, the clothes, the furs, the woman—none of them were his anymore. He had nothing. Wasn't that so? After sixteen years, he was back where he had begun. For the second time, it was all being taken away from him. Only he wasn't nineteen anymore. He was thirty-five. With nothing. Only himself, and this icy rage that was filling his mind and heart.

Then the choking sensation in his throat died away. Suddenly he felt very calm, and realized the blood must have drained from his face. He caught a glimpse of himself in the dressing table mirror, and he was as white as chalk. His face looked like a skull, he thought. Except for the eyes, which were those of a madman.

Céline must have thought that too, he realized, because she recoiled in her chair. He came toward her and saw her shrink back in fear. *She believes I'm going to strike her. And she's right. I will. If she makes any move to stop me.* He was thinking very clearly. The way you do, he thought, when you're very angry, or very frightened, after the first crazy panic dies away.

But when he had come up close, he ignored her and reached past her to the jewelry box on the table. It was open. She had been making her selection for the evening when he came into the room. Usually her maid, Sonya, helped her to dress, but Sonya was out. Suddenly, he realized why: she'd obviously been sent ahead to tell Céline's husband what was about to happen. Céline had known all along. Amazed, he realized it didn't matter. He opened the jewelry box and began to withdraw its contents. The diamond necklace. The diamond and sapphire bracelet. The emerald tiara. The ruby brooch. The diamond ring with the emerald setting. The emerald earrings. Céline was very fond of emeralds; they matched her eyes.

"Nicholas, what are you doing?" she gasped.

He was methodically stuffing his pockets with the contents of the jewelry box. It was very full. He'd bought her many of the things himself; some of them she had brought with her from her former life. He took only what he had given her. The topaz earrings. The bird-of-paradise pin. Some of these items were less valuable than others, but everything would be useful, he thought, if he was not murdered along the way. He knew that he didn't care.

"Nicholas, stop!" she cried. "Those jewels are mine!"

But she didn't dare move to stop him. Fortunately for her, Nicholas thought. He would have hit her. In fact he wanted to, quite badly, but he restrained himself. Calmly he picked up the earring from the dressing table and added it to the other things in his pockets. Then he reached for her. Her hands flew up in front of her. He struck them down and reached for the earring in her earlobe.

"Nicholas, damn you!" Her hands were trembling but she unscrewed the earring. She made a move to put it down on the table.

"Give it to me, Céline."

Unwillingly she dropped it into his outstretched palm. "You're mad," she whispered. "You're insane. Why are you stealing my jewelry? Give it back. Please, Kolya, put it back."

"No."

"At least the emerald earrings. And the diamond ring. Those two things. Only those. Won't you, Nicholas, please?"

"Go to hell."

He turned his back on her and walked out of the room.

In his own bedroom, he found his suitcase on the closet shelf. He threw it onto the bed and began to pack. He had no idea where the servants were. They'd probably deserted the house. But he didn't need them. It was all over. His mind raced as he emptied the jewelry from his pockets into the suitcase. Tonight he would stay with Sasha, and sell everything he owned for cash for the journey to Manchuria. He would keep the jewelry. He would use it to try to begin again. It seemed senseless, even meaningless, but the will to survive was strong in him in spite of his hopeless rage. At that moment to escape, to live, was all that mattered.

When he finished packing, he descended the stairs to the front door. He sensed that the house was strangely silent. Céline was already gone. Damn her, he thought savagely, let her go!

Outside in the shadows of the porch, with the front door slightly ajar behind him, he looked up and down the street. Then he felt a coldness settle over his mind. So Stepan had been right, he thought, realizing he didn't have to wait until tomorrow for the Cheka. They were here. Halfway down the block, on the opposite side of the street, three men were standing on the pavement studying house numbers. They began to cross the street as he watched. They walked purposefully, overcoats flapping around their legs. *Policemen. Unmistakable.*

He moved quietly back into the house, closing and locking the door again. He would use the back door, he thought, and go through the servant's quarters. Pavel, the chauffeur, was still in his room above the garage, because the light was burning, but the house itself was empty. Nicholas felt a renewed surge of fury at leaving everything here for the taking. But he had no choice. Possessions were meaningless now.

As he slipped through the back door into the snowy garden, he heard the urgent chiming of the front doorbell. But he didn't look back.

And so now here he was. In this boxcar, jolting its way over the Trans-Amur line to Vladivostok. And here in the teplushka, sleeping now, was a lovely girl with gypsy eyes who'd been thrown violently into his path.

Did they have any future, he and Daria? *Was* there a future?

The jewelry was safe on his person, except for those times when it seemed likely they would be searched. Then he divided it into canisters of tea, covered by dry crumbly tea leaves. The canisters were too small to conceal weapons, and so far they'd been ignored.

When he reached Harbin, he thought, if he still had the jewelry, he would have a way to start again. At least there would be something to build on; he wouldn't have to start completely from the bottom. He would have the jewelry and the cash. Perhaps. If he ever reached Harbin. If any of them did.

The train lurched, groaned metallically and pulled itself forward on the tracks. Nicholas realized with a start that they were moving again.

Chapter 8

In a log izba hidden in a pine forest deep in eastern Siberia, while Daria and Nicholas followed the Amur River, Lev Omansky sat on the edge of a narrow bed. He was barely listening to his companion, a peasant girl who was called Marisa. He was thinking about the war. He and Yuri would join their comrades soon, in a fighting unit near the Ussuri River. But right now they were still working with the muzhiks. Today Yuri was in the nearby village; Lev and Marisa were alone. They had just finished drinking tea Marisa had brewed, and now the girl's broad, high-cheekboned face wore a speculative expression as she stood in the center of the floor, her hands clasped in front of her.

"I'm not supposed to be here, you know," she remarked.

Lev was biting a corner of his fingernail, a bad habit he always fell into when he was thinking. "Why not?" He didn't really care; it was just something to say.

"Because Kyril told me not to. He said if I set one foot inside this izba, he'd never speak to me again."

"Who's Kyril?" Lev's voice was absent; he was concentrating on other thoughts.

"My special friend, in the village. He's very strong. His arms look like tree branches. Thick, like this." She held her hand over her upper arm, to demonstrate Kyril's biceps. Then she glanced slyly at Lev to see if he was impressed. "And his legs are like tree trunks," she added.

Lev began to pay attention. He had a sudden, swift

vision of an enraged and gigantic muzhik bursting open the door of the izba, swinging an axe over his head and demanding to know what was going on. It was a situation he hadn't anticipated.

An hour ago he'd been standing alone on the shore of a frozen lake near the izba. He'd been struggling with his own fear. Yuri was looking over the construction of their bronevik in the village railway yard; tomorrow it would be Lev's turn.

The armored cars would be important in this war, Lev thought. The fighting would take place up and down the railway line. There'd be a battle for every length of track, every siding, every bridge, every tunnel and depot.

Soon. Soon. He wished he wasn't scared. He tried to distract himself by thinking of a name for the bronevik. He knew that the Cossack regiments were naming their cars. The Avenger, for example. The Destroyer. The Merciless.

All right, we'll call ours the Liberator, he told himself.

He was looking across the frozen expanse of the lake. Far out from the shore, he saw three men fishing through a hole in the ice. The shoreline was uneven, broken up by fingers of land thickly covered with fir trees. Overhead the sky was a hard clear blue. Underfoot his boots were crushing pine needles. Behind him, squirrels with thick winter fur were chattering noisily and racing up and down the tree trunks. The air was cold, dry, fresh. It was a beautiful place.

But it was time to go back to the izba. He shoved his hands into his pockets. He was getting cold.

He began to tramp back through the pine and spruce and birch trees, through the snow. But when he emerged from the trees and came in sight of the izba, his muscles tensed. He stood silent and alert, listening. Someone was walking through the forest, coming from the opposite direction. It couldn't be Yuri, not so soon. Who, then? His hand went to the pistol holstered at his hip. He stood very still.

A girl came into view, appearing from a clump of white birch. She was wearing a heavy woolen coat, with a woolen scarf wrapped around her head and tied under her chin, and she was carrying a basket.

"I've brought you some food."

He relaxed. Just a girl from the village. He hadn't seen her before.

"Did you walk here from the village?" he asked.

She looked mildly surprised. "Yes, of course."

The village was nine versts away. Yet she was rosy-cheeked and smiling. She didn't seem to think it was anything at all. Still a city boy, he thought wryly of himself, used to walking only as far as the nearest trolley stop.

"Come inside the izba," he said. "You must be cold."

"Cold? No, it's quite mild today." She shrugged. "But I'll come in and make you some tea, if you like."

Now, inside the cottage, she was telling him about Kyril.

He began to study her more closely. It occurred to him that Yuri wouldn't be back for an hour or two. And the unknown Kyril, formidable as he sounded, was probably occupied far off in the village. Marisa looked very scrubbed and clean, and she smelled of soap. She had a sturdy, full-breasted peasant body, with thick legs and plump thighs, apparent even through the long woolen skirt she was wearing.

He struggled against the thought that was forming in his mind. Still, she'd brought up the subject of her friend Kyril for a reason, and it wasn't hard to figure out what it was. Did she know she was being provocative? She was beginning to blush, embarrassed at her own audacity, but she stood her ground and met his eyes calmly.

I'll be working toward my goal, he told himself swiftly, as speculations raced through his mind. By establishing a friendship, I can introduce her to new ideas and thoughts, and then she'll be able to pass them along in the village. It will have nothing to do with bourgeois exploitation.

Ha. He was lying to himself and he knew it. But he said, in a casual tone of voice, "What do you and Kyril do when you're alone together?"

"Oh, nothing very much. You know. The usual things."

Noncommittal, but promising.

He yawned. "You know, I'm not used to all that fresh air. Standing by the lake all that time made me tired."

"Maybe you should have a nap."

Very promising.

"Maybe I should. Just for a while." He bent over and began to pull off his boots.

"I should leave," she said, watching him. "I'm expected at home."

"Oh, not just yet. Why don't you stay for a few minutes?"

"But if you're going to take a nap . . ."

Lev stood up and began to unbuckle his belt. "Come and join me under the covers."

"Oh no!" Marisa's face turned bright pink. "That wouldn't be right. It would be improper."

"Not if you keep your clothes on. After all, you have a long walk back to the village. You should rest first."

"It's not such a long walk," she said hesitantly. "It's only nine versts." But her hand was plucking uncertainly at the edge of her skirt.

Lev felt a rising surge of excitement. Marisa had just sealed her own fate, whether she realized it or not.

But it wasn't quite that easy.

When he had gotten beneath the covers, in his underwear, she came and sat on the edge of the bed. "I'll only stay for a minute or two," she promised.

Lev watched her from under his eyelashes. The game was beginning, he decided, as she began to take her boots off. She knew the rules, and he didn't. The thing to do was understand them without being told, and then follow them faithfully to the prize.

All right, Marisa. I'll play your game, if you like.

First rule: no looking. The prize remained hidden. Marisa crawled under the blanket, fully dressed except for her boots.

Second rule: no admitting anything. This seemed to be basic. You never acknowledged what was going on, even while it was happening. You pretended to be concerned for her comfort.

"Marisa, wouldn't you be cozier without this long skirt?"

Hesitation, while she pretended to think it over. Then a little voice. "Yes, perhaps I would."

Fine. Off with the skirt.

"How about this heavy blouse? Aren't you getting warm?"

"Yes . . . a little."

Then the same charade about the woolen stockings. The chemise. The long petticoat. Christ, she still had a layer of woolen underwear, this was taking forever. Lev was becoming impatient, but he saw that Marisa's eyes were innocent, and her face impassive. He sighed, and continued the game.

The underwear took more persuasion.

"I couldn't do that!" Shocked blushes covered her cheeks. Apparently Kyril had been willing to settle for basic satisfaction, without possessing the naked luxury of all that soft pink flesh. But Marisa was built on heroic lines, which became more clear as each layer of clothing fell away.

He summoned his determination and marshaled his skill at argument, sharpened by years of dialectical debate in sidewalk cafés. He began to whisper in her ear. Little by little she weakened. She shrugged out of her chemise. Abundant warm curves suddenly spilled free, and his eyes widened in amazement. With renewed energy he directed his efforts to the final obstacle.

"Lift up your hips, Marisa."

"Why?"

"We'll just slip this off . . ."

At the last minute, with the underwear halfway down her hips, she balked. "I don't think I should do this."

Patience, patience. "Why not?"

"It isn't right."

"Nothing will happen," he said soothingly.

"Are you sure?"

"Of course." If she would believe that, she would believe anything.

The underwear slid down and away. He was stroking bare flesh. He bent to kiss her; she kept her lips prudishly pursed, maintaining the fiction of her virtue. But against his hands her breasts were heaving, and between his fingers, her nipples were straining, taut and erect.

Cautiously he slid one knee between her legs. The plump thighs parted obediently, following some inner command. She was still adhering to the rules: above the shoulders, all was calm withdrawal. But below, as he eased himself between her legs, everything was warm, clasping, moist, and fiercely welcoming.

She was an amazing girl.

Sensation rolled up, and he stopped thinking. Suddenly he was caught. Ambushed. Entrapped. Clamped in this deep hot cave of flesh that was sucking out his life. But if he was dying, then he didn't care . . . Hold on. Not yet. Not yet. Ahhh . . .

Marisa, you peasant bitch, I think I love you.

But when he rolled away from her, panting and drained, he felt the first pang of guilt. Maybe he'd betrayed his ideals after all, he thought in sudden depression. Certainly he had betrayed Daria. They had never made love.

But they'd never made any vows, either. Only a promise regarding that far-off day when they'd meet in Harbin.

Still, Daria was a vision and a dream he was clinging to until he reached Manchuria.

He fought down the guilt.

"Marisa," he asked, "will you come back tomorrow?"

She was dressing, replacing the layers of clothing one by one. "I'm not sure."

Then he remembered he wouldn't be here tomorrow. He'd be at the railway yard. He laid his arm across his eyes. Should he tell Yuri about Marisa? Leave it to fate. Maybe Yuri would find out for himself.

He sighed. There was no need for regret, he told himself. For a little while he'd forgotten about the war.

Chapter 9

The train was moving again, but it was moving at a crawl. There were more halts, more delays. The faded red boxcar was shunted onto sidings in remote depots to wait for clearances. Snow blocked the tracks. They experienced shortages of wood. Outside the car the forest was giving way, and the passengers saw fewer trees and more stretches of the barren land where only the scrubby bush called *saksaule* could grow. But sometimes they heard a cracking noise like the sound of a gunshot, and knew they had passed a birch grove where a tree had exploded in the cold.

Then at last the landscape began to change. Little by little, day by day, the temperature rose. Outside the open door appeared patches of swampy marshland and stretches of thick black mud. Clouds of mosquitoes rose up from the swamps in buzzing fury. Blotches of vivid green grass burst out of the mud. Wildflowers struggled up from the melting snow.

The river, too, was starting to thaw. Grinding, gnashing roars suddenly boomed into the air as chunks of ice broke apart and swirled in the suddenly free water.

Spring, Daria thought wonderingly, listening to the thunder of the ice. This endless journey would end. There was a destination after all: Vladivostok. What would she do when she reached it?

Everyone looked starved and thin, she thought. Even Nicholas. But he was still proud, still the Man of Ice. He still carefully shaved every morning. He still retained his air of elegance, although she saw lines of weariness in his face, and the skin was stretched more tautly over his cheekbones, making him look harder and more gaunt.

She glanced over at him where he stood by the open door. His eyes were very blue under the arched eyebrows. He looked impossibly handsome, even now, and impossibly far away.

She stared down at her hands. I must make my own plans, she thought. I can't depend on anyone else. She felt a strange twist in the region of her heart and fought it down.

She began to worry about money; her funds were dwindling. The purse Alexey had given her with their savings was growing thinner by the day. Everything was so expensive. She was always shocked to hear the prices of food and soap and clothing at the depots where they stopped. Although she told herself she should be used to it by now, she grew angry and indignant every time she made a purchase. It was simple robbery, she told herself. There was no other place to buy what was needed. So prices rose and there was no choice but to pay.

She sighed. She wondered if any of her letters had reached Alexey. But the thought of her grandfather was an aching bruise, slowly fading, but still painful, and she turned her mind back to Vladivostok.

She could join Ludmilla and Boris and try to reach Harbin with them. Once she reached Harbin, she would try to find her grandfather's cousin Victor, who worked for the Chinese Eastern Railroad. That had been the original plan. But she couldn't think that far ahead. It was too exhausting just living in the present.

And struggling against her dreams. Why do I see your face every night when I close my eyes? she thought, forcing herself not to glance up at Nicholas. In the blackness behind her closed eyelids, before she fell asleep, she saw the planes and angles of his face, the arch of his eyebrows, the curve of his mouth, the shadows beneath his cheekbones.

But I would feel the way I do even if I had never seen you, she thought despairingly. Even if I were blind and didn't know what you looked like, and knew only the sound of your voice, and the touch of your hand, and heard the things you say . . .

No. No. It was hopeless to dream. The time he had spoken about, that night by the door, when they could be alone together, was only a fantasy; it wasn't real, it would never come true, and she must put it out of her mind and stop dreaming.

She lay back on her shelf and closed her eyes.

The train crept on, into spring.

At last the locomotive inched its way onto the long steel railway bridge leading into the city of Khabarovsk; it was the beginning of May. Below the span of the bridge, the waters of the Amur shone burnished yellow, stained by the silt washed down from the clay banks on either side of the river. The ice was melted.

They approached Khabarovsk Station with the door open. The day was unexpectedly warm. Winter was truly over. Outside the door they could see the slopes of hills covered with soft green grass, and around the slopes, on level ground, row upon row of wooden barracks. Khabarovsk was a garrison town, headquarters of the Fifth Siberian Army Corps, and it was a river port as well, situated at the juncture of the Amur and Ussuri Rivers. Somewhere there would be wharves, a jetty, and a steamer landing. It was a railroad city, too, one of the three major terminals of the East: Khabarovsk, Nikolsk, Vladivostok.

The train began to crawl and stop, crawl and stop. Nicholas felt a sudden stab of foreboding as he stared out of the open door. He saw big canvas tents set up along the side of the tracks, just outside the station. Huge metal cauldrons of water kept boiling by charcoal fires were sending hissing clouds of steam into the air.

And there were people lined up outside the tents. Wretched lines of men in army khaki stood hunched over in misery with fever burning on their cheeks. Some faces showed ominous dusky splotches of purple-red. A second line of men was emerging from the other side of the tents, this group wrapped in blankets, with naked legs showing pitifully white beneath the edges of the cloth.

A few harassed-looking men and women were moving

109

along the lines, medical personnel, some throwing bundles of clothing into the cauldrons of water.

It was very clear, Nicholas thought in slow horror, what this was. In Kharkov he'd seen newspaper photographs of scenes like this during the Serbian epidemic in 1915. Thousands had died.

Typhus.

And he himself—oh Lord. He bowed his head, swallowing hard. He felt the fever flush rising along his cheeks and forehead. His face was burning. Swallowing only confirmed his fears, emphasizing the rasping, aching pain along his throat.

But it wasn't typhus. It couldn't be. He was almost sure. This was a recurrence of an illness he'd had in St. Petersburg after a winter of poverty and hunger, when he was nineteen. It was a form of influenza. It must be.

But could he be *sure?* Absolutely sure?

The train pulled into the station and halted. The station was imposing: a handsome stone terminal building and a long platform stretching to either side; a railway shop with varied goods for sale; a whole system of signals, semaphores, and winding tracks. They had come out of the wilderness and into a city.

The door rolled open with a clang of metal. Three men in uniform leaped into the car. Each wore a small red-and-white ribbon twisted in his lapel. "Out! Everybody out!" one of them called. "This car must be evacuated!"

Silence greeted this announcement. Then one of the passengers called back, "Who are you?"

The answer snapped. "I am an officer of the Czech Brigade." The speaker folded his arms. "Take your luggage with you when you leave. All your possessions. Make sure you haven't left anything behind. You won't be coming back."

Another stunned silence fell.

Commandeered, Nicholas thought sickly, putting his head into his hands. What about the Khabarovsk commissar? Was he cooperating with the Czechs? Not likely. This would be a quick coup. They were taking the train; the passengers were being forced out, into a typhus-ridden city. And he was feeling too weak and feverish to resist.

A young man in civilian clothes had hauled himself up into the car. His eyes were ringed with dark circles; he wore a white armband marked with a red cross on his sleeve. "What's going on here?"

"These people must leave the train."

"Not without a medical inspection."

"There's no time for that. They have to leave at once. This train is needed."

The young man sighed wearily. He raised his voice, looking into the car. "Is anybody sick in here?"

"Why?" Peter No-Name called back.

"If you are, you'll have to be quarantined."

"In those tents?" Boris asked hoarsely, clasping his baby in his arms. Ludmilla sat beside him, her eyes wide with fear.

"I'm afraid so. You won't be allowed to leave the station if you're ill. We can't risk spreading anything."

Typhus, Nicholas thought, still with his head in his hands. He must get out of here. He wouldn't allow himself to be quarantined. Not in those tents. Unless . . .

He gritted his teeth. Unless he had typhus. If he did, he would turn himself in, he thought. But first he had to be sure. He had to get into the city, away from the railroad station, then locate a place to be alone, strip off all his clothes, search for the repulsive little creatures that caused the fever. He didn't believe he'd find them. He'd been careful. But when you'd been isolated on this train with people like the gypsy woman and the ex-convict, you could have acquired anything.

"Everybody out!" the Czech officer was shouting again. The young man with the red cross armband was leaning against the wall with his eyes closed, his face a mask of fatigue. Passengers were slowly dragging their possessions down from the top shelves of the boxcar, realizing numbly that they were being stranded in Khabarovsk.

Nicholas told himself he had to start moving.

"Listen, starosta, I need money."

Peter No-Name had suddenly appeared by his elbow. Nicholas could hear his harsh breathing, and he raised his head. Waves of dizziness washed over him as he did so, and he closed his eyes for a moment, but the ex-convict was too absorbed in his problem to notice. Beads of sweat were glistening on the man's upper lip.

"I didn't plan on this," Peter No-Name said, muttering half to himself. "Everything would have been all right in Vladivostok. But Khabarovsk, that's a bitch, that's a story from a different opera." He cursed softly under his breath. "I need quick rubles."

"Why tell me?"

Peter No-Name barked out a nervous laugh. "Maybe you have some spare cash." He quickly lifted his hand. "No, no, I don't expect you to hand out money for nothing, of course not, but listen, starosta, I have something to sell. Something you can use."

"What is it?"

Peter No-Name leaned down and lowered his voice. "It's a revolver. A little Italian gun. Small enough to fit in your pocket, and no one the wiser. I've kept it hidden in a secret place . . . it will be very useful to you, believe me."

"If I'm not searched and arrested."

"It's bedlam out there on the platform. It's a madhouse. They won't search you."

Nicholas began to think about the offer. Think straight, he told himself; ignore the dizziness. Reason this out. The man's reassurances were worthless, of course; a weapons search was always possible, even likely. But if he moved very quickly and got away from the station and into the city, he might be able to evade it. A gun would be useful in Khabarovsk. Especially if, as he suspected, he was in for a bad siege of influenza.

Alone.

His resolve was growing firmer by the moment, that he must be alone. He couldn't risk taking anyone else with him. Not under the circumstances. Not ill as he was, infectious, feverish, breathing contagion, barely able to look after himself, much less someone else. He glanced at the fidgeting ex-convict. "Do you have bullets?" he asked.

"Bullets. Everything."

"How much?"

"Thirty-five rubles."

Nicholas frowned. He said nothing.

Peter No-Name licked his lips. "Listen, friend, I can't

take less than thirty. That's my bottom price. Believe me, it's a matter of necessity. Take my word for it."

This time Nicholas believed him. He made up his mind. "All right, thirty rubles. Where is it?"

"Right here."

The exchange was made swiftly. Nicholas slipped the revolver and the box of bullets into his pocket, and Peter No-Name drifted off with his thirty rubles like a wisp of smoke.

Nicholas stood up, forcing himself into motion, and took down his suitcase from the tier above.

"Nicholas, are you feeling well?"

The girl's voice was a soft huskiness behind his back. It was the sound he'd been dreading. He closed his eyes again for a moment. Blackness swam dizzily behind his eyelids. *Daria. Dear Daria, go away. I'm ill. I have a fever, and my throat is a red blaze of pain.* It could be typhus or influenza; but either way, it was contagious. He looked into her dark, worried eyes. She was so lovely. She didn't deserve to sicken with whatever he had caught.

"What that man told us—about leaving the train . . ."

"He meant it, of course." Nicholas turned away slowly, keeping his face impassive. "What are your plans?"

"My—my plans?"

"Yes, we must all think very fast now. We may not have much time."

She swallowed. "Ludmilla and Boris asked me to join them."

"That's a good idea," he said quickly. "They'll be excellent companions. It will be much better for you than traveling alone."

She was silent for a moment. Then she whispered, "Yes . . . much better."

Nicholas took a deep breath. Keep on with this, he told himself. She must go with them. He must force her to. "Daria," he asked, "do you have any money?"

"Do I—"

"If not, I can lend you a few rubles. You can pay me back eventually in Harbin. I'm sure we'll meet there some day."

She flushed immediately. "You don't have to say that."

"Perhaps I want to."

"Why?" Her voice was angry. "For a few stolen kisses?"

"Don't be a fool. Because we've been friends—at least I like to think so—and because I'll worry about you—"

He realized it was the wrong thing to say. He was feverish and not thinking straight, and he was being clumsy, making blunders. Pull yourself together, he warned himself, try not to make this even harder.

"There's no need to worry about me," Daria said tautly. "I'll be fine. I can look after myself."

Can you?

"I suppose, then," she added, "it's time to say goodbye." She held out her hand. "Good-bye, Nicholas. Good luck. I hope you reach Harbin safely." The huge dark eyes were shimmering with unshed tears, but she blinked and her voice was steady. "Perhaps you're right, and we'll meet there some day. I hope we will."

Oh, Lord. He groaned inwardly, struggling with the fever. He tried once more. "Daria," he said faintly, "on a journey like this you make friends and then say good-bye when the journey's over. It happens all the time . . . it's . . ." *Useless, useless, save your breath, you clumsy fool.* He took her hand. He knew his own was dry and hot, and he withdrew it quickly. There was nothing more to say. "Good-bye, Daria."

Go away. Damn you, go away. Now. Quickly. Before I—

There was a soft rustling sound, light footsteps, and he knew she had left.

He was starting to shiver. What was it? Fever? Regret? Anger? His hands were shaking as he buttoned his jacket. It was a warm day, but he was already racked by the fever chill. He told himself to forget it, forget how he felt, forget everything, and get himself out of this station. Fast. With the jewelry and the gun, he had no chance if he were stopped.

He went over to the open door. As Peter No-Name had said, the long platform was a confused, crowded bedlam of men in uniform, railway officials, medical workers, refugees, vendors, onlookers and droshky drivers —*isvostchiks*—who were looking for passengers to transport into the city. The line of droshkies waited to his right, each carriage hitched to a patiently standing horse. Some of the isvostchiks lounged on the seats behind their horses, idly picking their teeth and looking over the crowd. The whole scene was bathed in spring sunshine.

No, don't take a droshky, Nicholas thought feverishly, as the warm sunshine fell across his face. He felt the fever rise along his throat and pound against his temples. It was an ugly, familiar sensation. It had been spring the last time too, he remembered. Another river: the Neva. Thawed, running swiftly beneath the little stone bridges of Petersburg. That watery northern city. A long time ago. 1902. Another world. Before the war. Before the revolution.

He passed his hand over his eyes. It was fever whispering in his head. He must think clearly.

No droshkies, he told himself. Too dangerous. If they suspected he had any money at all, the isvostchiks would be on him like wolves. He was a stranger and a refugee with no friends. If he was attacked, he had only the revolver; it might not be enough. Don't take the chance, he thought. His best hope lay in the appearance of poverty. And the poor had no kopeks for droshkies.

He would have to reach the city on foot.

He waited for a moment when all the backs seemed to be turned. A commotion had arisen in another car, and one man, purple with anger, was being hauled out onto the platform by a Czech officer. Hoarse shouts and cries rose into the air; no one was watching him.

Now.

He flung his suitcase onto the platform. It landed unnoticed close to the edge, near the tracks. Then he scanned the milling crowd, searching for the stationmaster.

Yes, over there. The stationmaster was holding a match to the bowl of a pipe held between his teeth. He was easy to recognize in his official red cap and his uniform.

Nicholas leaped to the ground. He straightened his jacket. He hadn't shaved this morning—there hadn't been time—and he knew that stubble covered his cheeks. His eyes were bloodshot with fever, and his whole appearance was disreputable, but it would have to do. Perhaps it would even be an advantage.

"Stationmaster!" he called in a loud angry voice.

The man looked up from his pipe.

"Over here!" Nicholas called. He folded his arms across his chest.

The stationmaster peered through the crowd, identifying Nicholas as the person who was calling, then slowly he walked forward, taking his time about approaching, shouldering his way through the mob. Finally he reached Nicholas.

"Who are you? What do you want?"

"What the hell is that?" Nicholas pointed to the suitcase.

The stationmaster stared, and then shrugged. "Somebody's valise. How the hell should I know?"

"Why is it lying on the platform?"

"Listen, there's all kinds of luggage around here. I can't keep track of everything—"

"You'd better keep track of suspicious packages and parcels. Including unclaimed suitcases. That's your job. If you don't do it properly, you may find yourself in a great deal of trouble."

The stationmaster slowly took his pipe out of his mouth. "Who the hell are you, to be telling me my job?"

"Never mind. Just pay attention to what I say."

"Didn't you just get off the train?" The man's eyes narrowed in suspicion.

"That's right."

"Then what—"

Nicholas stepped close to the man, and took hold of his arm. "Listen," he said in a steely, low voice. "I just got off the train. That's correct. But do you know from where?"

"How should I—"

"Have you ever heard," Nicholas said through his teeth, "of twenty-two Lubianka Street?"

"Twenty-two—"

"It's an address, comrade. In Moscow."

It was the address of Djerzinsky's Cheka. The stationmaster's face twitched in nervous apprehension. Yes, he'd heard of it. Even here in Khabarovsk, that address had its own lurid notoriety. The man glanced uneasily into Nicholas's eyes. Céline had said, in a quarrel just before the end, that Nicholas resembled Felix Djerzinsky—the same ice-cold blue eyes of the man from Poland, she'd claimed tearfully. Nicholas saw no resemblance at all, but right now he welcomed the comparison.

"Maybe I'd better see what's inside the suitcase," the stationmaster muttered.

Nicholas let go of his arm. "I'll take it," he said. He bent and picked it up, putting it under his arm. "I'll inspect it myself. In the depot." He glared once more at the stationmaster. "I hope, for your sake, that the contents are innocent. Otherwise . . ."

He let the sentence trail off ominously. The stationmaster nodded. "Yes, yes, look it over, tell me what you find. I'll take action."

With a last angry stare, Nicholas strode off toward the depot. He had no intention of entering the building. Behind it, he knew, was the road leading to the city.

Daria, still in the teplushka, moved toward Ludmilla and Boris. They were gathering together their belongings. Ludmilla held the baby, who was coughing weakly, in a fierce possessive clasp. Most of the passengers were still slightly dazed, Daria saw, still not fully awake to the fact that the train journey had come to an end.

And she herself—oh, God—her mind was in a numb, disconnected whirl, aching with pain, and she could hardly realize what had happened. It was over. She'd said good-bye to Nicholas. Perhaps they'd meet in Harbin. *Will we, Nicholas?* Would she ever see him again? Or would she only see his face in her mind, and hear his voice like a fading echo, before she fell asleep at night, or in those quiet moments when her guard was down, and she forgot, and the thought of him came back like the stab of a knife . . .

Her whirling thoughts were suddenly interrupted by a woman's voice cutting through the murmur of nervous conversation in the boxcar.

"Please collect your belongings and come with me. All of you. As quickly as possible." Her voice held a note of weary authority. She was standing in the doorway, and like the young man previously, she wore an armband marked with a red cross.

"Why do we have to come with you?" someone asked, after a moment.

"It's for your own protection." She looked around the car and passed a hand over her forehead. "Is everyone here? I hope no one's left without permission."

Daria saw, after a swift glance around at the passengers, that two people were missing. The ex-convict, Peter No-Name. And Nicholas. But she didn't say anything, nor did anyone else.

Lowering her eyes, she went to her shelf to find her suitcase.

Ten minutes later, after a babble of confused objections and bewildered mutterings, the passengers found themselves outside in the sunshine, divided by sex into two disorganized groups, and waiting outside the entrances to two big canvas tents.

Daria, waiting with Ludmilla, felt the warmth of the spring day fall across her shoulders. She caught the faint scent of grass and wildflowers on the air. It was almost overpowered by the odor of human bodies and unwashed clothing all around her, but if she closed her eyes and concentrated she could sense it, and she found it comforting; it reminded her of the meadow at home.

"What are they going to do?" Ludmilla muttered, still holding the baby.

"Have some doctors examine us, I suppose." Daria tried to smile. "It will be all right, Ludmilla. Don't worry."

Ludmilla was searching anxiously for Boris in the men's group.

"Women with small children, please come with me." The woman who had spoken to them before was now walking up and down the line. Ludmilla, with a frightened glance at Daria, moved to her side. "The rest of you," the woman went on, "will please remove all your clothing as soon as you are inside the tent."

"Everything?" someone asked.

"Yes, everything," she replied firmly. "Even your underwear. You must strip to the skin."

"What will we wear?" another woman yelled out. "Blankets?"

"You'll get your own things back after they've been inspected. If they're contaminated, they'll have to be

118

boiled—that's very important. But you'll get them back, I promise."

Daria had reached the inside of the tent. It was floored with wooden planks that were dripping wet and slippery underfoot, and it was crowded with shivering naked women. Hesitantly she began to undo the buttons of her blouse.

When she was naked and had made a pile of her clothing, following instructions, she joined the others. Now what? she wondered, crossing her arms over her breasts. How quickly you lost the sense of your own identity in a situation like this. It was—

Oh! She caught her breath in a startled gasp of shock. Water was suddenly striking her body in a hard warm stream, assaulting her face, hitting her eyes, making her choke and splutter, soaking her hair, jetting fiercely over her skin. All around her women were shrieking and squealing, throwing protective arms over their faces. The water continued to spill over them, coming from everywhere, inescapable, reaching every corner of the tent. You couldn't get away, no matter how you ducked, no matter where you turned. The plank wood floor was running with deep streams of water. She was blinded.

After the first moments of shock, when she had blinked and could see again, dimly, through rainbows of moisture, she realized that the water was coming from patched rubber hoses being wielded outside the tent.

It must be necessary, she told herself desperately, surrendering to the streams of water. There must be a reason.

When the hoses were finished at last, one woman sidled up to Daria. "Have you heard what they're going to do with us now?" she muttered.

"No, I haven't heard anything."

"Keep us here, at the station. We won't be allowed into the city. They say they can't afford a typhus epidemic, so all the train passengers will be kept here in tents and not allowed to go."

"But surely they'll let us continue on our way?"

"Maybe, maybe not." The woman shrugged. "The soldiers are taking all the trains. How can we leave? And they say the Japanese have landed troops in Vladivostok.

They'll be in Khabarovsk soon. *That* will be something to look forward to."

"I don't understand why Japanese would be here," Daria said, confused.

"Ha." The woman curled her lip scornfully. "The Japanese have their eye on all this territory. Ever since they won the war in 1905. They have an army in Manchuria too," she added, ominously. "Did you know that?"

"No. I thought Manchuria was Chinese."

"It is. But it's ruled by a warlord, Chang Tso-lin. And they say Chang Tso-lin is a Japanese puppet."

Daria didn't know whether to believe all this.

"You'll find out," the woman said darkly. "The Japanese own all kinds of things in Manchuria. Iron mines, the warlord's government, the South Manchuria Railway. And now, with the civil war going on in Siberia, they're hoping to grab this part of the world too."

Daria stared at her silently.

The woman sidled closer. "Listen," she said, "do you know how the Japanese treat civilians when they take a city?" She lowered her voice and began to describe the use of bayonets.

Daria shuddered. "We'll have to leave Khabarovsk," she whispered. "They'll have to let us go."

"Will they?" The woman's eyes were somber, and heavily underscored with dark circles, like purple bruises. "We could be here for years."

I won't believe that, Daria told herself fiercely, wiping her wet face with her hand and blinking beads of moisture from her eyelashes. *I won't be stranded here for years. Or even weeks.*

I'll do something. Somehow.

Chapter 10

The railroad station was safely behind him. Somewhere ahead of Nicholas lay Khabarovsk. He forced himself to keep walking.

Every now and then an official automobile chugged past on the muddy road. Sometimes a droshky went by, with the driver shouting to keep clear and the horse's hooves churning up gobbets of mud onto the roadside. Overhead, whenever he looked up, he saw a soft blue sky dotted with clouds like fluffy white wool, and he realized dimly that it was a beautiful day.

But he seldom looked up. It made him dizzy. He wasn't perspiring; his body was burning with a dry heat. That was a very bad sign, he thought. He wondered with an odd, feverish detachment why he was doing this. What was the purpose of walking on? There was no end to this road. It stretched to infinity. And it was uphill all the way. Khabarovsk was built on hills. It would be so easy just to give up. Or return to the station and put himself into the hands of the doctors.

But he knew that if he did, he might never get out again.

Doggedly, one step at a time, he kept going.

There was an end, after all, to the road. How long had it taken him? An hour or two? No, not that long. But he'd lost all sense of time, imprisoned in the hot, aching cage of his fever.

He stood breathing sharply, gasping, looking down at

the green slopes he'd just climbed, running steeply down to the banks of the Amur, with the wooden structures of the city clinging to their sides. He blinked and rubbed his eyes. At the bottom of the hill, the river was a yellow-brown dazzle in the sunlight. Hurting.

Don't look back.

He turned and kept on going. He found himself on a sidewalk where there were other people. Shops. Droshkies. Automobiles. Carts. The chatter of voices. Lemon-yellow sunshine. The odor of sewage. He saw the city, but through a fever haze.

He realized he was walking again, and his boots were thudding on wood, sounding hollow in his ears. He was on a raised elevation, a wooden sidewalk constructed of wide planks, built up high over the muddy street. A lucid thought whispered through the fever: don't stagger too close to the edge, or you'll fall off the platform. Below the sidewalk waited the mud, thick and black and viscous, the oozing mud of spring.

He turned a corner onto a wide street. Facing him across the road was a store with a German name: Kunst and Albers. He'd heard of it; they had another store in Vladivostok; it was well known. He realized that he was on the main avenue, Muraviev-Amursky.

He had to stop. He couldn't keep going without stopping to rest. He didn't know how much longer he could force himself to keep moving.

The revolver was a comforting weight in his pocket. It had been worth the thirty rubles, he thought.

He saw that he was standing in front of a shabby storefront with a name painted over the door: The Illusion. That was appropriate. He wanted to laugh, but his throat hurt.

Then, as he noticed a grimy waterstained poster tacked up by the entrance, he realized it was a cinema. The colors of the poster were faded and smeared, but it was legible: Charlie Chaplin and Marie Dressler in *Tillie's Punctured Romance*. He recalled vaguely seeing that before. Kharkov. 1914? 1915?

He passed a hand across his forehead and felt it burning hot. He struggled against the depressing self-pity of

122

illness that was beginning to seep into his mind. He recognized it, the insidious gray companion of the fever, whispering, whispering, give up, give up, it's so easy to give up.

Not yet.

He glanced right and left. Another sign hung over the street, a few doors away. The Belvedere Hotel. Peeling paint flaked away from a splintery board, and he imagined what it must be like inside. But he realized, with a grim certainty, that he had no choice; he would have to make the Belvedere Hotel his destination. It was close and available. He had come almost to the end of his resources, and the fever was raging throughout his body now, aggravated by the long walk up the muddy slope of the hill. The Belvedere Hotel would have to do.

He set his jaw, walking again, and steeled himself to face the desk clerk and the formalities of booking a room. From the looks of the place, it shouldn't take too long; he doubted they would ask many questions. It was probably just as well. There was a soviet in Khabarovsk; though he could not remember the name of the local commissar. But the long arm of the Cheka might extend this far.

The squalid surroundings of the Belvedere Hotel would have their good points; he must try to remember that.

He thought of it again, fifteen minutes later, as he carefully locked the door of his room behind the departing back of the manager, a swarthy Greek with liquid dark eyes, a soiled shirt, and a pot belly hanging over his belt. The man had said little except to ask for a week's payment in advance.

He looked around, putting the key on top of the bureau to the right of the door. There was no toilet; the facilities were at the other end of the dark, grimy hallway outside. But there was a large tin basin, a pitcher of water, and a cotton towel. He saw them all on top of the bureau. They assumed you'd brought your own soap. Well, he had.

A big cracked mirror was set in a wooden frame over the bureau. Yellow waterstains blotched the walls. Dusty sunlight fell through the window overlooking the Muraviev-

Amursky and cruelly illuminated the cracked linoleum of the floor. As Nicholas watched, a large rust-colored cockroach scuttled into the baseboard.

There were things to be grateful for, though: few questions asked. And the bed—a narrow iron bed made up with a tan cotton blanket and coarse yellow sheets—strategically faced the door. He would not have to move it.

But before he could throw himself down on the bed, he had things to do.

First, he had to undress. He did it carefully, one piece of clothing at a time, scrutinizing each one for a sign of the little crawling creatures that spread typhus. Nothing. Then, when he was undressed and trying to keep his teeth from chattering in the burning chill that had overtaken him, he searched himself, skin and body hair. Again nothing.

This wasn't typhus. It was influenza.

He tried not to think of the fact that influenza was potentially as dangerous as typhus. Especially in his run-down state of health. Wearily he went to the bureau and poured water into the basin, to wash in. He stared at his own naked reflection in the mirror. He had lost weight. He could almost count ribs. And his eyes . . . glazed with fever . . .

Must eat something.

No, it was useless to think of food; the idea only nauseated him. And the enormous effort required to shave was beyond him. He finished washing and pulled on his underwear, not bothering with the rest of his clothing, then took the revolver from the jacket he'd left on the floor, and sat on the edge of the bed to load it. He broke it open and fumbled for the bullets, moving very slowly. He knew it was only a matter of moments before he lost consciousness. He'd pushed himself too far.

He laid the loaded gun carefully on the small table beside the bed, near his hand. The leather pouch with the jewelry he put under the pillow.

Was the door locked? Had he remembered to do that? It was too late. He couldn't get up to investigate because the room was spinning dizzily, and the fever was rising like a scarlet flood of pain to engulf him, and he had to lie back . . . close his eyes . . .

He woke up in darkness. His head was still burning, and he was shivering uncontrollably. Footsteps were going by on the wooden platform outside the window, thud thud thud, then dying away into the distance. A streetlamp reflected sickly yellow light onto the mirror.

The floor was probably crawling with cockroaches, he thought, but it didn't matter. The inside of his mouth was so dry he couldn't swallow, but that didn't matter either. The only important thing right now was to stop this shivering.

He crawled under the blanket and pulled it up to his shoulders. It helped just a little. He felt if he touched his body anywhere, he would burn his hand.

If someone came through that door right now, would he be able to fire the gun? He didn't know.

Time passed, in a fevered hell. The night ended, and hot yellow daylight flooded the room. A fly buzzed in through the open window. Nicholas kept waking and sleeping, in a shallow, uneasy state of semiconsciousness. His temperature rose. He kept shivering. Once he had to get up, pull on his trousers, and let in an old man with a mop to clean the room. He leaned against the bureau, watching the old man with feverishly glittering eyes. But the janitor was stooped and bleary-eyed, interested only in finishing his work and getting out. He never looked up. When he was done he shuffled back out into the hall with his mop and bucket, and Nicholas locked the door again.

The sun set, and darkness came.

By the third day, tossing on tangled sheets, with cracked lips and burning head, he recognized the truth.

He knew he was going to die.

He licked his dry lips. He should have stayed at the station after all, he thought. But what was the difference? In a fleeting moment of clarity he realized that the influenza was draining his will to live, but the moment passed and he sank back into delirium.

Once he thought of his father. Sergei Nicholaevitch had lived to forty-six. Nicholas had wanted to pass his forty-seventh birthday, just to outlive his father. What a stupid goal. Senseless. He wouldn't reach it anyway. Not even come close.

He passed out.

125

He woke up thinking it was a dream; the door was rattling. Someone was shouting outside in the hallway. The old man? No; he'd come and gone.

He fumbled for the revolver, thinking, so they've come for me.

In helpless disgust he realized he was too weak to hold the gun. Grinding his teeth with rage, letting the revolver clatter onto the table, he fell back on the pillow. In the next second he had passed out again.

When he opened his eyes, he was staring up at a face. He was hallucinating, he thought, or else he was dead. Could dying be that easy? No, because he was still in this room with the cracked mirror—and there was still a fly buzzing around somewhere, he could hear it. And he could smell the faint odor of sewage coming from the open window, just like Khabarovsk—

And the face he was staring at was Daria's.

Chapter 11

Nicholas, you mustn't die, Daria thought. She touched his forehead and felt it burning hot. Oh God, he was hot everywhere, and crackling dry. A deep, fearful dread that she'd come too late haunted her as she stared down at Nicholas's face. He'd closed his eyes again. How strange to see him with a four-day growth of beard. And half-naked. But those thoughts were only at the bottom of her consciousness, submerged by her growing panic that he was going to die.

No, he mustn't die.

Unconsciously she clasped her hands tightly in front of her as she tried to collect her thoughts and not submit to the panic. She would need a supply of fresh sheets and towels from the manager. And boiling water for tea. And a cot for herself to sleep on. The room would be crowded, but it didn't matter.

The manager was still standing in the doorway, frowning, jingling his keys in his hand. She turned to him, composing her features into stern, set lines and began to make her requests. After some grumbling and objections, he said grudgingly that he would see what he could do. He banged the door behind him as he left.

She prayed that she would have enough moral force to get what she'd asked for. She wished she were older, more formidable, with a sharper tongue. She would have to develop a sharp tongue, that's all! She knew if it were

127

the other way around, Nicholas would have no trouble having his requests filled.

Where could she start? That pitcher of water, the basin, a clean towel. She soaked the towel in the tepid water from the pitcher, then wrung it out and sponged Nicholas's face. She needed clean water too. Maybe she ought to write out a list. No, she could keep it in her head; she wasn't likely to forget, not under these circumstances . . .

She pulled over a chair, the only one in the room, a wooden slat-back with a cracked leg, and sat down at Nicholas's bedside. His eyes opened.

"How did you find me?"

Not delirious, thank God. Not at the moment anyway.

"There aren't that many places to stay in Khabarovsk. I just inquired at all the hotels I could find. I described you."

"How did you get the manager to let you in?"

Daria smiled. "Do you remember that market with the dancing bear, when you said I was your niece? I said that too, and that we'd been separated by accident. I think the manager was relieved. He didn't want the responsibility, if . . . if . . ."

She couldn't finish the sentence. Nicholas only nodded wearily and closed his eyes again.

Please don't die.

Suppose she hadn't escaped from the station last night? Suppose Nicholas were here all alone in this room, dying . . . no, no, she mustn't even consider that thought. It mustn't happen.

The memory of the railroad station came back to her. She saw again the big canvas tent set up on the grass, crowded with people who were clasping their children, clasping one another, frightened, yet resigned to their fate. *Avos.* Whatever happens is the will of destiny. *Nichevo.* What difference does it make? She couldn't quite achieve that resignation. In the darkness of the tent, she could see the flickering orange-red lights of candles, and here and there the red twinkle of a cigarette. Somewhere to the right, beyond the canvas walls, people were moaning: typhus victims, lying on blankets on the open ground. Some of them would die tonight, she thought.

Horrified pity ran through her. She tried to imagine how it felt to be stricken, after the crawling lice had invaded your body and your clothes: the weak, uneven pulse, the racing heartbeat, the purple rash spreading over your body, the burning temperature, the struggle, the weakening, and the surrender. She had seen some of the filthy bodies, before they were washed by the hoses, crusted with dirt like a second skin; not even the streams of water could take it off, it had to be scraped. And the rags of dirty clothing being flung into the cauldrons of boiling water . . . how could they let that happen? Oh Lord, perhaps they couldn't help it.

"What are you thinking about, my little friend?"

She started, peering up into the shadows. The woman's hoarse, husky voice was familiar, as was the shape of her wide woolen skirt. Zora, the gypsy from the train, was standing above her.

"I'm wondering what's going to happen to us all."

"I'll read the cards for you, and let you know. I promised to do that on the train, remember?" Zora took a pack of playing cards out of the pocket of her skirt and riffled them with her thumb; slapslap of cardboard. Daria saw the gleam of her teeth as she smiled.

"I can't pay you, Zora. I have no money to waste on fortune-telling."

"I'm bored. You can pay me some other time."

Zora squatted down and took a candle from her other pocket, lit it, and stuck it on the wooden floor in a blob of wax. Her face leaped eerily out of the darkness, lit from below by the wavering flame of the candle. Sunken eyes, sunken cheeks, tangled hair, thin hawk nose . . . like her lover the Yellow Hawk, Daria thought. She was afraid to have her fortune told by Zora, but she was ashamed to admit such a cowardly, irrational fear. When Zora held out the greasy cards, she obediently pulled out two, taking them gingerly, by their edges.

Zora's clawlike fingers turned the cards over. Ace of Spades. Jack of Clubs.

"Too bad," she muttered.

Daria felt a shiver of dread. "What's too bad?"

"I see a swift parting," the gypsy mumbled. She scowled down at the cards. "And I see . . . very clearly . . . the

129

death of a blue-eyed man." She held out the pack again. "Pull two more."

"No. No more."

How horrible. How stupid. I won't believe this. Not a word. Shuddering, she tried to put the sudden memory from her: Nicholas, on the train. Looking strangely flushed. A set look of pain around his mouth. And blue eyes . . . the bluest eyes she'd ever seen. *The death of a blue-eyed man.* Was he ill? She had thought so, until saying good-bye had made her forget. *A swift parting.* Surely that parting had been brutally swift!

"Go away, Zora," she said, turning her face aside. "I'm tired, I want to sleep now."

With a low laugh, pocketing her cards, the gypsy woman stood up. "The cards don't lie, little one. They never do."

She began to thread her way among the sleeping, restless bodies in the tent.

Daria was left with her fears. Second by second, minute by minute, she grew more afraid. The conviction came over her that she had to escape from the tent and find Nicholas. It had nothing to do with the cards. He was ill, Daria thought; she would have known, but she'd been too stupid to realize it before, too wrapped up in her own misery. What a fool she was. She must find him. Leave—right now. Before dawn. She would walk to Khabarovsk. She was used to walking. Even in the dark. She could follow the road. And if it was dangerous, well, she would have to chance it. Perhaps it would be less dangerous than in daylight. Soldiers were sleeping in their barracks, officials were home in bed; she could reach the city in darkness and begin her search at first light.

Stop thinking about the cards.

She had a more immediate problem: she had to get out of the railroad station.

Say good-bye to Ludmilla and Boris? No, they would try to stop her. She would leave them a note. She found a scrap of paper and a pencil in her suitcase, and scribbled a hasty letter, blinking back tears.

So many good-byes! Would they ever meet again? Perhaps not. In Saravenko little changed from year to year, there were few good-byes, only births and deaths; but since she'd left home, since that night at Chita Station, there had been only good-byes.

After leaving the note, she took her suitcase and made her way out of the tent.

Just as she'd feared, there was a military patrol guarding the platform. She could see dark shapes with caps and rifles standing alongside the tracks. In the other direction, kerosene lamps illuminated the typhus-stricken bodies on the grass. A few doctors and nurses were moving back and forth among them.

The young doctor, she thought, the one with the tired face, he'll help me. I know he will. He reminded her of Lev; she remembered that Lev had once been a medical student in Kiev. If it weren't for the revolution, he would probably have become a physician himself, like his father.

It was useless to think that way, she told herself. If it weren't for the revolution, she would still be in Saravenko, with Dedushka. And Nicholas would still own an iron foundry in Kharkov. Everything would be different.

Or would it. Could you change your destiny?

As if she had called him, the young man she had been thinking of walked over to her from the grass. "What's the trouble? Are you ill? Do you have any symptoms?"

"No, I—"

"Then why aren't you sleeping?"

"I was wondering when we could leave here."

"You'll be informed of that as soon as possible." His voice was tired, speaking the words by rote. "Please go back into the tent."

She had already offered, the day before, to help nurse the sick. But they were still wary of spreading the infection. Her offer had been refused.

"I haven't been near any of the typhus victims," she said.

"I know that."

She dropped her suitcase to her feet. "Please," she said urgently, "please, you must help me."

He frowned. "What do you mean?"

"Give me permission to leave."

"I'm sorry, that's impossible."

"Please!" She stared up at him desperately. "Please—

it's terribly important! You don't know how important it is! I—I can't explain. But it's a matter of life and death."

Suddenly she was very sure that it was. Her voice trembled with sincerity.

"Everyone says that." For the first time she heard a note of uncertainty in his voice. It gave her hope.

"It's true! If you let me go, you'll be saving a life! Isn't that your job?"

"My dear young woman, don't exaggerate."

"I'm not exaggerating! Can't you tell—can't you *see*—when someone is telling the truth?"

She persuaded him, finally. By the passion of her desire, and refusal to let him walk away, her grasp on his sleeve, and unashamed tearful pleading—she would have begged on her knees, if she'd had to—she convinced him to let her go. He spoke to the soldiers in weary acquiescence, and they passed her through. She was on the road to the city.

And now she had found Nicholas.

Was Zora right? she wondered fearfully, sitting at his bedside, watching him toss feverishly on the rumpled sheets. "I see very clearly . . . the death of a blue-eyed man . . ."

Without realizing what she was doing, sitting in the broken chair, remembering the tent, she had begun to sing under her breath. It was a sign of tension; she always sang to herself when she was upset; she'd done it since she was very small, and had been afraid of thunderstorms. She'd outgrown her fear of thunder, but the habit of singing had stayed with her. It was a song of her childhood, about a spirit who lived in a tree trunk.

Nicholas's eyelashes suddenly lifted. She was looking into depths of dark, intense blue.

"Where's your balalaika?" he said clearly.

"I—I left it at home in the izba."

"Ah. Then I'll have to buy you another."

Just as suddenly as he'd awakened, he fell asleep again.

Where's that manager with everything I asked for? she thought desperately.

She stood up and began to pace the room.

Chapter 12

Nicholas sat bolt upright in bed. What the hell—? It was pitch dark. A dark shape was curled up in a cot beside his bed, breathing rhythmically and slowly; all he could see was a back and the gleam of white cotton.

Of course—it was Daria. She was sleeping in her chemise, he could see that, now that his eyes were accustomed to the darkness.

She'd found him. On her own. Somehow, she'd gotten out of the railroad station and made her way to this room. She'd been brave and resourceful, and he would have to find a way to thank her.

But why had he awakened so suddenly?

Then he realized why. He was soaking wet. The sheets were soaked. He ran the palm of his hand down his face and across his bare chest, and brought it up dripping wet. He was sweating. Finally. His body was drenched with perspiration. And his head was clear. The fever was gone. He touched his forehead with the back of his hand: cool and damp with sweat. He cleared his throat, very softly, testing: no heat, no flare of pain.

With a low groan of relief he fell back against the pillow. Weak, yes, and trembling, but with relief, not delirium. He became aware of something else, a welcome, familiar discomfort: his stomach was hollow. He was hungry.

"Nicholas, are you awake?" Daria was sitting up in her cot.

"Yes."

"I fell asleep—I didn't mean to!"

"How long have you been here?"

"Two days." Her voice was a soft whisper. "I've been so worried—are you all right?"

"Yes, I'm all right. I'm sweating."

"You're—" He heard a little gasp. "Oh, Nicholas, thank God!" She scrambled out of bed and came to stand beside him, switching on the bedside lamp. They blinked at one another in the sudden light. "That means the fever's broken!"

He nodded.

Daria's eyes widened. "Your sheets are soaking wet. If you can get out of bed, I'll change them for you. I have clean sheets on the bureau—I had to promise the manager extra money before he'd bring them—he wants to charge extra for everything, you'd think he was parting with diamonds—"

Nicholas remembered the jewelry pouch and withdrew it from under the pillow before he climbed out of bed. He put it on the table, then leaned against the wall, weak-kneed. Daria was already stripping the bed and bringing over clean sheets. She wore a cotton lace chemise cut tantalizingly low across the bosom, revealing creamy-white swells of flesh every time she bent over. For a slender girl, she had a surprisingly lush figure.

Oh Lord. I must be getting better.

He squinted across at himself in the mirror. He was wearing only cotton underpants. Too thin. He would have to start eating, and gain back some weight. At the moment he could have put away a seven-course meal.

Daria had finished making up the bed, and bundled the wet sheets into a corner of the room. "How do you feel?" she asked, turning and brushing back her hair.

"Hungry."

She caught her lower lip in her teeth. "I only have a little black bread and cheese left from my own supper—"

"Fine, I'll take it."

He sat down on the edge of the bed, and she brought over the bread and cheese, wrapped in a napkin. "I hope it's not too stale. I try not to keep too much food here— you know, because of the cockroaches. And I boil all the

134

water, before I drink it—you *are* hungry! I'll make some tea."

"Daria, before you do that go over to my suitcase, like a good girl—it's there in the corner—open it up, and you'll find a bottle of brandy. Can you bring it here? And a glass of water." He glanced up. "What's wrong?"

She hadn't moved. She was staring at him, and he saw tears in her eyes. "Why didn't I think of that?" she burst out. "Tea! And clear soup! That's all I could think of! Why didn't I think of brandy? How stupid!"

"Whatever you did, it was exactly right. You probably saved my life."

"Do you think so?" she whispered. She whirled and went to the suitcase, kneeling down and looking for the brandy. When she found it, she brought it over to him with a glass of water. "Tomorrow, as soon as it's morning, I'll go out and buy more food." She sat down on the chair. Her voice was matter-of-fact again. "Nicholas, everything is so expensive! The prices they want for bread and eggs—"

"We have to get out of here," he said grimly. He took a long swallow of the brandy. The taste was smooth and fiery, and he was going to keep it down, there was no nausea, and he was still perspiring. "Khabarovsk is a trap. Especially if Japanese troops are on their way."

"That's what a woman said to me at the railroad station." Daria frowned, worried. "But she said there aren't any trains, at least not for passengers."

"Damn! If I weren't so shaky on my feet, I could start investigating tomorrow."

"But you're not recovered yet."

He took another swallow of brandy and leaned back against the pillow. "At least you don't have to worry about money. I have some left." He drained the glass and set it on the table. "We'll talk about it in the morning."

The brandy and the food were making him sleepy.

Daria stood up and turned off the light. "Good night, Nicholas."

"Good night."

When he woke up again, it was broad daylight. Another fly was buzzing in and out of the window. He could still smell the sewage stink from outdoors and hear the clatter of droshkies, the hoarse shouts of the isvostchiks, the thud of bootheels on the wooden sidewalk, the cry of a peddler selling melons. He lay back with his arms under his head and stared at the pattern of sunlight on the cracked ceiling and watched the dance of dust motes in the air, and knew he was glad to be alive. Just to be well again—without fever—seemed to make up for everything in the past, everything he had lost. At least at that moment. Even here in Khabarovsk, stranded, with no way out. But they'd find a way. As soon as he could get on his feet . . .

Daria came awake on her cot. "Look at that sun! It must be late! Why did you let me sleep so late?"

"I just woke up."

"I meant to get up hours ago and find us food."

"You needed the sleep."

She stood up and reached for her skirt. "I won't be gone long. There's a market on the next road. Of course there's a better one at the foot of the hill, near the river— Chinese people run it, and their prices are cheaper—"

"Here." Nicholas took his wallet from the bedside table and tossed it to her. "Take what you need."

She caught it quickly. "All right. I won't pretend it doesn't come in handy— Oh!"

"What's the matter?"

"All this money! Do you trust me?"

"Of course I trust you."

How incredibly innocent she was about money, he thought in sudden amusement. She was staring down at the wallet. It wasn't very much at all; most of his cash was still hidden in the suitcase. But she seemed to think it was a fortune. Well, that was what came of growing up in a small Siberian village. She certainly was not extravagant. No, just the opposite, he thought drowsily; she would have to learn how to spend money. Some day, when he made his fortune again . . . when they reached Harbin . . .

Daria had hastily washed and dressed and was preparing to leave. "I'll be back as soon as I can," she said with her hand on the doorknob.

"Daria?"

"Yes?"

136

"Do you think you can find me cigarettes?"

"I'll try."

She was back within half an hour with hard-boiled eggs, salted fish, cheese and black bread, a jar of raspberry jam, two bottles of red wine, fresh milk, and two jars of pickled beets. And a box of cigarettes. When he had eaten, he lit a cigarette and drew the smoke down into his lungs.

There was only one more thing he wanted. "Daria, will you do something else for me?"

She was taking the cigarette out of his hand and crushing it out in a saucer. I wanted to finish it, he thought. But his eyes were closing. Suddenly he was falling asleep.

The next time he woke, the sun was setting. He must have slept all day, he thought. But he was feeling stronger. Daria had gone out again while he slept and visited the market by the riverfront. She'd found a big piece of ham, some roasted lima beans and onions, and some pickled watermelon rind. He ate it all.

"We have practically nothing left for breakfast," she said in amazement. "Only some bread and jam."

"I'll go out myself in the morning."

"No, you won't! It's too soon!"

"I can't stay locked up in this room much longer."

"At least a day or so. Yesterday you were delirious!" Then she sighed. "I can see that you're going to be a very difficult patient." She went over to the bureau and picked up a basin of soap and water.

When she'd brought it to the table, Nicholas directed her to the suitcase. "You'll find a brown pigskin case, with a gold clasp—there's a razor inside. Shall I help you?"

"No, stay where you are, I can find it."

Crouched by the suitcase, she found the case, opened it, and took out the razor. "How beautiful!" she exclaimed, holding it up.

The razor was one of the few things Nicholas had carried away from Kharkov. The blade, which he kept carefully honed, was imported steel from Germany, and the handle was polished rosewood, inlaid with ivory. He'd owned it for years.

Daria brought it to him. "Shall I shave you?"

He looked at her dubiously. "Have you ever shaved anyone?"

"No. But I'm willing to learn." She made an experimental gesture with the razor, waving it in the air.

Nicholas watched her warily. "Maybe we'd better leave the lessons for another time. I think I'd better get up and do it myself."

"No, don't get up. I have a hand mirror. I can hold it for you—at least I can help that much."

She found the mirror in her own suitcase, a silver-backed mirror with a filigree handle, and came back with it to the bedside.

"Fine. Now just sit on the edge of the bed and hold it up—not so low, pick your arm up a little—yes, like that —very good."

When he was finished and had wiped his face with a towel and lain back against the pillow, he felt even better. He sensed a rising impatience within himself to be up and making plans, doing something, finding a way to leave Khabarovsk. But he knew she was right, he needed another few days. It would be senseless to have a relapse. Especially now, when he had the responsibility for both of them. It had just happened; neither one of them had planned it that way. But here they were, thrown together in this room, and one way or another they would have to get across the border to Manchuria. There was no question of abandoning her now. He began to think about the trains.

"How did you get away from the railroad station?" he asked.

"A very nice young doctor helped me—he gave me a safe conduct—you may remember him, he came into the boxcar the morning we had to leave."

"No, I don't remember." That whole morning was a blur of pain and fever in his mind, and he was just as happy to forget it. Then he wondered, in a flash of jealous suspicion, exactly what she'd done to get the doctor's permission. He said, in a mild tone of voice, "It must have taken quite a bit of persuasion."

"Yes, it did! But somehow I knew he would help me. You see, he reminded me of someone."

"Oh? Who was that?"

Daria blushed. "A young man in Saravenko named Lev Omansky. He came to organize the peasants' soviet. I think I mentioned him once before."

"Yes, I recall you did."

She'd claimed he was her lover, and then denied it. But he wondered how far they'd gone, how well they knew each other. Another stab of jealousy cut into him. "You must have been good friends."

The blush grew deeper. "Quite good."

"In that case," Nicholas said casually, "I'm surprised he sent you off all alone on the train. Knowing your grandfather couldn't come. Letting you travel by yourself to Manchuria wasn't a very responsible action, it seems to me."

"Oh no, you don't understand! He's very deeply involved in politics—he believes in his cause. He has to stay in Siberia."

Why was she defending this unknown young man? Nicholas found himself disliking him intensely. He was a Bolshevik as well. That was all the more reason to dislike him. "I don't think he's the kind of person you should be associating with," he remarked.

"You don't even know him."

He knew he was being unfair. But it was hard to fight down the little surge of possessive jealousy that had overtaken him. He knew that buried within him, lurking at the bottom of his mind, was the spoiled, arrogant young man who'd pounded his fist on the desk in his father's study. He had been struggling against that buried self for years. Perhaps some day he'd be successful. More likely, he would always have to struggle.

Daria was looking slightly offended. "I wish you wouldn't give me advice, as if you were my grandfather," she said suddenly. "You're not that old."

"No?"

"No. You're only thirty-six. That's not—" She bit her lip.

"How do you know that?"

"Oh, well." She made a helpless little gesture with her hand. "I looked at your identity card. It's in your wallet."

"I'm ashamed of you." But he couldn't help smiling to

himself. She looked so confused and red-faced. "What other fascinating information did you find out?"

"Nothing important. Just about Kharkov, and being a civil engineer, and that you're not married—" She stopped again in confusion.

"I would have told you that if you'd asked me."

"Now you're angry."

"No, I'm not angry," he said. "We have too many other worries, important ones, to be angry over silly things."

A look of relief came over her face.

"Daria, listen," he said, deliberately changing the subject. "When you go out to shop in the next day or so, I want you to be on the alert for gossip. Try to find out anything that could be helpful to us. Anything about the political situation, or transportation, or crossing the border —anything you hear that could be useful."

"I will, Nicholas."

Damn, I wish I were strong enough to leave right now, he thought, clenching his fist in sudden frustration. Get up, get dressed, and get us away from here. But he knew he couldn't chance it. Not for another day or two. He would have to be patient. He must make a complete recovery before facing the risks that lay ahead.

Two days later he was pacing the room like a caged tiger. He'd been doing nothing but eating and sleeping, and he knew he'd gained weight. He'd gotten dressed for the first time and had to use a wider notch on his belt. It was an encouraging sign. Now he was impatient to get out.

Where the hell was Daria? She'd been gone a long time. He tried to control his irritation, knowing it was the result of his confinement with not enough to do. One more night in this room, he thought, and to hell with that cot . . . and sleeping in low-cut chemises.

The door opened and Daria came in. She was looking pale, and tiny beads of perspiration gleamed on her upper lip. She set her bundles down on the bureau, then wiped her face with a handkerchief.

"What took you so long?" he demanded.

"I stopped at the Public Gardens for a glass of lemonade. It's very beautiful there, Nicholas. The park is on top of a hill, with flower gardens and apple trees and a church.

And at the very top is a big statue of Count Muraviev on a pedestal. He's looking out across the river, with a scroll in his hand . . ."

"Daria, please, I'm not interested in travelogues."

"I'm sorry."

She turned aside. He saw a fleeting look of pain cross her face, and she winced slightly. He was instantly suspicious.

"What's wrong with you?"

"Nothing. I'm just tired and hot."

"That's not true."

"I told you, it's nothing."

"Daria, don't lie to me! If you're ill, I want to know about it."

"I'm not ill." She pressed her lips together and lapsed into stubborn silence. He walked over to her and took her by the shoulders, realizing why she wouldn't answer. "Very well. If it's only your time of the month."

She flushed. "Do you have to know everything?"

"Yes. Everything about your physical condition, and I'll be just as frank about myself. It's important—there's no room in your life for girlish modesty. We have no one to depend on but one another, and we have to trust each other, and not keep secrets."

"All right. But—"

"But what?"

"But in a way, when you were sick and delirious—it was horrible, and I was so worried—but there was something about making the decisions myself, when you had nothing to say, and I was completely in charge, that was very nice!"

The sweet corruption of power. He tried not to smile. *Oh Daria, what will I do when you grow up?* And she would. He could see her changing already, growing more self-reliant and mature.

"Tell me what kind of gossip you heard outside," he said, letting go of her shoulders.

She took a breath, thinking back. "I met a girl in the Public Gardens, when I was having the lemonade. We just struck up a conversation. Oh, Nicholas, it was so sad! She was an actress; her name was Svetlana, and she'd been with the First Studio of the Art Theater in Moscow.

They were touring when the revolution broke out. They were in Saratov and they were afraid to go back to Moscow, so they just kept moving east, until they got to Khabarovsk. And now she has no work; she couldn't find anything to do. But she had to keep herself alive, so she . . . she moved to Kopek Hill." Daria looked at him with huge dark eyes. "Kopek Hill is a place where soldiers go to visit women," she whispered. "The women do what Zora did, on the train."

"I guessed that much."

"But it's so terrible! She wasn't like Zora at all! She was more like . . . like me!"

"You can't break your heart over all these stories, Daria. The East is probably full of women like Svetlana."

"I suppose so."

She was still troubled. He drew her forward, intending to comfort her. But the caress grew unexpectedly intense. After a second or two, her arms went up around his neck, and she moved closer, raising her face, and he bent to kiss her. Suddenly they were locked in an embrace that went on longer, much longer, than he intended.

The door opened.

"I hate to interrupt you and your *niece*," snarled a voice behind him, "but I came to find out how long you intend to stay here."

Damn. She'd forgotten to lock the door. Nicholas let go of Daria and turned to face the manager, who was standing in the doorway.

"Don't you knock before you open doors?" he asked coldly.

"I did. Nobody answered. You were too busy."

He was lying; he hadn't knocked at all.

"What difference does it make to you how long I stay here? I've paid you."

"I'm going to have to report you to the city officials. You've been here a week; that means a police report."

He might be telling the truth, or he might just be looking for a bribe, Nicholas thought. In either case, it was a bad sign.

"The police might be interested in the activities of this young lady too," the man added. "She needs a special card, you know, and a permit from the doctors, to do what she's doing."

You son of a bitch. Nicholas's face darkened, and the man stepped back. "You can let me know tomorrow," he said. "But no later."

"You'll hear from me tomorrow. Now get out."

He left, leaving the door ajar. Nicholas slammed it shut, and turned the lock. He turned to Daria, who was looking pale, still standing by the bureau.

"Did you hear anything about the trains while you were out?"

"Yes, Svetlana told me. She said they've all been taken by the soldiers. The Czech Brigade quarreled with Commissar Trotsky over the telegraph, and now they're fighting their way back west along the railway. Svetlana hears a lot of things on Kopek Hill."

"What else?"

"Japanese troops have already landed in Vladivostok, and they're probably on their way here. They already have spies and paid informers in Khabarovsk. No one can tell who's working for the Japanese and who isn't."

"They'll fight on the side of the counterrevolution," Nicholas muttered, searching his pockets for a cigarette. "Hoping to grab eastern Siberia for themselves when the fighting's over. It's what they've wanted for a long time."

The Japanese were tough, resourceful fighters. They'd proved that in 1904. But their cruelty to civilian populations was notorious.

"And they say Hetman Kalmikov and his Cossacks are approaching from the west," Daria added.

Ivan Kalmikov, the twenty-seven-year-old boy bandit. Khabarovsk was a tinderbox. Damn it, if they'd been able to cross the border at Chita and reach Manchuli, they'd be in Harbin by now, and out of this trap! He had a vision of himself arrested, imprisoned, shot. The jewelry gone . . . and Daria, alone, without money, and nowhere to go but Kopek Hill.

"You said something when you first came in," he said, half to himself, "that I should have paid more attention to. It was my fault, I was irritable, and didn't let you finish. It was about the statue."

"Count Muraviev?"

"Yes. Tell me about it again."

"It's a beautiful bronze statue, high up on the hill on a granite pedestal. He's holding a scroll, and facing the Amur River, way down at the bottom—"

"Of course! The river! The Amur is open for traffic—it has been since the beginning of May! I haven't been thinking."

"Oh, you're right. This is where the Amur meets the Ussuri." Daria paused, biting her lip. "If we could find passage down the Ussuri to Vladivostok—"

"No, Daria, not the Ussuri. Upriver, not far from here, the Amur meets the Sungari. And the Sungari flows past Harbin, in Manchuria." He looked at Daria without seeing her, thinking about the Sungari. It was not a large river, but it was deep enough for steamer traffic. And it flowed straight into the heart of Manchuria. "We could forget about Vladivostok, and the railway," he said slowly. "If we could get across the border on the river . . ."

"Could we, Nicholas? Wouldn't we be stopped at a customs station? I hear people saying they're slipping over the border on foot and trying to make their way overland to Harbin."

"It's almost thirteen hundred miles from here to Harbin. Do you want to attempt it on foot?" He laughed and went over to her again, gripping her by the shoulders. "No, first we'll try the river. If that fails, we'll think about the next step. But it's worth a try."

"All right, Nicholas." She rested her head against his shoulder. "I'll see about it tomorrow, if you think it's the right thing to do."

Not you, sweetheart, he thought, stroking her hair. This is something I'll have to do myself.

He woke at dawn the next morning. He had to go down to the wharf and look for a steamer.

As he got out of bed, wide awake, the idea of action filled him with new energy, and his restless impatience of the day before died away, replaced by cool wariness. He started to get dressed, moving quietly so as not to wake Daria. He was beginning to feel like himself again, and he knew that his mind was functioning clearly, freed of the last lingering shreds of the fever. He pulled on

144

corduroy trousers and low boots, then a short-sleeved blue cotton shirt open at the throat. The day would be warm and sunny, you could tell that already. He distributed the revolver, the jewelry, and the wallet in his pockets, then wrote a short note to Daria, telling her to stay inside the room with the door locked until he returned. Then he let himself out into the hall.

He went quickly through the small, dirty lobby. The man at the desk was someone he hadn't seen before, probably the night clerk not off duty yet. He was yawning and reading a newspaper, slumped behind the desk, and didn't look up as Nicholas went by.

Then he was outdoors in the early morning sunshine. Lord, it felt good to be outside! Fresh air, clear warm light, a breeze on your face. He felt as if he'd been caged for years, instead of a week. But even in that short time, the mud beneath the sidewalk had begun to dry in the sun. Soon it would be choking dust. Shopkeepers were unlocking their doors; a water wagon rumbled by with a clop-clop of horses' hooves. Looking to either side, he could see small wooden booths like ticket stalls at either end of the block. Chinese merchants were setting out goods for sale: kerosene, fresh fruit, matches and cigarettes, little jars of oil. He hadn't noticed them before.

This time the walk was downhill, to the riverbank. He went slowly along the wharf, looking at the steamers rocking at anchor. The Russian mail steamers were of no use, he thought. They would travel back up the Amur, in the direction he'd already come. A Russian freighter was too dangerous; he and Daria could easily be handed over to the authorities for trying to cross the border illegally. A Japanese fishing trawler? Possible, but he didn't really trust the Japanese. He held it in the back of his mind.

On the other side of the road, facing the river, a fruit and vegetable market was already bustling with energetic housewives who'd come early to get the best selection. Life went on, in spite of war. He heard the quick, up-and-down singsong of Chinese dialect. Here was fresh fish, laid out on shavings of ice. The fish would be sold by midday.

Nicholas stopped and looked up at the hill rising steeply above the river. As Daria had said, there was a green stretch of Public Gardens, with bright flowerbeds and apple trees and tables set out under canvas awnings. Higher still, the gold onion dome of a church glinted in the sun. Tiny and straight at the very top, past a gravel parade ground, the statue of Count Muraviev, Governor-General of the Amur Province in 1854, gazed down over his former territory.

Nicholas began to walk again, strolling along the wharf. A small, rusty freighter was loading cargo. Sweating Chinese deckhands, naked to the waist, were lowering huge red-and-white cans of insect powder through the open hatches into the hold. The deck was a jumbled clutter of winches, oilcans, boxes, bales, crates, and coiled ropes. Still onshore, waiting to be loaded, were burlap-covered bales of furs. Stone marten, squirrel, weasel, silver fox, sable . . . the soft fur spilled out here and there from the burlap coverings, pairs of bright black eyes still attached to the heads.

Nicholas looked more closely at the steamer. It had a wood-burning engine. An internal combustion engine would be of little use on the river, he knew, unless you had space to carry your own fuel, and there was no room on that deck for extra cargo, that was clear. The steamer would have to stop and load wood every day or so. But the forests here were deep and thick, untouched for centuries, and there'd be no shortage of wood for fuel.

"Good morning, my friend! You like my boat?"

A fat Chinese man wearing a captain's cap at a rakish angle over his eyebrow was grinning at Nicholas from the deck. His belly spilled out in lavish abundance over his sagging belt.

"It's a very fine boat."

"I think so too." The captain hitched up his pants. "Full cargo. I think I'll make a little money—I can use it."

"Do you own her yourself?"

"No, but I take my commission on the profits." He chuckled. "Sometimes the owners come along—we keep a couple of cabins handy, just in case." He waved at a square, boxlike structure rising midships from the deck, obviously housing cabins and the captain's quarters. Above it was the pilothouse, windowed all around. "Not this time, though," the captain added. "Just me and my crew."

"How big is your crew?"

"Eight deckmen, and my pilot." He laughed heartily. "And me, of course. I'm Captain Li."

"How do you do. My name is Nicholas Federovsky."

Captain Li nodded and touched his hand to his cap.

"Tell me, Captain." Nicholas hesitated, subduing a sense of rising excitement before asking his next question. It had to be the right answer. It was a Chinese crew and captain—and Chinese ownership too, he was almost certain—and so the answer had to be the one he was hoping for. "Where are you bound?"

"Upriver along the Amur, until we reach the Sungari. Then south to Harbin." The captain frowned at one of the deckmen and cuffed him on the side of the head, muttering something in Chinese before turning back to Nicholas. "It's a long trip."

"Two or three weeks?"

The captain laughed again, jiggling his huge belly. "Not on the *Kwan Yin*!" So that was the name lettered on the prow in Chinese: the *Kwan Yin*. The Goddess of Love and Mercy. Nicholas's hopes soared at the name. "We take our time," the captain went on. "We have to load fuel every day. And we anchor every night. No sense risking the boat after dark on the Sungari. We can do plenty of business during the day, at the riverports."

And that engine wouldn't take much steam, Nicholas thought. Not from the looks of the rest of the boat. Patched and leaky steam pipes, probably . . . plenty of breakdowns. If Captain Li didn't like to steam at night, he could not have have too much confidence in the pilot.

But it didn't matter. Nicholas was looking for a way out of Khabarovsk into Manchuria, and he had a feeling of deep sure certainty that he'd found it.

"Do you mind if I come aboard?" he asked. "To look around?"

"Help yourself." The captain waved expansively at the deck. As Nicholas walked up the plank, Captain Li casually unbuttoned his trousers and urinated over the side, into the river. Then he buttoned himself up again and held out his hand to Nicholas. "Welcome aboard. Do you know about boats?"

"Not much. I'm a road engineer by profession."

147

The captain looked roguish. "I hope you build good roads where you come from. In China we have a saying: a road is good for ten years, and bad for ten thousand!"

As the captain laughed at his own joke, Nicholas tried to place the haunting sickly sweet fragrance that wafted around him. Not perfume. Not hair lotion. Something else.

Of course. It was opium. Somewhere in his quarters, convenient for use, the captain kept an opium pipe.

Nicholas took a deep breath. That would make things much, much easier. A good passage fee for two illegal passengers who must hide from the border patrols until Manchuria would buy Captain Li a great deal of opium.

"Show me the owners' cabins," he said with a smile. "I'm curious. That is, if you're not too busy."

When he returned to the Belvedere Hotel and unlocked the door of the room, he found Daria sitting nervously on the edge of her cot. "Where were you?" she exclaimed, jumping to her feet. "I've been worried!"

"Visiting the riverfront."

"But you shouldn't have gone out! How do you feel?"

"Fine. Perfect." He went over to her after locking the door, and kissed her on the forehead. "I've found a steamer bound for Harbin. The captain is sailing in two hours."

"A steamer! Really? Will it be safe? Is it a Russian steamer? Nicholas, how did you—two hours! We haven't even had breakfast!"

The words came tumbling over themselves. He laughed and drew her over to the bed, then sat down and pulled her across his lap. "All right. Calm down. Two hours is quite a long time, really. We don't have much to pack, and we can have something to eat on the way. It's a Chinese steamer called the *Kwan Yin*, with a very pleasant captain who smokes opium."

She nodded, listening.

"It will probably be safe, because the captain claims to be on good terms with the customs and border officials, who probably won't search the cabins. The steamer seldom carries passengers, anyway."

She nodded again.

"If we stay out of sight at the customs station, I think we'll get by."

She hid her face against the side of his neck. He could feel her trembling against him, and he began to caress her gently. She nestled closer.

"We have to hurry," she whispered.

"I know. But stay where you are for just a minute."

She sat quietly, and after a moment he felt a rising tide of the desire that had been suppressed for so long, and would not be denied much longer. With a sigh, he buried his face in her hair. "I would like to make love to you right now," he murmured, speaking almost to himself. "If things were different . . . if we were already lovers . . . I would take you now."

The words alarmed her; he could sense the sudden tension in her body. He'd been indulging in a personal fantasy, but he was going too fast for her. She couldn't picture that kind of physical intimacy, which would be simple and beautiful and uncomplicated as sunlight on a meadow. He tilted her face to his and kissed her softly.

He'd promised her privacy, and lots of time. *Very well, my dark-eyed little gypsy. Don't look so worried. I won't force you.* He wanted a passionate and responsive woman in his bed, he thought, not a resentful child, and if it took patience, then he would just have to be patient. But not very much longer . . .

He set her on her feet and stood up. It was time to clear out of this room and leave Khabarovsk behind them. The *Kwan Yin* was waiting.

Chapter 13

It was spring in the Ussuri region of Siberia; late May. Lev and Yuri had joined their fighting unit. On either side of the railroad tracks, in the wild marsh and forest country north of Nikolsk, the narrow, rutted roads were little more than footpaths. The spring mud had already hardened to dust, baked by the hot sunshine, but both roads looked empty. So did the tracks. To the left of the tracks, beyond the road, stretched an expanse of tall, gray-green marsh grass, tall enough to hide a man if he crouched low enough. Only the low hum of cicadas vibrated across the marsh; everything else seemed still. Beyond it, even further to the left, frogs croaked in the shallows of a lake.

Lev and Yuri lay flat on their bellies in the grass, close to the railroad track. They were careful to keep their heads down.

"Hand me the binoculars," Lev muttered. "I want to take another look."

Yuri silently pulled the leather strap over his head and handed him the binoculars.

Lev raised himself up cautiously. Was anything moving on the other side of the track? Could he spy any activity in the woods? No, nothing. The area could have been deserted, but he knew better. It was crawling with the enemy.

He raised the binoculars to his eyes, supporting himself on his elbows, and peered through the waving grass, sweeping the field glasses from side to side. Straight ahead were

the deserted railroad tracks, running south into the flat-
lands, running north into a fold of hills. Past the tracks,
on the right-hand side of the road, a small cornfield was
empty and abandoned, except for a lonely looking peasant's izba in its center. The ground of the cornfield was
furrowed with shell tracks. Their own shells had made the
tracks, Lev thought. The shells were sent by their own
artillery batteries hidden in the hills to the north, where
they were bivouacked. And the Czech field guns, damn
them, were hidden in those woods.

He squinted through the binoculars at the woods just
past the cornfield. Silent trees leaped into focus: glossy
pines, firs, and cedars; a few graceful birches; some walnuts
and cork oaks. He heard the chirp of the birds, the hum
of cicadas, the whisper of a breeze through the marsh
grass. Nothing else.

The bastards wouldn't move, he thought, sweating
through his shirt. He wiped sweat out of his eyes and
looked again. The enemy was waiting. In the woods, he
knew, was a company of the Fifth Czech Regiment; maybe
a hundred men, mostly infantry, equipped with rifles. And
forty or fifty Ussuri Cossacks. And at least three machine
guns.

And those two field guns.

They had to take out the heavy artillery before they
could advance—before they could clear the track. Until
they did, the supply trains couldn't move, the armored cars
were stopped, they were crippled. They'd be forced back
from the railroad line into the countryside north and south.

The Czech Brigade was fighting well, Lev thought, too
well for his peace of mind. Little by little, the Czechs were
battling their way west along the railway line. They must
be stopped somehow. He wondered how this skirmish
would end.

"Can you see anything?" Yuri whispered.

"Not a damn thing. They've got perfect cover under
those trees. And they must have been digging trenches all
night, because I think they're dug in solid."

Yuri swore softly under his breath. "We'd better get
back," he said. "We're not doing any good here."

Lev nodded, slinging the binoculars around his neck and
adjusting his rifle strap.

They began to wriggle through the grass, to the north, back to the hills.

By nightfall, hidden beneath the hills in their bivouac, they'd built their fires to keep off the mosquitoes. If you didn't do that, you'd be tormented. This was one hell of a country, Lev thought, seated by the fire finishing his dinner. You froze to death in the winter, you were eaten alive by mosquitoes in the summer. You couldn't win. He set down his plate. Dinner hadn't been bad. Somebody'd gone rabbit shooting yesterday in the meadow to the north. Tonight they'd had stewed rabbit and potatoes.

The shelling had started again. Bursts of fire from their own batteries lit up the night, answered by the Czech guns down in the forest. Neither side had found the range; shrapnel was falling well short of their bivouac, but he knew that their own shells were doing little damage in the wood. We're just wasting ammunition, he thought. Because the Czechs could hold that position forever. Or as long as it made no difference. *Because if we don't get a supply train soon . . .*

Someone came from the area of the field telephone hut to his left and squatted beside him. The hut was a makeshift structure of rough branches and grass. "Come on over by the hut. We're having a battle committee meeting."

Lev turned his head to see the hut. "It looks as though they've started already."

"Well, hurry up."

He got to his feet. They had no officers; all decisions were the responsibility of the battle committee. The system was a fulfillment of the promise made by Lenin and Trotsky when they'd taken power from the Provisional government. The evils and abuses of the old Imperial Army would be swept away. There would be no more corrupt officer class—no more autocratic military hierarchy, no more executions and floggings. The power would return to the people, to the common soldiers, where it belonged.

Lev sighed. He was in no hurry to join the meeting. A battle committee was a shining ideal; it was a dream of justice brought to life. A free army—free to discuss and argue and reach a common decision. But he had to admit, in the depths of his mind, that in a tense battlefield situation such as this, it created problems. And if that Georgian hothead Takashvili insisted on haranguing everyone and refused to compromise . . .

Damn. He told himself not to get angry, not to lose his temper, to have patience with Takashvili, they were all comrades.

He lingered by the fire, delaying. Sprawled out along the hillside, laughing, eating, and smoking cigarettes, were the partisan fighters who had joined them from the surrounding countryside. Peasants, carpenters, blacksmiths, fishermen, coal miners, farmers. They were led by a man who called himself Vanya.

"It's good enough," he'd growled in a voice that was deep and rough with his years. He couldn't have been more than sixty, but he looked older. He'd lived hard. "I've been known by many names, and I've answered to them all, but here I'm only Vanya. Little Ivan. A son of Mother Russia. This is all I have to give." He'd held out his hands, big calloused hands scarred by old cuts and wounds, seamed in the cracks by black coal dust. Vanya had been a miner in the Suchan coalfields. He'd been waiting for years—working and waiting, organizing and hoping—for the day when the revolution would succeed. There were thousands like him, Lev thought, watching the red twinkle of cigarettes on the hillside, and listening to the sound of deep laughter. They were the true sons and daughters of the proletariat, the rightful inheritors of the new Russia. He himself, son of a prosperous Jewish doctor in Kiev, raised in a big white house with white pillars beneath linden trees, could only look at a man like Vanya and envy and admire him with all his heart, wishing he himself owned that seamed and grizzled face, that big scarred body, that iron-gray beard, those tired eyes, those massive stooped shoulders, and that patient, rock-hard courage.

But he never could. He hadn't lived Vanya's life. He could only keep doing what he was doing, and try to keep remembering why he did it.

Boom. An artillery shell burst in the trees below. It would fall short. Lev turned to the hut.

When he reached the meeting, held in a circle around a fire near the hut, he sat down quietly beside Yuri, cross-legged on the ground. The fiery Georgian, Anton Takashvili, was on his feet, running a hand through his curly dark hair and arguing hoarsely in a deep, emotional voice. His normally high color was flushed even deeper across his cheekbones. The men teased Anton, saying his red-and-white complexion was as pretty as a girl's. But there was nothing girlish about his quick hot temper, or his big fists, or his stocky shoulders, or his deep muscular chest. He was small in stature, but he made up for it in a dozen other ways.

"What are we going to do?" he demanded. "Sit here another three days, trying to find the artillery range? Like blind moles?"

"We're trying to decide that, Anton," someone said patiently. "If you'll just keep your mouth shut for a minute—"

"Why should I keep my mouth shut? I don't hear anything! Just a lot of stupid talk that gets nowhere!"

"Each of us has a right to be heard—"

"Only if you have something to say! I'm the only one with a plan! So let me talk!"

"What kind of plan do you have?" someone else asked in a weary voice. "You haven't told us a damn thing."

"You haven't let me finish!"

"That's enough, Anton," Yuri put in. "You have to listen once in a while, like the rest of us. We know what you're going to tell us, and it's—"

"Who have you been listening to?" Takashvili demanded, turning on him with a hard stare. "The Jew over there that you stick to like cement? Your friend Lev Aronovitch?"

"What the hell kind of remark was that?" someone asked angrily. Lev felt himself get hot from the neck up. Easy, he told himself, easy. You've heard that before. It's nothing new.

But he hadn't expected it here. Somehow, he hadn't. He stopped listening to the argument that was rising up heated and emotional around him, and concentrated on ignoring Takashvili's remark. He looked down at the ground and pulled up a blade of grass. What had he expected? That centuries of anti-Semitism would be wiped out overnight? That they would all love one another like brothers and comrades and forget the past?

Yes. Goddamnit, yes. He had.

He felt Yuri's hand on his arm, restraining him, and he settled back, fighting down the surge of anger.

Takashvili was calling for action. "We'll rush them, that's all. Take our chances. There isn't any choice."

"We're outnumbered, Anton. They're professional soldiers. We've got a bunch of coal miners and peasants. The only way is to knock out the heavy artillery—those two field guns."

"How?"

"We owe it one more try," Lev said quietly. "One more reconnaissance. Maybe a patrol, just before dawn, if we can spot the location of the guns—"

"What's the matter, Omansky, are you scared to attack?" Takashvili stood, breathing heavily, his arms folded.

"No more than anybody else," Lev replied, controlling his anger. "I just think that before we risk an all-out attack, we should try once more—"

"Aahh!" Takashvili turned aside with an angry gesture. "Just the sort of advice I expect from your kind. I don't want to hear it."

"What kind is that, Anton?"

The Georgian turned again slowly to face him. "The son of a stinking Jew."

Lev took a deep breath. It was tension, that was all. Everyone was on edge, and tempers were quick, and they were saying things they didn't mean . . .

But this time Lev couldn't talk himself out of it. He sprang to his feet, tense with fury, and leaped for Takashvili's throat. He took the Georgian by surprise and knocked him off balance. Before Takashvili could recover, he caught him with a hard right fist in the stomach, just above the belt. Takashvili doubled over, grunting. "You bastard—"

He made a quick recovery and, still in a crouch, came back at Lev with both fists cocked, landing his left hand hard on Lev's cheekbone.

Lev hurled himself forward, bearing Takashvili down with the weight of his body. Within seconds they were tumbling over and over on the ground, panting harshly, landing blows wherever they could.

Lev was dimly aware of angry shouts and hands trying to pull him to his feet, away from his opponent. He struggled furiously, trying to shake them off. Takashvili, equally furious, was being dragged away along the ground.

"What the hell is going on here?" someone demanded. "Who are we fighting? Each other?"

"Lev, calm down." Yuri was muttering in his ear. "Leave him alone, for God's sake, he's a madman, he doesn't know what he's saying."

"He knows." Lev was on his feet, breathing in long deep gasps. The bruise on his face was sending aching rhythmic pulses of pain along his cheek. He squinted past the fire with his fists still clenched, trying to see Takashvili.

"The enemy's down there in the woods, remember? Not up here."

"Well, I see that young men still have hot tempers!" A deep rumble of laughter boomed into the darkness. Footsteps crunched on twigs, and the heavy-shouldered figure of Vanya, the coal miner, appeared in the firelight. He stood with his hands in the pockets of his shabby trousers. Faces turned to him. Whenever Vanya appeared on the scene, he commanded attention, shambling and ragged as he was. Lev forgot his aching cheek and his anger at Takashvili as he wondered where that effortless authority came from. From inside, he knew.

"What's the fight about?" Vanya rumbled. "What did you decide? What can I tell my partisans?"

Uneasy silence fell. Finally someone said, "We haven't reached a decision yet, Vanya. We'll let you know as soon as we do."

"Don't take too long. You may kill each other first." He laughed again. "Listen, I know what your problem is. You're worried about the Czech field guns, am I right?"

There was another uneasy silence. Then one of the young men shrugged his shoulders. "We haven't been able to find the range. Not yet, anyway."

"And you won't." Vanya shook his shaggy head. "Not unless you know exactly where the guns are hidden."

"How the hell can we know that?" The question was explosive and angry. Anton Takashvili had joined the group. He avoided Lev's glance, but Lev saw with a twinge of satisfaction that a dark bruise was puffing up underneath his eye. "They've got plenty of underbrush and tree cover down there. We'll never spot them from the hills!"

"True, true." Vanya put his hands into his pockets and nodded slowly. "I think I'll have to go and find them for you myself."

One by one they sat down again by the fire. Vanya squatted down easily on his haunches, sifting dirt through his hands as he spoke. This time no one interrupted. His plan was simple: he would walk down the road, in the role of an itinerant tramp, and wander past the wood. He'd be stopped by the Czechs and questioned in the forest, and his own two eyes, searching the trees, would seek out the location of the guns. Then he'd return, crawling through the marsh grass, and describe exactly where they were. The range would be found. The guns would be destroyed.

Simple. Too simple?

"Will they believe your story, Vanya?"

"Why not? The countryside from here to Irkutsk is full of tramps. Beggars. Homeless ones. Every road, every village is swarming with people who have nowhere to go but the top of the next hill, nowhere to sleep but the bare ground, nothing to eat but what they can beg or steal." Vanya laughed richly. "Do I look to you like a man of wealth? Wouldn't you believe I'm a tramp?"

They would. They all had to admit it to themselves.

"They'll ask to see your papers," Yuri muttered.

Vanya patted the breast pocket of his jacket and winked. "That's my winning card, comrade. I have a Czech-French passport. Don't ask me how I got it. Ask my clever friend in Vladivostok. That is, if you can find him!" He lowered his massive body to the ground and stretched out his legs with a grunt. "I'll tell you something. I know the Czech commanding officer down there; his name is Captain Stefan. I used to see him in Vladi. Not that he ever saw me! He's one of those honorable types—an officer and a gentleman, rules of warfare, all that kind of thing. He'll let me go when he sees the passport. He won't like it, but his conscience won't let him do anything else. Not to an unarmed civilian."

Vanya stopped speaking and peered at them from under his bushy gray eyebrows. Everyone was thinking.

Lev spoke finally. "Suppose," he said, "you're questioned by the Ussuri Cossacks instead of Captain Stefan."

"Ah, well, in that case!" Vanya bared his teeth in a grin. "You'll have to think of another plan yourselves! I won't be able to help you!"

"It's a pretty sneaky trick," Takashvili muttered after a moment.

"So it is! So it is!" Vanya glanced up. "So tell me, my fine Georgian friend. Are you also an officer and a gentleman?"

Takashvili gave him a wry, unwilling smile, made slightly wolfish by his half-closed eye.

More thoughtful silence. They'd be risking Vanya's life. But if he succeeded in spotting the guns, they'd win the skirmish. The supply train could move, and the track would be clear. It would be worth it.

All right. Tomorrow, midmorning, when the sun was high and the light was clear. Vanya would tramp down the dusty road to the forest. They'd try it.

"Listen, Vanya," Lev said, edging close to him as the meeting broke up. "Let me come with you. Two pairs of eyes are better than one."

"And yours are younger than mine, is that it?" Vanya clapped him on the shoulder.

"Why not? I'm a pretty good actor." He remembered the time in Saravenko, in Daria's izba, when he'd impersonated the simpleminded villager. He was secretly a little proud of himself for that. He thought he'd done a pretty good job that night. And tomorrow he would have a black-and-blue cheekbone, that would add a disreputable touch.

"Too dangerous, comrade," Vanya said regretfully. "One tired old man coming down from the hills may not worry them too much. But with a young and healthy companion, they'll be suspicious. They'll suspect me anyhow, but I may pull it off. If I go alone."

Unwillingly Lev nodded. Vanya was right. Hell, it was going to be a tense day tomorrow, watching Vanya leave, and then waiting for him to come back . . . wondering if he would.

That night he couldn't sleep. He lay awake in his blanket on the ground listening to the whine of mosquitoes in the darkness and stared up at the sky. The night was cloudy.

You couldn't see anything; there was no moon, there were no stars. What if it rained tomorrow?

The old man would go anyway. He had eyes like a hawk. He could see in the dark, after all those years in the coal mines. Lev felt a surge of affection for the old man—and a twinge of fear.

He turned over on his side and tried to sleep.

By the middle of the next afternoon, they were in the middle of another artillery duel with the Czech guns. Back and forth, burst, boom, puff of smoke, hail of shrapnel raining down from the hills, then the savage answer from the trees. Pop-pop-pop came the deep stacatto chatter of the machine guns, punctuating the boom of the heavy artillery.

Lev, lying belly down with his rifle on the hill, watched in fascination as a dreamlike scene unfolded below him. A shell ripped across the little cornfield and exploded beneath the peasant's izba. The cottage blossomed like a flower. Slowly and gracefully it grew into petals of smoke, splinters and thatch. Then it collapsed like a ballerina's skirt. Now only a heavy purple pall hung over the ground where it had been.

Had there ever been a cottage there at all? Or only that pathetic heap of rubble?

He wiped his sweating hand along the side of his trousers. Where the hell was Vanya? They'd seen him go down the road hours ago, ambling along by the railroad tracks, kicking up dust, whistling to himself, as if he had nothing on his mind except his next meal. He'd been accosted by men who'd appeared out of the trees, prodded him in the back with the butts of their rifles, and shoved him into the forest, protesting his innocence. They hadn't seen him since.

Someone was below him at the bottom of the hill. Vanya? No. This man was in uniform. Not one of their own. He put the rifle up to his shoulder and sighted along the barrel. Take your time. Don't hurry. Remember it will drift to the right. Squeeeeeze . . . but gently, gently. Whine of the bullet. Recoil. Get ready to fire again. Don't raise your head too fast. Now look, cautiously.

He peered over the hill. The man was lying very still, face down, his hand flung out at his side. You learned to recognize that stillness, even from a distance. You could be fooled, but not very often. There was something very final-looking about a corpse.

He settled back, wondering why he always felt sick. But he would never tell anybody, not even Yuri.

He had to reload, the magazine was empty. He opened the breech and then fumbled for the cartridges across his chest.

A low, excited voice came from behind him. "Vanya's back!"

A surge of happiness and excitement went through him. He forgot the dead soldier and raised his head. "They let him go?"

"Yes, and he saw the guns! He's drawing the positions now, in the dirt!"

Lev had to stay where he was until he was relieved, but it was all right, they didn't need him, the artillery-men would figure out the range now, and maybe, maybe by nightfall . . .

Oh Vanya, damn you, you did it.

An hour later, the gun batteries were ready to start shelling again. This time the men knew where to place their shots. Vanya had returned from the forest with deadly accurate information. Now all they had to do was act on it.

A plan was hastily sketched out. They couldn't encircle the enemy. The forest was too deep on the right flank, and they didn't have time to advance through the trees. They had too few men to cover the enemy's rear, to the south, and so the Czechs had two escape routes. They'd have to be content with a retreat.

It would be enough.

"Yuri and I will scout on the left flank," Lev said tensely. "We were there yesterday, in the marsh grass, and we know the terrain. I'll carry a field telephone and let you know when to send reinforcements."

Heads nodded.

"I'll come with you," someone said. Lev looked around in surprise at Anton Takashvili. "I need some action," he growled, hefting his rifle. "I'm sick of popping shots from

160

this hilltop. Why should you be the only ones to get close?"

Lev grinned. "Think you can see to fire?"

"Listen, comrade, I still have one good eye!"

It was the closest the Georgian would come to an apology. The tensions of the night before had dissolved in the hope of success. Lev agreed quickly, glad the quarrel was set aside. The three of them set out down the hill.

When they were hidden again in the marsh grass, Lev let out his breath in a sigh of relief. It was always a bad time, wriggling through that grass. Your back prickled, right between the shoulder blades, all the time. You were blind, with your head down, and you couldn't hear anything because of your own breathing, the sound of your own body rustling along the ground, the pounding of the blood in your own temples, and you expected any minute to be knocked flat by the steel fist of a bullet.

He told himself he had too much imagination for his own good. He licked his lips and tasted salty sweat. Yuri was aiming carefully across the tracks, into the shadowy trees. So was Anton. He flopped over on his stomach and raised the rifle. But they couldn't fire. Not yet. It was too soon to give themselves away.

The shelling was about to start. He heard the first boom, and the answer.

Seconds passed. Minutes passed. A quarter hour. How long? He listened tensely, trying to hear, to distinguish sounds. *Damn.* He set the rifle down and unhooked the telephone from his belt, wound it up, praying it would work this time. *Come on, come on.* He heard a crackle of static in his ear, then a voice. He put it to his mouth and whispered, "Stop the shelling. I think we have them."

Within moments the artillery fell silent. Only the whang of rifles now, and the deep bass pop-pop-pop of the machine guns, and the tuneless hum of cicadas in the marsh, like a counterpoint.

No shelling. *No shelling. None.*

"Yuri . . . Anton . . . I think we got the guns . . ."

"Keep listening, Lev," Yuri whispered. "Let's make sure."

He listened harder. But he still didn't hear anything. He tried to picture what was happening in the forest.

Were the Czechs cursing furiously, in helpless rage at the wily old tramp who had given them away? Yes, probably. Weeping in frustration at the wreck of their field guns. Planning their retreat.

Retreat. What a beautiful word. When it meant the enemy.

"We're spotted," Anton said suddenly.

"Where?"

"Over there, at eleven o'clock. Under the birch tree. See him? See his cap?"

Yes, they could see the Czech rifleman now. He was kneeling beneath a tree, sighting along the barrel of his rifle.

"He's too far away, Anton. We're out of range."

"Not for long."

Takashvili stood up in a half crouch and began to run forward toward the tracks.

"Anton, are you crazy?" Yuri whispered hoarsely.

The Georgian only laughed.

"Come back," Lev called desperately.

It was too late. Takashvili was already scrambling up the embankment and across the road. When he reached the tracks, he stood up, legs wide apart, back straight, and raised the rifle to his shoulder. He was two hundred yards from the birch tree.

Crack. The rifle spoke. The Czech soldier toppled to one side like a rag doll.

Takashvili turned with a triumphant smile to Lev and Yuri. It only lasted for a split second, as rifle fire burst from all sides, from everywhere in the forest, right, left, center, twenty, thirty, forty rifles all firing at once, whang, whang, whang, taking vengeance for treachery, speaking in rage. Blood spurted from holes in Takashvili's jacket. He fell heavily across the tracks, sprawled on his back with his arms outstretched, fingertips just touching the stock of his fallen rifle.

"Oh Christ," Lev muttered hoarsely.

"Madman," Yuri whispered. "Madman. What did he do that for? He should have known! Why did he do that?"

"I don't know." Lev wiped his knuckles across his mouth and swallowed hard. "We'll have to go get him Yuri."

"Now? Don't be crazy. We can't get him now."

"We can't let him lie there. Besides, there's his rifle, and his cartridge belt—"

"Later, Lev. When the battle's over. After the retreat." Yuri put his hand on Lev's sleeve.

Later. Lev stared at the sprawled, motionless figure on the railroad tracks. That had been Anton Takashvili. He had fought with the Georgian last night, and now Anton was dead. It would go on like that, he knew; perhaps he would be next. He looked to the west, dragging his eyes away from Anton's body. *Think about something else. About Harbin. About Daria waiting there.* He held onto the thought. Daria must be there. It had been so long since that night at Chita Station. It seemed a lifetime ago to Lev. But he remembered just how she had looked, could see how it would be when he met her again.

He'd made up a fantasy about their meeting in Harbin, and whenever he had time he embellished it with details. He wondered if he had changed, if he was a different person, if his fantasy would come true, and he decided no, he was no different, he would always feel the same way.

It never occurred to him that Daria might have changed.

Chapter 14

The sun was setting across the river, turning the water to a sheet of hammered gold. It lay golden-orange and perfectly round on the western horizon, slipping with tantalizing slowness into the depths of the water, far off between the Manchurian hills, where it would drown in a final blaze of fiery crimson. But not yet. The breeze was rising, ruffling the surface of the water, making little patterns of crescents in the center channel between the sandbars. Daria could smell the strong, wet, muddy odor of it coming to her on the breeze, mixed with machine oil, freshly cut pine logs, and the rich fragrance of Nicholas's cigar. He'd bought the cigars yesterday at one of the river stations and now, after their early dinner, he was savoring one slowly. They sat on crates on the afterdeck, in comfortable silence, surrounded by stacks of fuel logs and coiled ropes.

Daria wondered if she needed her shawl. She'd brought it with her, folded on the deck.

No, not yet. The sun was still above the horizon. The days were beautiful and warm, although at night a chill crept over the river and a fog often rose, and you needed to sleep with a blanket.

"Do you want your shawl?" Nicholas asked.

"I don't think so."

She glanced out at the water, not wanting to stare at him. He looked dazzling. He was leaning back against a stack of crates, with one foot on a pile of ropes, drawing on the cigar, wearing a thin white cotton shirt open across his chest. He was bronzed by the sun; they'd been sitting on deck every day since boarding a week ago. He had gained back all the weight he'd lost in Khabarovsk, and now she was bewildered and dazed by intensely blue eyes and even white teeth against tanned skin, a strong, brown, shapely throat rising from the open shirt, muscular bare arms, and a broad chest covered with crisp dark hairs.

It was all very different from the teplushka, where you huddled in your clothes against the cold. *I didn't know. I didn't think . . .*

"Look," she said, just to say something, "the men are back from camp." She pointed to shore.

The *Kwan Yin* was moored on the Manchurian side of the Amur. A high hill rose from the riverbank, with a temple to the goddess of mercy halfway up its face, its curved pagoda glinting scarlet against the grass. At the foot of the hill was a gold-mining camp worked by Chinese miners. Two red poles topped with gilt balls marked the *yamen* of the mine superintendent—his official residence, larger than the other log shacks.

Now the men were streaming back to the camp from their day at the mines. The faint chatter of voices drifted across the water.

"I hope their dinner is as good as ours was," Nicholas said lazily.

The cook on the *Kwan Yin* prepared meals in a small iron box. The box was like a miniature kitchen, no more than a foot and a half square. The cook did wonders with it, producing meal after meal of noodles, vegetables, rice, pieces of pork or fish or chicken, sauce, all delicately spiced and served steaming hot in lacquered bowls. After eating, the crew always rinsed their chopsticks carefully in the river and stowed them away on deck. Now they were seated on the foredeck with their legs drawn up and their knees touching their chins, conversing among themselves with soft bursts of laughter. It was their time to rest. The captain had retired to his quarters and his opium pipe, as he did every evening after dinner.

Daria laughed. "If you don't stop eating so much," she said, "you'll be as fat as Captain Li."

"Fine." Nicholas exhaled a cloud of smoke. "It will be a sign to the world of my wealth and prosperity, evidence that I can afford to eat well and often." He smiled lazily. "Will you still love me when I have two bellies like a Buddha?"

"Yes," she said seriously, not matching his teasing tone. "But you won't get fat. Not you."

"It could happen to anyone."

"But you're not like anyone." Her face was still very sober.

Nicholas sat forward. "Daria, my sweet girl," he said, "I think you see me through a pink haze." A tender, amused expression came into his eyes. "I'm not looking forward to the time when the haze lifts and you see me as I really am, with all my shabby little faults."

She turned her face aside stubbornly. She hated to hear him criticize himself. A tow barge was moving past on the water, heading for the Russian shore. The wake behind it was straight as an arrow. Not a Chinese vessel, she thought irrelevantly, since they weren't worried about *fêng shui*. Water demons always followed a straight line, the captain had told them; the *Kwan Yin* followed a slightly zigzag course to confuse the demons.

"How peaceful it is when we're anchored," she said.

"Yes. No live sparks showering the deck, no rumbling wheel, no clanking rudder. It's very serene."

They were making extremely slow progress. Sometimes they were grounded on sandbars and the crew had to push them off with iron-tipped spars and a makeshift arrangement of chains and pulleys wrapped around the capstan. Sometimes they were caught in a swift-moving current and took an hour or two to move a short distance. The *Kwan Yin* couldn't afford to overwork her steam engine, risking an overheated boiler and an explosion. Nicholas often spent time in the engine room, helping the fireman to check the water and steam gauges.

Every afternoon they stopped at a wood station to load fuel. The split logs of pine and birch would be piled on the shore and the crew, bare-chested, smooth, slender torsos glistening with sweat, would make countless trips back and forth across the plank, carrying stacks of logs to be clattered thumpingly on the deck.

She remembered the day they had cast off from Khabarovsk. Captain Li had been shouting orders as the crew fastened canvas covers over the hatches and secured them down with weights. The anchor winch had been creaking as the dripping anchor was raised up from the water. The youngest crew member, little more than a boy, had been poised by the deck rail with his long pole for sounding the river depths. The pole was painted in foot lengths of black, white, and red. The boy constantly plunged it into the water, harpoon fashion, to test the depths as they steamed. And then had come the final, breathless moment of backing out into the channel and starting upriver.

Had it only been a week ago?

"You're very pensive," Nicholas said.

"I was remembering the day we left Khabarovsk. It seems so long ago."

"Not so long really. But the river doesn't change. There are just these low banks, and the forest on either side, and the little villages, and the bends and twists of the river. And then another vista, the same as before. And the hills, always looming ahead, never seeming to come any closer . . . one loses track of time."

"But it's done you so much good," she said suddenly. "You've had time to rest and gain weight. You're all recovered."

"Yes, quite recovered." He glanced at her with an odd expression. Then he tossed his cigar stub over the side into the water. She heard a tiny plop as it disappeared. She felt herself grow hot all over. She was suddenly recalling what he had said in the Belvedere Hotel, the day they'd left. *If things were different, I would take you now.*

It was what she'd wanted, in the boxcar, the night she'd waited for him to come back from the depot. She'd wanted it so much. But perhaps she'd known all along it wasn't possible, not on the train. Everything *was* different now. They were almost alone. The crew spoke only Chinese, except for Captain Li; Nicholas only communicated with the fireman by signs. She had a frightened feeling there was no more avoiding what she longed for yet shrank from. There was no running away; not here, on the *Kwan*

Yin. After all her brave words on the train, it was time to face that, and she was frightened.

I can refuse. Nicholas will never force me.

But perhaps he wasn't thinking that at all. Maybe he'd forgotten all about what he'd said in the hotel. Maybe she was just imagining the look in his eyes. Maybe things would stay the way they were . . .

"I sometimes wish nothing would ever change," she said with a little catch in her voice. "Like the river. I wish everything would just go on and on, and never end."

"It's never possible, Daria. We're changing every minute, every second."

"Perhaps I don't want to change."

"You won't be able to help yourself. None of us can." He paused. His voice gentled. "Daria," he said, "will you let me help you?"

"I don't understand—"

But she did. A tiny shock of fear and anticipation had run through her. She glanced at him and saw that his eyes were very steady, and very blue, and she knew what he was asking.

"Come here for a moment," he said.

"I'm comfortable where I am."

"Very well." He paused, and then said quietly. "If that's your choice."

She had just made a decision. She knew that. It was more than the decision to stay where she was, without crossing the tiny distance to his side. It was the decision to . . . to . . . She suddenly wanted to cry. *Now I'll never know . . . what it might have been like . . . what I have lost.* Yes, after all, she was the same Daria Petrovna who had flung herself into his arms in the boxcar in the depths of a Siberian winter. She was rising to her feet and moving to stand beside him.

He reached up and drew her down across his knees. "Now tell me why you look so troubled."

How comforting it was to feel his arms around her. She suddenly sighed and buried her face in the side of his neck, inhaling the delicious sweet and spicy fragrance of his skin. She whispered something very low.

"I can't hear you, with your face hidden like that."

168

She raised her head to look in his eyes. "How wonderful you smell."

He bent to kiss her mouth. "Daria, darling," he said against her lips, "we are going to have to do something about us. Very soon. Tonight."

Her heart lurched. She forgot pride and false modesty, and put her arms around his neck. "Oh, Nicholas, I'm so frightened."

"Why are you frightened? Do you believe I'll be cruel or unkind to you?"

"No . . ." She hesitated, and then said in a rush, "But I'm afraid that you'll be disappointed in me. That I'll be a terrible lover. That I'll just lie there like a stick of wood without knowing what to do, and that I'll be all frozen and rigid and awful, and you'll be so disgusted with me that you'll never want to speak to me again."

"Daria, don't think that way." His arms tightened around her. "My sweet girl, don't you know you mustn't worry about anything like that? If you're any of those things you said, it will be my fault. Not yours. Because I was clumsy, or thoughtless, or impatient. You must never blame yourself. Put it out of your mind."

She gave an unwilling nod.

Nicholas laughed ruefully. "I can see that you don't believe a word I've said. I'll have to convince you another way." He patted her hip. "Stand up."

Her eyes widened. "Now?"

"Yes, why not?"

"But it's so early! It's barely sunset! Look, there's still a sliver of sun over there, on the horizon—"

"Right now." He set her firmly on her feet, standing himself, and took her hand. "Unless you're planning an evening at the opera, or a dinner party. But we've had dinner, haven't we?" He considered her thoughtfully. "You can't complain of a headache, because I won't believe you. And you can't use the other classic feminine excuse, because you gave yourself away in Khabarovsk, before you left." He raised an eyebrow. "So I'm very much afraid that you're trapped."

In spite of her nervous anxiety, she couldn't help laughing. Feeling happier and more at ease, she went with him into the little passageway that ran the length of the covered deckhouse, midships. The captain's quarters were at the rear, but his door was closed. Captain Li would be lost in his dreams and his pipe, and would not hear anything, or appear again on deck, until early morning. Nicholas's cabin was the first on the right.

Nicholas was unlocking the door with a big iron key. He always kept the door locked, even when they were sitting on deck. She knew he kept a revolver in the low cupboard that formed the headboard of the bed, and thought perhaps he didn't want it stolen.

They stepped over the threshold. She heard a metallic click as he locked the door again. There was no going back, she thought, wondering at her own calm.

The cabin was softly illuminated in the twilight shadows. The sun was almost gone, and out on the river the water glimmered in the faint light of dusk. She could hear the soft slap-slap of the current against the sides of the boat and feel the slight sway of the deck beneath her feet, as the *Kwan Yin* rocked at anchor. The length of flowered cotton that served as a curtain was drawn back, revealing the night, and on the far shore, the Russian side, a line of black fir trees made a spiky pattern against the deep blue sky. It was like an illustration in a child's picture book, *Little Child of the River*. But that river had been the Volga, not the Amur, with towpaths along the narrow stretches, and boatmen hauling great lengths of twisted rope along the paths, dragging the boat with straining muscles, and chanting their song . . .

Nicholas had taken a box of matches from his pocket and was about to light the wick of the kerosene lamp that swung from an iron chain in the center of the ceiling.

"No, don't!" she exclaimed, not realizing she had been about to speak.

"I'll turn the wick down very low."

"But the light is so pretty as it is. The shadows are so soft."

"Very well." He put the matches away. "If you prefer twilight." He came over to her and put his arms around her. "I can see why you do," he said against her hair. "It makes you look very lovely and mysterious. If your eyes tilted just a little more, you could be *Kwan Yin* herself."

He tipped up her chin. "Daria, will you be merciful to me?"

"I?" She didn't understand.

"Yes. You have no idea of your own power, but you will be much stronger than I, some day. You will be able to hurt me in ways I can never achieve. I can only use force and bluster, and pretend to be strong. But the subtle, inner ways of hurting that are so much more painful and lasting and sink so much deeper into the soul . . . those will belong to you."

Her heart was beating very fast. She didn't believe him. She rested her face against his shoulder. "I could never hurt you."

"I hope not."

After a moment she became aware that he was unbuttoning her blouse. She felt a wild, fleeting sense of panic and wondered if she would please him, if he would be disappointed, if he would compare her to other, more beautiful women he had known. She felt intensely relieved that the kerosene lamp was still dark, hanging silently from its iron chain. But in the next second all her feelings were drowned in an urgent, pulsing excitement that rose between her legs, as the blouse slipped to the floor and he drew down the straps of her chemise, baring her breasts.

She thought she would die if he said anything.

But he said nothing, only kissed her mouth very gently, keeping his hands at her waist. She heard a soft, slithering noise, and realized her skirt had fallen to the floor.

She wondered why it was so different from the way it had been in the Belvedere Hotel. They had been undressed then too, she in her chemise, and Nicholas almost naked. But it was not the same at all. She was breathing very fast. The chemise was a puddle of cotton lace at her feet, and his hands were very warm on her bare skin. . . .

He had folded her close, and was telling her to get into bed now, under the covers. She obeyed quickly, grateful to hide her trembling nakedness beneath the sheet. The bed was under the curtain, and she could see the sky from where she lay. Night had fallen. She saw a bright silver moon, but no stars, in a deep black velvet depth of sky.

Nicholas had stripped off his shirt. She heard the chink of metal as he removed his belt and laid it on the cupboard beside a stack of cotton towels, a water basin, and the lacquered dish he used as an ashtray.

He sat down on the edge of the bed to take off his boots. She turned over on her side and studied his back. No blemishes. Nothing, not even a birthmark. Only smooth, tanned skin, rippling with muscles running in satiny perfection over the length of his spinal cord. Unable to resist, she reached out her hand to touch him.

He swiftly drew off his trousers and underwear, then, naked, turned to get under the covers.

Why was it, she thought, as he slid in beside her, how was it possible, that people looked so much bigger with their clothes off than they did when they were dressed? You'd think it would be the other way around.

But she had little time to wonder about that. She felt herself engulfed in a new flood of sensations, as the warm hard length of Nicholas's body suddenly moved close against her, and her breasts were crushed against his chest, and his mouth sought hers, and everything in her yielded in a great rush of surrender.

There was no thought now of self-consciousness or anxiety. She was filled with a fierce, deep happiness. This was exactly where she wanted to be. Always. Forever. *Just hold me and do what you're doing. Yes, and kiss me there . . . where your mouth is.* She arched her back and strained against him, lifting her breast as he took the nipple between his teeth.

But alarm ran through her when he took her wrist and guided her hand between his legs. She snatched it away as though she had been scalded.

"Daria . . . sweetheart . . . don't you care for me?"

"Yes . . . of course . . . you know I do."

"Then don't pull your hand away like that."

Hesitantly she let him put it back where it had been. Her fingers curled around warm, hard flesh, throbbing delicately beneath her touch like the heart of a bird. It was hers, to do with as she wished. Her alarm ebbed away. There was nothing to be afraid of. It was Nicholas, as much as the tender curve of his mouth or the sound of his voice, and her touch became less timid and more loving, and she heard him sigh and thought with swift joy that she was pleasing him.

The deep, steady pulse between her legs had grown more intense. She felt no shame or hesitation about parting her thighs when he slipped his hand between them, only the ache of wanting. No one had ever touched her there. But she felt herself opening like a flower under the gentle exploration of his fingers.

"Damn," he said very low. He raised himself up on one elbow and looked down at her. She saw his face in the moonlight, grave and intent, with shadows in the sculptured line of his cheekbones. "You are lovely and desirable and you're ready for me—more than ready—and I wish I didn't have to hurt you."

She felt a tiny thrill of fear. "Then don't."

"But I'll have to—just a little—I hope not very much—and you'll have to be brave, and try not to mind." He was settling her back against the pillow as he spoke, with his hands on her shoulders. "You won't like like it very much," he murmured, kissing her mouth, "not the first time. But the second time, I promise you, I'll try to make you happy."

In spite of herself, she was tensing. He stroked her gently along the line of her waist and hip, and she relaxed again and felt the slow tide of response well up once more from that dark mysterious place in the center of herself that wanted . . . wanted . . .

Oh!

Shocking pain ripped through her. She gasped. She was being torn apart.

Nicholas was moving, doing something, she had no idea what. He was just a dark moving shape above her in the moonlight, and the water was still slap-slapping against the side of the boat, and she hurt . . . She could hear his long, deep breathing and wondered what was happening to her. Why was this a marvelous experience? It was marvelous and thrilling to lie naked in his arms, to be caressed and kissed in secret, intimate ways, and lie close together in the warmth of the bed . . . but *this!* How long would it go on? She tried to blink back the tears.

A long, shuddering spasm ran through Nicholas's body, and then he lay still, his face buried in her throat.

After a moment she wondered what he was thinking. "Did you like that?" she asked wonderingly.

"Yes. Very much."

"But why?" She couldn't help herself; the question asked itself.

He raised his head. He had a strange, unreadable expression on his face, half tenderness and half regret. "How can I explain it to you?" he said, kissing her cheek, and stroking back her hair. "If I say there is a buried streak of cruelty in all of us that glories in having its own way with a beautiful, helpless creature entirely at its mercy, will you understand?" He brushed away a lingering tear on her cheek. "But you see, if it weren't for that streak of cruelty, that particular kind of excitement, then what has just happened would never have taken place, and you and I would never be able to take the next step on the road we still have to travel."

She was content to lie here safe and close, now that the pain and violation were over. There would be no next step, she resolved. Only this closeness and intimacy, and being held and kissed gently, and the low tender sound of his voice. That was all she wanted. She was aware of a strange fluttering between her legs, where he was still imprisoned, like the beating of a bird's wings against the sides of its cage, and an odd stir went through her, taking her by surprise.

He lifted his hips, beginning to withdraw. Then he reached past her to the headboard, helping himself to one of the towels. She came to the horrified little realization that she was lying on a wet patch of blood. She could feel the stickiness of it beneath her on the sheet, and on the inside of her thighs as well. But what was even worse—her cheeks flamed—was the fact that Nicholas was cleaning her off very gently and thoroughly with a moistened towel.

"I could have done that myself," she whispered, shamefaced.

"Lie still, I'm almost finished." He slid another towel beneath her, to cover the bloodstain, and threw the first one on the floor. Then he settled back and drew her against him. "Now I think it's time for you to go to sleep."

"No, not yet." But she was beginning to feel drowsy. The shock and strangeness of her experience were catching up with her, her eyes were starting to close, and she felt very warm and protected in the circle of his arms, with her head buried in the curve of his shoulder.

He kissed the top of her head. She was starting to fall asleep. Her eyelashes fluttered down across her cheeks like little black fans, and her breathing slowed and steadied, and after a moment Nicholas disengaged himself from her arms and arranged her against the pillow, where she sighed without waking, and reached up behind him for a cigarette.

When he struck the match, he could still see tearstains on her face in the tiny flare of light. She looked like a punished child, disciplined for something she couldn't comprehend and worn out with the effort to understand. He resolved to do everything in his power to make her happy, now that the necessary unpleasantness was over. It had been nothing like what she expected—no roses in the moonlight or romantic violins.

He turned over on his back and drew on the cigarette, staring out at the black sky and listening to the creak of the boat against the current. It had been a long deprivation for him. But that was over now. From now on she would sleep here, beside him. She would be a wonderful mistress. Lord, how narrow she was in that untouched place. Every move was a shock wave of sensation—not that he intended to explain that to her—but he couldn't remember when he had experienced a climax that was deeper or more intense. He was stirring again at the memory. No, not yet. Let her sleep.

He had a brief pang of wondering if he was being selfish, indulging himself. Should he have stayed away? Left her alone?

No, it wasn't possible. This moment had been inevitable, he told himself, since that first encounter at Chita Station. *The goddess of destiny pulls the strings, and all we can do is dance.*

He moved to put out the cigarette in the dish behind him. Seeing the stack of towels made him slightly angry, as he remembered Céline's silver and blue bathroom in Kharkov, with the blue porcelain bidet. Then he told himself to be grateful for a clean bathroom on this boat. *Think of the Belvedere Hotel.*

The bathroom here was in the passageway between the cabins. It was a plain, functional room with a toilet and shower, but no bathtub. But it was always scrubbed clean, and he couldn't really complain.

God, but he hated being poor. Living in poor surroundings. Not having the right conveniences. Wearing clothes that never quite fit. He found it almost intolerable. But he intended to get it all back, in Manchuria.

If he lived to reach Harbin, he'd make his way back. He'd vowed that once before, on a stone bridge crossing the Neva. But he had been nineteen then, and it had taken him a long time. Now he was thirty-six, and he had the cool judgment of maturity, the steel willpower of a man who'd struggled for many years, and a certain capacity for icy detachment that he'd acquired with the death of his father. Perhaps, he thought, he was a Man of Ice.

He refused to admit to himself that he'd inherited anything from his father. Sergei Nicholaevitch, with all his Slavic emotionalism, his weaknesses for beautiful women and well-tailored clothes, for expensive cigars and vintage wines . . . Nicholas shared those tastes, but he would never admit it. He told himself he was nothing like his father; he never would be.

He lay back and thought again about rebuilding his fortune in Harbin.

He still had the jewelry.

On that thought, he let himself fall asleep. He drowsed lightly, for how long—an hour? Not two, surely, for the moon was still high when he came wide awake.

Daria was still sleeping, with her hand curled under her cheek, like a child. He drew down the blanket to the foot of the bed and let it slide to the floor. Moonlight was falling directly into the cabin, and lit her with silver. No, she was not a child. Far from it. The slender, lush curves of breast and hip, the long graceful lines of thigh and calf, were not those of a girl.

She stirred at the cool breeze on her body and moved onto her back, flinging out one arm. She would wake soon. He lightly stroked the silvery nipples with the tips of his fingers, bringing them to life, then cupped the full soft breasts, running his hand down the curve of her belly to the feathery softness below. Her eyes fluttered open.

"Nicholas?"

"Yes, darling?"

"Oh, but . . . oh! What time is it?"

"I don't know." Then, smiling: "Why, do you have plans?"

"No, but . . . what happened to the blanket?"

"I took it off. I wanted to look at you."

He was reclining on his elbow, with one knee bent, still caressing her with one hand. She sat up, still flushed with sleep. "What are you doing?" she whispered.

"Just this. Don't you like it?"

"Yes, I . . . yes—"

In a swift, unexpected move, he pinned her back down against the bed, then slipped one arm under her hips, raising her up with the other until her breasts were flattened against his chest. He covered her mouth with his own and parted her lips, forcing his tongue deep, and she moaned, and tried to move away. But there was nowhere for her to go. She was caught. He used his thigh to spread her legs apart.

"Don't," she managed to say.

"Don't what?"

"Don't do what you did before, Nicholas . . . please . . ."

"Are you afraid I'll hurt you?"

He had poised himself above her, still clasping her firmly beneath the hips, tilting her body upward. He was taut and throbbing, and fully ready and he knew that she was too, although she wasn't aware of it. Her eyes were pleading.

"Promise me something, Daria," he said, ignoring the silent plea in her eyes.

She bit her lip.

"That you will never say no," he went on, keeping her immobile. "Not ever again. That whatever I ask you to do, from now on, you will do willingly and without question . . . because you trust me."

"I—"

"Promise me that."

Unwillingly she nodded.

"Now stop fighting me. I'm going to make love to you."

"Didn't you do that before?" she whispered unhappily.

"No. I only took you. That's not the same thing at all."

Her breasts heaved, and he knew that she wanted with

every fiber of herself to protest, but she had promised, and so she prepared herself to endure her martyrdom. She closed her eyes.

He guided himself within her, using his right hand to moisten her first with the swollen tip of himself. He blessed her silently for being so ready

"Oh!"

Daria's eyes flew open as she caught her breath in a gasp of wonder and astonishment. Her back arched. Her arms went up around his neck, clinging tightly, and her gasp turned into a long strangled moan back in her throat, ahhh . . .

Not yet, my love. Not quite.

He pulled her against him, offering all of himself. *Now. Take me, darling. For you.*

Tiny earthquakes of sensation were exploding in him with every . . . single . . . move. *Good Lord. It would take every ounce of concentration to make this last. But it will be . . . worth it . . . yes, darling, we have a long way to go. And I have wanted you for so long . . . and you're giving me everything of yourself . . . and, my God, you like it so . . . and you're telling me in so many different ways. . . .*

"Nicholas!" she cried. "What's happening to me, I—"

She was shuddering from head to foot. He held her close, watching her face, until she slowly relaxed in his arms, then hid her face against his shoulder, unable to speak.

He brushed back the damp hair from her temples. *But we have only begun. You are back at the foot of the mountain. But we will climb up again . . . because you're mine. My own sweet gypsy girl . . . and you can't go anywhere at all. Not until I say so, not until I release you. Not for a long long while. . . .*

He caught her wrists in one hand and raised her arms above her head, supporting her waist with his other arm. She looked up at him wonderingly. Her eyes were heavy-lidded, glazed with passion. Her lips were parted, and slightly bruised. She was breathing in long, deep pants; a tiny river of perspiration gleamed between her breasts. He lifted her up until her breasts were slippery against him, and buried his face in her throat. *No tricks, my love. Not this time. Nothing clever, no variations . . . I will only love you as long and as well as I can, until I have made you happy . . .*

He kissed her tenderly, lowering himself across her body, and she clasped him between her thighs. It wouldn't be long now, he thought, feeling a pang of regret, not wanting the end to come.

"Do that just once more," he whispered against her cheek.

"Do what?"

He gathered her close, inhaling the fragrance of her hair. *Oh sweetheart, don't you even know? What a long way we still have to travel together, you and I . . .*

Chapter 15

"Sometimes I think we should offer to carry wood," Daria said pensively. She was sitting up in bed, hugging her knees. The swinging lamp in the ceiling, with its wick turned low, cast soft light on her body, turning her skin to rose and ivory. A week had passed since their first lovemaking. But it seemed to her like a lifetime. The *Kwan Yin* was approaching the juncture of the Amur and the Sungari, and Captain Li had told them that if all went well, they would reach it by tomorrow.

Nicholas was lying back across the pillow with one arm under his head. She traced with her eyes the line of dark hair that ran from his chest across his stomach. His face was relaxed, and his eyes were half closed. He looked like a big lazy cat, ready to bask after making his kill. She loved to see that expression on his face. She had memorized all his moods, and sometimes pictured them in her mind before falling asleep. The light of suppressed amusement when she had said something unintentionally funny and he was trying to be tactful. The intent, inward look of concentration when he took possession of her and she was reduced to a moaning, clinging creature who was all body and no mind. The quick flare of anger in his eyes when—once—she'd mentioned Lev Omansky. She wouldn't do that again, she thought. It was strange to think that he was jealous, after she had given herself so completely, but it seemed to be so, and she had resolved to avoid the subject.

"The men were working so hard today," she said. "When we ran out of fuel, before we came to the wood station and they had to go ashore with saws and axes and cut down their own trees and chop them into logs. Do you think we ought to help?"

"No. We would lose face. Not that I object to physical activity; in fact it would be welcome. But doing menial work would mean a loss of status in their eyes. And then anything might happen. We're dependent on their protection, you know. They could turn us in at any time until we've crossed the border."

"I never thought of that."

"Ah well, why should you? It's enough for one of us to worry."

"You shouldn't have to do all the worrying," she said seriously.

"Very well, suppose we take turns. Alternate days. Would you like to do the worrying tomorrow, or the next day?"

"I don't believe," she said, lying back against him with a sigh, "that I can do it at all. I'm too happy."

She turned her head and saw their clothes still scattered across the floor, where they'd flung them in the haste of urgency earlier in the evening. A thrill of remembrance quivered through her as she recalled being sprawled here, upon this bed, with every nerve focused upon the intimate center of herself, where she was caught and held, where sensation, like liquid flame, was melting and flickering up and down, like hot lightning, and the secret crevices of her body were shuddering beneath the assault of Nicholas's mouth and tongue. *Oh stop, please, before I explode, or scream . . .*

He kissed her mouth, afterwards, and told her to taste herself—spiced honey. Heat ran through her at the memory.

"What are you thinking about?" he asked.

"Nothing."

"Liar." He laughed softly. Then his voice grew serious. "Daria?"

She looked at him quickly.

"Starting tomorrow," he said, "for a few days, you must remind me to withdraw before the end."

"Oh, but why?" She sat up straight. "That's not fair—it's almost the best time of all!"

"I know, darling, but it won't be safe. Just for a few days."

She blinked. "You don't want me to have a baby," she said after a moment.

"No."

"But I wouldn't mind that." It was something she secretly hoped for.

"Some day. But not right away. Not until after we've reached Manchuria and I can establish myself and look after you the way I would like to. We have no idea what we'll find there. Refugees and hardship and overcrowding . . . a cold winter on its way. If you're expecting a baby, it will be that much more for us to worry about."

There was no arguing with him when he used that tone of voice. She lowered her eyes.

"Will you remind me?"

"Yes." But she knew she wouldn't have to. He never forgot anything. "I wish you were human, like other people," she muttered rebelliously. "I wish you made mistakes once in a while." She stared down at her toes.

"Still wrapped in the pink haze?" He pushed back the curtain of her hair, which had fallen over her face as she studied her toes. "I think I'll have to live on these memories, some day. When I'm a tired old man, and you're still young and beautiful."

"You'll never be old." She turned and flung herself across his chest, gazing down into his face. "I know exactly what you'll look like years from now. Just some gray here, and here—" She touched his mustache and his temples, "And a few wrinkles at the corners of your eyes, and maybe here around your mouth—but you'll still be marvelously handsome, and lean and erect, with those blue eyes, and you'll wear wonderful clothes and carry a walking stick, and all the young girls will sigh and wonder who you are, when you walk by—"

"Where do you get these romantic ideas?" He laughed. "Have you ever seen a walking stick?"

"No, but I've read about them. And I've seen pictures." She paused. "Have you?"

"Yes, as a matter of fact. My father used to carry one. He thought he was very dapper."

"Was he?"

"I suppose so."

"Did he smoke with a cigarette holder?"

"No, he smoked cigars."

She pictured Nicholas's father, smoking a cigar, carrying a walking stick, wearing a fur-lined coat, with a fur hat tipped over one eyebrow.

"Now tell me about your mother," she said. "Was she beautiful?"

"She was considered to be. In a cool, statuesque sort of way."

He seldom spoke about his parents, and always tried to change the subject when she asked. She knew he wanted to change the subject now, but she persisted. "Did she have blue eyes?" she started to say, but didn't finish the question, as he pulled her down across the bed and moved above her.

"Yes, but I much prefer passionate black-haired girls with dark eyes—except when they ask too many questions."

He bent to her mouth, silencing her, as they began to explore again, slowly, this time without haste, and began to lose themselves once more in a cresting wave of desire that rolled up and poised and never dissolved, only continued to mount, until Daria knew that soon she would be begging to be taken . . .

But she didn't want to. Not quite yet. She struggled to a sitting position and put both hands against his chest. "Let me," she whispered. With gentle pressure she moved him away and forced him back down against the pillow. She threw one leg over his, to keep him from moving, and then bent her head and flicked her tongue over the flat hard nipple on his breast. His breathing quickened. She bit him, and he caught his breath. She began to move lower, with soft little kisses, pleasing him with all the ways he had taught her and adding inventions of her own. She heard him groan, and he threw one arm over his eyes, and reached down blindly to tangle his fingers in her hair.

Yes, now it's your turn, she thought with a secret surge of triumph, and became more ardent and more inventive.

She had a moment of amazed wonderment as she thought of herself only a week ago, frightened and anxious and totally, incredibly ignorant of this body that thrilled and possessed her in ways she had never dreamed of . . . that she had learned to know with every part of herself, as she was known in return . . . and of this wild, shameless abandon that was lost to everything but itself. *Was that I? So ignorant, so unknowing?*

Then she forgot everything as the long, slow pulses rolled up to engulf her, taking her by surprise, as always, and she heard herself moan deep back in her throat. An iron door clanged shut in her mind, closing off everything except the awareness of what was happening now, right now, this shocking, astonishing sensation . . .

"I can't think back to the way I was before," she said sleepily when they lay quietly again.

"Now you're a sophisticated woman of the world."

"No, I'm not silly enough to believe that. I know better." She lifted her face. "Unless you'd like me to be. I could try to learn."

"No, I wouldn't like you to be. I like you the way you are. Mine." He spoke lightly, with teasing affection, but she saw the quick little flare of jealousy in his eyes. *Are you mine?* she wondered suddenly. When they reached Harbin, would Nicholas meet beautiful, elegant women who would capture his attention? Would he grow bored with her, and forget her?

The thought was unbearable to her.

"As long as you always came back to me," she said, "I would be happy. As long as you didn't send me away. I wouldn't care if you make love to every woman between here and Shanghai."

"What an absurd idea. I have all I can do to take care of one small dark-haired girl, who's managing to keep me very busy."

"Good." She curled up against him, preparing to fall asleep. The last thing she saw before her eyes closed was the kerosene lamp swaying gently back and forth on its iron chain, swinging from the ceiling of the cabin, and for one half-dreaming, half-sleeping moment she thought, *I almost wish we never reach Harbin.*

Chapter 16

"When the fog lifts," Captain Li said softly, "you will be able to see Manchuria. We've come to the Sungari."

A thick, clinging fog surrounded the pilothouse, drifting against the windows like white cotton wool, and bringing the *Kwan Yin* almost to a halt. The engine had rumbled down to near silence, and the boat crept forward slowly, trembling and shuddering, as the pilot squinted anxiously through the fog, struggling with the wheel and listening for the shouts of the boy on deck who was sounding the channel.

"The river is very narrow here," Captain Li said. "It's choked with little islands, and the channel twists and turns between them in a tricky way. If the fog continues, we'll have to anchor."

Nicholas drew slowly on his cigar. He thought it would be wise to anchor at once, since they'd already run aground on sandbars several times; but it wasn't his place to say anything, so he only nodded. Daria was on deck, keeping out of the way of the crew, wrapped in her woolen shawl. Captain Li inhaled his own cigar, removing it from his mouth and turning it in his fingers with a grunt of approval. It had been a gift from Nicholas, who thought it was prudent to stay on good terms with the captain, although his cigar box was almost empty and there was no telling when he would find more.

"But I think it will lift," the captain went on. "I know

these fogs on this stretch of the river. They come on suddenly, and they depart the same way. Ah . . . look."

A patch of light was gleaming through the window, and the swirls of white were moving, drifting, sliding away, as though someone were breathing on them and blowing them aside.

Captain Li chuckled. "It's just as I thought. Soon we'll be able to raise steam and continue to the customs station. By evening we'll be moored in the Sungari."

Like magic, a scene was appearing before them as the fog rose. Bright sunlight shone on blue water. Low, forested banks rose on either side of the river, climbing more steeply beyond the point where the Amur joined the rushing current of the Sungari. Tall poles were fixed on both shores, marking the change in the channel. Oil lamps on the poles waited to be lit at nightfall: red on the right bank, white on the left. The pilot was moving his head from side to side, studying the poles carefully, keeping them in line. The *Kwan Yin* picked up steam.

Here at the mouth of the river were steamers and barges and rafts, some rocking at anchor, some, like the *Kwan Yin*, navigating the channel that twisted between the small green islands covered with scrubby bush that dotted the river.

"Slow down," Captain Li muttered to the pilot. "You'll swamp them in the wash."

A pine raft had come up on the port side of the boat, and was rocking dangerously in the wash from their passage. As the *Kwan Yin* slowed its speed, the occupants of the raft grinned and waved and shouted thanks.

"When we reach the customs station," Captain Li said, turning courteously to Nicholas, "perhaps it would be best if you stay in the cabin, out of sight."

"Yes, you're quite right," Nicholas agreed. He decided to go down on deck and find Daria and alert her to stay hidden until they were safely across the border.

He found her on the afterdeck, leaning on the starboard rail, which was pitted and scarred with burns from the live sparks that flew from the funnel. She had discarded her shawl. Now that the fog had lifted, the sun was hot.

"Do you see those bushes on shore?" She raised her

voice against the noise of the clattering engine as he came up beside her. "I think they're wild roses. I wish we could go on shore and pick some."

"Maybe tomorrow."

"And the ones with the leafy fronds are peonies, I'm sure of it!"

Her face was glowing with interest as she stared at the shore. This was all new and fascinating to her, Nicholas thought. How young she was. In some ways she was very young for her age. But not in others. Her face was beginning to lose the girlish roundness it had had when he first met her, and hollows were showing under her cheekbones, revealing the woman she would become, disclosing the haunting beauty that would be hers in years ahead. Faint purple shadows made stains beneath her eyes, and he felt a stab of guilt, seeing them, knowing he was using her very hard, and telling himself he should stay away.

But he knew he would not. She was always so eager and responsive, quickening with desire at the slightest touch, and his good intentions always dissolved in a renewed flood tide of passion. Then he would pull her to him with a sudden, rough impatience to have her. Once he had taken her on deck, in full view, seated across his lap, fully dressed, unbuttoning his trousers and draping her skirt across them and easing himself under the concealment of the cloth, silencing her scarlet-faced protests with the assurance that no one was paying attention, and even if they guessed what was happening, the Chinese weren't prudish, they wouldn't care. . . .

But this river journey wouldn't last forever. Not even with Céline, he thought, that first year, had it been this way. But the idea of Céline made him feel guilty again, and he told himself it was despicable to make comparisons. He pushed the thought away.

As though she had read his mind, Daria asked casually, "Who is Céline?"

He glanced at her, startled. "Where did you hear that name?"

"You said it in your sleep last night."

Damn. He hadn't buried it deep enough. "Someone I used to know."

"In Kharkov?"

"Yes."

"Was she your mistress?"

"What difference does that make?"

"She must have been very beautiful."

It was time for some diplomatic lying, he thought. "From a distance she was attractive," he said casually. "But she had flaws."

"Oh? What were they?"

"For one thing," he said, improvising as he spoke, "her eyes were set too close together."

"Mmm. I suppose that is a flaw."

"She was also," he went on in a new inspiration, "quite flat-chested."

"Really? How unfortunate for you." She was looking much happier. It was an area in which he had paid Daria some extravagant compliments.

"It would have been, but at the time I didn't know what I was missing." He cleared his throat. "Now, though, I'd be very dissatisfied."

"You're probably lying," she said with a contented little sigh, leaning on the rail, "but I don't care."

"We'll have to go into the cabin very soon. We're coming to the customs station."

"That means that by tonight we'll be in Manchuria!"

If nothing goes wrong, he thought, covering her hand with his own on the rail.

Later—much later—he wondered if the journey had come to an end. They were sitting in the cabin with the door locked and the flowered curtain drawn across the window.

He glanced away from Daria's strained face, seeing her sitting quietly and listening to every sound from outside. He was straining to listen himself. The anchor ropes had been cast down, mooring the steamer, and the *Kwan Yin* was now rocking gently with a soft slap-slap slap-slap against the sides of the vessel. He knew they were moored beside a splintery pier. But he was more concerned with what was happening on deck.

Voices were audible through the closed door, rising and falling. First a harsh tone, stern with authority; then the chuckling, placating murmur of Captain Li in response. Bootheels were making a constant thud-thud-thud back and forth across the deck. Every few moments there was a grinding, scraping noise as boxes and bales were hauled up through the hatchway.

This was taking too long, Nicholas thought, gritting his teeth. It should have been over by now.

He forced himself into outward calm. There was nothing to do but wait, he told himself. Conversation was impossible; so was any kind of movement. He couldn't take the risk of lighting a cigarette. They could only wait.

But damn it, it was taking too long . . .

He tensed. Someone was rattling the doorknob of the cabin.

"What's in here?" said the harsh voice.

"Nothing. Owner's cabin." Captain Li's tone came easily in response. "We keep it locked when not in use. To keep it clean."

Daria's eyes turned to Nicholas in a silent question, huge and dark and worried. He tried to look reassuring, but he felt his hands clench themselves into fists.

"Open it up," said the voice.

"Yes, of course." A pause. "I'll find the key. It's in my quarters."

Another pause. Then the sound of throat-clearing. Then loud hawking and spitting. "Never mind. I've spent too much time here already." A rusty laugh came grating through the door. "You're a fat-bellied old pirate, Li. But I'll trust you this time. Now let's talk about what you owe me."

Footsteps were walking away. In a silent breath of relief, Nicholas reached for Daria's hand. This time, he thought—this time—they had been lucky.

By the next day the *Kwan Yin* had moved from the Amur into the Sungari, and the pattern of the journey resumed its rhythm. They stopped each afternoon at a wood station and watched the long line of crewmen travel back and forth across the plank with stacks of logs. They passed villages, just scatterings of huts along a single-track dusty road, where the *Kwan Yin* loaded and unloaded cargo, oats and soybeans and pressed dried tea, and the cook bought supplies of bread and milk, eggs and chickens, butter, soy flour and tobacco. Nicholas found another box of Manila cigars.

They experienced delays. A steam valve leaked and had to be patched with white lead and wrapped in blankets, slowing down their speed even more. Fogs forced them to anchor, sometimes for an entire morning. Treacherous sandbars, built up over the winter, rose too suddenly under the channel to be detected by the sounding pole, and ran them aground. Once they bumped on a snag and tore a hole in the stern, and it took a whole day and night to repair it.

Other river traffic went by. Pine rafts. Barges. Steamers.

The scenery changed. Russian log huts had given way to village dwellings roofed with thatch, and joss sticks burned in the doorways; these were Chinese *fang tzu*. The riverbanks grew higher and steeper, thickly covered with pine and birch trees, and they could see pine logs being dragged up the slopes by teams of horses and oxen. Sometimes naked villagers were bathing at the river's edge, their bodies very white and slender in the sunlight, and the people waved and laughed at the boats going by.

The village women who came down to the shores had slanted eyes and ivory skin, and the bread they sold was Chinese-style, round and flat with holes in the center, strung on a string. But the women weren't Chinese, the captain told them.

"They are Manchu. You see? They have large feet."

The custom of foot-binding was still followed by the Chinese villagers here in the remote north. But the Manchus had never followed that custom.

Days went by, and Daria and Nicholas lost track of time, more deeply absorbed than ever in their discovery of one another. Everything else was fascinating but remote, like a panorama cast on a screen. In the afternoons they went ashore and strolled the tiny villages, followed by a crowd of curious, giggling villagers, who commented loudly to themselves on the appearance of the strangers.

"What do you suppose they're saying?" Daria whispered to Nicholas.

"They're saying that you have very big feet, and I'm as hairy as an animal, and they're wondering if I'm furred all over."

"That can't be true."

He laughed. "I think it is. From what the captain tells me."

Often, from the deck rail, they saw smoke curling up from the forest, where woodcutters were burning charcoal. Sometimes herds of ponies were grazing on the banks, slipping and sliding with their hooves to keep their footing. The horses with bred along with cattle as a source of income.

But there was another, more sinister, source of income in this country.

One afternoon Nicholas stood with Captain Li by the rail, as a raft approached. Daria was asleep in the cabin. The raft people were offering a live pig for sale, holding it up squealing in their hands, shouting its virtues, and the captain called for the cook to come and buy it. There would be steamed pork for dinner.

Then Captain Li leaned over the rail and called out a rapid question to the men on the raft. One of them grinned, displaying broken teeth, and shook his head. *"Mai yo hunghutze."* The captain looked relieved.

Nicholas had caught one word: *hunghutze.*

Bandits. The scourge of Manchuria. He and Daria had left behind the revolution and the war and the agents of the Cheka, but they weren't safe yet. This wild, unpopulated country was infested with bandits. The hunghutze were lawless men who terrorized the villages and the countryside, some of them ex-soldiers of the warlord, some of them bankrupt farmers who had turned to banditry, some of them just murderous criminals.

"What did he say about hunghutze?" Nicholas asked the captain.

"He said there are no bandits in the area."

"Do they travel on the rivers?"

"Sometimes. They have boats. But usually they stay farther south, near the kaoliang fields, where they can hide in the tall stalks and not be seen."

The flat, marshy plain around Harbin, Nicholas knew, was good country for growing the sorghum called kaoliang. But perhaps they would be lucky and not find bandits on this stretch of the Sungari.

They steamed on, slowly, haltingly, but making progress, as the river wound between the steep banks, with the hills always looming ahead, and little by little came closer to their destination.

One afternoon they moored by a village with a decayed houseboat at the top of the riverbank, the dilapidated wreck guarding the entrance to the village and the start of the narrow, dusty road. It was an opportunity to go onshore.

But neither Daria nor Nicholas heeded it. They were inside the cabin in the deckhouse. The flowered curtain was drawn, filtering muted sunlight into the cabin, hiding them from view.

Nicholas picked up her wrist and brought it to his mouth, then turned it over and kissed the palm of her hand. She cupped her hand around the strong line of his jaw, then moved it around to where the thick dark hair curled at the nape of his neck. *How beautiful you are. And I love you so.* She twisted a lock of his hair around her finger. One of the crewmen would have to cut it tomorrow, she thought. Or she would do it herself. There were no barbers in the villages. The men let their hair grow long, and braided it into pigtails that fell down their backs. The women rolled their hair into buns covered with ragged hairnets.

The few white men who lived here, mostly Russian woodcutters and fur trappers, let their hair grow wild and tumbling past their shoulders. Their beards flowed across their chests.

She sighed and stirred. She was still sitting facing him, naked across his lap, on a small wooden chair. Their clothes were in a heap on the floor. The bed under the window was smooth and untouched, still made up; they had never gone near it.

Their passion had been too urgent, too demanding. It was hard to remember the urgency, now that the passion was spent. But they hadn't even bothered to undress completely, before she'd lowered herself across his thighs and sheathed him within herself. She'd still been wearing her blouse and chemise; Nicholas still had on his shirt.

Only then, when the first hot need was answered and she was straddling his legs, feeling his length throbbing within her body, had he stripped off his shirt, taken off the rest of her clothes, and pulled her down upon him.

She'd lifted her breasts in her hands and offered them to his mouth one at a time; now she could still feel them tingle at the tips.

The sudden, rushing climax had taken them both by surprise.

Nicholas took a deep breath. "Daria," he said, "Daryushka my love, I've been thinking."

"About what?"

"About you. And me. And what's to become of us."

A sick, nervous feeling moved in the pit of her stomach. She wondered if she would like what was coming.

"I thought at first," he went on, "when you gave yourself to me, that you would be my mistress . . . and that you would be a wonderful and exciting lover. But I realize now that I was wrong."

Hot tears sprang into her eyes. *Don't. Don't. Don't say any more.*

"You see," Nicholas went on, "my feelings are not what I expected." He took her face between his hands. "Because I'm in love with you. And I don't want you to be my mistress. I would like you to be my wife." He studied her face, looking very grave. "That is, if you feel the same way."

The tears brimmed up and spilled over, streaming down her cheeks. She couldn't say anything, she was crying too hard. He held her close and kissed her throat.

"Perhaps I shouldn't have said it. Perhaps I should have waited until we reached Harbin. One grows superstitious; so much has happened. We never got to Manchuli. Or Vladivostok. Something always prevented it, but it seems, now, that we're so close to our destination . . ."

Up on deck, Captain Li was frowning. His usually jovial face wore a dark expression as he stared out at the barge that was making its way back into the channel. Bad news, he thought. If what they'd just told him was true, then he'd have to revise his plans about Harbin. He'd have to dispose of his cargo in Sunsing. That was very bad. It would mean a serious loss in profits. The owners would be very displeased.

He sighed, longing for the opium pipe that awaited him on the shelf in his quarters. No, too early. He couldn't console himself yet with the pipe of dreams. He would have to wait.

And he would have to inform his passengers too, he thought. Where were they? In their cabin, absorbed in one another. They had been no trouble at all; well worth the passage fee. You hardly knew they were there. They didn't even eat very much, at least not by his standards.

Should he knock on the door and tell them now?

No, it could wait, he thought. This bad news could wait. There was still a little distance to go on the river before they reached Sunsing.

Chapter 17

June became July as the *Kwan Yin* approached Sunsing. Above the border in Siberia, the war continued. Today in Siberia it was raining. On a small spur of the Trans-Siberian Railway, somewhere to the north of Nikolsk-Ussuri, the armored car called the Liberator stood in a gray drizzle. Plating was bolted onto the sides of the bronevik, and a gun turret was mounted on its sandbagged roof. The gun stood silent. The gunner was lying dead on the ground. All around the car, on the grass and on the slopes of the railway embankment to either side, corpses lay looking at the sky with sightless eyes. The drizzle was washing the dead, bloody faces with gentle moisture.

Inside the car, lights were burning. Men with hard, impassive faces and slanted black eyes stood leaning against the walls, holding rifles with fixed bayonets. They wore the uniform of the Japanese Twelfth Division.

A stocky man in a lieutenant's uniform bent over a figure slumped in a chair. The officer's name was Lieutenant Haneda. He straightened and spoke to a soldier who was standing behind him. They held a rapid conversation, and suddenly the enlisted man stepped forward and lifted his rifle high in his hands, butt forward.

The lieutenant stopped him with a hand on his sleeve. No, not yet. He had other plans for this one.

Lev slumped forward in his chair, against the ropes which bound him to it. He was dirty and bloodstained, his uniform was ripped, and beneath the unshaven stubble on his cheeks his skin was gray. The bruises and marks of a vicious beating were visible on his face. His eyes were closed.

Consciousness flickered across the surface of his mind like a streak of crimson lightning, bringing with it the awareness of pain. He tried to retreat back into blackness and peace, but it was eluding him. He groaned. He came awake.

In his ears was the hoarse, harsh, gasping sound of someone's breath—his own.

Every time he breathed, something stabbed him viciously, painfully, in the chest and lungs. Every breath was its own little torture. Sweat poured down his body.

Broken rib, he thought. When they were using their boots on me . . . before . . .

Something sticky and wet was running down the left side of his face. He licked swollen lips. A salt taste. Blood.

He opened his eyes and raised his head. His vision blurred. He saw a dizzy swirl of colors and shapes. Nausea rose in his throat, and blackness swept over him, but only for seconds. It receded again, and his eyes came into focus.

He saw a pair of narrow black eyes in a flat-cheekboned face swimming out of the darkness above him. The eyes were studying him coldly.

The mouth moved. It spoke. "What's my name?" A rough hand reached forward for his chin and grasped it in steel fingers, forcing it upward, so that Lev had to stare into the face. "Do you remember my name?"

Lev jerked his chin away; the movement brought back the sick dizziness again. But he remembered. "Haneda," he muttered.

Crack. The lieutenant brought his open palm down savagely across Lev's face, hurling it to one side. Pain. Red, jagged streaks of pain. "Use my rank when you speak to me. Pig."

What was his rank? Oh Christ, what was his rank?

"Lieutenant," Lev croaked. "Lieutenant Haneda."

"That's better."

I'll remember that, you stinking bastard.

If I live through this.

His memory was coming back. The memory of crimson

horror. He didn't want to remember, but he couldn't help it.

This morning. Was it this morning? Daybreak?

Yes, this morning.

They'd been fighting the Czech Brigade along the railway line, as they had been since May, when Anton Takashvili had died. In the five weeks since, they'd made slow progress. It was still a battle for every length of track.

This morning he'd been hiding in the marsh. He'd gone to the nearby village the night before to get information from the cooperating peasants, and he'd spent the night in an izba. Just as the sun came up, he'd been returning to the train through the tall grass.

But as the dawn broke, he'd watched an unbelievable sight by the armored car.

As the sky lightened to gray, he'd seen row upon row of Japanese troops rising up from the concealing grass on either side of the railway embankment like monstrous flowers, their rifles fixed with glittering bayonets, the red bands on their caps camouflaged by clumps of grass or smears of dirt.

Then the bloody horror began. Their own Maxim machine gun chattered desperately from the top of the train, the gunner feeding cartridges like a madman, firing blindly into the oncoming rush, until, in just seconds, he was overcome. The Japanese swarmed up over the train brandishing their rifles like clubs, smashing bones and heads with vicious, savage fury, then using their bayonets—oh, they were good at that. Men were tossed screaming onto the ground on the points of those bayonets like shovelfuls of coal, bleeding and dying, their own blood choking in their throats.

He'd seen Yuri tossed to the ground with his guts torn out, shrieking for help, then gurgling into silence.

Oh Christ. He didn't want to think about that.

He'd tried to fire his own rifle, stumbling through the coarse grass, half-crazy, not knowing what he was doing. Then a rifle butt came from nowhere—he hadn't even seen it—shattering his head into a thousand slivers of pain, and he'd fallen face down on the damp, squishy ground, smelling rotting vegetation and tasting dirt.

A booted toe turned him over. Then it was smashing into his ribs. Then again . . .

Two voices were speaking. He couldn't understand them. Then words he could recognize were being hissed into his ear by a squatting figure.

"The lieutenant says we are to keep you alive. You will be an example for the others to see. We will deal with you more thoroughly when we have more time."

Later, they'd had more time.

They'd taken him back here, to his own armored car. And they had been very leisurely.

"Cigarette?"

Haneda was crouched down in front of him. Lev peered at him through bloodshot eyes, and slumped against his ropes. Was this another trick?

"Take it, you don't have much time," Haneda said pleasantly. He held a cigarette to Lev's mouth. Lev inhaled, feeling the stabbing pain of his rib; then the smoke was moving deep down in his lungs. He exhaled, still savoring the smoke.

What were the Japs doing here? he thought brokenly. They weren't supposed to be here . . . had they joined the war?

You goddamned idiot, of course they have.

The Japanese had intervened against the Red partisans. They'd sent troops into Siberia to fight the revolution. It was foreign intervention in the civil war, just as everyone had predicted.

But he couldn't think straight now. He was so tired. He didn't even have the energy to hate Haneda anymore, or despise the Japanese troops. He only wanted to be left alone, to die in peace.

Then, in the next moment he felt icy terror: *I don't want to die. Not that way. Please . . .*

His eyes widened. He hoped desperately he would be able to keep silent, not beg. He pressed his lips together.

The lieutenant had snapped his fingers, and the enlisted man had handed him a rifle. Haneda had wrenched off the bayonet and handed back the rifle. Now he stood facing Lev holding the naked bayonet by its leather grip.

Lev's body tightened in desperate anticipation.

No! They'd promised to let him live . . . he would never

live through that! *But maybe they lied. They lie through their teeth . . .*

Why did he think of his grandparents? His mother's parents. And Sabbath night candles, flickering in a darkened room. And the sound of prayers. His father had not been observant, but his grandparents were pious Jews, and he'd visited them often as a child, in their small village outside Kiev.

Blessed art thou O Lord our God, King of the Universe, who distinguishes between light and darkness. Blessed art thou O Lord our God, King of the Universe, who created the light and the fire. No, Zaide! I don't believe in your God! Forgive me! I have gods of my own . . . *Blessed art thou O Lord our Lenin, who gave to me my faith . . .*

Except now—now—

Haneda stepped forward, took a firm, hard grasp of Lev's hair, and pulled his head back. He raised the bayonet. Lev tried frantically to pull his head away. Haneda gripped him more tightly, holding him steady, and ran the tip of the bayonet lightly over his cheek, drawing a thin trickle of blood. "Here, I think," he muttered. "It will look very well. Keep steady and don't move. I am going to brand you like the pig that you are."

Not castration after all.

"Prepare yourself, Bolshevik scum," Haneda said. He raised his arm.

Lev saw the bayonet flash silver before his eyes.

Aaaagh . . .

Someone screamed, a terrible, hoarse scream. It was himself.

Pain. And blood, streaming down his cheek.

He was abruptly released. His head fell forward on his chest.

"Now," Haneda said, "I have marked you well." He stepped back and wiped the blood from the bayonet with his thumb and forefinger. "You have been branded with the mark of O-Ameratsu-O-Mi-Kami, goddess of the sun. Now you will return to your fellow soldiers and display that sign, and you will tell them that we have arrived, and that we intend to stay. Make sure you tell them that, Bolshevik pig."

No. Lev had one last thought before the blackness came

Chapter 18

"You understand," Captain Li said regretfully, "that the Chinese Eastern Railway in Manchuria belongs to the White regime. It's still in Russian hands."

As the captain spoke, he crossed his arms and placed the palms of his hands on his forearms, just above the wrists. It was a curiously old-fashioned gesture, not suited to the clothes he was wearing. He should have been wearing a brocaded silk robe in blue or scarlet, embroidered with golden dragons, fashioned with wide full sleeves to hide his hands.

Nicholas, who was struggling with suppressed anger and regret, mingled with a fatalistic certainty that something—something—had been bound to go wrong, couldn't help noticing the gesture. The only thing more archaic, he thought, would have been the hands-on-thighs, head-lowered, bending-at-the-waist posture of the kowtow.

But why should the captain kowtow to him? At the moment he, Nicholas, was in an extremely precarious position. He and Daria were about to be put off the steamer at Sunsing. They would be stranded in the heart of bandit country, with Harbin still over a hundred miles away.

It was not a long distance by rail, he thought bitterly. But there was no railway here; the Chinese Eastern tracks ran west, into Mongolia, to link with the Trans-Siberian Railway at Chita. No, they would have to reach Harbin some other way.

And pray they didn't run into hunghutze along the route.

Just then, Nicholas thought, he would have given all the jewelry he was carrying for an automobile—not that the roads were safe.

"The orders are clear," Captain Li went on. "No Chinese vessel may approach the railway bridge across the Sungari at Harbin. The White Russian officials are worried about the war and the strategic importance of the bridge. They fear sabotage. Armed soldiers are posted all along the span, with orders to fire on any vessel that approaches too near."

That bridge, belonging to the Chinese Eastern Railway, was the only link between Vladivostok and Siberia, now that the war was raging across the Amur and Ussuri branches of the railroad. No wonder the White regime was anxious about its safety. The Chinese Eastern had been built with Russian money, using Russian workers, and the land had been leased to Russia in 1896 by the Chinese government. Harbin, originally a railway village, was still Russian in character.

"They can't stop traffic for very long," Nicholas said, reaching into his pocket for a cigarette.

"They will allow White Russian barges and steamers only."

"But for how long?" Nicholas turned to lean against the rail. They were standing on the foredeck. "This embargo will have to be lifted very soon." He stared out at the opposite shore. The high, forested riverbank seemed more sinister now.

"Yes, that may be so." Captain Li lifted his shoulders. "But I can't afford to wait in Sunsing. For a variety of reasons."

Hunghutze was one of them, Nicholas thought. He struck a match on his thumbnail and bent his head to the cigarette, cupping the flame against the breeze from the water. "Yes, I understand." Li would unload his cargo in Sunsing and then steam back down the Sungari to Khabarovsk, he thought. But that did him no good at all. There was no going back for himself and Daria.

He tossed the dead match over the rail into the water.

No, there was nothing to do but continue, and see what

202

possibilities presented themselves in Sunsing. As he took a breath and inhaled the muddy smell of decaying vegetation coming up from the river, mixed with the fishy, machine oil odor of the deck behind him and the faint tobacco pungency of his own cigarette, he felt sure that the goddess of destiny was laughing.

They reached Sunsing the following afternoon. Nicholas and Daria stood on deck, watching the town approach as they steamed through the crowded river traffic: shouting bargemen, raft-vendors hawking fresh vegetables, floating garbage, Chinese square-sailed junks, shallow-draft cargo steamers. A few boats already at the dock were being unloaded by half-naked dock coolies who struggled back and forth with enormous bags of soybeans.

"It's walled," Daria said softly. "I didn't expect that."

So many of the cities in China and Manchuria were walled, Nicholas thought, for there had been so many centuries of invasion and conquest.

Sunsing's wall was low and built of mud. Above it they could see wooden houses built on piles. Here on the west bank of the river, which swept past the Western Gate, they could see the dock outside the wall, and the gate above it, at the top of a flight of broad stone steps. The gate was very wide, to allow carts and caravans to pass through. Water carriers were running up and down the steps to the river with poles and buckets slung across their shoulders, surefooted on the slippery stone. Other gates in the wall would open out to the east, north, and south.

A strange odor of incense, excrement, sweat, dust, and overripe fruit drifted across the water. But it was not unpleasant, Daria thought. She told herself she would associate that odor with Sunsing from now on. That, and the bright sunlight dazzling on the river, and the up-and-down singsong of the raft people, and this sense of motion, approaching closer to the dock every moment, while she herself stood motionless, surrendering her will to whatever the fates had in store.

Her moment of reflection came to an end as they bumped against the dock. With a creak of winches and a slither of ropes, the anchor splashed into the water and the wooden plank went down.

Captain Li came up beside them.

"I wish you good luck," he said to Nicholas, holding out his hand. "In China we call it good joss."

"Thank you. I wish you the same."

"We have a saying: a pair of golden lilies must be bought with a water barrel of tears. But perhaps you won't have to pay so high a price."

Half an hour later, Nicholas and Daria were standing at the top of the broad stone steps, which were slimy with water and the grime from countless bare feet. From behind them came the rhythmic chanting of the dock coolies: *hai yo, hai yo.* To their left lay an empty grassy field surrounded by trees. Beyond the field was a graveyard, marked by cone-shaped mounds of mud. Facing them, straight ahead loomed the high wide Western Gate, its great brass-studded door pushed back against the wall.

An eager young coolie was carrying their baggage, and had offered to show them to the Hotel Manchuria, which was just within the wall. "Only a few short steps!" he'd promised.

Daria thought the name sounded very grand; Nicholas had been wryly skeptical, advising her not to expect too much.

They were waiting to pass through the gate, but the small door beside it for foot traffic was closed and barred until the doorkeeper returned from wherever it was he had gone. Meanwhile Daria was fascinated by the colorful scene before her. A steady stream of carts was passing through the Western Gate, drawn by mixed teams of mules, ponies, donkeys, and oxen, and piled high with hemp mats, bags of soybeans, barrels of salt, wicker baskets of bean oil, and squealing live pigs. Traffic was suddenly held up in a long line as a pony stumbled and overturned its cart, spilling beans all over the ground. Mule drivers cursed and shouted, men scrambled for the beans, and young boys raced about scooping animal droppings into woven baskets with little shovels.

Finally the overturned cart was righted, the beans were collected, the shouting died away, and traffic moved again.

Daria glanced over at the empty field to her left. The

trees around it were very lovely, she thought, willows, oaks, and birches. But something odd caught her eye. Big round objects were dangling from the branches . . . what were they? A sick feeling moved in the pit of her stomach as she began to suspect.

"Come this way, come this way," the young boy with their luggage was saying, tugging at Nicholas's sleeve.

"Why?"

"To see a spectacle!"

He was urging them to the edge of the grassy field. Others were moving in that direction; a crowd was collecting, and Daria could hear happy, excited chatter begin to rise. Impelled by the surge of traffic, they followed the crowd.

Suddenly two gray uniformed men on horseback came riding through the Western Gate: soldiers of the warlord. Two others followed, in the same gray cotton uniforms with peaked caps. Behind them stumbled a line of men, ragged and filthy, roped together with their hands behind their backs.

"Hunghutze," said the boy excitedly.

The bandits were grinning and laughing. Some of them shouted remarks that made the crowd burst into laughter. An onlooker ran forward and shoved a piece of fried dumpling into the mouth of one of the men. who chewed comically and bowed his thanks. More laughter arose.

Daria, in disbelieving horror, was close enough to the trees to confirm her suspicion about the big round objects. They were human heads, tied to the branches by their long black hair, twisting and swinging in the breeze that rose off the river. A faint smell of rotting flesh moved on the air.

She dragged her eyes away, swallowing hard.

The soldiers had dismounted. One of them was now holding a rusty scimitar in both hands. The chatter and laughter died away. An expectant hush fell over the crowd. The man with the scimitar hacked off the rope of the first prisoner and led him forward, forcing him to his knees on the grass. The man obediently bent his head, exposing his neck, and the soldier yanked him by his hair, pulling his neck taut.

Those rust-colored stains on the scimitar weren't rust at all, Daria thought in sudden horror.

"Daria, let's go." Nicholas's voice was hard as he took her arm. "You don't want to watch this."

"They're going to—"

"Yes, it's an execution ground."

They began to push their way out, turning their backs on the field. Suddenly a long sigh went through the crowd, and tension seemed to ebb.

They've cut his head off, Daria thought sickly. Now they'll tie it to the tree with the others.

The hush fell again, and she could sense the crowd holding its breath once more. The second prisoner was being led forward, she thought. They were going to execute all of them. But none of the bandits still roped in line were displaying any fear. They still grinned and joked with the onlookers, waiting their turn to kneel in the grass.

"How can people watch!" she burst out, turning to Nicholas, when they were free of the crowd. "It's horrible!"

"It's supposed to be an example, to discourage banditry and thieving." Nicholas added drily, "It doesn't seem to work very well." Then he frowned, and she wondered what he was thinking.

"We'll have to wait until this is over," he said slowly, "before I can speak to those soldiers. But I think they may be receptive to an offer."

"For what?" ·

"Hunghutze ride horseback in this country. That means there are horses and saddles available."

Daria shuddered. It seemed a little macabre to bargain for the property of a decapitated bandit. Of course the bandit had probably stolen the animal in the first place.

"Won't a horse be expensive?" she asked.

"Yes, but we need transportation, and I doubt if I'll find a motor vehicle in Sunsing. A horse might be a good investment." He looked thoughtful. "If I'm successful, we can start out tomorrow, first thing in the morning. After a proper night's sleep." Then he smiled down at her. "Do you think you can sleep in a real bed, with no deck swaying and rocking underneath you?"

"I don't know—it will be very strange!"

By the time she was ready to fall asleep, hours later, she had almost adjusted to the odd sensation of being in a real bed—a four-poster made of cheap varnished pine, with a curtain around it—and having the floor steady beneath her, with no lapping water outside the window, no creaking deck, only this motionless quiet, protected by the curtain. It smelled of dust but how luxurious it was to have so much room for stretching.

Nicholas, on his side of the bed, was stretching too, enjoying the unaccustomed spaciousness. Their lovemaking had been gentle and tender, because they were both tired, both anticipating the problems of the morning. She knew he had been pleasantly surprised at the Hotel Manchuria. The room was plain but clean, with tall glazed double doors opening onto a narrow verandah, and bare board walls—with knotholes affording a view into the room next door—and a washstand shadowed by the curtain of the bed. The sheets were freshly laundered.

A Chinese servant had brought them hot towels and steaming little cups of tea when they arrived.

Now all the events of the day were tumbling through Daria's mind in spite of her weariness. That hideous execution scene—though she hadn't watched it, she imagined it vividly—and then the purchase of the horse and saddle from the solder, who was employed by the Manchurian warlord, Chang Tso-lin. The little luggage coolie had translated while the negotiations went on. They'd been long-drawn-out; bargaining was a ritual here. Nicholas had also bought two saddlebags, and tomorrow they would pack them with their belongings, leaving the suitcases behind.

The horse was a pale gray mare with white markings, and Nicholas had renamed her Chaika.

"Seagull—how pretty—why do you call her that?"

"It was the name of a gray pony I had as a child."

Daria had never seen the sea. Some day, perhaps, she would see the ocean, and hear the cry of circling gulls.

She had new clothes, purchased from one of the open-fronted little shops that lined the narrow street within the wall. The alleys were called *hutungs*, she had learned. Now she possessed a blue cotton tunic and trousers; they would be more practical than her skirts for the traveling that lay ahead. She would smooth down her hair, twist it into a knot at the back of her head, and fasten it with hairpins. With the high-necked tunic buttoned at the throat and the wide blue trousers, she would look from a distance like a Chinese girl.

Nicholas was turning down the wick of the oil lamp by the side of the bed. She wondered what it would be like to be married. Would it be different?

"Were you faithful to that woman?" she asked suddenly. "The one in Kharkov?" She didn't like to say Céline's name.

"Why in the world would you ask a question like that?"

"I don't know. It just occurred to me."

He yawned and pulled up the blanket.

He hadn't answered the question, she noted. Nor did he intend to, it seemed. He was settling down to sleep. That meant the answer was no. She wasn't really surprised. She could picture how it must have been in Kharkov. Women would be attracted to him, inevitably, and begin teasing little flirtations, and he would be flattered, and interested, and respond to their overtures. One thing would lead to another . . . then he'd feel guilty, and hope he'd been discreet . . .

"Would you be angry if I was unfaithful to you?" she asked sleepily.

"Yes."

"Very angry?"

"Yes."

She wondered what he would do. Turn into the Man of Ice, probably, and never speak to her again. It was an extremely unpleasant speculation. "You do have faults after all," she said. "I'm beginning to see that now."

"That's too bad. I was hoping to be a god of perfection for just a little while longer."

"Are you jealous?"

"Yes."

"Are you possessive?"

"Yes."

"Do you get impatient and angry with people when they do stupid things or make ignorant remarks? Even when they don't know any better?"

"Yes."

She smiled in the dark. "Never mind, I think I can forgive your faults. As long as you never get impatient or angry with me." She would never be unfaithful anyway, so that was nothing to worry about. She raised herself up on her elbow to kiss him good night, then settled back against the pillow and closed her eyes, ready at last to fall asleep.

In the morning, as they packed the saddlebags, Nicholas told her what he had learned from the dining room waiter the night before.

It was always better to travel through the open countryside with an escort. Best of all was a caravan, since the caravans paid tribute to the local bandit chieftains as a matter of policy, ensuring their safety. But few camels set out at this time of year from the Temple of the Skylark in Mongolia, and there were none in Sunsing at the moment.

However, if they could catch up with a Manchu peddler called Cha Ho, who traveled with an oxcart, he might be able to lead them to the outskirts of Harbin. Cha Ho was well known in this part of the country. He was said to be traveling south.

"His name means Two-Branched River," Nicholas said. "It refers to his birthplace."

"Is he here in Sunsing?"

"No. He was last seen in Lung Ta Chan—the Village of the Dragon Pagoda. It's just outside the Southern Gate."

The Village of the Dragon Pagoda, Daria thought. How romantic . . .

But the village was not romantic at all. They came upon it soon after leaving the Southern Gate, which even now, just at dawn, was noisy with carts, oxen, mounted soldiers, and pedestrians in their traditional blue cotton, carrying baskets of produce. The day would be clear and sunny; blue sky was already beginning to appear above the clouds of dust rising from the road. They rode into Lung Ta Chan's one narrow road in their own cloud of dust, Chaika patiently bearing their weight, to find naked children surrounded by milling pigs, ducks, and chickens, open-fronted mud huts with thatched roofs, barking yellow dogs, and mounds of steaming manure. Smoke obscured the interiors of the huts; the villagers were cooking their breakfasts of millet and the heavy cereal odor drifted out onto the road.

But the Dragon Pagoda itself almost made up for everything else. Daria could see it at the end of the road. She sat before Nicholas in the saddle, looking at the temple's roof, gracefully curved to discourage fêng shui. A small stone dragon guarded the entrance, flanked by two stone lion-dogs. How pretty it was, all of wood, painted scarlet and gold.

She wondered, scanning the village and remembering the beheaded bandits, if that would be China. Squalor and loveliness. Wisdom and cruelty. Serenity and horror.

Harbin, of course, would be Russian in character and flavor. She knew it was often called the City of Nichevo— the spirit of what-does-it-matter, nothing-can-be-done.

But Harbin was more than a hundred miles to the south.

Now, approaching closer to the pagoda, she could see inside. Beyond the door, in the shadows of the temple interior, a stone altar was surrounded by the fragrant smoke of incense from burning joss sticks.

An oxcart stood in front of the entrance, piled high with all kinds of peddler's goods, from hairnets to tinware.

"Cha Ho is around somewhere," Nicholas muttered.

"There he is, coming out of the temple!"

A small man in a blue quilted jacket, with a felt cap pulled down over his ears in spite of the warmth of the day, was climbing up to the seat of the oxcart. His cheekbones were so high that his eyes almost disappeared, and his eyebrows were invisible beneath the cap. His skin was dark brown from the sun, and it was impossible to tell his age. He could have been anywhere from twenty-five to fifty.

"Are you Cha Ho?" Nicholas asked, hoping the man spoke Russian.

Fortunately, he did. "Yes, that is I." The small man grinned. "Ni liao tao—how do you do! You wish to buy something? Blankets, pots and pans, knives and forks? Chopsticks?"

"Perhaps."

"Beautiful blankets from Mongolia, soft as a cloud? A jar of Tiger Balm Lotion, to perfume the lady's hair? Or perhaps a little powdered ginseng root, to mix with your wine. To make your nights full of power and strength, and please the young lady."

"All those things sound very fine," Nicholas said politely. "But I would like to know something first. Is it true that you're traveling south?"

Cha Ho hesitated.

"I was told that in Sunsing," Nicholas added. "You see, we would like to travel with you. Since you know the way and we are strangers."

Cha Ho suddenly laughed. *"Yang kweitze!* Foreign devils! You wish to travel with me?"

"If you don't object."

"It's hard going. I sleep in my oxcart. The first night or two, you'll have to sleep on the ground."

"Perhaps we can buy some of your Mongolian blankets, to soften our rest."

"Ah! Perhaps so!" After a moment he narrowed his almost invisible eyes to tiny slits. "You would have to take the risk, along with me."

Risk, Nicholas thought. The peddler must be referring to bandits. "Have you heard any news of hunghutze?"

Cha Ho grinned, showing a gleaming gold tooth. "I have heard that many went to join their ancestors yesterday on the execution field outside the Western Gate. Perhaps it will be quiet in the countryside for a little while."

"I hope you're right."

"Well well, I will have to think about this. After all, you could be hunghutze yourself. You could be planning to rob me on the roadside and steal my wares."

"I assure you I am not."

"It's never safe to trust a person with blue eyes. That's a well-known fact!"

Nicholas sighed inwardly. "There's nothing I can do about the color of my eyes, Honorable Peddler," he said courteously. "I come from a land above the border, which is much younger in wisdom than that of your esteemed ancestors. But if you will accept my most humble as-

211

surances that I wish only to share the pleasure of your companionship and your vast experience of the road, I believe you won't be sorry."

Cha Ho was silent for a moment. He seemed to be weighing in his mind the phrases he had just heard. Then he nodded. "I will make my decision after I have concluded my business in Lung Ta Chan," he said. "Perhaps you can be trusted after all."

"When will your business be concluded?"

"This afternoon, at the Hour of the Monkey."

That was some time after three o'clock, Nicholas thought, Captain Li had told him. "We'll be happy to wait," he said aloud. "Shall we stay here at the Dragon Pagoda?"

"I think it will be best if you wait on the road." Cha Ho pointed south, past the pagoda, where the village ended and the countryside began. "Wait beneath the large willow tree near the meadow. Do not choose the oak on the right-hand side of the road. It's the home of green forest devils."

"I'll be sure to avoid the oak."

"If I haven't arrived by the Hour of the Rooster—" Five o'clock, Nicholas thought swiftly—"then you must continue on your way without me."

"I understand," Nicholas said. He gently urged Chaika into motion, and they took their leave of Cha Ho and moved out onto the road.

When they were seated beneath the willow tree, on the edge of a small meadow bright with yellow lilies, pink-and-white wild peonies, and hovering golden butterflies, and Chaika was grazing peacefully on the grass, Daria unpacked the food they had brought from the Hotel Manchuria: cold roast pork, pickled beets, wheat cakes and clay bottles of samshu wine. After they had eaten, she felt sleepy and leaned her back against the tree trunk.

"Will Cha Ho come, do you suppose?"

"It's hard to tell. If he doesn't, we'll go on by ourselves."

Nicholas was lying full-length at her feet, unconsciously graceful as he always was, chewing on a blade of grass, thinking his own thoughts. Probably about hunghutze.

But it was difficult for her to believe in the dangers of banditry as she gazed up through the feathery leaves of the willow tree and listened to the faint barking of the *wonk* dogs, in Lung Ta Chan, almost musical from this distance, and felt the wine warm in the pit of her stomach.

They had been awake before dawn. Now it must be —what? The Hour of the Snake? She realized she was going to fall asleep.

When she woke, the sun was in the western half of the sky. A sound had awakened her. She got to her feet, realizing that Nicholas was standing beneath the willow tree, holding Chaika's bridle, looking north. A rattling, jingling, creaking noise was coming down the road, growing louder and louder. In the next second, Cha Ho and his oxcart appeared, swaying from side to side on the narrow track. He halted when he reached the willow tree.

"No green forest devils?"

"We haven't seen any."

Cha Ho flashed his gold tooth. "If you're coming with me, the young lady might like to ride in the oxcart!"

Daria hesitated for only a moment. She would have preferred to ride with Nicholas, but she knew it would be easier for the mare if she didn't. They had miles of hard riding ahead, and Chaika was already laden with saddlebags. "Thank you," she said. "I would enjoy that." She climbed up beside Cha Ho on the oxcart and found herherself looking out over the broad, hairy back of the ox.

"The day after tomorrow," the Manchu peddler said, glancing up at Nicholas who had already swung himself into the saddle, "with luck, we will sleep beneath a roof."

"Where?"

"At the Inn of the Green Parrot. I've stayed there before. It's in the territory of Shih Lung, the Stone Dragon —but we will pray to avoid that encounter!"

He picked up the reins, slapping them against the sides of the ox, and urged the huge animal into motion. The cart groaned and creaked into motion again. Chaika snuffled and sidestepped, then settled down to a graceful trot by the side of the cart, happy with her lighter load. They turned south, facing the territory of the Stone Dragon, to leave the outskirts of Lung Ta Chan by the southern route.

Chapter 19

From the north the Inn of the Green Parrot was approached through a stretch of light forest, trees and underbrush rustling with life: squirrels, rabbits, deer, foxes, wood mice, pheasants, partridges, and grouse. The fiercer wildlife—the timber wolves, bears, wild pigs and Siberian tigers—remained lurking in the deeper forest, closer to the foothills of the Khingan Mountains on the Mongolian border. A few miles to the west of the inn, past the small stretch of woodland on its borders, was a little lake surrounded by a swampy marsh. Here hunters found waterfowl of all kinds: swans, geese, wild ducks, herons, snipes, pelicans, and cranes.

The inn itself was hidden from the road by a high wooden stockade of willow and oak branches. The gate in the stockade could be barred against hunghutze, although it would not resist a determined assault. It was meant only as a delaying device.

Beyond the stockade was a muddy courtyard crowded with animals: tethered horses, braying mules shoving and crowding one another at the water trough with bells tinkling around their necks, grunting pigs, squawking chickens, barking dogs, silent, slinking cats—and one noisy green parrot in a wicker cage hanging by the door, hopping up and down on a bright yellow feet and adding its raucous parrot voice to the general bedlam. Mud, dung, and cornstalks littered the ground.

The inn was a low, sprawling building of mud and logs,

built up against a stream convenient for watering the animals. Its interior consisted of one large common room, with a sleeping platform, or *k'ang*, along one wall and a big wooden table and chairs against the other. The smoky kitchen and the four tiny guest rooms, each with its own *k'ang*, opened out along the rear, through a doorway hung with skins.

It was almost dinnertime. Tantalizing odors from the kitchen floated out to the common room, where a small, wiry, bald-headed man with bright blue eyes sat at the table, slouched on his spine, drinking steadily from a clay bottle of wine. The fringe of hair above his ears was streaked with gray, but it still showed traces of its original brilliant orange-red. He still wore his cartridge belt strapped around his chest, although his rifle hung from its leather strap on the back of the chair. At his feet lay a handsome black-and-tan Gordon setter, its head on its paws. Absently, he scratched the dog's ears as he swallowed his wine.

The man's name was Brendan O'Reilly. He was originally from Belfast, but now he claimed Vladivostok, Shanghai, Harbin, and various points east as his home. And was glad of it.

Be damned to Belfast, with its greasy yellow fogs and everlasting rain and black smoke, and mean gray streets, and dark hallways smelling of boiled cabbage and piss. He'd never go back, if he had any say in the matter.

Brendan's stomach growled.

Christ Almighty, where was his dinner? He'd shot a full bag of partridges today out at the lake, with the help of Drum—he fondled the dog's ears affectionately—and now Hao, the innkeeper, was back there cooking them up. But what did the man think he was doing, starving him to death?

He threw his head back and roared in the direction of the kitchen. "Hao, you damned bloody Chink, what the hell's taking you so long?"

Hao appeared in the back doorway, wiping his sweating face with a corner of his apron. "The partridges have to be cooked. It takes time."

"You've had enough time to cook an ox, for the love of Christ!"

The innkeeper shrugged and spread his hands. *"Mei yu fa tzu."*

"Mei yu fa tzu in yer eye!"

But in spite of his fierce words, Brendan sat back and grinned to himself, pouring himself another glass of wine. That was the answer to everything around here. *Mei yu fa tzu.* It can't be helped. It was the exact equivalent of the Russian word *nichevo,* accompanied by the same fatalistic shrug of the shoulders. Nothing you can do about it. Why not just accept it?

Damn right. Not a bad way of looking at things, once you learned the trick.

This country suited him. He'd been here for six years now.

He swallowed. The wine was hot and spicy, warming his belly. Kaoliang wine, distilled from the sorghum plant that was the major crop in this part of Manchuria. At the marsh this afternoon, Brendan had finished the whiskey he'd brought with him from Harbin, so now he was reduced to this local brew.

He glanced idly to his right, where a group of Chinese men were sprawled on the k'ang, talking excitedly and waving their arms. They'd had their own dinners, served in lacquered bowls with wooden chopsticks, and now they were deeply involved in the fist game, *pao chuan.*

Jesus, Mary, and Joseph, they'd gamble on anything. Brendan didn't mind a wager himself, particularly on a fine-looking horse, but the Chinese were incorrigible gamblers: Short stick, long stick; fan-tan; that painted-tile clack-clack affair they called *mah jongg.* Christ knew what. And this childish game, *pao chuan.* Hold out your fist, bet on the number of fingers to be extended, spread out your fingers—loser bought the wine. They could keep it up for hours.

But as long as they were happy, why should he care?

If that damned Hao didn't bring out his dinner in about two minutes—

Ah, here it came. Hao set the steaming plate in front of him: roasted partridges surrounded by noodles, vegetables, and rice. He decided to eat it with a knife and fork, although he was equally adept with chopsticks. Drum raised his head with a little whine. The dog had already been fed, he wasn't hungry; but because the setter had worked hard today, Brendan fed him some partridge meat with his fingers. Then he settled down to finish the plate.

When he'd eaten, he leaned back in the chair, loosening his belt. Hao was hovering anxiously, waiting for the courteous belch that meant the meal had been enjoyed, and Brendan good-naturedly obliged. Then he began to think about what he would do when he got back to Harbin. He still had plenty of money in his pocket, so he was in no hurry to make a decision.

With this civil war going on to the north, Red against White, you could always join one of those catch-as-catch-can armies being organized in Harbin by the Cossack hetmans. Semenov, Kalmikov, Dmitri Chernov, who was in Harbin looking for recruits—no, not Chernov; Brendan couldn't stomach the man. Orlov was the best of the lot, though none of them would part with much cash for an Irish soldier of fortune. The White Russians needed money, a great deal of it, and for all the hetmans were taking payment on the sly from the Japanese. Now *that* bunch didn't mind spreading it around, as long as they got what they'd paid for. They'd been moving into Manchuria little by little ever since the Russo-Japanese War in 1905. The arrogant little dwarf-devils were dreaming of empire, Brendan thought.

But he was up here on a hunting trip, and not in any rush to join an army again. The bars and brothels of Harbin still beckoned, and he still had a pocketful of Mexican silver dollars.

Brendan looked up with interest as a commotion arose at the door. Newcomers? That might liven up the evening. He heard the creak of wheels in the courtyard and some confused shouting as the Chinese boy who was the coolie-of-all-work went running out to see to the animals, the parrot squawking his one Chinese phrase—"Shut the gate! Shut the gate!"—and then the sound of footsteps. In the next moment three people appeared in the doorway.

Brendan was fascinated. Not by the little Manchu with the felt hat—he was too common a type to hold any interest at all—but by the other two.

White men. Or rather, a man and a woman. A young woman.

The man was startlingly good-looking. Something Slavic about the cheekbones . . . Russian probably, but not one of your peasant types; no, not with that casually arrogant way of carrying himself and the cool look in his eyes. There was good breeding there: you didn't acquire that lord-of-the-manor attitude overnight. He was a refugee, most likely, on his way to Harbin one step ahead of the Bolshevik secret police. Join the rest of the crowd, my fine lad, Brendan thought, you won't find an easy time of it in Harbin.

Not that Brendan cared. He felt himself instantly envious of the man, for the sake of the girl who was with him, looking up adoringly into his face. Proper little beauty she was, even in that Chinese peasant's outfit. Brendan preferred the tight-fitting, slit skirt *cheongsam*, which made the Shanghai bargirls look so appealing. But this girl possessed a vivid dark loveliness that fairly leaped out at you, and an exciting promise of sexual fire. You didn't see many girls like that around here. Few white women at all, as a matter of fact; and certainly not that kind.

He prepared to be friendly, however, and reserve judgment as they approached the table. The young woman smiled shyly, and he grinned back, hoping she would sit down beside him. But no such luck. Her companion, in a swift, smooth gesture, was pulling out a chair for her on the opposite side of the table and helping her to sit down.

Brendan couldn't help chuckling to himself. He knew he would have done exactly the same thing if the situation were reversed. He began to like the man a little more, seeing a chink in his armor: a flash of the jealous male protecting his property. It was an emotion Brendan could easily identify with, and it made the man a little more human.

Hao came over to the table, bowing politely with his palms pressed together. "Welcome to the Inn of the Green Parrot," he said in English. "I am the innkeeper. My name is Hao."

"How do you do." As Brendan suspected, the man was Russian, but he spoke excellent English. He introduced himself and the girl with him, whom he referred to as his wife, and the Manchu, who was called Cha Ho.

"I hope you will be comfortable here," Hao said formally. "Although I am only the humble native of a troubled province in the center of a civilization that crumbles and decays through sheer antiquity, I am honored by the privilege of your presence in my humble surroundings, and it is my hope—"

"For the love of Christ, Hao," Brendan said with disgust, interrupting the speech, "will you get these people something to eat? Save the bleeding introductions for later!"

"Yes, yes, of course."

"Any partridges left?"

"Yes, more than enough. I will see to it."

As he scurried away, Brendan shook his head. "They'll let you drop with starvation while they bow you to death around here. You're in a strange and heathen land, there's no doubt of that."

Nicholas laughed and extended his hand, introducing himself, and Brendan lazily shook hands and gave his own name. Then he yelled after Hao's retreating back, "And bring another bottle of wine and some cups, damn it, we're running low out here!"

"Yes, yes," the answer came floating back.

Within moments the boy came to the table with a tray of cups and wine.

"What is this?" Nicholas asked, after taking his first sip. "I didn't expect it to be hot."

"Kaoliang wine, heated and spiced. Be careful, it has a kick to it."

"Thank you, I will." Nicholas smiled. "You seem to know this country quite well."

"Aye, that I do. Been out here a few years. A man learns his way around after a while."

"In that case, perhaps you can answer a question for me."

"I'll do my best." In spite of himself, Brendan was flattered. He hitched his belt. If he didn't know the answer to the question, he would make it up.

"What is the purpose of the silver mirror over the back doorway? It doesn't seem to reflect anything."

Brendan grinned. As it happened, he did know the answer.

Daria refrained from giving Nicholas a puzzled glance. She was following the English with difficulty, but she was understanding Nicholas better than the bald-headed man, who spoke with an unfamiliar lilt. She had understood Nicholas's question, and wondered why he'd asked it. He knew very well what the mirror was for. Captain Li had explained on board the *Kwan Yin*. It was to frighten away fêng shui, who flew through the door in a straight line, saw their own terrible demon faces reflected in the mirror, and flew straight out again.

But Nicholas was listening with attentive interest to the man's identical explanation as though he'd never heard it before. The man was visibly pleased to be treated as an expert on local customs, and was going on to explain the purpose of the k'ang, and how it was heated with bricks in the winter. You could almost see him grow expansive. What a simple form of flattery, she thought, and yet how effective, instead of establishing yourself and your own competence in the first few moments.

She began to have an inkling of why Nicholas had been successful in business in Kharkov.

Then she stopped listening to the conversation as she stretched luxuriously in the chair. No jolting, no creaking—that oxcart was certainly harder on your bones than the deck of the river steamer! She thought of the narrow rutted track they had traveled, that led through marshes, woods, and villages. After a while she had become too occupied with the scenery, and the jolting oxcart, to worry about bandits. They'd passed over picturesque little wooden bridges, arched over rushing streams like paintings on silk screens, and slept under the stars on blankets. But Nicholas's arms were always around her, keeping her safe . . .

And on the next day she'd glimpsed the flash of a raven's wing in the treetops, heard the rustle of twigs in the underbrush as a hare leaped to startled safety . . .

But she was grateful to be here, at the inn, under a roof. To Daria, it meant sanctuary. A refuge. And the innkeeper's name was the same as Cha Ho's ox: Hao. It meant Good. Surely these walls were safe.

She tried to dismiss the uneasy memory of the stockade and the gate and the slightly sinister green parrot in its wicker cage hanging by the door. She had taken an immediate dislike to the parrot. Silly, she thought. Why should anyone dislike a bird?

But now dinner was arriving. It smelled wonderful. The bald-headed man, whose name she hadn't quite caught, was pouring more wine into her cup, and she thanked him before starting to eat, realizing how hungry she was.

After the meal was over and the dishes were cleared away and the men were sitting back smoking their cigars —Nicholas had offered his own, which the man accepted with alacrity, insisting on paying for the next round of drinks in return—she began to feel sleepy. No more wine, she decided, or she would fall asleep right here in this chair, with her head on the table.

Not that the men were likely to notice. They were absorbed in their conversation. She made one more effort to follow it. They were talking about bandits.

"Watch out for the Stone Dragon," Brendan was saying.

"I've heard that name before."

"Aye, Shih Lung is a notorious name around here. The village mothers scare their children with it."

"You don't seem very frightened."

Brendan laughed, and patted the stock of his rifle, on the chair behind him. "With my friend along, there's nothing much to worry about. They terrorize the villagers, those hunghutze, but they're a pretty cowardly lot when they come up against a man with a rifle." Brendan grinned. "Of course, for hunting bandits, this rifle isn't as good as the Springfield."

"American rifle?"

"Aye. Good weapon, the Springfield; I used it in Mexico. Can't beat it for accuracy and sighting."

"When were you in Mexico?"

"Nineteen ten. I fought with Francisco Madero until he got himself killed. Then I joined up with Pancho Villa."

He'd had to leave Belfast in a hurry that year, on the overnight steamer for Glasgow, with the police hot on his heels. There'd been a bit of trouble with Barclay's Bank—a few gunshots, bank guard grazed in the leg— nothing to speak of, but it was best to leave the country for a while. So he'd sailed down the Clyde on a freighter one pouring rainy night in 1910, cold and shivering, and ended in Vera Cruz.

"And after Mexico?" Nicholas asked, looking interested.

"Vladivostok, in 'thirteen."

Vladi, that stewpot of drunken Russian officials, drinking and card-playing army officers, counterfeiters, fur trappers and gold prospectors.

"That's when I met Chang Tso-lin," Brendan added. "The Old Tiger."

"Oh yes. The Manchurian warlord."

"Aye. We were both working for Japanese Army Intelligence then—it was after the war broke out."

"So then you came back with Chang to Manchuria."

"That I did." Brendan sighed contentedly. "Now, though, I'm on a hunting trip. No need to work for a while. I've still got plenty of Jap money in my pocket."

"So we have you to thank for the partridges." Nicholas smiled. "I wish I had a gun of my own; I'd come with you tomorrow."

Brendan looked regretful. "Too bad, I only brought the one." He shook his head. "I tell you, man, the hunting around here is magnificent. Just close your eyes and squeeze the trigger and the ducks fall right in your lap."

What a boring conversation, Daria thought. All about guns and war and shooting. She yawned.

"Are you sleepy?" Nicholas asked softly. "Would you like to go to bed?"

"Yes, I think I would."

"The boy will bring you a tub of hot water so you can bathe."

That was a wonderful thought. After splashing in those icy-cold streams along the road, she longed for a hot bath. But first she had a more urgent need. "Where do you suppose—" she began.

Brendan guessed her question.

"If you're wondering about the facilities," he said, "they're in a little shed out in the back. But don't expect too much."

Nicholas laughed ruefully. "We haven't been used to luxury, I can assure you. We've been traveling for a long time."

222

"That's good. Because what you'll find here is a hole in the ground."

Daria didn't care. First she would bathe, she thought, and then she would climb onto the k'ang and pull up the quilt, and then she would fall asleep and leave the men to their cigars and their talk.

But as she said good night and turned to leave the room, she had the sudden irrational fear that she would dream about green parrots. She told herself she was being a fool. Thank God, she repeated firmly in her mind, thank God for this safe haven. Stop being a superstitious peasant. Nothing bad will happen here.

She had almost convinced herself by the time she went through the doorway.

Chapter 20

"Keep your eyes on the Japanese," Brendan was saying. Clouds of cigar smoke were moving on the air. Spilled wine made gleaming puddles on the table. The Chinese men on the k'ang against the opposite wall, had grown quiet and sleepy. They would retire soon to their room. The kerosene lanterns hung around the walls were casting flickering red shadows in all four corners of the room, and the parrot in its cage outside the door was asleep with its head under its wing beneath a flowered cotton cloth.

"The Japanese are the ones to watch," Brendan went on. "Ye may not like them, but don't make the mistake of ignoring them. They pull a lot of strings in this country. They own railways and mines, and they keep an army here."

"I've heard the rumor that Chang Tso-lin is a puppet of the Japanese."

"That may be so. Aye, there may be truth in that story." Brendan nodded judiciously. He was very drunk, Nicholas thought, but he was holding it well. Only a thickening of his voice, and a slightly glassy look in his eyes, gave him away. He was still making sense.

Nicholas himself was drinking in moderation, just enough to keep the other man company. He was finding the conversation interesting. Along with the rambling, entertaining, often obscene anecdotes the Irishman told, were many useful bits of information. Since Daria had gone to bed, Brendan's conversation had taken a ribald turn.

Now he had launched into an exceedingly vulgar but amusing story about stealing Mongol ponies from a corral guarded by savage Mongol dogs. The brutes were blood-thirsty and vicious, but they had one weakness: they had a taste for human excrement. So you fooled them into thinking they had a treat in store by assuming the proper squatting position on the ground and creating the appropri-ate sound effects.

The Chinese men on the k'ang, half understanding, were beginning to giggle.

When you stood up and the dogs rushed over, sniffing for their prize, Brendan went on to explain, you had to move fast toward the corral. But the dogs quickly discov-ered the trick. So you repeated it. More crouching down, more sound effects. The stupid animals were fooled again, nosing around on the spot you'd left. This had to go on every few steps, over and over, run and squat, run and squat, until you'd reached the fence and could unlatch the gate.

Encouraged by his appreciative audience on the k'ang, Brendan was making his pantomime very vivid. You couldn't help laughing, the man was funny.

"And the moral of that story is," Brendan concluded, pouring more wine, "that it never pays to eat shit."

"In any way."

Brendan glanced at him shrewdly. "Damn right. Keep your bloody self-respect, whatever you do. The Chinks will respect you for it. Don't lose face." He sat back and belched thoughtfully. "Face and squeeze. The two great principles of life in the East."

"Squeeze is bribery?"

"Aye. Way to do business around here."

"Anywhere, I think." Nicholas smiled. "Methods of do-ing business don't seem to change very much from country to country."

Brendan said nothing for a moment. He drew slowly on his cigar, exhaling a cloud of smoke. Then he leaned for-ward with his elbows on the table, ignoring the fact that he was resting one elbow squarely in a puddle of wine.

225

"You know, I like you," he said. "Didn't think I would when ye first came in. Wrote ye down in me mind as one of them sniffy bastards who wouldn't give ye the back of his hand." His brogue had grown thicker as the night progressed. "But I was wrong." He chuckled. "In spite of the fact that ye're not drinkin' enough to keep yer throat wet."

Nicholas refilled his own wine cup from the bottle.

Brendan grinned approvingly. "Ye may do all right in Harbin," he said. "If ye keep yer nerve and use yer head. I think ye've got brains. Any jackass can pull a trigger. But a clever set of brains is harder to find."

Nicholas made a noncommittal answer, playing for time as he turned over in his mind exactly how far to trust this man.

He was obviously an adventurer and a mercenary, and not always on the right side of the law. Besides that, he was a crony of Chang Tso-lin, and like many of the Chinese warlords, Chang was said to be a former bandit.

Could you depend on this man's word? Nicholas wondered. Was he honest? Or would he say one thing and do another, concealing his greed at the hint you might have something worth stealing?

Nicholas hadn't liked the way he'd looked at Daria when they first came in. But he'd been perfectly respectful since then, not giving offense in any way.

And the man was obviously tough and experienced, afraid of nothing. A good man to have on your side in a fight.

But most of all, Nicholas was depending on his own instinct. He'd relied on the captain of the river steamer in the same way, and Li had not betrayed him. Sometimes you had nothing to go on but that inner voice, that deep irrational instinct that said gamble, take the risk, this man will be all right.

Brendan raised his wine cup. "A toast," he said. "*I loh ping an*. May your road be peaceful."

"Thank you. But I'm afraid that from here to Harbin, my road may not be peaceful." Nicholas set down his cup, making up his mind. "The peddler, Cha Ho," he said, "is afraid of hunghutze. He told me after dinner that he's returning to the north, tomorrow evening. He won't continue."

"I see. So ye're on yer own."

"It appears that way."

Brendan narrowed his eyes, waiting for Nicholas to say more. When he didn't, the Irishman remarked, "The peddler's no kind of escort anyway. What could he do, in case of attack?"

Nicholas only shrugged. He reached into his pocket, removed the small Italian revolver and set it on the table.

Brendan glanced at the weapon. "That won't do ye much good either," he said after a moment. "Not from a distance. Bandits always attack from the trees, or the kaoliang stalks, or the marsh grass. Ye need a rifle."

"How about yours? Is it for sale?"

Brendan laughed. "Offering to buy my gun?"

"On a temporary basis. Along with your services, of course."

"Well. That's an interesting proposition." He cleared his throat. "But why should I accept? Because I like yer face?" He sat back with his thumbs in his belt. "In other words, me friend, what can ye pay?"

The crucial question. Nicholas decided to lie temporarily, for the sake of prudence. "I'll write you a promise to pay. Name your price. I have friends in Harbin who will back me up."

"Do ye now!" Brendan threw his head back and laughed. "How drunk do ye think I am?"

Nicholas only smiled and said nothing.

Finally Brendan leaned forward again. His face sobered. "I like yer style," he said. "Ye could have done this another way. Hell, man, I'm going back to Harbin day after tomorrow. Ye could have just delayed and wasted time and waited till I was ready to leave, and then come tagging along, hanging on my coattails. I wouldn't have said a word, mainly for the sake of the lady. But ye didn't do that. Ye saw that I was a professional, and ye looked me in the eye and offered to pay. Fair and square, like a man should do. So I say fine. Come along." He extended his hand across the table. "We'll settle the price in the city. If ye trust me."

"Yes, I trust you."

Brendan grinned crookedly. "Seems as though you've hired a bodyguard."

They shook hands across the wine-smeared table.

Brendan emptied the last drops of wine into his cup with a regretful sigh. "Mind you," he added, "I'll not give up my hunting. I promised myself a last day in the marshes, and I intend to keep my word. It's what I came for."

"Fine. We'll wait here at the inn. We need the rest anyway."

"I'll be gone by sunup, and back by sundown. D'ye fancy roast duck for dinner?"

Nicholas laughed. "Very much. But I wonder if you'll be awake at dawn."

"Hao knows what to do. He comes into the room and pours a bucket of cold water on my head. Never fails."

On that note they rose to their feet and said good night. Drum, the Gordon setter, woke up and yawned, stretching his paws. The wine was gone; Hao and his boy were asleep; the Chinese men had disappeared into their room. The evening was over.

Nicholas entered his own small room, past the skin hanging in the doorway, down the short dirt corridor, and through the flimsy wooden door. Daria had left the lamp burning for him, with the wick turned low, but she was asleep on the k'ang. All he could see was her dark hair spread across the pillow. He began to undress very quietly. It was too late for a hot bath, he thought, he would have to wash in cold water. But there would be time for a bath tomorrow. It was just as well to have no plans tomorrow. The last few days had been hard; not so bad for himself, on horseback, but hard for Daria in that jolting oxcart.

He glanced around the room. It was tiny and without windows, just big enough for the k'ang, a crude little table with the water basin, the towels, and a china chamber pot painted with pink roses. The saddlebags made a shadowy heap in the corner on the floor beneath a shelf containing some tallow candles and a broken lantern. The shelf was thick with dust. Hao was a good cook, but his housekeeping left a lot to be desired.

When he was undressed and had washed in the basin, he eased himself under the quilt. The k'ang was comfortable, considering it was made of bricks. But there was another quilt beneath him. And after sleeping on the ground for two nights, even with blankets, this was luxury.

He stretched, feeling Daria comfortingly warm beside him. She was wearing a thin woolen nightgown. What a relief to be out of your clothes. Fortunately the weather had been good. He suddenly wondered what date it was. He hadn't seen a calendar in a long time, and a newspaper was a modern invention that no one had ever heard of in these parts. It must be July, he thought. He'd heard somebody say it was the Lotus Moon, probably Cha Ho.

He yawned, feeling sleepy, until Daria murmured and moved against him and he felt a swift upsurge of desire. But she was sound asleep.

He drew her closer and pulled up the nightgown. She protested slightly, still not waking up, until he drew the nightgown over her head and dropped it on the floor. Then she opened her eyes and smiled up at him sleepily. "How was your conversation?"

"Fine. Very interesting."

"Would I have liked it?"

"I don't think so."

"That's good. Because I was so tired . . ." She sighed and nestled in his arms. Then she raised her face. "Mmm, you taste of wine. It's making me drunk just to kiss you . . ."

Her conversation trailed off into small sighs and murmurs. They began to explore the deliciously familiar ways of pleasing one another, postponing by unspoken agreement the final moment of surrender and conquest, waiting until her need to be taken was as fierce and urgent as his need to thrust and conquer.

Nicholas wondered briefly if they could be heard. The walls were thin. Not that he was concealing their relationship, but he hadn't liked the first look on the Irishman's face when they'd entered the inn, and it was never wise to arouse another man's lust too openly. Particularly when the other man had no woman of his own. They would be traveling together soon.

But the Irishman was two doors away, and he was undoubtedly sprawled across his k'ang in a cloud of wine fumes, in a drunken sleep. Nicholas brought his mind back to Daria. He heard her moan of surrender, and they began to take the first steps toward that final, shocking moment of reversal when she became the master and not the slave, and he was conquered and would surrender in his turn.

Everything else was forgotten.

In the morning he woke to find bright clear sunshine and the clucking of hens in the courtyard and the smells of breakfast drifting out from the kitchen. He'd slept late, he realized, much later than he usually did. Daria was already dressed and out in the common room having her breakfast. He could hear her attempting to communicate with Hao in halting English, with a great deal of laughter on both sides. He remained in bed for a few lazy moments, staring at the ceiling with his arms folded under his head, thinking about nothing in particular, until the boy brought in his tub of hot water. Then he bathed and shaved and dressed in a leisurely way, and paid the obligatory visit to the shed in the back.

It wasn't a place you'd care to linger with the morning paper, assuming you had a paper to read.

When he entered the common room, he was hungry; it seemed like a very long time since dinner last night. O'Reilly had left hours ago, Hao informed him, but he had promised to bring back ducks for the roasting pan.

"Did it take a bucket of cold water to wake him up?"

"Oh, yes! *Two* buckets! He was very angry!"

The innkeeper promised to bring breakfast in a few moments as Nicholas sat down at the table. The peddler, he said, had unhitched his ox and taken it down to the stream to be watered. The other guests had departed. Now he himself would go out to the kitchen. After kissing him good morning Daria returned to their room to read a book she'd tucked into the saddlebag. She'd read the book twice before, but reading material was in short supply. Everything was very peaceful.

Nicholas settled back to wait for breakfast.

He heard a sound and looked up. He saw that the young boy who tended the animals had come through the front doorway. He'd been holding a water bucket, but his hand was trembling and he'd dropped it onto the floor, spilling a few drops of bright silver water at his feet.

The parrot was suddenly squawking in its cage outside the door.

Hao, who had just come into the room from the back doorway, caught a glimpse of the boy's face. Forgetting whatever errand had brought him into the room, he went over to the boy and began to question him sharply.

Nicholas frowned at the flood of excited Chinese dialect that followed. He couldn't understand a word. The boy was pointing behind him in the direction of the stream, and his eyes were frightened, darting from side to side like a terrified rabbit's. You could understand that clearly enough.

Warily apprehensive, Nicholas called over the innkeeper. Hao came unwillingly.

"What's the trouble?"

"Very bad, I'm afraid." Hao looked pale. "Some men are coming to the inn. They're at the stream, watering their horses."

"What sort of men? Bandits?"

"No, not bandits." Hao blinked. "They're worse than bandits." His voice suddenly became high and resentful. "They are Cossacks," he burst out. "Bad, cruel men. Bandits can be bribed or bought off—some are only stupid peasants with broken weapons. But these men are soldiers, and they are cruel. For no reason!" The innkeeper's voice dropped to a whisper. "If they find the young lady, your wife, it might be a bad thing. She is very pretty."

"How many are there?"

"Six."

Six against three, Nicholas thought. To defend her. No, the innkeeper and the boy would be no use at all. Six against one.

It seemed his luck had turned again.

But they'd be here soon. He'd have to think of something very fast. Either that, or take the chance that the men were good-natured and friendly. It was a very slim chance. Especially when you remembered the look on the boy's face.

He was no longer interested in his breakfast. He stood up, almost knocking over the chair. "Keep the gate closed as long as you can," he said to Hao.

"They will be angry if I keep them waiting!"

"As long as you can."

He turned and strode through the skin-hung doorway and entered their room. Daria was stretched out on the k'ang, reading her book.

"Daria."

She looked up. She sat up and closed the book. "What is it? Is something wrong? What's happened?"

"Nothing. Yet." He deliberately made his voice calm. "Some Cossacks are approaching the inn. I don't want to alarm you, but I think it's best if you're not here when they arrive. Just as a precaution."

He wasn't deceiving her with his reassuring words. He saw her face turn slightly pale, but she only nodded and said calmly, "All right. Where shall I go? Into the courtyard? Perhaps the oxcart, under that pile of blankets—"

"No, they'll be sure to search the oxcart. It's the first place they'll look. They'll be hunting for weapons, of course, but that's not a safe place." He thought swiftly. "You'll have to take a chance on the road. Hao will unbar the gate to let you out. They're coming up from the south, from the direction of the stream, so go to the north. Don't stop until you've reached the bend in the road and are out of sight."

She nodded, big-eyed, studying his face.

"Wait by the side of the road for the peddler and the oxcart. I'll catch up with you after I've saddled Chaika."

"Suppose—suppose you don't?"

"Why shouldn't I?" He smiled down at her. "These men have no quarrel with me. But in case I'm delayed, don't return here to find me until you're sure the Cossacks have left. No matter how long it takes. Will you promise?"

"Yes . . ."

One more precaution. He took her by the shoulders. "If for any reason," he said, "you have to come back here and you don't find me"— She drew in her breath, but said nothing—"then I'll leave you something in the water trough. A leather pouch. Don't forget to look for it."

She nodded again, her eyes huge, biting her lip.

"But that's not likely." He bent his head and kissed her swiftly and hard. "All right. Hurry now. Go to the courtyard and tell Hao to open the gate, then run as fast as you can. I'll come and get you soon."

When she had left the room after a last anxious glance into his face, he made himself relax by breathing deeply, then went over to the saddlebag and found the leather jewelry pouch hidden in the tea canister. He added most of his gold pieces to it, then tied the pouch firmly by its leather strings. Then, after slipping it into his pocket, he tucked the revolver into his other pocket.

The gun would do him no good, not now, and it might cause trouble. He'd have to do without it from now on.

No time to carry out the saddlebags. He'd have to make some conversation with the Cossacks before he took his leave.

He went through the common room and out into the sunny courtyard. Chaika was tethered in a corner of the yard, quietly cropping the few blades of grass that survived in the muddy ground. Hao was just rebarring the gate. Daria had left, then. She would be on her way down the road. Thank God.

Cha Ho was here, he saw, hitching up his ox. The peddler looked pale and frightened, and was obviously about to leave. Good. Nicholas wondered if his own face betrayed his tension. If only she had reached the bend in the road, and was out of sight.

He could hear hoofbeats now, outside the gate, and a whinnying of horses, angry shouting, and a pounding of fists against wood. They were here, demanding to be let in. And they were not in a very amiable mood.

The parrot was squawking in its cage again. Damn that bird. Can't somebody stop that racket?

Calm down.

Swiftly he removed the leather pouch and the revolver from his pockets and tossed them into the water trough. They sank to the bottom, invisible in the muddy water. The Cossack horses had already been watered at the stream, he thought, and so had Cha Ho's ox, and the trough was filled to the brim. It should be all right.

He went to Chaika and began to stroke the animal's mane, with his back turned to the gate. Hao was unbarring it now, screaming that he wàs moving as fast as he could. The parrot was in a furious rage, hopping up and down and making its cage swing back and forth.

Then the gate was open. The courtyard was suddenly

filled with horses and men, angry curses, complaints about the delay, and loud comments on the disgusting appearance of the yard.

"You stinking son of Han, what's in that cart?"

One of them had noticed Cha Ho.

"Only peddler's goods."

Nicholas heard the squishing noise of hoofs in mud as the Cossack approached the peddler. Then a loud crash; some of the tinware had gone tumbling to the ground. "Pull away those blankets, goddamn you, and let's see what's in that cart! What have you got there? Hunghutze rifles?"

"No, no, nothing like that."

"Well, move fast, or you'll feel this whip across your back!"

"Krylovsky, what's going on here?"

A pleasant tenor voice had spoken, edged with the hard steel of authority. Still with his back turned, Nicholas bowed his head. The icy certainty came over him that his luck, indeed, had turned against him. Because he knew that voice. There was no mistaking it. He continued to stroke the warm, velvety nose of the gray-and-white mare, but he clenched his jaw and stared down at the ground, breathing silent thanks that Daria had made her escape.

"Tell this peddler to hitch up his ox and get out of here. After you've searched the cart. The inn is full. No more guests."

"Yes, sir. But what about the one over there, Major?"

"Oh, yes. In the corner. Who is that?" A throat-clearing and a neigh from the horse. "You, there! Turn around!"

Nicholas turned around slowly and looked up to see, as he knew he would, the lean and handsome face of Dimitri Chernov staring down at him from the back of his mount.

The major drew in his breath. His eyes widened. His knuckles tightened on the reins. "Well," he said, and triumph flared in his hot and restless eyes, "I believe this gentleman can stay. Yes, I'm sure of it." He leaned forward across the saddle. "I have a feeling," he said softly, "that we have a lot to talk about."

Chapter 21

Major Chernov entered the inn, banging the parrot cage with the flat of his hand as he went by, making the bird squawk with fury. Inside the door he came to a halt, stripping off his riding gloves and looking around the room with taut satisfaction. Volchin was sitting on the k'ang with his rifle across his knees. Ryakov and Grigorovitch were leaning casually against the back doorway with their arms folded across their chests. Tuvorin was lounging here by the front door, equally casual, equally watchful. And Krylovsky was on sentry duty at the gate, to make sure there were no interruptions.

Excellent, he thought.

Here inside there were only the innkeeper and his boy.

And Chernov's quarry.

He stared under half-lowered eyelids at the man who was sitting at the table. He noted wary apprehension in the long-lashed blue eyes, and a set, hard look to the handsome jaw. But he observed no other signs of tension. Graceful posture. Straight shoulders. Steady hand holding a match to a cigarette. Casual ease, waving out the match, dropping it to the floor, crossing one ankle on his knee. But Chernov was not fooled.

He had come to this inn at exactly the right time, he thought. It was more than he'd hoped for. Destiny. He felt another surge of triumph as he tucked his gloves into his belt, raised his hand to his mouth and stroked his mustache, hiding the smile of pleasure that curled his lips.

He'd been waiting to meet this man again. He'd been thinking about it ever since that day in Siberia, last winter, when his quarry had escaped on the train. This time it would not be so easy.

This time Chernov would have things his own way. *As I would have then, if you hadn't been so clever,* he whispered silently to the blue-eyed man at the table.

But Chernov was in no hurry. He had time to think about it, he told himself. First there would be a game of stalk and pounce.

He glanced again at the strong, shapely throat visible above the open collar of the man's shirt, the muscular, tanned arms, the broad shoulders, and the lean hips, and thought idly that you never remembered exactly what a man looked like when you'd only seen him once. Of course it had been winter, that first time, and he had been dressed in winter clothes. Overcoat, gloves, fur hat.

He strolled over to the table, pulled out a chair, and sat down opposite the man, who only glanced at him with mild interest.

Very good. He was willing to play the game. Chernov decided to open the conversation. "It's thirsty work, riding all day," he said pleasantly.

"Did you leave from Harbin?"

Very nice smile. Even teeth. Yes, Chernov had remembered that. "Yes, three days ago. The city's a sewer. But what can you do, one needs money to carry on a war, and Harbin is the only place to get it." Chernov stretched in the chair and looked around the inn. "I'm ready for a decent meal," he remarked, "before getting back to Siberia."

"So you're going back above the border?"

"Eventually." Chernov smiled. "There's always time for a little detour. The war will wait. It's not going anywhere." A small silence fell. Then Chernov asked, "Do you happen to have another cigarette?"

"Yes, of course."

Nicholas offered his box of cigarettes, and Chernov helped himself. Volchin immediately got up from the k'ang, swaggered across the room, and struck a match.

As he turned to go, Chernov murmured, "Stay here for a minute, Volchin." Then he addressed himself to Nicholas. "I wonder if you know my name."

Nicholas shrugged. "No, I don't believe so."

You're a liar, Chernov thought. But how well you lied. Without a flicker of an eyelash. And with what cool indifference. "What's your business at the inn?"

"Just a traveler."

"For what purpose?"

"I don't know if it's necessary to tell you that." Nicholas inspected the ash of his cigarette. "Or if it's any concern of yours."

"But it might pay you to answer."

After a pause Nicholas said, "I think perhaps I won't."

"Why not?"

"Just on general principles."

So it was to be that sort of game, Chernov thought. His opponent would lose of course; the odds were against him. But it would make things more interesting. The major preferred an opponent with some fight. "I think," he said reflectively, "that I'll have to look at your identity papers."

Another small pause. Then, "I seem to have lost them," Nicholas remarked.

Chernov stubbed out his cigarette, making sure it was completely crushed. Then he murmured to Volchin, who had been standing by, waiting for orders, "Volchin, search him, will you? Find his papers."

Volchin went immediately to Nicholas's chair, looming behind him. "You. Stand up."

Nicholas remained seated.

"Stand up, I said," Volchin growled. "I won't tell you a second time."

"I'm sorry, did you say something?"

Volchin only snarled this time, and reached out his hand. Nicholas threw himself to one side, came up out of the chair and went into a crouch. After one surprised grunt, Volchin bared his teeth in a grin and came after him.

Chernov observed the scuffle coolly. Volchin wasn't having as easy a time as he'd expected. His opponent was quick, and he was using wrestling holds. They were evenly matched in height and weight. Volchin was obviously uncertain about whether to use his pistol. Now he was reduced to circling the other man warily, looking for an opening.

Finally Chernov sighed. "Grigorovitch, Ryakov—do you think you can put an end to this display of incompetence?" Grigorovitch weighed 250 pounds. That should tip the balance.

Finally Grigorovitch held Nicholas pinned by the arms while Volchin went through his pockets. Volchin, breathing hard, did it none too gently. He found the papers in Nicholas's shirt pocket and pulled them out triumphantly.

"Here you are, Major."

"In a minute." Chernov waved the papers away. He got up from the chair and strolled over to Nicholas, who was still being held by Grigorovitch. "What did you accomplish by that?"

"Obviously, nothing very much." He was catching his breath. "They seem to have been in my pocket all along."

"I suppose we'll have to look over your luggage. Just as a safety measure. You may have forgotten something else." He smiled thinly. "Commissars and Bolshevik spies are as thick as rats these days." He turned to Ryakov. "Search his room. Look for weapons."

"Yes, sir." Ryakov started for the back doorway, then hesitated. "Which one is his room?"

"Oh, for God's sake. Ask the innkeeper."

Ryakov nodded and disappeared.

"He's from Kharkov," Volchin announced suddenly. He'd been reading Nicholas's papers. "In the Ukraine. He must be a *svoloch,* Major. If he lived in the Ukraine."

"That doesn't necessarily follow." Chernov glanced casually at Nicholas. "And look at that straight nose. He's no Jew." He sketched a Semitic hooked nose in the air with his hand and then laughed. "Besides, I can smell a Jew when I come into a room. It's a talent of mine." He paused. "However. It's always best to make sure." He took a step closer to Nicholas, speaking very politely. "I'm sure you have no objection to our making sure."

Nicholas stared at him.

Chernov felt his amusement rising. He addressed him-

238

self silently to Nicholas: *you know what's coming, don't you?* But when he spoke aloud, his voice was crisp and businesslike.

"Lower your trousers."

Instant fury and outrage.

Chernov concealed his amusement. "Oh my dear man," he said lightly, "don't look so startled. It's a perfectly usual procedure. It only takes a moment." He paused again. "If you don't cooperate, we'll have to see for ourselves."

"Go to hell."

Chernov frowned. "You're behaving in a very suspicious way." He snapped his fingers. "Volchin, give me his papers."

Volchin handed them over.

"Now see if you can get this over with a little more quickly than you did before. With Grigorovitch to help you, of course."

Nicholas was already beginning to struggle violently.

Chernov walked over to the front door, where Tuvorin was leaning against the wall with his arms folded. He looked down at the papers. "You may have to give them some assistance, Tuvorin," he said absently. "The gentleman seems to be making rather violent objections."

"Yes, sir."

Tuvorin was a good man. Unemotional. Stolid. He'd carry this out in a very businesslike fashion. Chernov studied the papers as a new scuffle began by the table. It was taking all three to hold him down, apparently. But he only gave the scene a casual glance out of the corner of his eye. Grigorovitch had succeeded in forcing Nicholas into the chair, and had tied his wrists behind his back with a silk scarf. He'd also seen fit to stuff Volchin's rather grimy handkerchief into his mouth as a gag. Was that really necessary? Tuvorin had managed to get his trousers unbuttoned, in his usual methodical way, and yanked them down to midthigh. Dmitri had a quick glimpse of strong muscular legs and a flat, hard belly.

Above the gag, the blue eyes were blazing with fury and hatred.

"Not a *svoloch*, Major," Tuvorin reported.

239

"No, I thought not. All right, release him. Take that ridiculous handkerchief out of his mouth. And Tuvorin, come back over here."

Chernov remained by the door for a few moments, pretending to read. Let the man compose himself, he thought. He continued to speak to Nicholas in his mind. *It's too bad this little indignity made you so angry, my friend. But you'll be more than angry when it's my turn. When I have you stripped naked and prepared for the lash. Then it will be cold, crawling fear.*

He felt his own excitement rise at the prospect. He visualized the scene that was to come and forced himself to be patient.

He gazed down again at the papers. Strange, they had been born in the same year. Nicholas in early April; himself in early June. Two months apart.

He folded the papers neatly and walked back to the table. Nicholas, seated in the chair, was lighting another cigarette. He'd tucked in his shirt. His composure was restored. The blazing fury was suppressed. His hands were steady.

A remarkable display of self-control, Chernov thought admiringly. He was enjoying the game more every moment.

"Your papers," he said, holding them out. Nicholas took them silently and returned them to his pocket.

"Was it really necessary to make all that fuss? Over a procedure that happens every day? And as you see, it took no time at all. One would think you had something to hide."

"Suppose I'd been a Jew. What would have happened?" *Not a tremor in his voice. Admirable.*

"I'm sure you know. Various unpleasant things. Ending in only one way." Chernov sat down and stretched out his legs. "However, although you passed the inspection, I believe you may have some other disagreeable traits."

New wariness on Nicholas's part. The game had entered a new phase.

"For instance," Chernov went on, "you may be a liar." He twisted in the chair. His voice hardened. "And you may be too clever for your own good." He narrowed his

240

eyes. "For example, there was a certain matter of a railway bridge . . ."

Ah. You see, I remember. Did you doubt it?

But there was nothing. No reaction. Only a look of amusement on Nicholas's face. Chernov began to feel angry. The fear should be rising. There should be a display of emotion. Something.

"Do you really remember that unimportant incident, Major Chernov?"

"It's not likely I'd forget. *Nicholas Sergeievitch.*" He found himself staring across the table into intensely blue eyes. His voice suddenly thickened. "You're not the sort of person one forgets very easily, my dear Inspector Engineer."

He hadn't intended to say that. Nor had he intended to use such an emotional tone of voice. He heard the sound of his own harsh breathing. Silence had fallen. The men were listening.

Ryakov broke the tension. He strode into the room from the back doorway. Dmitri looked up with relief, clearing his throat. "What did you find in his room?"

"Something peculiar, Major. In the saddlebags."

Now, suddenly, he saw a flash of alarm in Nicholas's eyes. Why? The look was gone instantly, but it had been there.

"Peculiar? In what way?"

"Women's clothes, Major. In one of the saddlebags."

"Women's clothes. I wonder why that is." He began to tap his fingers on the table. He gazed at Nicholas coldly. "Are you traveling with a woman?"

"No."

"Then why the clothes?"

"I'm bringing them to a friend in Harbin."

"A poor lie."

Chernov suddenly received a brilliant and charming smile from across the table. "My dear Dmitri Pavlovitch. You've searched my room, and you've searched my person. Have you found anything besides myself?"

The disarming smile and the friendly tone of voice were extremely disturbing. They made Chernov more angry than ever. He felt himself losing control.

241

His voice turned icy. "Who is the woman? Some stupid cow?"

Nicholas didn't answer.

Chernov leaned forward with both hands flat on the table. "Do you fuck her nicely?" He spoke through his teeth. "Does she like it? How often? Every night?"

"You can save yourself the questions," Nicholas said calmly. "I told you, I'm traveling alone."

"Then why the women's clothes?" He paused. "Do you like to dress up in skirts?"

"I explained that. I'm bringing the clothes to a friend in Harbin."

"Harbin has plenty of clothing stores. There are ten for every block on the Kitaiskaya."

"These have sentimental value. They belonged to the woman's dead sister."

"How quickly you lie."

"I'm sorry if you don't believe me."

"I know what a liar you are. From past experience."

"I think," Nicholas remarked, "that your lunch has arrived."

Chernov flung himself back in the chair, taking long breaths. He decided to drop the subject. There was obviously no one else in the inn. What did it matter? There was a foreordained end to this encounter anyway. And he, Dmitri Pavlovitch, was in full control of the outcome.

He began to feel better. His breathing slowed. He pictured again in his mind the final outcome. It was a very satisfactory vision. *You'll strip well, my arrogant friend. So far you've been handled very gently. Although you don't think so.* But having his wrists bound by Grigorovitch for that particular inspection, which he considered so outrageous, wasn't very drastic. Not compared to what Chernov had in mind. Did he suspect? Probably he did. Dmitri smiled to himself.

Hao and the boy were distributing food around the room. At the table, the innkeeper offered food to Nicholas, who shook his head. No, nothing to eat.

Wise, Chernov thought, observing Nicholas. He would be better off with an empty stomach. *He can spare himself some extra humiliation later on.*

He settled his shoulders. "Allow me to buy you some

242

wine, Kolya," he said. He felt relaxed again. "In memory of our first meeting in Siberia."

He could almost see Nicholas set his teeth at hearing the familiar form of his name. He could almost read his thoughts: *only my friends call me Kolya.* With a malicious little smile, he waited for Nicholas to make the remark.

But Nicholas smiled instead. "Thank you, I believe I'll accept."

All right, play the game, damn you. I can wait.

Chernov turned his attention to the food. The innkeeper served the wine, and for a while the conversation ended. Finally Chernov pushed aside his empty bowl and refilled his wine cup. "I'm surprised, Kolya," he said, "you haven't asked me yet about Striabin."

"How is Lieutenant Striabin?"

"Poor Grisha. Too bad about him. He had his privates shot off in a skirmish near Lake Hanka. Fortunately, he died. Knowing Grisha, he wouldn't have wanted to live under those conditions."

There was a silence. Then Nicholas remarked, "People sometimes want to live under any conditions."

Chernov felt a sudden swift leap of speculation. Was this an overture? Was that arrogant resistance starting to crumble? Perhaps, he thought, after this is over—if I let you live—we'll be on another footing. But first Federovsky would have to learn a little discipline.

"I wonder if you're one of them," he said. "Those who want to live."

Nicholas didn't answer.

"But we'll find out, won't we?" He used a pleasant tone of voice, but the threat was unmistakable.

Nicholas gave him an even stare. "Just what did you have in mind, Major Chernov?"

Damn you. You called me Dmitri before.

"Since it concerns me rather intimately," Nicholas added, "I'd be interested to know."

"I haven't made up my mind yet." Chernov smiled. "It all depends on you."

"In what way?"

Chernov suddenly felt a savage, impatient anger. Let's stop this fencing! he thought. He was tired of the game. He was tired of having Nicholas thwart and defy him.

They could settle it right now. After they established how it would be—in the necessary way. That couldn't be avoided. *So you'll understand, Kolya, as the other men do, who is in command, and learn to submit. We can proceed from there . . .*

"You understand that I haven't forgotten your treacherous behavior at the railway bridge." He paused. "But I'm willing to overlook it. After a certain . . . apology."

"What does the apology consist of?"

"I'm sure you can guess."

"I'm very grateful to you," Nicholas said drily.

"And then I'm willing to make you an offer."

"What offer is that?"

"To come and join me."

"You must be joking."

"No, I'm serious. Join me up north. In Siberia."

"I'm no soldier."

"Remain a civilian, then. Choose what title you like. I could use a cool head to advise me, among these firebrands."

No. He was about to be refused. Nicholas was smiling ruefully. "Do you really suppose I'd consider an offer like that?"

Yes, if he knew the stakes. Chernov would make them very clear. "If it meant the difference between life and death, perhaps you would."

"And be forced to make apologies to you all my life? No thank you, Dmitri. I don't submit to authority very well."

Stubborn. Maddening. What would it take to persuade him? *No, Dmitri. Control this red haze of anger that's moving across your mind. Calm yourself. Wait.* "I thought you cared about your life."

"I do. I suppose most of us, given the choice, would prefer life to death."

Would we? Chernov suddenly stared off into space. He felt his hands clench themselves into fists. Was life so sweet for most people? Why? Not for him. It never had been. He wondered why they cared so much. Why they struggled and screamed so much just before the end. He'd watched them die, over and over, and heard them plead wildly for their lives, and wondered what it was they found so valuable.

He returned his gaze to Nicholas. "Then why do you refuse me so fast?"

"Your price is too high, Dmitri."

Still defiant; still unbending.

After a moment he said softly, "You've made a very poor choice."

No answer.

"I advise you to change your mind."

"There's nothing you can threaten me with. Except physical force."

"Don't look so scornful. It's very effective."

A charged and heavy silence settled over the room.

Finally Chernov reached down to his belt and unhooked the lanyard ring of his pistol. He looked down at the dull blue finish of the gun, hefting it, liking the heavy feel of it in his hand. Nicholas was watching him closely.

He broke open the gun and spilled the cartridges onto the table. Then he picked one up, stared at it thoughtfully and dropped it into the cylinder. He closed it and spun the cylinder with this thumb.

"Do you ever try games of chance?" He held out the pistol on his palm.

"I thought that kind of roulette had gone out of fashion. Even among Cossacks."

"I play it quite often." Chernov shrugged carelessly. "I always win." He narrowed his eyes. "Is your luck that good?"

"Right now it seems to be quite poor." Nicholas smiled. "You may lose one day."

"I never lose."

"You're very confident, Dmitri."

"Yes, I have fate on my side . . ." After a long moment Chernov opened the pistol again and reloaded the cartridges. Then he set it on the table by his right hand.

Nicholas crossed one ankle on his knee. "How is the war progressing?" he asked casually. "I've been deprived of a newspaper these past few weeks."

The war, Chernov thought. That bloody, unfinished business. More bitter than ever now. "The filthy Bolshevik murderers will pay for what they've done," he said bitterly. "The whole world knows them now for the savages they are."

The other five men growled assent around the room. Tuvorin began to curse long and fervently under his breath.

"What's happened?"

"Don't you know?" Chernov's mouth twisted. "They've murdered the Czar."

Nicholas looked up in genuine shock. "You can't mean it."

"The Czar, the Czarina, all the Grand Duchesses and the Czarevitch. Butchered like animals by the Bolshevik scum."

"But they were under house arrest in Ekaterinburg."

"And that's where they died. All of them. Shot to death, in the cellar of the house."

"Good Lord. That's monstrous."

"God save the Czar," Chernov muttered. "One of the Grand Dukes will take over. When we restore the throne."

"God save the Czar," the other men echoed in a ragged chorus around the room.

Chernov took a long breath. He passed his hand over his forehead. He pushed out of his mind the thought of the murderous outrage. Avenging the Czar could wait. He had something else to deal with right now. Something more immediately personal. It was time to bring this encounter to its fated conclusion. The waiting was over.

He raised his head. *No need for words, is there? You know the time has come. I can see it on your face.*

He picked up the pistol from the table.

"I'm suddenly very tired of this charade," he muttered. He stared across at Nicholas. "Your arrogance is beginning to sicken me, Nicholas Sergeievitch." He clicked off the safety catch of the gun and extended his arm, holding it out. "Say your prayers."

He saw a slight whitening in Nicholas's face, a widening of his eyes. But that was all. Nothing else? No pleas? No last request? No offers to bargain? No Dmitri, I've changed my mind?

Or did he know, after all, that Chernov wouldn't shoot. . . .

He lowered his arm. "Not this way."

"No, I thought not."

You son of a bitch. I'll break you yet. He turned his head. "Tuvorin," he said, "bring me the *tashur*." He clicked back the safety catch and replaced the pistol on his belt. Tuvorin walked over carrying the tashur, a thin bamboo whip in a leather handle. It was strong, supple, and dangerous.

Dmitri took the whip and tapped it against his fingers, considering.

"Seventy-five lashes," he said at last, taking satisfaction in Nicholas's surprise. Twenty-five was the usual punishment. Fifty was inhuman. Seventy-five, well, few men lived that long.

Nicholas stared down at the table. He wondered, for a weary and despairing moment, if this could have been avoided.

Suppose Daria and I had gone to Vladivostok, he thought. Suppose we hadn't been forced off the train at Khabarovsk. Suppose we hadn't stopped at the inn. Suppose . . . No, such speculation was fruitless. If you had an appointment with the Angel of Death, you kept it one way or another.

He had one last request to make. In case Chernov meant to carry out that seventy-five lashes—a death sentence. He'd hate to think of Daria returning to the inn to find a bleeding corpse covered with buzzing, crawling flies. It would make a hideous memory.

But he wouldn't do it. He wouldn't give Chernov the satisfaction of making the request. It was a sure way to bring about the worst. They'd hang him on the stockade post.

Maybe Hao would have the common decency to bury him.

"Take him outside," Chernov said carelessly. He glanced at the men. "Into the wood, outside the stockade. Strip him and tie him to a tree. You know what to do." He stretched in the chair. "Call me when you've done it. Don't take too long."

"Let's go, friend."

Grigorovitch's heavy hand fell on his shoulder. Nicholas tensed his muscles, wondering swiftly how much he could resist. But this time they anticipated him. Volchin appeared on his other side, grabbed his wrists and tied them behind his back with the silk scarf they'd used before.

The other three had already gone through the doorway. The parrot was squawking again.

"On your feet."

Then they were outside. It was a beautiful day. Sunshine. Cool breeze. That was something to be grateful for. Maybe, Nicholas thought, the breeze would keep the flies away. Chaika was there in the corner. Daria could ride her, if the mare wasn't stolen. And the Irishman could escort her to Harbin. He hoped she would remember to look in the water trough.

The gate was unbarred.

"Wait here," Grigorovitch said. He brought Nicholas to a halt inside the gate. His grip on Nicholas's arm was rough, but not unnecessarily so, considering his size and the victim's bound wrists. Volchin was standing a few paces to the left, lighting a cigarette. Neither one of them looked particularly happy.

They had been happy enough to carry out their instructions before, but a lashing was something else and they knew what it was like. They'd all felt the whip themselves. It made them uneasy. Who would be next?

But they would follow orders, Nicholas knew.

Maybe some day Chernov would be murdered by one of his men, he thought savagely. It helped to get angry. It pushed out the fear, and you didn't think so much about what was coming.

The fifth man, the one called Krylovsky, came back through the gate. "Found a tree, right at the edge of the road. Nice low branches."

"That didn't take long," Volchin said.

"Plenty of choice around here."

"Right, no shortage of trees!"

They all laughed, and Grigorovitch gave Nicholas a small shove. "Come on, we don't want to keep the major waiting."

Through the gate. Out onto the road. There was no sign of the oxcart. Or Daria. He thanked God she wasn't there, imagining Chernov's glee, forcing her to watch.

248

And then what? That didn't take much imagination. There were six of them . . .

Krylovsky, Tuvorin, and Ryakov had found a small clearing near the road, to the north of the inn. A spruce tree with low branches was growing at the far edge of the clearing. Tiny wood violets clustered around its base. Blue sky gleamed through the branches.

Two of the men were measuring off lengths of rope. They were matter-of-fact; they'd done this before.

"Do you need some help undressing?" Grigorovitch growled. "Or can you do it yourself?"

"If you'll untie my wrists."

"Hey, Volchin! Ryakov! Come over here and see he doesn't try anything!" As Grigorovitch yanked off the scarf from Nicholas's wrists, he muttered, "Make a run for it and you'll get your jaw broken."

"Better not do that, Grigorovitch," Ryakov observed as he approached with Volchin. "Don't break his jaw. Go for his kidneys. The major doesn't like people's faces messed up."

Sour laughter echoed from all three. Chernov didn't seem very popular with his men, Nicholas thought. He flexed his wrists and began to unbutton his shirt. Grigorovitch hawked noisily and spat on the ground.

"In the Novocherkassk barracks," he said in a low voice, "you didn't strip a man naked for a lashing. A bare back was good enough."

"Well, that's what Chernov wants. You know how he is."

Grigorovitch muttered something under his breath. "Hurry this up," he said to Nicholas.

Nicholas had taken off his clothes; they were in a neat pile on the ground. He took a deep breath, straightening his shoulders. The sun was warm across his back. Alive. A bird was chirping somewhere. Leaves were rustling. How long now? Tuvorin and Krylovsky were waiting by the tree. The other three were watching him closely. No chance.

"Listen," Grigorovitch said out of the side of his mouth, "if you're smart, you'll take a piss while you can. May save you some embarrassment later."

It was sensible advice, and Nicholas acted on it immediately.

249

Then they brought him to the tree, stretched out his arms and tied him by the wrists to the branches on either side. They made sure the knots were tight.

"Shall we tie his feet?"

"No, let him brace himself, Chernov wants this to last a while."

"All right. Call the major."

The bird was still chirping. The breeze was cool across his face, and there were no flies. He tried to move his wrists, but they'd done a professional job. He tried not to think about anything, to make his mind a blank. But his body was tensed. Waiting. He'd done everything he could, he thought. Hadn't he? Then: *Dear God, keep Daria away from here, that's all. Keep her away from Chernov.*

The major had arrived. He was walking over to the tree. Nicholas recognized the footsteps. He set his jaw and stared at the ground.

Chernov stopped by his side, and stood silently for a moment, tapping the handle of the tashur against the palm of his hand. Then he said softly, almost casually, "You know, I've been thinking about this for a very long time."

"You're lucky. Your dreams have come true."

"Defying me even now, I see. Is that all you have to say?"

"Just get on with it."

Chernov said nothing. He was deeply excited. This was a sight he had imagined over and over, and he could hardly believe in the reality.

He drew a long breath and stared at Nicholas's profile. What remarkably long eyelashes the man had. Surprising, in so masculine a face. What was he hoping to see? Humiliation, pleading, loss of dignity, a breaking down of defenses? But he saw none of those things. Only the simplest, most universal of human emotions. Fear of pain. Regret at dying.

Never mind, Chernov thought, he'll break before it's over.

He tested the ropes. Yes, they'd done a good job.

His gaze dropped to Nicholas's bare back. Unblemished. Smooth and lightly tanned, rippling with muscles—untouched. Well, not for long. Within fifteen minutes it would be different.

Like a ray of light through a fog, the thought came to him that he might be on the verge of committing an act he would regret for the rest of his life. He was about to destroy a unique and valuable personality, for no reason except his own whim and his own pleasure.

It wasn't too late. He could still change his mind. He could claim Nicholas had apologized, and have him cut down. Now, before things had gone too far . . .

No. No. The red fog closed in again, and the light dimmed in his mind. He'd waited too long for this satisfaction. He would not deny himself.

He stepped up close to Nicholas and spoke in a whisper. "Are you aroused by pain?"

"No."

"Are you sure?"

No answer.

"If not pain, then perhaps Krylovsky. He has the touch of a surgeon." Chernov paused. "He doesn't care to do that sort of thing, but he will if he's ordered." *Think that over.* "Shall I call him?"

"Do what you like." Nicholas's tone was coldly contemptuous. "What will you prove? Any skilled whore could do the same."

Chernov flushed angrily. No, that approach was doomed, he thought, feeling his facial muscles harden. The man was too sure of himself; he was not young enough to be uncertain. He was too self-confident, with too many years of sexual success behind him. A younger man would be easier to deal with, more easily shaken.

He turned away. "Volchin," he said, speaking through his teeth, "you first. When you're arm-weary, you'll pass the whip to Grigorovitch. We'll proceed from there."

"Yes, sir." Volchin began to strip off his jacket.

"Do you take your turn with the whip, Dmitri?" Nicholas muttered.

"No. I never carry out lashings myself."

"You only watch."

Enough. Enough. Chernov felt a savage surge of anger. He'd had enough of this man's cold, contemptuous arrogance. He could stand no more of it. He suddenly raised his arm, holding the tashur. He was about to break a rule. He was about to strike the first blow himself. The impulse was almost irresistible. But with a great effort, trembling, he fought it down. He lowered his arm.

Abruptly he walked away from the tree and handed the whip to Volchin, who was standing in his shirt sleeves. "Very well," he said thickly. "You can begin."

He lit a cigarette as he turned to face the tree. He stood very still.

Volchin made an experimental slash of the whip through the air. It made a sharp whistling noise. Then he flexed his shoulders, strode up to the tree, took his stance, and began.

Chernov watched silently, with intense concentration. After a while there was a rhythm to it, he thought. Always. The whistling, slashing noise, and the curious dull thud of bamboo meeting flesh, and the uncontrollable grunt as the man sagged against the tree, held upright only by his roped wrists. Otherwise, he hadn't made a sound. Blood was streaming down his legs and puddling on the ground.

How long would he last? If the men were careful, and not clumsy, and didn't sever tendons and expose the bone too soon . . . perhaps sixty lashes . . .

Whistle. Thud. A groan.

Stubborn. Defiant.

I've seen your kind before. You'll die without a word, damn you. . . . He felt a thickening in his throat. "All right, Volchin," he said suddenly, in a hoarse voice, "you're getting tired. Pass it on."

Chapter 22

Alive . . . yes . . . still alive . . . but the fiery pain was
blazing across his back like a bonfire, and a wave of sick
nausea swept over him again; he fell on one knee on the
road, half gagging with dust and pain. He'd done that before. Twice before. Three times before. He couldn't remember how many times. It was a hundred miles from the
clearing to the stockade. A thousand miles. A continent.
His legs were sticky-wet and crimson with his own blood,
and already the fever of delirium was raging in his body.

But it hadn't been seventy-five lashes of the tashur. No,
he wouldn't have lived through that. And when he moved
his shoulders, the pain was like fire, like seven hundred
licking tongues of flame; but it wasn't the pain of severed
tendons or ripped muscles. It was the screaming of tormented flesh—and flesh would heal.

Chernov had changed his mind. Nicholas could still hear
the strange, hoarse whisper of the major's voice, thick and
strangled, spewing out words, phrases, whispering in his
ear as Nicholas was cut down from the tree to kneel on
the blood-spattered ground. The remembrance made him
ill, and his stomach twisted with hatred and disgust, over-
riding the pain in his body. He'd stopped listening after a
while: Don't die, Kolya. I'll let you live . . . I want you
alive . . . I've changed my mind. Now that you understand
how it will be . . . now that you know. So that when we
meet again . . . in Harbin . . . it will be different. You
know it will . . . as I do . . . we understand each other now.

Yes, I'll be back in a month . . . maybe two. And we'll meet there . . . in Harbin. Promise it.

Oh, yes. I can promise you that, Dmitri. I've already promised myself.

"Can you hear me?"

"Yes."

"Do you promise?"

"Yes . . . I promise."

"Do you know where to find me?"

"I'll find you."

"Ask in the Metropolitan Café on the Kitaiskaya. They'll always know where I am." A pause. Harsh breathing. "Did you understand me?"

He nodded.

"Say it out loud. Repeat it."

"The Metropolitan Café . . . on the Kitaiskaya."

"Yes, that's it. Don't forget."

"I won't forget."

I promise you, Dmitri Pavlovitch, I won't forget. You should have killed me. That was your mistake.

He'd shut the rest of it out of his mind. There was more; on and on, a strange, disjointed babbling, half apology and half triumph, half regret and half feverish excitement. It was better not to listen.

Where were his clothes? He'd left them on the ground, in the clearing. After the shouting and the orders and the hoofbeats had faded away down the road, and Chernov and his men had departed, leaving him kneeling on the ground on the bloody grass, he'd stayed there for a while. He didn't know how long. And then he'd pulled himself to his feet and started to stumble up this dusty road. Back to the inn.

Suppose the gate is barred? Have to get in somehow. Some way. Pound. Shout. You can do that. If you have to.

First you have to stand up.

After a hellish age had gone by, half stumbling, half crawling, he came to the stockade. The gate was ajar. The Cossacks had left it open when they rode out of the courtyard, and apparently Hao and his boy had been too terrified to come outside and bar it again.

Into the courtyard.

It was empty now. The mules of the Chinese traders were gone, the Cossack mounts were gone, the peddler's ox was gone, O'Reilly and the dog were gone. There was only the parrot in its cage. And Chaika in the corner of the yard. And the hens, pecking and clucking around the door.

He fell on his hands and knees in the mud, gasping for breath. He knew he had to get up. There were flies in this courtyard, attracted by the animals and the dung, and now by the oozing, clotted blood that was blackening on his back. In a few minutes, if he didn't get up, he would be in torment.

Can't . . . make it . . . yet . . .

Buzzing of flies. Stink of mud. To his right was the water trough. Oily sheen of water. Pieces of straw floating on top. Underneath . . . the jewelry pouch? He wondered. *Later . . .*

He saw visions of flashing gems in front of his eyes. An emerald and diamond necklace. Green-and-white fire. He had bought that necklace in Kiev and paid too much for it. He'd needed the money for something else, but now he couldn't remember what.

Ah, yes. He'd gone to the Solovtsy Theater in Kiev that night with a business friend. They'd paid a visit backstage after the performance. He'd met the leading lady, a beauty with melancholy eyes and a magnificent, throaty voice. They'd spent the night together, one of those insane, abandoned nights that happen sometimes, when two people knew they would never see each other again. They'd exchanged only first names. She used a stage name, but her real name was—what was it?—Rachel. . . .

The next day, weary with lack of sleep and guilty at having betrayed Céline, he'd gone to a little jewelry shop off the Kreshchatik and bought the emerald and diamond necklace. Even after the bargaining, he'd paid too much, far more than he could really afford. But at home in Kharkov, Céline had been thrilled and delighted. She'd fastened it around her throat and flung herself across the bed wearing nothing but the necklace, and taunted him with wickedly tilted green eyes, daring him to be sorry he'd bought it. . . .

So of course he'd had to prove he wasn't sorry. . . .

Why remember that now? It was another world. Another life.

Daria, my love, I'm sorry.

Something cold was nosing in his armpit. Cold and wet. Silky fur. Rough tongue, licking his shoulder. Inquisitive canine growl. The cold wet nose against his face. He turned his head and saw the inquiring face of Drum, the Gordon setter, thrust into his own. The dog made a questioning whine. Nicholas sank back on his heels and buried his hand in the dog's furry neck. The rough tongue licked his wrist.

In the next moment there was a horse smell and splashing hooves and the creak of a saddle. Someone had ridden into the courtyard. Someone had dismounted.

"For the love of all that's holy, what happened to you?"

Footsteps squished in mud. A hard male hand fell on his shoulder.

O'Reilly was back.

"I seem to have . . . annoyed . . . some Cossacks."

Brendan squatted on his heels. He was silent for a while. Then he said, "Who was it?"

"Chernov. Dmitri Chernov."

"I should have known. He likes to use a Mongol tashur. I recognize the signs. Bamboo." He paused again. "Christ, man, you're a bloody mess. How bad is it?"

"I'm not sure."

"Well, let's get you inside and cleaned up and we'll take a look." Brendan rose to his feet. Then he frowned. "I'd carry you, but you're too heavy for me. Can you walk?"

"Yes . . . I think so, with some help."

When Brendan had gotten him inside the inn, into his room, and Nicholas had fallen face down on the k'ang, the sweat of his exertion streaking down through the oozing blood on his back, he was gasping, half-conscious.

Brendan strode out to find Hao. He located the innkeeper, cowering with his boy in the kitchen, and began to curse. Hao was the son of a rabbit. He was the spawn of a snake. He was a miserable turtle's egg. Why did he leave the man out in the courtyard? Never mind. Get busy. Hot water. Bandages. Ointment. Rubbing alcohol, you have some? Good. Kaoliang wine, make it two bottles. No, three. *Move,* or ye'll feel the back of me hand across the front of yer face.

"If you don't move fast," Brendan said ominously, "it will be *pu shang kao* with you. Understand? *Tung te mo?*"

Hao nodded. *"Tung te!* I understand!"

"Shang kao! That's fine! I'll give you two minutes." He held up two threatening fingers, and then left.

He sat down on a saddlebag in Nicholas's room as Hao came in with the basin of water and torn-up sheets for bandages, and lit a cigarette.

"Where's the wine?"

"The boy is bringing it."

"Let him drink the wine before you start."

Nicholas raised himself up painfully on one elbow.

"Drink the whole bottle," Brendan advised as the boy came in with the wine. "This is going to hurt."

Nicholas nodded, taking a bottle and tilting it up to his mouth.

"Give me one of those bottles," Brendan said to the boy. "I think I'm going to need it myself."

It hurt. You could see the white lines of pain on his face and hear the tiny whistle of indrawn breath as Hao cleaned up the blood and applied the alcohol. It was stinging torture, but necessary. You couldn't risk infection. Sure way to kill yourself. Especially out here, where there were no doctors, no hospitals. Brendan had seen men die from a flesh wound, just a scratch, when the wound got infected and swelled up and purpled, and the yellow pus began to ooze. It didn't take long. You died screaming with your own stink in your nose.

But this wasn't as bad as it looked. No permanent damage. There'd be fever for a couple of days, and bleeding for longer than that, and pain, a lot of it, but it would heal. It could have been worse. Considering.

Chernov. The worst of a bad lot. Half-mad. Maybe more than half. He was about finished; according to what you heard in Harbin, even his men couldn't stand him anymore.

"You'd better drink the second bottle," Brendan said. Hao was smearing ointment on Nicholas's back.

". . . need some food. Haven't eaten since last night."

"When you're finished, bring him something to eat," Brendan said to Hao.

The innkeeper nodded.

After Hao and the boy left, and Nicholas was wrapped in bandages, already slowly crimsoning with blood, he caught his breath for a few minutes. Then he looked over at Brendan. "I need to ask you a favor."

"What's that?"

"It's Daria. She should be back by now."

"That's right, man, where is she?"

"I sent her out before the Cossacks got here. Down the road. I told her to wait until they left."

"Just as well. They would have had some entertainment. You wouldn't have liked it much."

"That's what I thought, but . . . they've been gone for a while, and she isn't here." Nicholas finished the last of the wine and wiped his mouth with the back of his hand. "Will you go and look for her? Tell her it's safe now. Tell her I'm all right. I'd go with you, but . . ."

Brendan laughed shortly. "You'd fall off the horse. You'd better stay where you are. Get some sleep. I'll take a look around." He stood up, hitching his belt. "Which direction did she take?"

"North. The peddler went that way too. Maybe she rode on the oxcart."

"Right. I'll be back as soon as I can."

There was a small village to the north, Brendan thought. Maybe she'd sheltered in one of the *fang tzu*. As he went into the courtyard to saddle his horse he decided to look there first.

Nicholas felt himself slipping into oblivion on the k'ang. He struggled to stay awake. Better eat something first. Then the bliss of unconsciousness, thanks to the wine, strong and raw, searing your throat when you gulped it that way. He knew if he was ever going to get out of here and away from this cursed inn, he had to recover fast. When Daria gets here, he thought, we'll make plans.

He managed to keep awake long enough to eat a bowl of steamed vegetables and chicken when Hao brought it in, and exerted all his will power to keep it down and not retch, before he fell into a feverish sleep.

It was dark by the time Brendan returned to the inn. As he dismounted in the courtyard he' remembered the ducks. He'd never brought them inside. To hell with the ducks. What he wished he had, what he longed for with all his heart, was a quart of good Irish whiskey. Failing that, a bottle of cognac. What he'd have to settle for was kaoliang wine.

He walked into the inn. Hao was setting out his dinner on the table. He wasn't hungry.

"Bring me something to drink," he said heavily.

Hao began to leave.

"How is he?" Brendan asked.

"Sleeping."

"Aye. Just as well. Don't wake him."

He sat down at the table, throwing himself into the chair, and stared into space. This information could wait. Christ Almighty, how were you going to tell a man who'd been tortured with a tashur, who was tossing in feverish pain in a Godforsaken Chinese inn, what he had to say? It was enough to break anybody's spirit.

Brendan had ridden into the village to find wails of anguish, screaming children, frantically barking dogs, pitiful household possessions scattered in front of every hut, hand-wringing women, tight-lipped men, shrieking old ladies—the place stank of fear. He'd seen scenes like this before. He felt cold apprehension run up his back.

He reined the horse in front of a hut. The family huddled in the doorway. Ripped-up bedmats were thrown into the yard. Pots and pans were flung all over the ground. The people were wide-eyed and nervous. What did the foreign devil want? Was this more trouble?

"Hunghutze?"

No answer.

"Were there bad men here?"

This time the woman replied. *"Pu hao. T'ing pu hao."*

Bad. Very bad indeed.

He began to feel sick.

He asked another question. Where were the peddler and the oxcart? No answer. They were terrified. He persisted. A young woman. Yang kweitze. Have you seen her? Finally the woman pointed to the end of the road.

What he found when he got there was one slaughtered ox, a very dead Manchu peddler, the ruins of an oxcart with its goods ransacked. No girl.

Jesus, Mary, and Joseph. The damn fool must have re-sisted and gotten himself shot. Perfect prey. A pretty young woman and a fear-crazed peddler who couldn't think straight enough to appease a party of bandits. *You should have known better, Cha Ho.*

He rode back up the road to the *fang tzu,* and asked more questions. Was it the Stone Dragon in person? No. The Stone Dragon's bandits, then? No answer. That prob-ably meant yes. But the villagers would never commit them-selves. They were terrorized. You could beat them black and blue with rifle butts, and they'd never answer. They were more afraid of hunghutze than government soldiers or foreign devils. The menace of bandits was more im-mediate and more certain.

Where was the young woman? Did she go with the bandits?

He finally got an answer. A scared yes.

Did they harm her?

No answer.

Probably not. They had better uses for a girl.

Which direction? Where did they go? Where are they hiding?

That was totally useless. They'd been well taught not to answer that kind of question.

How many men?

Five.

Horses?

No horses. On foot.

Crafty. Stupid but crafty. On foot you could melt into the grass, or the kaoliang fields, without a trace. The bas-tards had a good head start. And they could have gone in any direction. Every peasant in the countryside would pro-tect them, out of simple fear. You could spend the rest of your life searching these marshes and plains and villages, and only break your heart.

Sad and angry, he turned back to the inn.

Aye, let the man sleep, he thought, sitting at the table. This particular story could wait.

He decided to stay at the inn. He had no urgent business in Harbin, and he'd offered to escort Nicholas to the city. Christ, he could do that much for the man.

* * *

By the next afternoon, when Nicholas finally woke and was clearheaded enough to hold a conversation, Brendan couldn't delay any longer. How much could the man take? Might as well get it over with. There was no way you could soften it.

"Have another drink," he said, lowering himself onto the saddlebag in Nicholas's room. "I have bad news."

A flare of suspicion and fear kindled in Nicholas's eyes as he sat up on his elbow on the k'ang, staring at Brendan. And then . . . ice. That was the only way you could describe it. The man turned to ice.

Brendan told his story in three or four sentences.

Silence.

Say something, damn it, Brendan thought, this icy calm is inhuman.

"We'll find them," Nicholas said finally. "We'll go after them."

"You're in no condition to travel."

"It doesn't matter. I'll manage."

"Which way? North, south, east, or west? The hunghutze could have gone anywhere. They hide like rats. In three hours they could be ten miles in any direction. And while you comb the countryside, they're moving on, laughing."

"Will you help me look?"

He was not even listening, Brendan thought. He sighed. "I'm going to tell you some facts of life," he said. "Although you probably know them, I'll remind you anyway. What you have here is a kidnapping. You understand what that means? A victim. With two ears, a nose, and ten fingers. That can be chopped off and delivered to you in a box. Then they begin on other parts of the body. Hands. Feet. And so forth. Believe me, they've done it. They won't hesitate. This is Manchuria, it happens all the time."

Brutal. Oh Christ, it was brutal, but it was the simple truth.

Another silence; a long one this time.

Then: "What can I do, Brendan?" Nicholas asked in a low voice. "What do they want?"

"Money. Wait for a ransom note. When you get it, you can start to bargain."

"Suppose there's no ransom note?"

This time it was Brendan's turn to be silent. He hadn't

told Nicholas yet about Shih Lung. The Stone Dragon had a profitable sideline selling concubines. But Nicholas would find that out for himself, soon enough.

"Will the government help?" Nicholas asked.

"They make a stab at it. But Chang Tso-lin can't do much about controlling bandits. Hell, he chops off a few heads here and there, but it doesn't do much good."

"Suppose I hire my own soldiers."

"To cover this area? You'll need to set yourself up as a warlord and hire an army. Costs money. Weapons, food, uniforms, sleeping quarters; it could take months, maybe more. Meanwhile the hunghutze have your wife, and they know you're out searching for her, and refusing to pay ransom—"

"So that's the best advice you can give me!" Nicholas spoke savagely. "Wait for a ransom note that may never come! Or pursue them, and risk having her murdered!"

"I'm sorry, Nicholas." Brendan's voice was gentle. "There's nothing more I can say. People have gone out looking for kidnap victims, and regretted it."

Nicholas closed his eyes. "It's not your fault . . ."

Finally Brendan said, "All right. If you want to go out searching, I'll go with you."

Two men on horseback, Brendan thought. Hunting, grim and desperate. Village to village, asking questions, getting no answers. Have you seen some bandits with a young woman? A white woman? No answers. Never any answers. Weeks of living outdoors, eating off the countryside, sleeping on the ground—on and on. Weeks. Months. Winter would close in while hope shriveled to bitterness, and your life crumbled away. Was the woman alive or dead? After a while he and Nicholas would be known and shunned in every village in the countryside.

"I have to think," Nicholas whispered. "And not act blindly. You're right." He was silent for a long time. Then he said in a low voice, "People can be bought. Information can be bought. Not out here in the countryside; they're too frightened. But in the city . . ." His expression hardened. "I'll find her. I swear it. I'll discover where they've taken her, and where they're hiding, and I'll go prepared. And then I'll get her back. However long it takes." He set his jaw. "I have an appointment with Dmitri Chernov," he said very low, "and by God I'll keep that too. In my own way."

"You'd better get some more rest," Brendan said.

Nicholas sat up, ignoring the bloody bandages on his back, and put his feet on the floor. He stood up and reached for his trousers.

"Where the hell are you going?"

"Just out to the courtyard. I left something in the water trough. I'm going out to find it." He was buttoning up his trousers. "I'll tell you an interesting fact, Brendan. With money you can accomplish many things. You can even find a girl who's been kidnapped by bandits. But it takes more than just some money. Moderate resources aren't enough. I can see that now. You can exhaust them too quickly. You need a large and constant income, and that brings power. I intend to get it. One way or another." He went to the doorway. "Will you come with me tomorrow to Harbin?"

"Tomorrow!"

"I'm in a hurry, Brendan. I've got a lot to do, and not much time to do it in."

Christ, Brendan thought, did I worry about his spirit? This man wasn't broken. Whatever was holding him together was holding like iron.

"You're a madman. I'll come with you to Harbin, but only if you'll wait another day." Nicholas started to say something. Brendan waved his hand. "I'll not be picking you up off the ground every few yards and putting you back in the saddle. You can wait another day. As it is, you'll be bleedin' all over your shirt."

"All right. One more day." Nicholas's eyes were blue ice. "But that's all. And then we go."

Chapter 23

They had roped Daria's wrists in front of her and tied another rope around her neck like a halter, fastening her to the man in front of and the man behind her. They marched single file through the tall grass, very rapidly, so that she kept stumbling; when she fell, they cuffed her until she got to her feet.

Before they'd left the village, they'd poured hot water on the ropes around her wrists, to make them tighter. Now the skin was being rubbed raw.

She was terrified and miserable. Her hair was tangled and her face was scratched. She couldn't bear to think about what had happened to Cha Ho and the ox, in the village. She was numb with fear for herself. But her true terror was for Nicholas. Where was he? Why hadn't he come down the road? What had happened to him?

She kept remembering Zora, and the gypsy's dreadful prophecy in the tent at Khabarovsk station: a swift parting; the death of a blue-eyed man.

If it's true, and Nicholas is dead, then I don't care what happens to me!

But she didn't *know*. Until she knew . . . And then the sick fear came back.

"Where are you taking me?" Her cry was wild; she couldn't help herself.

The hunghutze only laughed, gesturing that they couldn't understand her jabber. Only one man could communicate with her, a toothless old man with horrible breath and wisps of white hair on his chin. But she imagined he was kinder than the rest. Maybe she was deceiving herself; you needed some hope. They were all dressed in ragged odds and ends of clothing, some of them in tattered uniform jackets, some in coolie coats and trousers. One boasted tin medals on his chest. All of them were filthy. Old, young, she couldn't even tell, she didn't care. Except for the toothless old man they were a faceless mass. There were only five of them, but in her state of agitated horror, they seemed like dozens. Their weapons looked ancient and unsafe, and one of the bandits almost blew his foot off by accident, holding his rifle carelessly downward as he marched. They all thought that was hilariously funny.

But they'd managed to murder Cha Ho without much trouble.

Stumble on. Keep on going.

They were crossing endless marshes, and her feet were covered with mud up to her ankles. The sky was filled with the haunting cries of waterfowl. She heard the beating of wings and saw the soaring forms of ducks, wild geese, a pair of white swans, once a golden eagle against a very blue sky; the beauty of the day and the surroundings seemed to mock her. The coarse grass waved above her head.

"Where are we going?"

More gestures: keep your mouth shut, yang kweitze.

She had to stop. It was necessary! It was a call of nature. She told the old man, and thought, now they'll have to untie my ropes.

But they only untied her wrists, and she hastily rubbed them to bring back the circulation. They kept the halter around her neck, and stood by jeering while she crouched in the grass.

She decided desperately that the only thing to do was ignore it. *Ignore their taunts and jeers. If they see you don't pay attention, and don't respond, maybe they'll get tired of it, and stop.*

It helped a little. They left her alone for a while, stopping their jeers, and when they retied her wrists, the ropes weren't quite so tight.

The old man warned her, whispering in her ear, that if she tried to escape, she would be killed at once, like the

265

peddler. He wouldn't take part in it himself. Not him! He would never do such a barbarous thing! But the others! Ai ya! They were just ignorant bandits!

She decided he was as bad as the rest.

After a while she sorted them out and gave them names in her mind. Old Man. Tin Medals. Shaved Head. Cross-Eye. And the one who seemed to be the leader, swaggering and giving orders, she called Warlord.

The day wore on. She was growing exhausted and received more cuffs to keep her going. They were in a hurry. Why? To avoid pursuit? Yes, probably. They must have covered miles of this empty wilderness, unseen in this grass, so high a horse and rider would have to stumble right over someone to see him at all.

She gritted her teeth and determined not to show her fear and desperation, if she could help it. They only laughed at fear. Defiance seemed to give her some status. So she would have to remain defiant.

The next time someone cuffed her—it was Tin Medals —she yelled angrily and swatted at him with her bound hands as she struggled to her feet. He laughed, but stepped back and didn't hit her again.

That was obviously the only course of action. She hoped she could keep her courage.

They'd made no sexual advances. Another consolation. If they were going to rape me, she thought, they would have done it by now. Wouldn't they? But why were those women screaming in the village? Maybe the bandits were sated temporarily.

She hoped they would consider a yang kweitze untouchable.

The sun was setting. The sky was flaming crimson-orange-pink over the marshes, gilding the grasstops to red-gold and burnishing the surfaces of the stagnant pools of water to iridescent crimson. A pair of ducks flew overhead, black-winged silhouettes against the burning sky. It was the most beautiful sunset she had ever seen; it was splendor and glory in this unseen, uninhabited place, like the beginning of the world, and its beauty gave her comfort. She clutched the ragged edges of her courage around her.

After dark they came to a village, just a miserable collection of mud huts with the usual pack of yellow dogs yapping in the road.

A cry went up. "Ai ya! Hunghutze!"

Warloard and Shaved Head swaggered into a hut and drove out the occupants with kicks and blows, and Daria realized that this was where they'd spend the night.

Dinner was boiled millet and kaoliang, which the bandits gobbled greedily. She could hardly eat. But you didn't know what was ahead of you tomorrow.

They slept together on the k'ang, all six of them. They kept the rope around her neck, not taking any chances on her escape. It was impossible to sleep. They thrashed and made disgusting noises, constantly hawking and spitting on the floor, and they smelled vile, of sweat and garlic and a sickly sweet odor she recognized as opium. She realized that Shaved Head was continually chewing opium pellets.

But she didn't smell much better herself, she thought miserably. Would they ever let her wash?

The next day Warlord took pity on her, because, the old man said, she refused to beg or ask for favors. They attached the halter to an old village woman, threatening that the woman had better not let her escape, and reinforcing the threats with blows. Then they allowed her to go with the woman behind the hut to attend to her needs.

But it was outdoors, in the open, and there was still no privacy. The bandits stood around in a circle with their backs turned, but the village women came to gape curiously, nudging each other and pointing. See the foreign woman! She's just like us!

One tiny girl crouched beside her and solemnly offered a handful of leaves at the appropriate moment. Daria didn't know whether to laugh or cry. The child was so obviously trying to be helpful. Oh God, you might as well laugh.

The next days were a repetition of the first. The marching and stumbling, growing filthier every hour. Sleeping on a k'ang at night when they came to a village. The bandits seemed to know the location of all the villages, and managed to reach them by nightfall or a little after. They arrogantly took what they wanted from the villagers, demanding food and accommodations, and receiving it immediately. Warlord boasted of what he would do if anyone refused, but so far no one had.

She tormented herself with thoughts of Nicholas's safety, and tried to reassure herself over and over that he was safe and alive. She firmly pushed Zora's prophecy out of her mind. It was dangerous weakness to think of it. She needed all her strength.

They hadn't molested her, except for pokes at her body and loud boisterous comments on her appearance, which the old man didn't bother to translate. But they played sadistic jokes. Once they shoved her onto the floor of a hut and Cross-Eye ran over with a pot of boiling water, threatening to toss it. Genuinely terrified, she screamed and rolled aside, and the water splashed harmlessly on the floor beside her face. They roared with laughter.

She scrambled to her feet and shouted at them, calling them every name she could think of to relieve her feelings.

By accident, she discovered a way to entertain them. She began to hum under her breath as she marched, to keep up her spirits. They overheard, and encouraged her. They liked to hear singing. She thought hopelessly that she had nothing to lose. She sang the words out loud.

More! They liked it.

It was something to do. It kept her mind off her misery. At night, in the huts she would sing to them, and they sat cross-legged on the floor and listened quietly. She exhausted her repertoire, but they wanted to hear the same songs over and over again anyway.

They were like children, she thought. Cruel and horrible children.

Perhaps because of the songs, they allowed her to wash. The shower was just a petrol drum filled with water, rigged up behind one of the huts with a spigot attached. The village women came to stare, as usual, patting and pinching her and commenting on her skin. She was past caring. Just to be clean was heaven. But she had to put on her dirty clothes again, and they never took the rope from around her neck.

It occurred to her that they were going somewhere. There was a purpose to this marching. A destination. They weren't just wandering aimlessly. She had no idea where she was, except that they were traveling west, into the sunset; but the bandits knew, and she sensed their spirits rising as they approached an end to the trek.

She asked the old man one day as he sat beside her in the grass. "Where are we going?"

"Shih Lung Chan."

"What is that?"

"The Village of the Stone Dragon."

Her heart sank and she began to tremble. She was being taken to the Stone Dragon. She knew that name. Cha Ho had said it. Brendan O'Reilly had said it. She couldn't control the quiver in her voice.

"What will they do with me?"

"Don't worry. You won't be harmed. Shih Lung will sell you for a great deal of money."

That wasn't reassuring. She forced down her dread and made her voice steady before she spoke again.

"Soldiers will come to Shih Lung's village," she said firmly. "They'll take me away."

"We'll cut off your ears before they do that!" The old man cackled. "Then who will want to buy you? Big feet and no ears!" The old man lowered his voice to a confidential whisper. "Shih Lung never stays in one place. Two hundred armed bandits come and go in Shih Lung Chan, and they move all the time. Soldiers never find us. No one finds us."

"Soldiers have cut off the heads of bandits," she said. "I saw it myself, in Sunsing." She hadn't actually seen it, but the old man wouldn't know that.

The old man looked worried. "Not us," he muttered. But he got up and moved away.

Not long after that Tin Medals came over with a long-bladed knife in his hand and grabbed her by the ear. By now she had hardened herself to their jokes. He waved the knife in the air, slashing it past her earlobe and yelling wildly. She forced herself to ignore him, and finally he let go and walked away. But before he did, he turned and gave her a meaningful stare, letting his eyes travel up and down her body. She wondered with a chill of dread what he was thinking as he stood there hard-faced and intent, appraising her with his glance. Maybe he was thinking that the foreign devil was just another female. Maybe he intended to prove it. She wondered in sudden horror what she could do, how she could fight. She turned aside, pushing the thought from her mind.

That night they slept in the open, in a grove of trees beside a brook. The sky above them was covered with clouds, and Daria wondered miserably if it would rain tomorrow. So far she'd been spared that. All around her the bandits were sprawled in noisy, restless sleep. Beneath her body the ground was uneven, covered with twigs and lumpy clods of dirt. She closed her eyes, hoping she would sleep.

Then she opened them again, stifling a scream. Hot breath was moving over her cheek. Hands were running over her body, prodding and poking her. Someone was thrusting himself against her. Tin Medals was attempting to cover her body with his own, fumbling at her clothes as he did so.

To her own surprise, she wasn't frightened. She was just angry and startled and deeply indignant. She sat up and shrieked at the top of her lungs, trying to push him away.

All the others awoke. A babble of Chinese surrounded her. Warlord stood up, walked over to them, grabbed Tin Medals by his ragged sleeve, and hauled him to his feet. They began to argue. Tin Medals gestured violently at Daria. Spittle appeared at the corners of his mouth as he shouted. Warlord shouted back.

At last the argument subsided into grumbles, and Tin Medals looked sullen. Daria was untied and retied again, with Tin Medals placed far at the end.

She wondered, lying back against the ground, how long she would be left alone. Not very much longer. Reaction set in, and she began to tremble. She knew now that she would be protected until they reached Shih Lung Chan. But what would Shih Lung be like?

At sundown two nights later, they came to Shih Lung Chan. Warlord was leading the way. They approached through a field of kaoliang, the tall stalks waving above their heads, hiding them from view. Warlord was beating aside the stalks of grain with a bamboo staff he'd stolen from a peasant. Daria followed, roped to Warlord, with Tin Medals roped behind her. When they emerged from the protective stalks of grain, they were in the straggling, empty street of a deserted village. More kaoliang loomed ahead beyond the abandoned huts. The place looked eerie and desolate. They plunged into the second field, leaving the village behind.

They came to a clearing in the grainstalks, and Daria saw as they halted that the kaoliang had thinned and ceased. She looked up and shivered. She was standing in the shadow of a wall. It was a mud wall, fifteen feet high, with watchtowers at all four corners. Where had it come from? Out of nowhere. She couldn't hear anything but the howling of a dog, and then she heard the pounding of Warlord's rifle butt against the heavy wooden gate in the wall.

Someone shouted on the other side.

Warlord shouted back: a password.

Metal screamed. Bolts were drawn. *Creeeak* . . . the gate was opened. Now it stood ajar. She saw that the wall was six feet thick, and an archway passed beneath it.

Single file they marched beneath the archway. The gate slammed shut.

Fortifications. Watchtowers. Passwords. All at once, Daria knew she had entered the Village of the Stone Dragon.

Chapter 24

His companion looked fierce and grim, Brendan thought, glancing at Nicholas. But no wonder. He would himself, if he had to ride all day in that condition. He knew that the man was one dark purple bruise from the nape of the neck to the hips. You could see the set lines of pain around his mouth, even though the horses were using an easy gait now through this forest trail. Nicholas's khaki jacket was stained by dark red blotches across the back, where blood was still seeping through the bandages. The bleeding would stop soon. The bruises, though, wouldn't fade for weeks.

Nicholas's eyes were distant and brooding beneath the arched eyebrows. He spoke little. He hadn't bothered to shave for days, and dark stubble covered his cheeks and his chin. Bearded and mustached, with the gaunt cheekbones and the fierce scowl, he looked almost Biblical. If John the Baptist had worn a khaki jacket, riding breeches, and boots . . .

Still, the man retained a natural elegance. And Brendan couldn't help remembering the tender and affectionate way he'd spoken to his wife that first night at the inn. He saw no trace of that gentleness now. It was a sad thing, he told himself. Then he cursed himself for a sentimental jackass. Christ, he wasn't even drunk.

They were eating and drinking sparingly, going through this uninhabited stretch of wilderness, heading south toward the flat plains around Harbin. When their supplies ran out, they'd have to depend on what Brendan could bring down with his gun. And they'd have to drink water.

Well, he'd endured worse times. At least he had plenty of cartridges for his rifle, and there was no shortage of game. And the weather was good.

Drum, the Gordon setter, had been left behind temporarily with the innkeeper. They'd impressed on Hao, over and over again, before leaving the inn, what message he must give to the bandits, when the hunghutze sent word about the ransom. Nicholas's name. And where he could be reached.

"The Hotel Novy Mir, in Harbin. Will you remember?" Yes, yes.

The Novy Mir was Brendan's hotel. They rented rooms by the week or the month; it would be easy enough to find accommodations there for Nicholas. Unlike the Grand Hotel on the Kitaiskaya, which was always crowded with people coming and going, commercial travelers, staff officers, politicians, the Novy Mir was quiet. Harbin was a madhouse these days. Since the revolution and the war, the cabarets, brothels, and cafés couldn't handle the surge of business.

Finally, not trusting the innkeeper, Brendan had written down the name and address on a piece of paper and hammered it into the wall with four nails.

"Leave it up there until it falls apart," he warned Hao. "Don't take it down. Understand?"

"Yes, yes, I understand. *Tung te!*"

It was all they could do. They'd packed their food and wine, and left.

"Want to try an opium pellet?" Brendan asked now as they passed beneath sun-dappled branches. "I took some from Hao before we left. It will kill some of the pain."

"No. I don't want to get sleepy. Maybe I'll take one tonight, before we make camp."

Brendan nodded. "Aye."

After a while, Nicholas asked slowly, "Brendan, what do you know about the Metropolitan Café?"

"The Metropolitan Café? Everyone knows the place. It's a big meeting spot in Harbin, on the Kitaiskaya. The place is always crowded. White Russian officers, for the most part. They walk in with their uniforms and their epaulettes and their pistols, swaggering as though they

273

owned the world, and then they sit around and drink and argue and sing *God Save the Czar,* and quarrel for hours at a time." Brendan laughed shortly. "Jesus, you wonder how they get anything done."

"I wonder if they do."

"Think they'll take back the country?"

"No, Brendan. Somehow I don't." Nicholas's voice was grim. "I've made up my mind that there's no going back to Russia for me. I'm here now, in Manchuria, and this is where I'll have to play my game. Win or lose."

After that they fell silent. Brendan began to sing, softly at first, then louder, in a pleasant light tenor, enjoying the echo of his voice among the treetops. "Give a man a horse he can ride . . . give a man a girl he can love . . ."

When he stopped, Nicholas asked fiercely, "Do you think they'll hurt her?"

Brendan didn't have to ask what he meant.

"No, I don't believe so. Why would they? Unless you refuse to pay ransom." Brendan paused. "Too bad you couldn't have paid off the Mad Major. You would have saved yourself some pain."

"Yes, too bad. But Chernov had a different motive."

"Planning to meet him at the Metropolitan Café?"

"That's how I'll know where to find him. But I have a feeling that when we meet it will be in private."

The conversation ceased again. Once they passed an ancient crumbling *p'ai lou* by the side of the road, a Chinese memorial arch, built of gray stone, with faded characters inscribed on the arch and bird droppings obscuring the stone. There was no telling how long it had been there, or what it was supposed to mean. Centuries could have passed while it stood crumbling in the wilderness.

They kept going.

Toward sunset they approached the bank of a small river. Brendan said he believed it was the Ching Ho, but he wasn't sure. This country was crisscrossed with small streams and rivers.

Then he exclaimed under his breath, "For the love of heaven."

They reined their mounts, coming out of a grove of trees, and stared at the scene ahead of them. Black tents were pitched all along the banks of the river, running from north to south. Kneeling camels made long rows in front of the tents. Behind them loomed bales and bags of merchandise, piled up on the ground like little mountains. Campfires were already twinkling in front of the tents, and the pungent odor of burning camel dung drifted on the air, along with the smell of roasting mutton. Small shaggy horses were tethered everywhere. Dogs ran back and forth.

It was a scene straight out of the Gobi Desert.

"It's a Mongol caravan," Brendan muttered. "This is a bit of luck. We'll have plenty of company tonight."

"Is that the lead camel? The one with the pole?"

"Aye. And that bit of red cloth on top of the pole means they've paid their tribute to the bandit chieftain. Five dollars for each camel, Mexican silver."

"The hunghutze do well, don't they?" Nicholas said bitterly.

It was best to avoid the subject of bandits, Brendan thought. He should have kept his mouth shut. "See that flag waving on the pole? The one with all the writing on it?"

"Yes."

"It's a prayer flag. Every time the flag waves, the prayers go up to heaven and reach the ears of God." He grinned. "It's easier than saying a rosary, I'll tell you that. Saves energy."

"They're Buddhists, aren't they?"

"Aye. Tantric Buddhists, like the Tibetans. Only they don't worship the Dalai Lama, they have their own. He's in Urga, the Mongolian sacred city. They call him the Living God." He grinned. "Let's go. That mutton smells good."

They spurred their horses and rode down toward the river. Now they could see men moving among the tents and camels. Some of the types Nicholas recognized from Siberia; the peoples who moved freely back and forth across the border. Kirghiz, walking mincingly in high-heeled boots, with eagles' feathers stuck into their pointed caps. Buryats, small and bowlegged, wearing deerskin trousers and jackets. Mongolians in brilliantly dyed sheep-skin vests down to the ground, with long silver knives thrust into their belts. Old men with turbans on their heads, sitting cross-legged on mats, sucking on water pipes that gurgled and bubbled; not Buddhists, but Moslems.

As they came closer to the riverbank, the caravan dogs found them. Snarling, vicious brutes with coarse black hair and snouts like wolves, the dogs ran back and forth snapping at the horses' ankles, until Chaika reared nervously. Nicholas calmed her.

"Are these your famous Mongol dogs, Brendan?" he asked, a touch of humor momentarily lightening the grimness in his eyes.

"Aye. Don't get too close. They're nasty beasts, and they don't like strangers."

"Nohoi! Nohoi!" A small, bowlegged figure was toiling up the bank toward them, calling off the dogs. He moved uphill with the rolling, awkward gait of a man who'd spent most of his life on horseback. When he approached they could see he was a small brown man with squinting eyes and a friendly grin.

"Sain bina!" he said as he shooed away the dogs. "Greetings," he added in English.

Mongolian, Brendan thought.

"Greetings," he replied politely. *"Sain bina."*

"Who are you? Are you alone?" The man's English was quite good.

"Yes, we are only two."

"You wish to join our caravan?"

"Perhaps just for the evening. If you don't object."

"Why not? Perhaps Shaliva Gegen Zerang will offer you the hospitality of the desert." He grinned widely and waved at the camp spread out along the riverbank. "I know what he will say. He will tell you that you have only to observe etiquette, and every tent will be yours." He paused, then said to Brendan, "Of course you will have to give up your rifle." Then he added, "It will be returned to you when you leave."

After a moment Brendan lifted the rifle from around his neck and handed it down to the Mongolian. The man stepped back while Nicholas and Brendan dismounted.

"What's etiquette?" Nicholas asked out of the side of his mouth.

"Just eat everything they give you."

"What will that be? Sheep's tails?"

Brendan laughed. "I doubt it. They reserve that for ceremonial feasts."

The man approached and took the horses' reins. "Follow me," he said. "I will take you to Shaliva Gegen Zerang."

They followed him down the sloping bank of the river to a large black tent where a kneeling camel was chewing reflectively from a bag of dried barley and oats, tinkling a little bell around its neck every time it moved its shaggy head. A man was seated cross-legged in front of the tent flap. He rose to his feet as they approached. He was wearing ragged white trousers, a purple blouse, a long sheepskin vest dyed crimson, and a violet turban.

Their guide handed over Brendan's rifle and said something very quickly.

The man in the turban came up to them and bowed as the guide disappeared. "Greetings," he said in English. "Allow me to introduce myself. I am the lead camel driver. My name is Shaliva Gegen Zerang." He studied them for a moment, and then he grinned. "However, that is a very long name. Let me shorten it for you. Please call me Shanghai. Other white men have called me that."

"Shanghai. Very good. I'm Brendan. This is Kolya."

The man turned and gestured at his tent. "May I offer you the hospitality of my campfire?"

When Nicholas and Brendan were settled around the campfire, and the horses were attended to and the rifle put away, the man called Shanghai began to stir a pot over the fire, spooning food into the pot out of a wide-mouthed wicker jar. The food was a thick paste, smelling strong and spicy.

"What the hell is that?" Nicholas muttered.

"It's a kind of bread sauce. I don't know what the Mongol word is, but the Chinese call it *pao peitung hsi*. They make it out of mildewed bread, fermented in the sun, and powdered ginger, red and green peppers, soybeans and bean curds, and minced mutton and mutton fat—"

"All right. That's enough. If I'm going to eat it, I'd better not hear any more."

277

Brendan laughed. "It's not so bad. He'll add water and dough. When they're traveling, they live on it. Keeps you healthy. I think it's the red peppers."

He leaned back and began to explain his theory about hot red peppers, and how they cleaned out your system and kept away germs. The sun went down. The campfires blazed up crimson against the dark sky, and burning sparks flew up and disappeared against the blackness. The dogs quieted down and crept off to sleep. Someone began to sing in a high mournful wail, accompanied by the music of a flute.

The bread sauce, cooking over the fire, was beginning to smell better.

Shanghai brought them mugs of hot tea. Nicholas, after one long swallow, made a grimace behind his back. "Is this tea salted?" he asked Brendan.

"Aye. They add salt and mutton fat."

"Good Lord."

Brendan grinned. "Drink up. You'll get used to it."

When the bread sauce came, hot and spicy, served in bowls with chopsticks, Nicholas was hungry enough to eat it all. Plates of roast mutton followed, which they ate with their fingers. Shanghai sat down cross-legged to join them.

"Shall I tell you about that song the man is singing?" he asked politely.

"Please do."

"It's the song of Chikherli Bodena. It's an old Mongol tradition. It tells of a brave warrior who in the heat of battle kept his head and remained calm and self-possessed, and thus was able to shoot straight and drill his enemy's skull from ear to ear." Shanghai paused. "That's the meaning of Chikherli Bodena. A skull with a hole bored in it from one ear to the other."

Brendan laughed. "Are you a brave warrior, Shanghai?"

"I? No, I'm not a warrior. Only a simple man of the desert. I have simple desires. Just a good horse and a wide plain under God's heaven." He thought a moment, then added, "Still, as we say in the Gobi, a man's way is only one, that which is ordained by fate."

There was no arguing with the proverb, Nicholas thought. He leaned back on one elbow, trying not to wince at the pain as he moved, and stared somberly into the fire. The burning bricks of camel dung had shapes, if you studied them long enough. The head of a tiger, with two eyes, a nose, and a mouth, flaming like coals. Then the brick fell apart with a soft hiss of sparks, and the head disappeared. But over there . . . a falcon, with an open beak . . .

Shangahi was explaining to Brendan how they treated captured horse thieves in Mongolia. Horse stealing was the most serious of all offenses, he explained. The culprit was put into a box so constructed that he could neither stand up nor sit down. The box was put into a dark celler. The man was fed through a hole in the box, and it was never cleaned. He lived in his own waste.

"How long does he last?"

"Six months. Sometimes less."

"Ah, well. So it goes." Brendan stretched and lit a cigarette.

"Your friend is very quiet," Shanghai observed.

"He's tired."

Nicholas smiled and reached for his own box of cigarettes in his breast pocket. "Tired," he said, "and filthy, and battered, and feeling about as civilized as one of those camels."

Shanghai was silent for a moment. Then he said, "Nevertheless, I believe that some day, when you are shaved again, with a fine bath and a clean shirt and a new suit of clothes, you'll discover that you're still a gentleman."

"How about me?" Brendan asked. "Am I a gentleman?"

"No." The answer was prompt. "You are a roughneck."

Brendan laughed, and cuffed him in the shoulder. "A man of good judgment, I see."

They grew silent. The fire burned lower. The singing stopped, and the flute ceased to play. The camels closed their eyes, sleeping in their kneeling positions. Horses whinnied softly. Dark figures of men moved among the bales of merchandise, checking them over before going to the tents.

"I'll sing you a song," Shanghai said dreamily. "Shall I do that?"

"Why not?"

"It's a song of the camel drivers. I'll tell you first what it means." He looked into the fire and spoke softly:

When the flames of sunset gild my hair
I remember thee.
When the eternal snows change to purple and gold
I remember thee.
When the first star gleams to call the herdsman home
When the pallid moon is colored red
I remember thee.
When there's nothing else but all that is, and me . . .
I remember thee.
And so . . . I follow the caravans.

Then he threw back his head and sang the song. It was high and wild and in a minor key, and when he had finished, they were quiet again for a very long time.

Finally Brendan stirred. He cleared his throat. "What are you carrying in the caravan, Shanghai?" he asked.

At that an air of alertness seemed to come over the Mongol camel driver. The atmosphere around the campfire changed. Nicholas sensed it. He felt a little tingle at the back of his neck, and roused himself from the melancholy mood the song had put him in. Something was happening. Was it important? An instinct told him it might be. Brendan's idle question had made Shanghai straighten his shoulders, and now the camel driver's eyes were darting from side to side, studying each of the white men in turn.

Now why should that be, Nicholas wondered. Brendan's question hadn't been very startling.

Brendan didn't seem to notice anything.

"We are carrying jade from Khotan," Shanghai said at last. "Rugs from Kashgar. Musk oil, to use for perfume. But mostly . . . wool." He paused. "Bactrian camel's wool. Very fine, very valuable. Soft and light as a cloud. Hard to obtain. Worth much on the open market. Greatly desired by the woolen mills of England and America."

"Stop right there, Shanghai." Brendan grinned lazily. "You've got a line of chatter like a rug salesman. I'm not buying wool."

"No, of course not." The camel driver was still tense.

An instinct told Nicholas to change the subject. He struck a match to light his cigarette. He waited for a few minutes, then he remarked, "You have sturdy horses in this camp. I haven't seen the breed before."

The camel driver relaxed. "They're Ili horses, from the valley of the Ili River, in Chinese Turkestan. The best of the Asian breeds."

The conversation wandered after that, as Nicholas wondered about the significance of the Bactrian camel's wool.

Shanghai served them *kumiss,* fermented mare's milk, tasting sour and vinegary. But as Brendan remarked, it was better than drinking water.

Finally Shanghai rose to his feet. "I believe you are tired after your long day in the forest," he said courteously. He turned to the tent. "Would you like to sleep inside?"

"No, we'll stay out here," Brendan said. "Thanks anyway."

Shanghai bowed. "At sunrise I'll wake you for tea."

When he had gone into the tent, lowering the flap behind him, Brendan and Nicholas wrapped themselves in blankets by the campfire. "Stinks to high heaven inside those tents," Brendan said. "We're better off out here." He rolled onto his side. "Want some opium?"

"No, I'm tired enough to sleep without it."

"All right." He yawned. "Remember what I told you about the Japanese when you get to Harbin," he said sleepily.

"I'll remember."

"You may not like the little bastards, but they've got brains and money, and they're well organized. That's more than you can say for the Chinks, with all those tin-pot little warlords running around."

"Some day China will organize herself."

"Aye, some day. The sleeping giant wakes, and so forth. But meantime . . ." He yawned again. "I'm going to sleep."

Nicholas lay carefully on his side and turned his head to see the sky. He couldn't lie on his back; he wouldn't be able to do that for a long time. He wondered again about the wool. Then he looked at the dying fire. The flames were embers now. Embers and ashes.

A man's way is only one, that which is ordained by fate.
You couldn't deny the truth of that Mongol proverb, he thought.

He fell asleep.

In the morning, Shanghai was gone from the tent, but he'd left mugs of salted tea by the campfire. Nicholas drank his tea while he watched the pink-gold rays of the sunrise slant through the branches of the trees to the east. The river, to the west, was still half in shadows. Brendan was sleeping.

He got up and made his way down to the riverbank. Rows of camels and horses were lining the shore, being watered, and men with buckets were bringing water back to the tents for cooking. The camp was already astir and bustling with life. Food was simmering over fires. In the center of the river a wedge of ducks was swimming placidly, and in the shallows a long-legged heron was fishing for breakfast.

Nicholas stripped off his jacket and shirt and plunged his head and shoulders into the river. He could feel the bandages on his back sticking painfully to the clotted blood, but he thought the bleeding had stopped.

He used his shirt to dry himself, and put his jacket on over his bare chest. He had a clean shirt in the saddlebag. He'd left a bloodstained one at the Inn of the Green Parrot, for Hao to launder and wear, if the innkeeper wished. Nicholas had worn it the day after Chernov left, and thought it was past saving.

He would buy new clothes in Harbin, he thought.

Then he heard voices to his left. He stood up.

Shanghai, the camel driver, was in conversation with two strangers a short distance away. The men were Chinese, and Nicholas thought they didn't belong to the caravan. He saw their horses standing nearby, under a grove of trees.

The conversation was emotional. Hands were waving in the air. Voices were loud. Shanghai looked distressed, and then angry. He seemed to be arguing with the strangers. It went on for a long while.

Finally the two men shrugged and walked away, with a last loud set of comments. They mounted their horses and disappeared into the forest.

"Shanghai!" Nicholas called.

The camel driver turned his head. Then he walked over slowly to Nicholas. "Good morning," he said. He looked unhappy.

"Are those friends of yours?" Nicholas asked.

"They were to be . . . business partners." Shanghai shrugged his shoulders. "But something has gone wrong."

"That's too bad. Why don't you tell me about it?"

"It's a private matter."

"I'm on my way to Harbin. I'm just passing through. What's the harm?" He paused, and then he added, "Perhaps I can help you."

"You?" Shanghai stared into his eyes. Nicholas had the sense that this had something to do with the Bactrian camel's wool. He was curious, slightly interested. And perhaps a little more.

Shanghai's face kindled with a sudden flare of decision. "Yes," he whispered, "perhaps it is so. Destiny works in strange ways. You came here last night out of the forest, and perhaps it was for a reason that you shared my campfire." He sat down cross-legged on the ground. Then he gestured for Nicholas to join him.

Obviously he'd made up his mind to unburden himself, Nicholas thought, because his face was solemn. The camel driver had an excessively dramatic way of putting things, he thought wryly. But he sat down on the ground beside Shanghai and settled himself to listen.

The story could have been quickly told. Shanghai, however, related it in a long and roundabout fashion, with many references to destiny and the smiling face of Buddha and the silver moon of good fortune and the golden blossoms of fate.

It seemed that certain people—Shanghai wasn't mentioning any names—had made special arrangements for the valuable bales of Bactrian camel's wool. They had arranged to "remove" the bales from the caravan just outside of Harbin—in fact to steal them—and carry them on ponyback to the Harbin waterfront. There they would be delivered to a certain person in a warehouse. He, Shanghai, had been told the secret. He was to be amply compensated for the risk of closing his eyes at the right moment.

All was clear so far, Nicholas thought. This was a simple case of theft. It happened all the time, especially here, especially now. Lawlessness was a way of life in Manchuria.

The man in Harbin, Shanghai continued, would realize a handsome profit on his valuable merchandise. He, Shanghai, would become a rich man. Everyone would be wealthy and happy. Except, of course, for the Chinese merchants in the Harbin district of Fu Chia Tien, who had paid for the wool in the first place, and financed the caravan. But they were rich already, and so it didn't matter.

"But now you have a problem," Nicholas said, prompting him.

Yes, one flaw had developed, Shanghai explained. The man in the Harbin warehouse, receiver of the stolen bales of wool, had been unexpectedly knifed to death in a Pristan alleyway, two midnights ago. Pristan was the commercial center of Harbin.

"And so . . ." He paused, and looked at Nicholas out of the corner of his eye. "Will you betray me now? I will deny it, for the plan is ruined."

"No, I won't betray you."

Nicholas fell silent. He was considering what he'd heard. He could buy the wool himself, in Harbin. Wool for diamonds. Was that a good exchange? Yes, very possibly. Jewelry was worth cash. But cash was worth nothing unless you put it to use. Wool. Now, in the summer of 1918, in these wartime conditions, the woolen mills of Britain were probably standing idle. It was a place to begin, he told himself. A gamble. Diamonds for wool.

There would be problems. Details. A place to store the bales of wool. A way to resell them to make his profit. But maybe the problems could be solved.

"Shanghai," he said slowly, "I may have a solution for you. Tell me something. How long will it take for this caravan to reach Harbin?"

"Loaded camels move very slowly. We must break up this camp. I would say six days."

"And my friend and myself?"

"If you meet no bandits and your horses keep well—and you leave within the hour—you should reach the city by midday tomorrow."

That gave him four and a half days, Nicholas thought. It was not much time to make the necessary arrangements. But it was possible. Difficult and rushed, but possible.

"Can you get word," he said, "to your friends, to go ahead with their plan?"

"Yes, they will be camping here tonight."

"Then listen to me, Shanghai. I have an offer to make."

The camel driver raised his head. "Wait before you speak! I hear the *kilitai shobo*."

"What is that?"

"One raven. A very good omen!" He smiled into Nicholas's face. "If many ravens gather at sunrise, it signifies difficulties on the journey. But if one raven croaks at sunrise, it foretells a fortunate journey, and that you are about to reach your goal." He took a breath. "Now tell me your offer."

Chapter 25

Beyond the archway through the mud wall of Shih Lung Chan stretched an open compound of beaten dirt. Daria took a deep breath, fighting down her panic. She knew where she was: the Village of the Stone Dragon. Crude wooden shelters for horses stood around the edges of the compound; twenty or so were tethered in the shelters. Some of them were stamping their feet and whinnying nervously in their stalls. The area smelled of manure and horse sweat.

How would she ever escape from here? No one would ever find her. She was at the end of nowhere.

Through the compound, another heavy wooden gate faced her. Then the gate closed behind her. Now she was in a big central courtyard, ringed by low mud huts with paper windows. Inside the huts men on k'angs crouched over greasy cards or fingered painted mah jongg tiles; she could hear the sounds of talk, laughter, and the clack-clack of tiles.

She was looking at a hut across the courtyard that was bigger than the others, and she had a feeling of uneasy dread that it was the hut of Shih Lung.

Then a sense of relief swept over her as she felt the rope being taken from around her neck and her wrists being untied. The bandits must feel safe here, she thought, in their stronghold. She should have been downcast to realize that, but she felt so liberated without her ropes that she couldn't even care. With a deep sigh she began to rub her wrists.

Warlord was strutting around boasting to the other men of his exploits in the villages. She didn't need to understand his words to know what he was saying. His gestures were clear. She turned her face away, slightly sickened, as he pantomimed raising a rifle to his shoulders, and she knew he was acting out the murder of Cha Ho.

Men were pouring out of the huts now, to listen and to gape at her as they chattered and laughed. She kept her face impassive and her chin high, folding her arms across her chest. Where was Shih Lung?

There—someone was walking out of the big hut. Swaggering, with thumbs in belt.

Could this be the Stone Dragon?

If so, then Shih Lung was a woman.

She couldn't help staring in surprise. She hadn't expected that.

The woman was short and stocky. It was hard to tell her age—perhaps thirty. She strode freely on unbound feet. Her skin was brown and weather-beaten and deeply pitted. She wore a badly fitting uniform jacket. Cotton trousers one size too big were fastened by a rope around her waist.

Her face was very broad, and her eyes were very hard and very black.

After one cold, penetrating stare at Daria, sweeping her from head to foot, the woman turned to Warlord and held a long conversation in Chinese.

"Don't worry," the old man whispered in Daria's ear, "she can speak your language. She is very, very clever. She even taught herself to read the Chinese newspaper." He cackled. "But I'm the only one in the village who knows how to write. I still have to write all the ransom notes."

"Is that woman Shih Lung?"

"Of course." He looked affronted. "What did you expect?"

Daria was staring at the woman's hands. They were deformed. The thumbs were stretched out of shape, and the knuckles stood out at unnatural angles.

"What happened to her hands," she whispered.

"Common punishment for lazy servants. She was hung by her thumbs when she was nine."

"Nine!"

The old man shrugged. "Girl children are sold very young in north China. Shih Lung was born in a village near Tientsin. She was sold to be a servant when she was a small child."

"But it's horrible to hang a child by the thumbs."

"Her mistress wished to teach her obedience." The old man giggled again. "But she wouldn't learn. Her name was Ah Ting then."

The woman had finished her conversation with Warlord. She was swaggering toward Daria. Her black hair was hacked off raggedly at the ears, and fell in stick-straight bangs over her forehead.

"What have you to say for yourself?" she demanded in Russian in a harsh low voice, halting in front of Daria.

Daria set her jaw. "Please let me go," she said. "Your men had no right to bring me here."

The woman smiled scornfully. "When a ransom has been paid, you will be freed." She paused. "For you, the ransom will be high. Because you are young, and a woman, and a foreign devil." She scowled. "I hope you have someone to pay your ransom for you. Otherwise it will be very bad."

Daria lifted her chin. "Yes, I have a friend who will pay my ransom."

"I hope he's very rich." The words were meaningful.

Inwardly Daria felt sick. Where was Nicholas? Was he even still alive? And how could she reach him? And how would he pay a very high ransom? There was her cousin Victor. But he was only an employee of the Chinese Eastern Railway. . . .

She tried to look as scornful and confident as Shih Lung. Everything would depend on her courage, she thought. She had to believe Nicholas was alive, it would keep her going. She must forget Zora's prophecy. She must believe she would get out of here. Somehow.

"We will go inside the hut," Shih Lung said. "Come with me. You will eat and sleep, and then we will discuss your ransom."

The hut was bare, Daria saw, with a dirt floor. Clothes hung on wooden pegs around the wall. But there were two sleeping platforms, one against each wall. Was she to sleep here, then? If so, she would have her own k'ang. That was one small consolation.

One of the k'angs had a table beside it, with a tray of implements. But she was too tired to study it. She realized that she was exhausted. Too tired to be frightened anymore. She wasn't even hungry. She only wanted to rest. She could hardly stand up.

"Sleep, then," Shih Lung said angrily, seeing her sway on her feet. "We have time to talk, yang kweitze. You are not going anywhere."

Daria went over to one of the sleeping platforms and collapsed across it, closing her eyes. She felt herself sinking into a heavy, exhausted sleep.

Shih Lung sat down on her own k'ang.

Yao had done well, she thought, to bring this foreign devil. Perhaps a ransom for her would be valuable, perhaps not. It didn't matter; a young girl could always be sold. And this one—Shih Lung studied the sleeping girl with narrowed eyes. Filthy and exhausted, with tangled hair and grimy clothes. Shih Lung frowned; coolie clothes—but if you washed her and combed her hair and dressed her in silk and perfumed her skin, perhaps attractive. In the foreign way. Not to the Chinese taste, for a cultivated Chinese gentleman had no love for these big-boned foreign women with their large feet and cowlike breasts; but still, the brothels of Harbin and Shanghai catered to many tastes. That remained to be seen.

Good work, Yao. You have done well. Shih Lung is pleased.

She looked over at the tray next to her k'ang and her eyes softened.

Ah, her opium tray. She counted over the objects lovingly in her mind.

Her opium pipe. Old, weathered bamboo, of excellent quality.

The row of fine steel needles.

The opium, brown and viscous in its clay pot.

The smoking lamp.

A box of matches to light it with.

All ready, all waiting.

Soon, soon, she whispered to herself in her mind.

She lay back on the k'ang with a sigh of anticipation, delaying her pleasure, although her nerves were suddenly shrieking for the smoke of dreams. She wanted to think first. This girl had given her hope. She wanted to visualize the glory that lay in the future, the goal she had promised herself she would reach some day, when her dreams came true.

She closed her eyes and thought about her vision. Once, in her wanderings, she had visited the Imperial City of Peking and gazed at the walls of the Forbidden City. She had passed out of the city through the North Wall, beneath the *Te Sheng Men,* the Gate of Victory. Then she had mingled, like the humble coolie woman that she was, with the other travelers who flowed along the northwest road to the Valley of the Tombs, where the Ming Emperors were buried.

She had been Ah Ting in those days.

On her way she had passed a house with a garden. She had never forgotten it. That was her vision. That was her dream of heaven: that garden outside Peking. She had slipped unnoticed through the round weathered-stone moon gate of the house, with its red tile pagodas dreaming under the summer sun, and gazed at the garden, and a terrible hunger for it rose inside her soul. The flower beds. The wind chimes. The fragrant, jade-green grass. The glowing peonies. The soft trees, drooping like the hair of beautiful women. The little stone bridges over the azure streams. The polished stones of the rock gardens, amber-brown and silver-gray in the sunlight. The simple loveliness of it, the perfection, the dreamlike peace. *Mine. Some day this all will be mine.*

Ah Ting, a branded and beaten slave, how can you have such dreams?

But now she would make them come true, Shih Lung thought. She had come a long way since then, she told herself, a way of cruelty and blood, of death and anguish, but other people's sufferings meant nothing to her now. Was she not the Stone Dragon? Did she not command two hundred hunghutze? Ai ya! It was so.

And she would have that garden some day, or one just

like it. And then she would be at peace. And there she would die.

Meanwhile, she had her precious opium pipe. It was almost as good.

With a long, ragged intake of breath she sat up again and reached for the clay pot of opium. She would delay no longer. Her yearning was too intense.

First, she struck a match and lit the lamp.

When the flame was burning, she took one of the steel needles in her hand, and plunged it into the pot of opium. She brought it up with a ball of sticky opium paste on the point and twirled it in the air. Then she held the needle over the flame of the lamp, and listened to the little sizzling noise it made. The paste was swelling up, bubbling, becoming transparent, turning into a pearl of opalescent beauty. But it was more precious than pearls, she thought.

She had learned to smoke opium in a Shanghai brothel. She had been sold there by her mistress, who wished to be rid of sullen, lazy Ah Ting. But she was not a singsong girl, not to be used by men, for she was much too ugly. She was only a slave, to run errands, to fetch towels, to scrub floors, to change sheets, to be cuffed and beaten and made to work from dawn to midnight, and her only consolation was her pipe.

She had run away.

Shih Lung's fingers were smoothing the ball of opium on the point of the needle as she twisted it around in her hands. When the ball was flat against the needle, she plunged it again into the clay pot, brought it up with more sticky paste, and held it again over the flame. It sizzled, swelled and bubbled.

She had wandered alone after leaving Shanghai. She had gone north, to Peking, heading north toward the country where she had been born, hungry, footsore, half-starved, but free. Ah Ting was free.

But her freedom hadn't lasted. She had been captured by a band of renegade soldiers and made to be their servant and their concubine. She'd been sixteen, and she had been a virgin. Who had ever wanted ugly Ah Ting?

She hated the act of copulation, that sweating, grunting animal act that always left her sick and revolted at the pit of her stomach. She detested the sight of a male body, particularly with an aroused organ. Ai ya, those hideous purple veins, that distended flesh! Like an animal! Like a pig!

She schemed and plotted to get away from her tormentors.

She stole a knife and hid it under the pillow of her k'ang.

One night she slit the throat of her possessor just at the moment of his climax, and felt his hot, foaming blood spurting over her face and her naked breasts. And for the first time, hearing him gurgle to his death, she felt savagely happy. She pushed him away from her onto his back, with his throat gaping red and his trousers still open, exposing his nakedness, and she stood up and spat on his body.

Then she ran.

Shih Lung picked up her opium pipe. She was satisfied with the thick round ball of cooked opium on the point of the needle. She thrust the needle into the hole in the onion-shaped bowl of the pipe and pressed it down. She was almost ready. She leaned forward with the pipe in her mouth, over the flame.

After leaving the soldiers, she had grown crafty and cunning. She had learned to survive. She had learned that she had the ability to make decisions and to carry them out —she, the humble slave—and to command others, less intelligent than herself, and compel them to do her bidding. She understood torture and its uses. She had been taught it for years.

She went to Manchuria, and there she became Shih Lung, the Stone Dragon.

Now children wailed when they heard her name! Women shrieked, and men trembled! For she was Shih Lung . . .

She lay back with her head on the hard wooden pillow of the k'ang, inhaling the smoke of dreams. Deep, deep inside her lungs.

She thought of that garden in Peking. Soon her dream would come true. This girl would help her make it come true.

Fragrant, sweet smoke.

The world was fading.

Now . . .

She closed her eyes.

Soon I will not hurt. I will not feel pain. I will not feel anger. I will want nothing. Soon I will feel nothing but peace, and the cool happiness of drifting clouds.

For the poppy was the flower of joy.

And soon, as soon as she decided what to do with this girl, this foreign devil, she would have her garden.

Chapter 26

Brendan and Nicholas looked down from a hilltop upon the city of Harbin. It sprawled down the hillside to the banks of the Sungari River, gleaming far below like a ribbon of silk. The onion domes and minarets of the city's churches were glittering blue and gold and scarlet in the late morning sunlight.

"Across the river," Brendan said, "you'll find the suburb of Hailan and the Chinese town of Fu Chia Tien." He pointed.

Nicholas could see the lacy webbing of the railway bridge spanning the river. Down there on the waterfront, he thought, would be the warehouses and the docks and the waterfront coolies; but you couldn't see them from here.

Harbin, he thought. At last.

"Let's go," Brendan said, urging his horse. "I'm anxious to get there."

When they were down from the hillside, the gleaming vision of onion domes and minarets disappeared, giving way to dreary city outskirts. They rode through unpaved dirt roads lined with hovels, with the usual ragged children clustering in the open doorways, fingers in noses, and the usual barking *wonk* dogs snapping at the horses' ankles. A straggling barbed-wire fence guarded by lounging soldiers marked a police station.

Then the surroundings changed again. The dirt roads gave way to cobblestone paving. Buildings grew taller.

Streets began to stretch in all directions. A city began to close in around them.

"Here we are," Brendan said as they turned a corner. "This is China Street."

So this was the Kitaiskaya, Nicholas thought. He reined Chaika in the middle of the road as a bearded Sikh in a policeman's uniform and a turban suddenly blew a whistle. The Kitaiskaya: China Street. It ran from here, in Pristan, to the residential section of New Town, two miles away.

Horns were honking. Automobiles, rickshaws, droshkies, and taxis were crowding the road. Whistles were blowing. Traffic was stopping and starting. Big commercial buildings lined the street on either side: Tcherin and Sons Department Store; the Russo-Asiatic Bank, with armed guards on the sidewalk; the Grand Hotel with its imposing stone façade; a Russian church, with a twisted blue-and-gold onion dome. People. Crowds. Life. The electricity of a city, beating and pulsing all around him.

Twenty years ago this city had been a collection of wooden shacks built around a railway yard. It had grown with the Chinese Eastern Railway. Now the civil war above the border made it a center of intrigue as well as a prosperous commercial city. Women in silk stockings and smart hats and lip rouge strolled the sidewalks. Well-barbered men in tailored suits gestured with manicured hands as they walked. Shop windows displayed expensive merchandise. Khabarovsk, Nicholas thought, was a sleepy village in comparison.

Brendan was right, he thought, the city was overflowing. You could sense it.

Harbin was exploding, he knew. Currency speculation was rampant and uncontrolled, in spite of the efforts of the warlord, Chang Tso-lin, to stop it. Fortunes were made and lost overnight. Black markets flourished. Weapons were smuggled in, sold at quick, huge profits, and smuggled out again. The freight yards of the Chinese Eastern Railway were crammed with stolen goods.

It was wartime, and the atmosphere was frantic.

People were living in the freight yards too, huddled in abandoned railway cars. They were refugees with nowhere else to stay, those who had begun to pour in from across the Russian border fleeing the war, the revolution, and the

Bolshevik terror. Where would they go, how would they live, what would they do to survive? Most of them had no skills or professions, no ways of earning a living, only memories of a former life, and hopes of return.

They would have to be housed somewhere, Nicholas thought. In a few months it would be winter. The freezing, bitter-cold Manchurian winter.

But the refugees were not his problem, he told himself grimly. He was a refugee himself. He had a cold, rock-hard certainty that his fate would be different from theirs.

He'd told Brendan, on the way to Harbin, about the camel driver and the plan to steal the Bactrian camel's wool.

Brendan had laughed heartily. "So he's just a simple man of the desert, is he? A good horse and a wide plain under God's heaven?"

Nicholas had to smile. "So he claimed."

"Well, count me out of this scheme of yours, Kolya. I'm no merchant. I wouldn't know what to do with camel's wool."

"You sell it, Brendan, and you make a profit."

"Good luck to you, man. When you get rich, let me know. You can put me on your payroll."

"I may do that."

He'd made arrangements to meet Shanghai at the Hotel Novy Mir, at twelve noon, four days from today. He'd promised the camel driver some money at their next meeting, as a token of good faith. The rest of the payment would be made on delivery of the wool, at a place to be established when they met.

Now all he had to do was find the place and make sure he had the cash available.

He and Brendan were moving again, along the Kitais-kaya. Traffic was flowing.

Ah. The Metropolitan Café. Take note.

Many cafés lined the street. All were crowded. At the sidewalk tables you could see all kinds of people, all shades of color. Sikhs from India in turbans and beards. Siberians with slanted eyes and aboriginal faces: Kalmucks, Gilyaks, and Buryats. Chinese and Manchus, hard to tell apart in their blue cotton coats. Japanese, easily identified, in Western business suits, their eyes alert and watchful behind gold-rimmed spectacles. Europeans, big-boned and pink-faced, from Britain, Holland, Germany, Scandinavia.

And, of course, the White Russian officers.

They were conspicuous everywhere, swaggering in their uniforms, braid-heavy epaulettes swinging from their shoulders and pistols bulging at their hips. They were swarming into the public rooms at the Grand Hotel, crowding the tea shops, jamming the cafés, singing, drinking, talking, scheming, quarreling.

"Gentlemen, I give you—God Save the Czar!"

"A toast, gentlemen! To our meeting in Moscow, six months from today!"

"To our meeting in Petrograd! Three months from today!"

"They say Kolchak is coming to Harbin . . ."

"Kolchak doesn't know what he's doing. He's an ass."

"Semenov is gathering more men in Trans-Baikalia . . ."

"Semenov is a pig and a butcher!"

"Putilov just got here. To make sure nobody steals the Chinese Eastern from under his nose. Let the Bolsheviks try!"

"Anya, four more vodkas!"

But according to Brendan, Nicholas thought, the most influential, stealthy, and devious of all the groups in Harbin were the Japanese. Their influence in Manchuria was growing every month. Rumor said Japanese secret police were setting up a network of spies and paid informers to supply them with a constant stream of information. Nothing seemed too small or unimportant to escape their notice. Money appeared to be no obstacle. As well as information, they were purchasing fighting men and weapons in Harbin. Warlords, bandits, mercenaries, White Russian adventurers, counterrevolutionaries—which men were in the pay of the Japanese government? Who was being financed from Tokyo? Was Japan involved with the regime of Chang Tso-lin, the Old Marshal? Very likely. Was Japan deliberately causing disorder and upheaval in Manchuria and Siberia? No one in Harbin knew for certain, but everyone suspected.

And in Siberia, they'd entered the war against the Bolsheviks.

But Nicholas had his own affairs to think about, of a more immediate nature.

He considered again the branch of the Russo-Asiatic Bank two blocks behind him. He reined Chaika.

"Brendan, why don't you go on without me? Can you arrange a room for me at the Hotel Novy Mir?"

"Aye, that I can. Business to attend to?"

"Yes, for the next few days, I intend to be very busy."

"And as for myself," Brendan said, rubbing a reflective hand over his chin, "I have some cleaning up to do, and then I have some money to spend." He grinned. "By the time you see me next, Kolya, I'll be a helluva lot poorer than I am now."

They took their leave of one another, and Nicholas returned to the Russo-Asiatic Bank, along the Kitaiskaya. Inside, he asked to see a safe deposit box. They showed him to a small room in the vault, brought him a safe deposit box, closed the door, and left him alone.

He put all the jewelry into the box, emptying out the pouch, keeping only the emerald and diamond necklace.

He found some of his own things among the pieces. His gold watch. His ruby ring in the gold setting. He picked it up. He'd bought it a long time ago, in Kharkov.

He slipped the ring onto the little finger of his right hand. For luck.

Then he counted the cash. More than he'd thought, even after the steamer passage and the purchase of the horse and saddle. Good. He would need it all before he was through.

He kept only the cash he would need to use over the next few days, allowing for the purchases he wanted to make, and distributed the money into his pockets. He put the necklace into the leather pouch and, fastening it to his belt, stood up and buttoned his jacket. Then he locked the box with everything else inside and left the bank with his signed receipt.

Once he was on the street, he considered his next move.

Sell the necklace. Get that over with. He needed money to pay for the wool; buying clothes could wait until tomorrow.

He looked at the sky and judged it was somewhere between four and five o'clock. A jewelry store? No, he needed a more flexible bargaining position. Something else.

He remounted Chaika and when he was four blocks down the street, he stopped to ask directions from a young boy on the sidewalk, who answered him with a slightly terrified expression on his face. Nicholas realized how he must look; a foreigner on horseback, bearded, travel-stained, grim-faced.

He'd come a long way from a chauffeured limousine in Kharkov.

Following the boy's directions, he found his way to one of the Jewish sections of Harbin, a place of narrow streets and shabby houses, and dismounted in front of a small crumbling red brick building with a six-pointed star over the door. He entered the vestibule.

A tiny man in black wearing a skullcap and a prayer shawl emerged into the vestibule from an inner door. He scowled immediately on seeing Nicholas.

"Don't you cover your head when you enter a synagogue?"

Damn, he'd forgotten. "I'm sorry," he said courteously, "I'm not of your faith."

The scowl grew deeper. The question was unspoken, but quite clear: Then what are you doing here?

"I'm looking for a diamond merchant," Nicholas said. "Someone who deals in jewelry."

"Here?"

"Yes, I thought you might be able to help me."

Challenge. Cocked head. Squinting eyes.

"Why should I be able to help you?"

Nicholas sighed inwardly. It was going to be one of those conversations. But since he was already here, he decided to persist. He cleared his throat.

At last, after hedging and sparring back and forth, the old man made a concession. "Maybe Nachman Hirsch can help you," he said in a grudging tone.

"Does he know of a diamond dealer?"

The old man glared indignantly. "He *is* a diamond dealer!"

"I see. Where can I find him?"

More indignation flared at the stupid question. "You'll find him here, of course! Where else?"

"Yes, of course," Nicholas murmured. "Where else."

"Wait outside," the old man said, waving his hand. "They'll be out soon."

"Thank you."

Nicholas went outside to wait, leaning against the wall and lighting a cigarette. Within fifteen minutes men began to leave the building in groups of twos and threes. Nicholas stepped forward, dropping his cigarette onto the pavement and crushing it beneath his boot. "Excuse me," he said, "I'm looking for Nachman Hirsch."

Silence met him. Suspicious faces turned his way.

"Is he here?"

No answer.

"I have some business I'd like to discuss with him," Nicholas added politely. "It's quite important."

Another suspicious pause fell over the group. Then a man with an iron-gray beard sighed deeply. "I'm Hirsch," he said. "What can I do for you?"

"Do you think we could have a talk?"

Hirsch looked him up and down. "Naturally," he said, "if someone shows up looking like a wild Cossack, he wants to talk to Hirsch. It's never the ones in the fur coats; they always want to talk to somebody else. That's my luck." He walked over to Nicholas, leaving the other men behind. "All right, whoever you are, what do you want to discuss?"

"Do you think we could go somewhere private?"

Hirsch glanced at him shrewdly. "Oh," he said, "like that." He shrugged. "We'd better go to my house. It's just down the street. You can have a glass of tea, you could probably use it."

After tea and boiled chicken in the living room of the crowded little Hirsch dwelling, Nicholas and Nachman Hirsch settled down to business. Nicholas, on the sofa, produced the necklace, and Hirsch, in a facing chair, screwed a jeweler's glass into his eye. He inspected the necklace for a long time. Then he took the glass out of his eye. He scowled. "Where did you say you bought this piece?"

"In Kiev."

"That's right, you said so before." Hirsch paused. Then he shook his head. "How much did you tell me you paid for it?"

Nicholas told him again.

Hirsch pulled his bottom lip. "Excuse me," he said, "I don't like to be so blunt. But I think, Mr. Federovsky, you were cheated."

Nicholas settled back and smiled, reaching for his cigarettes. The bargaining had begun.

At the end of an hour, they'd reached an agreement.

"So you accept my offer?" Hirsch said. He seemed almost sorry to have the discussion at an end.

"I have no choice. My back is against the wall."

"You didn't do so bad." Hirsch sat back and grinned. "Did you just get here? Did you just arrive in Harbin?"

"Yes, this afternoon." Nicholas settled against the sofa, putting the necklace away again, careful to keep his bruised back an inch or two away from the sofa cushions.

"What are you going to do with yourself? Stay in Harbin, or move on to Shanghai?"

"I believe I'll stay. I'm thinking about going into the wool business."

"Is that so? Import-export? I have a friend, Herman Levy, who does very well in that field. Leather, wool . . ."

"Maybe he could give me some advice," Nicholas said pleasantly. "Maybe I could help him too. A traveler hears gossip. Some of it is useful."

Hirsch looked interested. "I'll send you over to see him. Since you're new here." He tilted his head. "Who knows, maybe Levy wants a partner. I can see that when you clean yourself up, you'll make a good appearance. And you're a Christian, that doesn't hurt."

Nicholas wasn't interested in a partnership. But he thought it would be helpful to speak to Hirsch's friend. The Jews of Harbin were reputed to control much of the city's wealth; an acquaintance could be valuable. And if the profits were high enough on the camel's wool, he had no objections to sharing them.

First, though, he needed a warehouse.

"Who would my competitor be in the wool trade?" he asked.

"Quite a few people. One of the biggest is a man named Liu. A Chinaman. I understand he has a caravan coming in from Mongolia in a few days."

Very good, Mr. Hirsch. Very helpful.

"Where does Liu keep his goods? In his own warehouse?"

"No, there's a comprador named Wang Tien-shan who represents the warehouse owners." Hirsch grinned, seeing that Nicholas didn't understand. "A comprador is an agent. A middleman. The Chinese like to do things that way, through a third party. Wang has an office over in Fu Chia Tien, across the river."

"You wouldn't happen to know him too, would you?"

"Wang Tien-shan? How would I know him? The Chinese keep to themselves."

"Yes, that's true."

It was time to conclude his conversation with Nachman Hirsch, Nicholas thought. He was ready to find his room at the Novy Mir and go to bed. He stood up. "Well, Mr. Hirsch, you've been very kind. I won't impose on you any longer. Thank you for your hospitality."

Hirsch accompanied him to the front door.

"I'll be back in a day or two with the necklace," Nicholas said on the doorstep. "Will you have cash for me? Gold, if possible. Not paper."

"It may have to be Mexican silver dollars."

"That will be acceptable."

They shook hands.

Now the Novy Mir, Nicholas thought, as he left the house.

In the small hotel lobby, after he had found a stable for Chaika, he discovered that Brendan had engaged him a room on the third floor. But Brendan wasn't in.

"Mr. O'Reilly left word that he'll be out until very late," the Russian desk clerk reported.

Nicholas smiled to himself. He'd expected that.

He paid a week's rent in advance, and had his saddlebag brought upstairs.

The room, he found, was small but comfortable, with an easy chair, a writing desk, and a large closet.

Best of all, it had its own bathroom.

Nicholas turned on the tap in the bathtub. Hot water. How long had it been? He stripped off his clothes, leaving them on the floor, and unwound the bandages from his back and chest, gritting his teeth against the pain of tearing them away from the clotted blood. Then he got into the tub, relaxing and letting it fill with steaming water.

Civilization.

Tomorrow he would shave. Not tonight.

Before he fell asleep, he resolved to put all thoughts from his mind except what lay ahead of him in the next few days. No remembering Major Chernov, or the Inn of the Green Parrot, or Daria's kidnapping. He couldn't afford to think about any of that yet. He would have to concentrate only on Harbin, until these first days were over. It would take all his willpower.

He woke up early and went to a café for breakfast. Afterward he stopped and bought three sets of silk underwear in a shop, returned to the hotel, undressed, and put on a set of the new underwear. Then he shaved off his beard and got dressed again. His hair and mustache needed trimming, but he would have that done some other time.

Now he had to pay a visit to Fu Chia Tien.

He took a taxi across the river and dismissed the driver on one of the narrow, odorous streets of the Chinese town. He might have been in a different city, so completely had the Russian atmosphere disappeared. Faded banners with Chinese characters flapped from the windows, meeting and mingling overhead. The fragrance of frying noodles filled the air. Rickshaws crowded the road, with the rickshaw coolies screaming for pedestrians to get out of the way, get out of the way. Peddlers dodged between people's legs with trays of hot food on poles across their shoulders, crying their wares in high, rhythmic singsongs. Dumplings! Meat pies! Chu po po! The street was lined with open-fronted shops, many of them doing business on the sidewalk. Crowds of blue-coated Chinese strolled up and down, shopping, bargaining, some of the men carrying bamboo cages with pet larks swinging in their hands.

He began to walk, and passed a barber shop. The barber stood outside, honing his razor, but Nicholas was looking for something else. He finally came to a halt beneath a canvas awning in front of a little store with an open front. Inside, in the shadows of the interior, a silk-robed merchant stood with his hands in his sleeves in front of a long counter. Bolts of cloth were piled on shelves behind him.

The sign overhead, extending into the street, pictured a needle and a pair of scissors.

Yes, this was what he was seeking. A tailor shop.

The tailor's apprentice, a young man in a long blue gown, came out to greet him, bowing and smiling, and ushered him inside.

He was taken behind a flowered curtain at the rear of the shop to disrobe, and the tailor himself came in with a measuring tape. His apprentice followed with bolts of cloth over his arm. When Nicholas had selected enough material for three suits, the tailor took measurements.

He fingered the silk underwear appreciatively.

"Can you get me more?" Nicholas asked.

"Oh yes!"

"And four or five silk shirts."

"Certainly." The tailor smiled broadly.

"Good. I'll need one suit and one shirt as quickly as possible."

"Day after tomorrow?" The tailor paused. "Perhaps tomorrow afternoon, if I hurry."

"No, day after tomorrow. But in the morning."

"Very good. You shall have it."

When he was finished with the tailor, Nicholas stopped for lunch at a small restaurant.

After that, he was ready to find Wang Tien-shan.

He discovered the comprador's establishment on a wide, quiet street shaded by trees. Bustle and clamor were absent here, although the shopping street was only three blocks away. Nicholas was facing a high wooden gate painted red and set into a thick wall of stone. He rang the bell beside the gate.

A blue-robed employee answered the bell, guarding the entrance with his body. After a glance at Nicholas's face he spoke in Russian. "Yes? What is it you wish?"

Beyond him, over his shoulder, Nicholas could see a wide courtyard bordered by shade trees. Rooms were open on all three sides, where robed men were conversing and drinking tea over lacquered tables. The atmosphere was cool and hushed.

"I would like to see the Honorable Wang Tien-shan."

"Have you an appointment?"

"No."

"Have you a business card?"

"No."

"Then I'm afraid it's not possible."

"I see." Nicholas paused. "I've just arrived from the north, and I have news of a very grave nature."

The employee regarded him impassively. "Perhaps you might relate it to me."

"It's for the ears of the Honorable Wang Tien-shan only."

"I'm sorry. He is busy."

"I must insist," Nicholas said.

The man began to close the gate.

"If you refuse to let me in," Nicholas added, "I'll be forced to lean on this bell without stopping. It will be very disturbing to your customers."

"You will not do that," the man said angrily. "I'll call a policeman and have you removed."

"Do that. Until he arrives, your customers will be very upset. I can make a great clamor, I assure you."

"Why are you being so rude and insistent?"

"Because it's important that I speak with Wang Tienshan."

"Send him a message in writing."

"My news is too urgent."

The man scowled angrily.

"May I know your name?" Nicholas asked.

The man set his jaw. "My name is Mr. Tsai," he said with dignity.

"Do you see that bird in the tree, Mr. Tsai?" Nicholas gestured at one of the trees in the courtyard. A brown thrush was seated on one of the lower branches.

Tsai followed his gesture. "Certainly," he said, turning back to Nicholas. "It's a brown thrush. A most ordinary, unremarkable bird."

"I believe it will fly south when it leaves the tree. I believe it will fly straight ahead." Nicholas paused. "I'd be willing to bet on it. Would you disagree?"

A gleam of interest came into Tsai's narrow black eyes. He hesitated. Then he said softly, "The bird will fly east, when it leaves the tree."

"Or west?"

"Perhaps."

"If the bird goes east or west, Mr. Tsai, I'll leave quietly, without any disturbance. But if it goes south, will you agree to announce my business to Mr. Wang Tien-shan?"

Tsai looked again at the bird. It was busily smoothing its feathers with its beak.

"I can make a very great disturbance, until the police arrive," Nicholas repeated softly.

"The bird will fly east or west," Tsai repeated half under his breath. "I will wager on it."

They waited. The bird was very occupied with its feathers. Finally it lifted its wings and flew off. Straight ahead, to the south.

Nicholas let out his breath. He had not considered what he would do if he'd lost.

"Come in," Mr. Tsai said, standing aside from the gate. He bowed from the waist. "I will find Mr. Wang Tien-shan."

Nicholas entered the courtyard and prepared himself to wait.

Half an hour later, he was escorted to one of the side rooms, invited to sit down, and served tea in a handleless cup.

More time went by.

"You wish to see Wang Tien-shan?"

Nicholas got to his feet at the sound of a low and cultured voice speaking excellent Russian. He was facing an elderly Chinese man in a dull blue silk robe, with his hair in an old-fashioned queue down his back. He wore a round buttoned cap on his head, in the style of the late Manchu dynasty, and his hands were tucked into the wide blue sleeves of his gown. His expression was politely inquiring.

Nicholas bowed. "Yes, I have news to tell him."

"Mr. Tsai was very vague."

"I explained to Mr. Tsai that my news is for Wang Tien-shan only."

The man paused. "Who are you? Where do you come from?"

"My name is Nicholas Federovsky. I come from the city of Kharkov, in the Ukraine. I have crossed the northern border only a short time ago."

"How do you know Wang Tien-shan? Who sent you?"

"Many voices in the city speak of Wang Tien-shan."

"You are not known to him or his family. You have no introduction or card. Why should he speak with you?"

"I have news that may be of great importance to him." Nicholas paused. "Perhaps Mr. Tsai explained that."

There was a longer pause. Finally the man gestured with a slender hand. "I am Wang Tien-shan. Please be seated. We will speak."

They sat down facing one another across the table. Wang folded his hands.

"How old are you?" he asked.

"I am thirty-six."

"I am sixty-one." Wang paused. "Have you children?"

"No. I am unmarried."

"I have five sons and three daughters." Wang cleared his throat delicately. "And seven grandsons." He poured tea. "What is your business or profession?"

"I was once a civil engineer. But I no longer have a business or profession. I have been impoverished by the revolution in my country."

"I see." Wang took a sip from his teacup. "Do you come to me for assistance?"

"In a sense."

"Why do you not go to your own people?"

"Because, Honorable Wang, I have information regarding one of your people."

The comprador raised his eyebrows.

"Information regarding a theft of wool from the great Merchant Liu."

A subtle look of interest flickered over Wang's face. But he only said mildly, "Theft? Why, then, do you not go to Mr. Liu?"

"He is very busy. He would not see me."

That lie, Nicholas thought, was not intended to be believed. But it didn't matter. The rituals would be observed.

After a while, when more formalities had been completed, Nicholas described, in very vague and general terms, the plan to steal the Bactrian camel's wool from the caravan. Wang nodded.

"Such things often happen. Sad to relate, there are many dishonest men in our land. And profits have been made from such dishonesty." He frowned. "Why do you tell me this story?"

"I have an opportunity to obtain the wool myself, from the thieves. If I might bring it to you, Mr. Wang, for storage in one of your warehouses, you might hold it in safekeeping for the Merchant Liu."

For the first time Wang smiled faintly. "Very thoughtful."

"Surely Mr. Liu would reward you generously for that action. When he discovers it."

Nicholas met his eyes across the table.

Liu, of course, would never hear a word about it. They both knew that.

Finally Wang set his teacup aside. "You understand, of course," he said, "that I only represent the warehouse owners. I cannot make such a decision by myself."

"I understand."

"Still, the Merchant Liu has a reputation for generosity." He paused to let the significance of that sink in, and then stood up. Nicholas rose to his feet. "I will consult with the owners," Wang said, "and inform you if any of them has space for these bales of wool."

"I hope the answer will be favorable."

"If you'll return here tomorrow afternoon, I will give you my answer."

"Thank you, Honorable Wang."

They both bowed. The conversation was over.

One and a half days gone.

Now, unexpectedly, Nicholas had hours to himself. He bought a pair of white jade cuff links in Fu Chia Tien, for the time when his new shirts would be ready. Then he returned to the hotel, with nothing to do until tomorrow. He found himself sleeping, in weary gratitude for the respite. He hadn't realized his utter exhaustion. He felt he could sleep for days. His back was stiff and aching, but scabs were forming over the wounds. The flesh was still dark purple, but the color was fading to yellow around the edges.

The next afternoon he went back again to see Wang Tien-shan.

After the formalities, when they were again sitting over cups of tea in the courtyard, Wang came to the point.

"I have spoken about your proposition," he said, "to Madame Sung."

Nicholas waited politely.

"Madame Sung owns many warehouses along the waterfront," Wang went on. "She wishes to meet you first before making a decision."

"I see."

"Madame Sung is a widow. She has had much recent tragedy in her life. She doesn't wish to make a mistake." Wang lowered his eyelids. "It will require much tact and diplomacy to persuade her."

Nicholas began to feel weariness overtake him. He wondered if he was up to dealing with an elderly Chinese widow.

But he'd come this far. "I'll be happy to meet Madame Sung," he said. "Can you arrange it, Mr. Wang?"

"I have already arranged it. With your permission, of course." Wang sat back. "She will see you at four o'clock tomorrow afternoon."

That didn't leave him much time. The day after that, Shanghai would be arriving in Harbin. If the widow were stubborn—

But I have nothing to lose, he told himself tiredly.

"If you will tell me how I can reach Madame Sung," he said, "I will keep the appointment."

"Where are you staying, Mr. Federovsky?"

"At the Hotel Novy Mir."

"Madame Sung will send her car for you tomorrow at half-past three."

They both stood up.

"I'm very grateful for your efforts on my behalf," Nicholas said.

"I'm sure you are." Wang lowered his eyes suavely. "I wish you good luck in your endeavor." He smiled. "I believe you will find Madame Sung . . . most interesting."

Two and a half days gone, Nicholas thought.

The next morning he visited Nachman Hirsh and collected his money for the necklace. He put it into the safe deposit box at the bank. Then he found a barber shop. He leaned back in the chair as the barber flung a towel around his neck. "Everything."

"You wish hot towels on your face?"

"Yes."

"Cologne?"

"Yes."

"You wish a manicure?"

"Everything."

The barber summoned the manicurist, a young Chinese girl in a slit skirt cheongsam, as he began to lather his shaving brush. Nicholas closed his eyes.

An hour later, shaved and barbered, he crossed the river again to Fu Chia Tien. His suit was ready at the tailor shop, a dark blue cashmere. And one of the cream silk shirts. He fitted the white jade cuff links into the cuffs as the tailor patted and straightened the jacket. The apprentice brought in an armful of neckties. The tailor held one out. "This?"

Nicholas glanced over. "No, not that." He selected another one.

When he was finally dressed and was adjusting his tie, the tailor stepped back and beamed appreciatively. "Such elegance! You are a very fine gentleman! You do me credit!"

Nicholas looked at himself somberly in the mirror. The tailor and the barber had done a good job. The grim-faced stranger of the wilderness was gone, replaced by the old Kolya Federovsky, with the familiar and comforting feel of silk against his skin, and the ruby ring flashing on his finger. Time had rolled back. He was himself again. But only outwardly. Too much had happened to be the same inside. Strange, that it didn't show. A visit to the barber; some new clothes . . . but the inner wounds were invisible.

He still had so much to do.

Daria was still lost.

Steeling himself to keep going, he arranged to have his other clothes delivered to his hotel when they were ready, and then went outside to find a taxi. He must return to the Novy Mir in time to keep his four o'clock appointment with Madame Sung.

Chapter 27

The Chinese widow, Nicholas realized, did not live in the Chinese town of Fu Chia Tien. She lived, apparently, in the wealthy residential section of New Town.

He glanced out of the limousine window, drawing on his cigarette. The chauffeur-driven Benz sedan was rolling through broad, tree-shaded avenues lined with spacious houses of stone or wood set back on well-cared-for lawns. The grass was a uniform shade of glowing emerald. Many of the lawns displayed landscaped flower beds, bright with color.

Very nice. New Town, it seemed, was a most desirable place to live.

No desperate, haunted-eyed refugees moved on these quiet streets, he observed. There were no people visible at all, in fact, except for a gardener here and there.

Some day, he thought, when Daria is back . . . He wouldn't let himself consider any other possibility. Instead he thought about some day living in New Town.

Then he wondered what he would say to Madame Sung. It was difficult to know in advance, until you met the woman. He just had to hope he wouldn't violate courtesy in any way, or commit some unsuspected breach of etiquette.

It would be a little more complex than eating bread sauce and drinking kumiss in a Mongol caravan, he thought.

Above all, he told himself, he mustn't come to the point too quickly in the conversation. That applied as much to the Mongolian camel driver as it did to Wang Tien-shan. All these peoples of the Orient liked to approach a subject obliquely. Dealing with them required patience. You had to move step by step; you had to take one thing at a time, wary, testing, hoping your judgment was delicate enough to warn you of the right moment to speak. . . .

The chauffeur was turning a corner. Now the city had disappeared. They were not on a paved street but a quiet country lane. No lawns stretched by the roadside, no houses, only trees and tall uncut grass. The smell of sun-warmed grass was in the air, and the fragrance of wild-flowers, and the chirping of birds, and the low hum of cicadas.

Odd, he felt as though he had stepped through a doorway into some other time and place. He wasn't usually fanciful. He felt slightly annoyed with himself.

The automobile was bumping gently over the ruts in the road. They hadn't yet passed another house. They continued past waving grasses and occasional groves of willow trees. More birdsong and the rustle of leaves filled the air.

Madame Sung, it seemed, liked privacy.

For the first time Nicholas wondered if he were being led into a trap. He'd trusted Wang Tien-shan, believing they understood one another, but now he had begun to ask himself uncomfortable questions. He dismissed them as more foolish fancies.

The automobile came to a gentle stop. The chauffeur got out and ran around to the back door, opening it and gesturing for Nicholas to alight.

He was standing on the dirt road, facing a high wall of weathered yellow brick. Tree branches drooped over the top of the wall, and he could see the graceful curves of a red tile pagoda through the leaves, the rooftop of the house which was hidden behind the wall. The hush was very peaceful. Somewhere far off he heard a fountain splashing. He felt another strange sense of premonition, but this time the sensation was pleasant. Now the yellow bricks of the wall seemed welcoming and mellow, whispering a greeting—or was it the rustle of the leaves? He'd never had imaginings like these before. He needed more sleep, he told himself, passing a hand over his eyes. He must be more weary than he'd realized.

A gatekeeper was opening the door in the wall. The man was young, brawny, and armed with a rifle.

Yes, there was always the danger of kidnapping in Manchuria. Guard yourself . . .

Inside now. Gatehouse to the left. Another wall straight ahead, more yellow brick, another gate, and a huge brass gong in a metal frame.

Sound vibrated in the air. The gatekeeper had struck the gong. The inner gate opened noiselessly, and a manservant stood bowing, with his hands in his sleeves. He wore a black silk robe embroidered with scarlet dragons.

"This way please, Honorable Guest." His voice was low and courteous. "You are expected."

Nicholas had grown accustomed to hearing his own language. He followed the manservant through the second gate.

He was in an inner courtyard, wide, spacious, with flowering shrubs and fruit trees, silver birdcages in the branches, with larks fluttering inside.

Straight ahead, on either side of a round moon gate, crouched two lion-dogs of blue porcelain, with scowling faces and huge blue paws.

"Follow me, please."

He went through the moon gate, past the lion-dogs. A stone pavilion lay beyond. Then they entered a long, dim corridor floored with mahogany polished like black glass. The manservant's felt slippers made a soft whispering sound against the floor.

Another curving moon gate let in light at the end of the corridor.

The splash of the unseen fountain grew louder.

He came out of the moon gate into a garden. Sunlight fell across his shoulders. All around him were grass and flower beds. In the center of a rock garden gleamed a turquoise pool where the fountain was splashing. Within the pool glinted the now-and-then fire of golden carp.

But he was more interested in Madame Sung. He stared. He was fascinated. She'd been sitting on a stone bench beneath the overhanging branches of a willow tree, and now she rose to her feet as he emerged from the moon

313

gate. How wrong he'd been. She wasn't elderly at all. She was exquisitely beautiful, small and slender as a porcelain figurine, but with the warm living tint of rose in the perfect oval of her face. Her hair was black and glossy, framing a fragile-boned face, and coiled at the back of her neck. Her tiny breasts rose and fell beneath the blue silk of her gown, perfectly outlined by the clinging fabric to the last detail of the small, pointed nipples, and he imagined he could see the hollow of her navel, molded by the blue silk, and the faint shadow of the mound between her thighs.

All his preconceived ideas vanished. Wang Tien-shan had been right, he thought in bemusement. He found Madame Sung most interesting.

She was standing quietly with her hands folded, waiting for him to approach. He realized the manservant had disappeared.

As he walked toward her, she extended her hand. "I am Madame Sung," she said softly. "Welcome to my humble house."

He took her hand and murmured his own name. He forgot about being a stranger, and a refugee in a foreign country, and acted as he would have done at home. In a natural and spontaneous gesture, he raised her hand to his mouth and bent his head and touched his lips to the cool, scented flesh of her hand. She smelled of sandalwood and jasmine.

She withdrew her hand, looking slightly startled. He wondered, still bemused, if it was the custom to kiss a woman's hand in China. But it was too late now.

Madame Sung gestured at the stone bench. "Won't you sit down?"

"Thank you." He seated himself on the bench.

She sat down beside him with effortless grace. "May I offer you some jasmine tea?"

He saw that jasmine tea was steaming on an ivory table near the bench. Thin blue-and-gold cups and saucers stood waiting beside the teapot. He accepted the offer of tea, and she poured two cups with the same flowing grace with which she seemed to do everything.

He reminded himself of why he had come as he accepted his cup of tea. But here in this quiet garden, behind these high walls, with the tinkling fountain splashing somewhere behind him, the fragrance of sandalwood and jasmine drifting on the air, and this delicately beautiful woman seated beside him, it was difficult to keep his mind on warehouses and bales of wool.

He made the effort.

Madame Sung smiled. "I know you have come to discuss business," she said, "but you must forgive our customs. We find it impossible to come straight to the point, as Westerners do. At least those of us who have been brought up in the old ways, as I have."

"Certainly," he said gravely. "I've already met Wang Tien-shan."

She laughed at that. "He's extremely old-fashioned. His family has served my husband's family for many years. He is a good friend."

"I'm grateful to him for arranging this meeting. It's kind of you to see me."

"It's not . . . usual," she said. "But there has been much sorrow and unhappiness for me in this house, and I wanted to see you here, in these surroundings, before I decided what to do about your offer." She turned her head to look at him over the teacup. "Do you believe, Mr. Federovsky, that walls and houses and gardens have a life of their own?"

"No, I'm afraid I don't."

"But they do. They have an aura. There are . . . vibrations in certain surroundings that respond to each individual presence as it enters or departs. For good or evil."

Good Lord. Did she mean that?

She laughed again, a low musical sound. "I can see that you're skeptical."

"Surely there can be nothing evil in this beautiful garden."

"It's tactful of you to say so. But I've tasted bitterness in this garden. There are fêng shui hovering in the branches of this willow tree. They are unseen, but they are very powerful."

Demons in the willow tree? She couldn't believe that. She was a well-educated and cultivated woman.

"I hope they'll stay away from now on," he said. "If I can do anything to dispel them, I'll be glad to try."

He wasn't making any more sense than she was, he

thought, discussing demons as though they perched at his shoulder.

"Perhaps you can." Madame Sung looked pensive. "Tell me, what year were you born?"

He reminded himself that asking someone's age was a perfectly normal question here.

"Eighteen eighty-two."

She considered for a moment. "The Year of the Horse. You represent the *yang*, or male principle. Perhaps that's why the fêng shui seem to have withdrawn." She smiled wistfully. "I was born in the Year of the Monkey, and my husband was born in the Year of the Dog. They were both years of the *yin*, or female principle. It was unlucky for this house."

"I'm sorry if your husband met with ill fortune."

"You must have heard of it, surely."

"No, I've only just arrived in Manchuria. I know nothing about events on this side of the border."

"Shall I tell you what occurred?"

"Yes, if you like."

"It was a year ago. It no longer pains me to speak of it." She set down the teacup and folded her hands in her lap. "When Chang Tso-lin, our warlord, first arrived in Manchuria in 1911 he issued a warning against currency speculation. My husband, and certain others, paid no attention. Last year nine of them were summoned to Chang Tso-lin's yamen in Mukden and confronted with their crimes. Half an hour later they had been tried, condemned, and beheaded in the courtyard." She smiled sadly. "Justice is swift in our country."

"I'm sorry, Madame Sung."

"Chang Tso-lin was quite merciful. He allowed me to keep my property and my house, and took only reparations for my husband's crimes."

There was very little else you could say, Nicholas thought. They certainly didn't waste time here with courts and appeals and trials.

"And now perhaps you will explain to me about Mr. Liu, and the Bactrian camel's wool." Madame Sung looked slightly mischievous. "I'm sure you are anxious to reach the real point of your visit."

316

As a matter of fact, he wasn't. The caravan and the bales of wool seemed remote and unreal, and he was being curiously affected by the surroundings. Maybe she was right. Maybe houses did have an aura, an atmosphere, for good or evil. He wasn't sure which this was.

He wondered how much Wang had told her as he began to explain his story. She listened courteously, remaining very still, not even moving her head. There was an oddly erotic quality about her stillness. He found his mind wandering as he spoke, although he hoped she couldn't tell.

Then she leaned forward to set down her teacup. As she bent he examined the row of tiny silk buttons down the back of her gown. They ran from the nape of her neck down to the small of her back. Each was fastened by a small silken loop. How long would it take to unfasten all those buttons? Endlessly long. How many could you manage to undo before she sprang away scarlet-faced and called for help? Four or five. If you were quick.

No, you wouldn't have to unfasten the buttons at all. Clearly she was wearing nothing under the gown. All you would have to do would be to pin her down against the grass and keep your hand over her mouth so that she couldn't cry out, and then raise the gown . . . and when she was helpless, you could release yourself with your free hand . . .

I must be mad. What am I thinking of?
Fêng shui.

He realized that his thoughts were becoming embarrassingly obvious, and hoped she would be polite enough not to notice. *Blame it on demons, my dear lady.*

Maybe in this country such a noticeable reaction was considered a compliment. A tribute to the lady's beauty and femininity.

He forced his mind back to the conversation.

Madame Sung's ivory cheeks were stained pink. He had the uncomfortable feeling that she was aware of his desire. But she remained very calm, and continued to discuss the warehouses.

"I don't believe, Mr. Federovsky, that you are a bad or evil person," she said, folding her hands on her lap. "I don't believe you would bring any more ill fortune upon

317

my house. I see no reason why you shouldn't go ahead with your plan to obtain the wool, and bring it to my warehouse."

He murmured something, realizing that she was giving her consent.

Madame Sung heaved a sigh, lifting the tiny, perfect breasts beneath the silk. "I'm not a businesswoman, and I dislike the responsibility of ownership. Yet I cannot leave it all to Wang Tien-shan. The burden is mine."

"Perhaps you might sell the warehouses."

She looked at him in genuine surprise. "Yes, I was thinking exactly that. Before I go on my journey—"

"Are you leaving Manchuria?"

"Soon." She waved a slender, graceful hand, dismissing the subject. "If I found the right person to buy the warehouses . . ."

"Is that why you asked me here, Madame Sung? To see if I was the right person?"

He'd had no idea he was going to say that.

"No, of course not. How could I know such a thing?"

"Nor could I. And yet . . . now . . . it seems exactly right. I'm a newcomer to Harbin, as you know. But I've had experience in my own country with owning property, and the responsibility doesn't trouble me."

Warehouses. Storage space. In Harbin, where stolen goods were pouring in and out every day, every hour. You could charge whatever you liked, he thought in sudden excitement. You could fill up the space and empty it out with dizzying speed. Each turnover would mean more profit. You could make a fortune. If you weren't timid. And you were willing to take risks.

"Could you afford such a purchase?" Madame Sung asked wonderingly.

"Yes." He thought quickly. If he sold the wool at a good profit, and could get a bank loan against the jewelry and the cash—if not the bank, then a moneylender. And if she was willing to take a chance . . . "I think I might."

"I must have time to think about such an idea."

"Of course."

She fell silent. He wondered what she was thinking about. The idea of warehouses had stirred him, and the

318

emotion was mingling with his previous arousal in an intensely erotic way. He began to feel reckless.

There were times, he thought, when you could not make a mistake. Certain times when the gods were smiling. When the fêng shui had been driven away. And right now, he almost believed that the demons had flown away from the willow tree. Away from the garden. Away from the house.

"Will you show me your house, Madame Sung?" he asked. "I realize it may be discourteous of me to ask, but I don't believe I'll have a chance like this again. And I have an idea that your home is very beautiful."

She hesitated for a moment, and then she said, "Of course. I'll be glad to." She stood up. "It's built around courtyards. There are many pavilions. Here in the garden, we are facing the south pavilion."

Nicholas rose to his feet. "I see. Is that where you sleep? Facing the garden?"

She drew in her breath a little, but she said calmly "No. I sleep in the east pavilion. I like to see the sun rise."

"If I owned a house like this, I'd make the same choice." He paused, looking down into her eyes. "May I see your bedroom?" he asked quietly.

For a moment he wondered if she were going to call the manservant and the gatekeeper and have him thrown out. But instead she made a helpless little sound deep in her throat and flung out her hand. She turned her face aside. "I must tell you something," she whispered, "before we go any further. I can see that we must be honest with each other. Although it is very painful for me."

"I'm sorry. I don't want to cause you pain."

"No." She raised her chin. "You make me feel proud. And womanly. You see . . . those are feelings that have been absent from my life for a very long time."

Nicholas started to say something, but she stopped him. "Do you know what it means," she said in a whisper, "for a woman to drink the cup of vinegar?"

"No."

"We say that in China, when a husband brings a second wife into his house. A young, beautiful woman, to share

319

his bed. And you, the first wife, must drink the cup of vinegar."

Nicholas said nothing for a moment. Then he began slowly, "I always thought—"

Madame Sung gave a rueful laugh. "Yes, you thought the concubine system was an accepted way of life among my people. Perhaps it is. But it is bitter to be rejected and cast out. To be lonely, no longer wanted. I spent hours of bitterness in this garden, after my husband brought home his second wife." She paused and lowered her eyes. "That was five years ago," she whispered.

My God. Five years. He caught her hand, brought it to his mouth, turned it over and kissed the palm. "My dear Madame Sung, may I know your name?"

"Mei-ling."

"Sung Mei-ling. It sounds like bells."

She smiled mistily. "How kind you are." She took a deep breath. "Now, if you like, I'll show you the east pavilion."

She led him through the house. They passed through pavilions with cool stone floors, covered with rugs that were silky and faded with age. Silk screens depicted seasons of the Moon Year. White T'ang horses glimmered in porcelain. Black-and-gold lacquered chests spoke of great antiquity.

Her bedroom, in the east pavilion, was dim and spacious. The sun was in the west. The sky above the terrace beyond the open double doors glowed a deep shining blue. Pots of flowering shrubs stood around the terrace.

The bed itself, against the far wall, was draped with a covering of pale apricot satin. Mei-ling's fragrance of sandalwood and jasmine was very strong, and Nicholas felt slightly dizzy and a little out of place. This was a very feminine room. He felt like an intruder. The bathroom door was open, to his right, and he had a glimpse of peach-colored tiles and a round sunken bathtub. A dressing room adjoined it.

"Is this what you expected?" Mei-ling asked, turning to face him.

"Yes. It's exactly what I expected." His unease suddenly vanished, and he caught her to him, feeling her slender body and fragile bones melt against him. How delicate she was. He would have to be very careful, he thought. She would break, surely, if he handled her too roughly.

"May I stay here for a while?" he asked.

"I . . . I think so."

He found her mouth with his own, and kissed her very gently and very thoroughly. She trembled in his arms. Her lips were sweet and cool and tasted of jasmine.

"It has been a very long time," she said, sighing and drawing back. "I feel very shy and timid. Like a young girl."

"I would like to make love to you. Will you let me?"

After a moment she whispered, "You have brought the yang principle into this house. Here and now, it is more powerful than the yin."

It was her way of consenting. He caught her close again.

She laughed shakily, resting her head on his chest. "Will you permit me to withdraw for a little while?"

"Of course."

"I'll remove this cover before I go." She drew out of his arms, went to the bed and pulled off the apricot satin, letting it fall onto the floor. The sheets and pillowcases were ivory silk.

When she had disappeared into the dressing room, Nicholas undressed slowly and thoughtfully. He had to remember not to turn his back, or he might shock her with the sight of his bruises.

Standing in his shirt, tie, and underwear, holding his trousers, he found his cigarettes and matches in his trouser pocket and laid them on the bedside table. Then he took off the rest of his clothes and got between the cool silk sheets of the bed.

The scent of jasmine surrounded him. He lay on his side, smoking a cigarette. His desire had ebbed during the walk through the pavilions of the house, but now it was rising again. This atmosphere was dreamlike and very sensual. He felt detached and aroused at the same time. He thought of ivory silk, and jasmine, and the taste of Mei-ling's mouth. He wondered if she would cry out at the moment of her climax, or if she would become very still and silent, looking inward.

He became aware that she was coming toward him from the dressing room. He crushed out the cigarette. Her hair was loose and spilled down around her shoulders like black silk. She wore a sashed robe, and with one slender hand she held it closed around her throat.

She sat down on the edge of the bed. She was like a bird, he thought, poised to fly away.

"Have you changed your mind?" he asked.

"No."

"Then will you kiss me?"

She leaned forward and brushed his lips with hers. He pulled her down and searched her mouth more intimately, and felt her quiver in response.

She drew back, took a breath, and ran her hand wonderingly over his chest. "You are strange to me," she whispered. "The men of my race are not so hairy."

"Does it upset you?"

"No." A faint blush stained her cheeks. "I . . . I thought it would. But it is only . . . different."

This time, as he caressed her, he untied the sash of her robe, and crushed her naked breasts against him. "Is that very different?" he said against her mouth.

"No . . ."

"Then no more questions. From now on, Mei-ling, I'll discover you for myself."

After all, she cried out at the moment of her climax. Her eyes glazed, and her fragile, delicate body shuddered beneath him as though she were being shaken by an earthquake. Her hand reached up blindly to stroke his face, and she cried out something he couldn't understand. Then she yielded herself in a hot, wet flood of surrender. When she had subsided, she lay very still in his arms. He felt tender and excited, and thought he would give himself very soon. He was afraid of hurting her. The sweet hidden intimacy of her was like that of a young girl, for she had been untouched for a long time, and the bones of her body were almost childlike in their delicacy. He moved slowly, gently, and after a while her back arched, as she began to respond again.

When he gave himself, she shuddered and breathed a long sigh, and surrendered once more.

He remained within her, afterward, holding her in his

arms, not withdrawing. He thought he would keep her here, and not let her go. He wondered if he was drunk on the scent of jasmine. He had certainly never imagined, a few hours ago, that he would find himself here, in Madame Sung's bedroom, naked between silk sheets, with this strange and beautiful woman imprisoned beneath him. No, never. He would have said it was impossible.

But she was very real.

"May I go?" she said, half laughing, half shy.

"No. You may not go."

"How long must I stay?"

"Until I give you permission to leave." He kissed her mouth. "That won't be for a long while."

"Then I suppose I must submit . . ."

She remained quiet, breathing softly and quickly, like a trapped little bird. The tiny, perfect body was very exciting to him. He began to think about what had just happened, reliving it in his mind, and as he thought it would, after a while the memory brought him to life again. Wanting, wanting. Growing hungrily. Stirring. Seeking out her hidden places. Searching within her. *Give me your secrets. Let me know you.*

But she was so very small, even this was enough to bring a startled and wondering expression to her face.

Only wait. There will be more.

When he had taken her for the second time, they were both quite spent. He allowed her to leave, and when she returned from the bathroom, she was wearing the robe, and her face was washed.

He brushed back the long, straight black-silk hair as she sat down on the edge of the bed. "You look like a very young girl."

She gazed at him with a strange, unreadable expression on her face. "Do you think so?" Then she looked down at her hands. "I am older than you."

"I don't believe you are."

"But it's true." She paused. "I am forty-seven years old."

He was taken aback. She looked no more than twenty-five. He'd been aware she was older than that. Still, the truth surprised him.

"You must have discovered the secret of eternal youth."

How many times had he said that, in how many bedrooms? It was just something you said. This time he meant every word.

"Are you sorry now, that you have been my lover?" she said.

"Of course not. Why would I be sorry?"

"Perhaps I am not like the other women you have known."

"You're not. You are yourself. You're Mei-ling."

"You have been very good to me," she whispered as he reached up to the table for a cigarette. Then she said softly, "Now we must heal your injuries."

He turned to look at her. She stretched out her hand and touched his back. "What has been done to you, Nicholas? Who did such a thing?"

Of course she would have noticed. She would have from the beginning.

"Soldiers."

"They must have been very bad evil men."

"Some day, I believe someone will answer for it."

She stood up, tightening the sash of her robe. "Will you turn over on your stomach?" He hesitated. "Please," she said.

After a moment he turned over on his stomach and rested his cheek against the pillow. Mei-ling ran her hands over his back. She had a light, fluttering touch, like the brush of a bird's wing.

"Stay where you are for a little while. Do not move."

He realized that she had pulled a velvet rope behind the table. But he was feeling drowsy, lying against the pillow. He was vaguely aware that she was speaking to someone at the bedroom door, in a low musical singsong. Then time passed. Other people entered the room. He sat up. The manservant in the black-and-crimson dragon robe, aided by a pretty young Chinese maid, was wheeling in a tray of covered dishes.

He wondered if she was compromising herself, allowing the servants to find him here like this, in her bed. She didn't seem to mind. She was dismissing the servants and picking up a small covered jar from the tray.

"Lie down, please."

"Is that supper, on the tray?"

324

"Yes."

"I'm very hungry."

She smiled. "After I have finished, we can eat."

He stretched out again on his stomach. She took some ointment from the jar and began to rub it into his back, slowly, gently, one area at a time, making sure she had completed it before going on to the next. Her touch, and the feel of the ointment, were remarkably soothing.

"What is that?" he asked drowsily.

"Oh, many things. Powdered ginseng root, and herbs and medicine. It will prevent scars."

"There'll always be scars."

"Yes, but very light ones. They will fade. They will be very light and fine."

When she was finally done, he sat up again and they ate the food in the covered dishes on the tray. There was amber-colored wine as well, with a strange exotic taste he couldn't identify. Mei-ling refused the wine, saying she never took spirits, so he drank it himself, wondering what it was. It probably wasn't polite to inquire about the food or drink, he decided, and he was extremely hungry.

He finally smoked his cigarette when they'd pushed the tray aside.

"Will you stay now," she asked, slightly wistfully, "or do you have an appointment?"

"No, I have no appointments. I told you, I'm a stranger here. I have nowhere to go and nothing to do."

"But that will change. Perhaps very soon. You will be busy in Harbin before long. People will know who you are." She smiled. "Would you like to go to sleep?"

"If you'll come to bed with me."

"Very well." She began to rise. He caught her by the wrist.

"Where are you going?"

"To put on my nightgown."

"No, don't do that. Stay as you are. Only take the robe off."

She hesitated, but after a moment she shrugged off the robe and slipped beneath the sheets, He folded her in his arms, burying his face in her throat, feeling her hair a spill of black silk across his arm.

Jasmine. Silk. Warm, smooth ivory flesh. Woman scent. Slender thighs. Tiny breasts with tips like rosebuds.

He would have sworn he was exhausted. Drained. But it wasn't so. He wanted her again. Desperately. Urgently. With a swelling, bursting need that was more intense than before. He whispered, "Mei-ling . . ."

"Yes."

"I must make love to you again."

Her protests died away as she surrendered.

Even then, with her struggling, slender body at his disposal, yielding and moist, and her narrow hips caught between his hands, molded against him, there was no end to his need. No bottom to his desire. No way to reach the top of the mountain. Only this driving urgency, this swelling need.

His passion should have been slow-moving, hard to waken, half-asleep. Not this bursting flame.

He heard her speaking, from very far away. "Nicholas? Tell me how you feel."

"As though I could go on forever, my love. Like this. At the bottom of an ocean. On the edge of a volcano. Beneath the sea. Until your hair is tangled with pearls and coral, and the seas dry up. Until the world comes to an end." *What was he saying?*

Suddenly, she sat up. With strong small hands she pushed against his chest. "Stop. Please stop."

"No, you mustn't stop me. Not now."

He tried to make her lie down again, but she struggled. "Listen to me. Please listen."

"Later. Afterward."

She threw her arms around his neck and whispered in his ear. "If you'll listen, it will be something you'll like."

She pushed him down against the mattress, on his back, and he struggled, fearing the pain. But there was none. He closed his eyes and allowed himself to relax against the bed. The cool silk was suddenly soft and slippery against his back, but there was no pain. Only for a moment. Then he was stretched out full-length on his back for the first time since Chernov had cut him down from the tree.

Mei-ling was reaching out for the bedside table. Why?

Was she pulling the velvet rope? No, he must be imagining it.

Then she was lying beside him, covering his face with little kisses. He still needed her. He was still throbbing.

"Why did you go away?" he said, pulling her close.

"It will be all right. Everything will be all right. You must forgive me, I didn't know."

Forgive her for what, he wondered.

"Lie still," she said, "just for a moment."

"How can I lie still, when you are so beautiful and I still want you so?"

"Oh, it will be——" She stopped and caught her breath, looking toward the door. He raised himself on his elbows.

Someone was standing in the bedroom door. He made out the small, lithe figure of a girl in a long robe. Mei-ling said something very quickly in a very low voice. The girl entered the room, moving with feline grace, and came over to the bed.

Nicholas sat up. "Who are you?" he asked angrily. "What are you doing here?"

"I am Yum Li."

He thought perhaps she was the maidservant who had come into the room earlier.

In one swift, graceful movement she was taking off the robe. Then she was standing naked by the bedside.

Mei-ling was silent.

"What——"

"Don't," Mei-ling said suddenly. "Lie back, as you were."

Warily he lay back against the sheet. Mei-ling stretched herself across his chest.

The girl called Yum Li climbed up onto the bed. She straddled his thighs. Then slowly she lowered herself down until she was encasing him. He drew in his breath. She was hot, moist and clinging, with a fierce muscular urgency that pulsed with demand. Fiery sensation went through him.

Mei-ling brought her mouth down on his, and forced her tongue deep into his throat. He groaned and pulled her closer. She writhed against him, rubbing herself like a tigress against his body.

327

Yum Li, straddling his thighs, was a heaving sea of molten lava. He strained to thrust himself within that heated flesh.

Mei-ling raised her body and lowered her breast into his mouth. He took it greedily, holding her pressed against him with one arm around her waist and the other across her slender buttocks. She drew away until he released her and she fell across him with a little cry and found his mouth with her own.

Yum Li, encasing him, was clinging tighter, demanding, wanting, asking for everything, his life's blood, pulsating in and out like a hot cave of flesh. Mei-ling's tongue was exploring deep inside his mouth, searching and wet.

With a final moan he arched his back, lifted his hips and exploded into Yum Li.

It went on and on. Unceasing. Mei-ling was holding him, caressing his face, saying things, uttering wordless little cries, as he shuddered without end, crying out . . . for Daria.

He was quiet again, at last. He realized that Yum Li had disappeared. He and Mei-ling were alone again, still stretched side by side on the silk sheets of the bed.

He began to feel angry.

"Who is Yum Li?" he asked.

"She is the maid."

"Do you always share your lovers with the maid?"

"Oh, don't! Don't be angry!" She sat up, and he saw the distress on her face. "I didn't know what to do. I was so afraid you would injure yourself . . . it was the third time . . . and Yum Li is very skilled in the ways of love . . . and if you just went on and on for hours without relief . . ."

He began to realize what had happened. "Mei-ling, was I drugged?"

"Yes, the servants did it. They knew you were here, and they wanted me to be pleased, because I've been lonely for so long. Don't be angry."

"Something in the wine?" She nodded. "What was it?"

"Some mixture they know of. Opium and saffron, ginseng root, cantharides, other things . . ."

"Good Lord."

"Are you peaceful now?"

"Yes."

"Are you calm?"

"Yes."

"Then I'm glad."

She sighed, and he drew her across his chest. "And what about you? Are you happy?"

"Oh, yes." She sighed again and laid her cheek against his and whispered, "You have been endowed with much to bring a woman joy and happiness."

He tightened his arms around her. "I wish it had been you, instead of Yum Li."

"But I'm content. I have had great pleasure. It will console me, when . . ." She left the sentence unfinished. She drew up the top sheet and covered them both, as they lay back against the pillows. "Now shall we go to sleep?"

He woke to find himself alone. The sun was streaming across the stones and shrubs of the terrace, beyond the open doors, and he wondered what time it was.

Today, he remembered, he was to meet the camel driver at noon, in the lobby of the Hotel Novy Mir.

He thought it must be after nine o'clock, from the angle of the sun.

Did all that really happen, last night? Yes, from that aching feeling of overindulgence, it had.

He felt angry and annoyed with himself, at his failure of control.

For a moment he seemed to see a vision of his father, Sergei Nicholaevitch, seated at the foot of the bed, jauntily smoking a cigar, with the familiar, amused expression on his face. *My dear boy, you will never learn. Give up trying. It's useless. I can tell you from long experience, that you needn't bother to make the effort.*

I'm not you, Father.

Sergei Nicholaevitch only winked, and waved the cigar, and the vision disappeared.

He heard the soft patter of felt slippers against the floor and sat up. He saw that Yum Li was entering the room. She carried a silk robe over her arm.

She was polite and respectful, as though nothing had

329

happened. "I have brought you a robe to wear," she said, holding it out. "It belonged to Mr. Sung, and so it will probably be too small." She giggled, covering her mouth with her hand, as he put on the robe. The sleeves only covered his elbows. They should have come down to the wrists, he thought.

He got out of bed, tying the robe.

"Shall I draw your bath?" she asked.

"If you would. Where is Madame Sung?"

"She will meet you in the willow garden. After you've had your breakfast."

He wondered where his clothes were.

He entered the bathroom. Yum Li was filling the sunken tub.

She helped him off with the robe, and into the tub. He stretched out in the warm, scented water. The stiff ache of his back felt almost healed.

"I will shave you now," Yum Li said.

She brought a basin, soap, and a razor, and knelt by the side of the tub. She was very quick and skillful.

"Mr. Chen is bringing your clothes and your breakfast," she said. "Your clothes have been laundered and cleaned."

He closed his eyes. "That's fine. You've thought of everything."

When he was dressed and had eaten breakfast on the terrace, he went to find Madame Sung in the willow garden.

He discovered her seated on the stone bench. This morning she wore a gown of rose-colored silk. Her hair was coiled again at the back of her neck in glossy perfection, and she looked very cool and remote and untouchable; the porcelain figurine of yesterday. Last night might never have happened, he thought. He was aware of himself impeccably dressed, as yesterday, wearing his silk shirt, which had been beautifully laundered, and his cashmere suit, which had been immaculately pressed; the servants had even polished the jade cuff links.

Those two people of last night had never existed. It was all a dream.

No, he wouldn't accept that.

"Mei-ling," he said, going toward her, "I missed you when I woke up."

"Nicholas! Good morning." She smiled. "I hope you do not mind. I needed some time to myself, before I spoke with you. I wanted to think."

He sat down next to her on the bench. "About what?" He picked up both her hands and kissed the palms.

She withdrew her hands gently. "You mustn't treat me as a lover," she said, misty-eyed. "Not today."

"Why? Is today so different from yesterday?"

"Yes. Because I'm happier than I was yesterday. You've given me back my pride and my fulfillment. So that when I go on my journey, I will be content."

"You keep speaking of a journey. Are you going back to China?"

She didn't answer for a moment. Then she said softly, "Farther than that." Then she smiled. "But it doesn't matter, because you have your own life—and your own love. We have had our time together."

"Why do you say that, Mei-ling?"

"Because it is true. Is there not someone in your heart?"

He hesitated. He knew that he could lie, but he didn't want to.

"You see," she said quietly, "I am right. And so it is best if we say our destined farewell. Please . . . do not say anything. We must follow our own paths, and they lead in separate ways. You must deal with Wang Tien-shan from now on. I shall instruct him to cooperate with you in every respect. If you wish to make arrangements to buy the warehouses, I shall agree to it, and try to make everything as easy as possible."

"But not personally."

"No, not personally." She touched his face lightly with the tips of her fingers.

"I'll be very sad, not ever to see you or this house again."

"Do you really care for this house?"

"Yes, it's very lovely. As you are."

"Then perhaps . . ." She looked around the garden for a long moment. Then she sighed deeply. She stood up. "We must say good-bye now," she whispered.

He rose. "I won't forget you, Mei-ling." How strange this was, he thought.

"Nor I you."

"Will you kiss me good-bye?"

"Yes."

She went into his arms, and he kissed her gently, tasting jasmine. Then he left the garden, leaving her standing beneath the willow tree, a still, small figure in rose-colored silk. He wondered if she'd meant it; that they'd never meet again.

In the back seat of the chauffeur-driven black sedan, returning to the Hotel Novy Mir, he forced his mind to what lay ahead.

He would meet the camel driver. Arrange for a meeting tonight at Mei-ling's warehouse. Then go to the Russo-Asiatic Bank and take out the money he needed. Late tonight, after midnight, the bales of wool would be brought to the waterfront, and he would pay for them.

He would use the time in the afternoon to buy something for Yum Li. Perhaps a pair of earrings. He would have it sent to the house, without a card; she would understand.

In the days after that, he would meet with Hirsch's friend Herman Levy, to discuss selling the wool. Then the purchase of the warehouses with Wang Tien-shan . . .

Then, for the first time, he allowed himself to think of Daria.

He bowed his head. Where was she? How long had it been since he'd seen her, running out of their room at the Inn of the Green Parrot, with Cossacks at the gate? Was she safe? Was she frightened? When would he see her again?

Have courage, darling. I'll find you. I swear it.

Chapter 28

Daria was ill and weak. She could barely hold herself upright in the saddle. They'd left the Village of the Stone Dragon ten days before, on a journey to an unknown destination, and now they were traveling on ponyback through a barren wilderness. She'd grown accustomed to the small, shaggy pony, and the unfamiliar Chinese saddle, and she was managing to conceal her fear and panic at being taken deeper into the wild plains and mountains. But her illness was draining her strength.

She thought there were about fifty bandits in their group. They were riding single file, except for herself: Shih Lung rode at her right hand and Yao, the man Daria had called Warlord, on her left, both holding rifles ready in case she tried to escape. But she was feeling too weak.

She knew they were traveling west, into the sunset. But Shih Lung refused to explain anything more.

She'd screamed at Shih Lung, back in the Village of the Stone Dragon, before they'd left.

"Where are you taking me?"

Shih Lung had yelled back, equally angry, equally shrill-voiced. "Why do you keep asking questions?" Her face reddened. "You're a miserable turtle's egg! You will learn to do as I say! Without questions!"

"Never! You can't force me! You can keep me prisoner, like the evil person that you are—but you can't make me keep silent!"

"I will beat you!" Shih Lung snatched a riding whip

from its peg on the wall and brandished it furiously. She began to advance on Daria, clutching the whip. "I'll teach you to keep silent!"

"Go ahead!" Daria clenched her fists, eyes blazing, holding her ground. "You're a cruel, bad woman, but I'm not afraid of you!"

She was afraid, but she dared not show it. These scenes were frequent between herself and Shih Lung. So far she hadn't been beaten. She suspected that Shih Lung was saving her for another purpose. But she still felt sick with fear sometimes, before she fell asleep.

She kept remembering what had happened to Pei Pa-tien, the White Wolf, a rival bandit chief Shih Lung's men had captured a week ago. They'd hung him by his thumbs in the courtyard, and while he was hanging, they'd burned his body with hot irons. He'd screamed all night, until the morning, when he was dead. The memory gave her nightmares.

But she couldn't show fear in front of Shih Lung or the others. Fear excited their cruelty.

Shih Lung flung the riding whip on the floor and stamped her foot. "In two days we're leaving on a journey. Far and long. Prepare yourself."

"Where? Where are we going?"

"You'll discover that when we arrive."

Daria changed her tactics. She calmed herself and made her voice reasonable. Up to now Shih Lung hadn't relented to her pleas, but she had to keep trying. She had to.

"Shih Lung—why won't you write to my friend in Harbin? Ask him for ransom?"

Shih Lung shrugged her shoulders. "How do you know he's in Harbin?"

Daria didn't know; she was horribly afraid for Nicholas; but she had to keep hoping.

"Ask the innkeeper at the Inn of the Green Parrot. Surely my friend left word where he could be found."

Shih Lung's narrow black eyes grew thoughtful and speculative. "Perhaps I've already done that."

"What did you find out?"

Another shrug. "What's the difference? If your friend is alive, he's only an engineer. You told me that. Such men cannot find work in Harbin, there are too many refugees looking for employment. He can't pay a high ransom."

"Try! Write to him! You must release me, Shih Lung!"

"I must do nothing. You cannot give me orders. If you do, I will beat you."

Around and around. Over and over. She'd drooped with weariness. But there was nothing else to do.

Now they were on this mysterious journey, going west, and her hope was ebbing.

They were traveling over vast plains of barren brown earth, and uphill over narrow rocky trails. She thought they must be approaching the foothills of the Khingan Mountains. The villages were poorer, and more miserable and farther apart; mostly Manchu. A sprinkling of Mongolians was beginning to appear.

Somewhere to the north, she knew, were the tracks of the Chinese Eastern Railway. Shih Lung had told her they would avoid the city of Tsitsihar, which was located on the railway line.

She wasn't sure of the month, but she believed it was the Moon of the Hungry Ghosts. Captain Li had explained that once, on the river steamer: it was the time of year when the ghosts of people's ancestors came out of their graves and roamed the earth, looking for food and drink; they must be appeased by offerings. It meant the end of summer and the approach of autumn. Sleeping out at night in the mountain passes, you shivered with a sudden chill.

Now this illness had come upon her. She suspected it was from bad water. Stomach cramps and diarrhea and vomiting first, and now a constant low fever and a dull, persistent ache in her stomach. She was losing weight, and her lips were beginning to crack with dryness. She could barely eat. It was a struggle to stay in the saddle during the day. She had to drag herself to her feet every morning.

Shih Lung glanced over from her own pony with a narrow-eyed frown.

"Are you no better?"

"The same as yesterday."

Shih Lung hawked and spat on the ground. "Weak foreign devil." But her face was worried. "If you keep getting weaker, you will die."

"Perhaps I will. That would serve you right, Shih Lung. You'll get no ransom then."

"Don't threaten me." But Shih Lung's voice carried no confidence. Daria knew she was worried. She wants to keep me alive and well, she thought. She has some purpose in mind. But she was feeling too miserable to wonder what it was.

If I get better—if I just stay alive—I'll get out of this. I'll reach Harbin. I'll find Nicholas.

But her own confidence was waning.

And they were still traveling west, always west. Toward the sun setting behind the mountains like a ball of crimson fire. The chattering line of bandits on ponyback, ahead and behind. Shih Lung and Yao on either side. Rising mountain foothills in the distance. The tireless, even gait of the shaggy pony. And this constant fever . . .

She decided something was seriously wrong with her stomach. Maybe dysentery. Did people die of dysentery? Yes, of course they did, from weakness and dehydration.

She didn't want to die. The fierce desire to live, and escape from the bandits, kept her going.

The old man told her one night that Shih Lung had considered taking her to a doctor in the city. They could turn north to Tsitsihar.

"But there are foreign doctors in Tsitsihar," he explained. "Missionaries. Shih Lung doesn't trust foreign doctors. Everyone knows they kill you with their needles. No one comes out of their hospitals alive."

"That's not true. It's nonsense."

"The Stone Dragon has another plan. Don't worry, she'll save your life."

Why? Daria wondered wearily, as she lay back in her blanket on the ground. Why am I so important to her? *Oh God, I wish I could get better. I could face this with more courage.*

One afternoon they rode into a town. It wasn't much better than the villages: one dirt road lined with one-story mud buildings. The usual smell of garbage, and the usual flies. A dog squatting to defecate in the middle of the road, and a man beside the dog with his robe raised, doing the same thing. Some mules, oxen, and two-wheeled donkey carts milling around. But still, it was more than a village. There were shops, a silk merchant, a grain warehouse, a Chinese inn surrounded by a mud wall. The road was wide, and extended at least half a mile.

Seated on the ground in front of one of the buildings was a gaunt young man with a ragged red cloak flung over his shoulders. In front of him was a large square box of sand, and beside him was an incense burner. In his hand was a bamboo stick. His eyes were half-closed; he seemed drugged.

Opium, Daria thought. She'd seen it so often by now. Everyone smoked opium in this country. It was as common as drinking vodka at home.

Shih Lung yelled an order, and the column halted. The Stone Dragon swung herself down from the saddle and strolled over to the seated young man. With an arrogant gesture she flung coins across the box of sand.

The old man rode up beside Daria. "That man's a fortune-teller," he whispered excitedly. "Now he'll summon the spirits to predict the future."

The young man had gathered up the coins, putting them away in his clothing, and was lighting the incense burner. Daria could smell the pungent fragrance as the smoke began to rise. The young man began to sway back and forth, seated on the ground.

"He's inviting the spirits to come out of the mountains," the old man whispered to Daria.

The fortune-teller was holding the bamboo stick extended over the sand now. It dipped down, as though of its own free will, and began to make marks in the sand, tracing odd curving patterns over the surface.

"See?" the old man said. "The spirits are causing the stick to write. They're sending a message."

"Those aren't really characters, are they?" The patterns didn't look like any Chinese writing Daria had ever seen.

"He has to interpret them, of course. That's how he earns his fee."

Shih Lung was crouched down listening to the young man explain the marks in the sand. Then she stood up, swaggered back to her pony, and remounted.

She considered Daria impassively for a moment. "You and I will sleep at the inn tonight," she said abruptly. "Tomorrow we'll cure your illness."

337

"How do you intend to do that?" Daria felt very weary.

Shih Lung pointed to the end of the road. "Down there is a settlement of Golds. They are a people with Manchu blood, but no one knows where they really came from. They are a strange people, and they have powerful ways of curing. Their shaman will cure you."

"Shaman?"

"Yes, their spirit doctor. I'll pay him well. It's worth it to me."

She was wasting her time, Daria thought, closing her eyes for a moment, if Shih Lung believed a case of dysentery could be cured overnight by some primitive shaman, or spirit doctor. But let the Stone Dragon try. She didn't care anymore. She was too weak and tired.

The next morning she rode with Shih Lung and Yao, one on either side, to the end of the road, to find the village of the Golds. It was just a collection of mud huts, the poorest and most squalid she'd seen so far. She looked around dull-eyed at the dungheaps, the strewn garbage, the rotting vegetables, the scavenging dogs, the naked babies toddling in the dirt. Was she to be cured here?

But the hut of the shaman was somehow different. She couldn't tell exactly why. Perhaps it was the spirit doctor himself. He stood in front of the hut, waiting for them to dismount. He was leaning on a tall spear, taller than his head; the shaft was covered in snakeskin. He wore a fantastic headdress of horns and fur that fell to his shoulders. Beneath it, his face was very wrinkled, and his eyes were narrow, like those of the Chinese or Manchus. Around his neck were four leather thongs, and dangling from them, down to his chest, were four large circles of hammered brass. They clashed musically whenever he stirred. He wore a pair of deerskin trousers and a deerskin shirt, and wound around his hips was a deerskin apron cut into long fringes that reached to his thighs.

She'd never seen anyone like him.

An old woman stood in the doorway of the hut, peering out at them.

Shih Lung dismounted and went up to the shaman, starting a conversation. They spoke for a long time. Shih Lung turned once and pointed to Daria, shaking her finger; then she returned to the shaman. Money changed hands. Finally Shih Lung summoned Daria.

She went reluctantly, climbing down from the saddle, wondering what was to come next. She imagined disgusting rituals, perhaps something horrible to eat or drink. But she thought she had nothing to lose. She couldn't feel worse; she couldn't be in a more hopeless situation. This was all part of the same nightmare that had begun the day of her capture.

The shaman took her arm and led her into the hut. His touch was gentle. She had expected something else, something fiercer. His appearance was so barbaric, she'd thought he would clutch and grab. But in a strange way, he seemed to be displaying compassion.

After all he's a doctor, she thought. Then she wondered at herself. What a strange term to use for a primitive tribesman.

He sat her down in a crude wooden chair by the open window of the hut. The old woman went to stand behind her. Shih Lung and Yao were waiting outside. They were squatting below the window, smoking cigarettes. Daria could hear them conversing in Chinese. Somewhere a baby was wailing. The hut smelled of incense, garlic and boiled millet.

She felt a curious sense of calm, and folded her hands in her lap.

The shaman had brought over a skin-covered drum and a small hammer, and he sat down facing her with the drum between his knees.

The old woman placed her fingertips on Daria's back.

The shaman began to beat the drum. He closed his eyes. A tense, drawn look came over his face. *Boom-boom, boom-boom, boom-boom.* Insistent, monotonous, compelling. The rhythm began to echo inside her head.

The shaman began to sweat. His look of concentration deepened. His cheekbones stood out stark and gaunt. His face paled.

Boom-boom, boom-boom, boom-boom.

Now she heard nothing but the drum. It was a part of her breathing. It was matched to her pulse and her heartbeat. It was making a wild, primitive music, steady and rhythmic. *Boom-boom, boom-boom, boom-boom.*

The shaman was beginning to look ill.

The old woman said something and shifted her fingers on Daria's back. The shaman altered his beat very slightly, and Daria felt herself shudder. She closed her own eyes. The drumbeat was her own heartbeat. She felt something happening inside her body. An altering, shifting, changing, drawing out.

She thought, from the look of concentrated anguish on the shaman's face, that he was drawing her illness into himself.

What a strange, mad idea.

But she couldn't think, with that wild, insistent drumming.

The old woman suddenly cried out and removed her hands. The drumming stopped. The shaman's head drooped; he looked on the point of collapse.

Daria sat wonderingly in the chair. The dull ache in her stomach had gone away. The feeling of nausea that had been with her for days had disappeared. She was actually hungry.

I believe I'm well.

How could that be?

The shaman hadn't moved. He sat with his body curved over the drum, breathing harshly.

The old woman helped Daria to her feet, and led her to the doorway of the hut.

Shih Lung sprang up.

"Are you better?" she demanded.

"I . . . I think so. But I don't understand it."

"He's a very good spirit doctor."

Daria glanced back at the hut. She wondered if the shaman would be ill.

Imagine if a real doctor grew ill, every time he cured a patient. There would be no doctors . . .

But she felt remarkably light and free of physical discomfort as she rode back with Shih Lung to join the other bandits. She began to think again about where they were going. Why they were traveling, what purpose the Stone Dragon had in mind. They were avoiding the railroad tracks, so she probably wasn't being sold to a city brothel. Was that good or bad? What were her chances of escape, here in these wild mountains? And how would anyone ever find her?

If Nicholas is still alive . . .

Shih Lung felt deeply satisfied with her investment as she rode beside the foreign devil. It had been worth paying the shaman for his healing, she thought. You could see the girl improving in front of your eyes. Already pinkness was returning to her cheeks, and the sparkle of health to her eyes.

Good. Shih Lung wanted the girl to look her very best when she was presented to Bogdo Khan. Because the Mongolian lama was very wealthy.

Everyone knew the lamaseries of Mongolia were corrupt. The lamas were supposed to be celibate monks; and those who wandered the plains and steppes, like the nomads, those who went from village to village ministering to the people, were very often pious. But those who lived within the monastery walls—they were rich, corrupt, idle, with many concubines and wives. They fed off the people. The lamaseries were the curse of Mongolia.

Yet the people believed in the lamas, and supported them in luxury.

Bogdo Khan was one of the richest of all the lamas, Shih Lung knew.

He would be on the Manchurian-Mongolian border to attend a festival, away from his monastery, living in a *yurt* in a village south of Solun. Shih Lung intended to find him.

He had never, to her knowledge, had a foreign wife. He had married two Manchu princesses, and gotten many children on them, but he accepted that as only proper, for he claimed to be descended from the Mongol princes of the Ten Banners of the Cherim League.

But a foreigner, young and pretty, with fair white skin . . . Bogdo Khan might be pleased by such a wife. It would lend him much prestige.

Shih Lung knew he was a vain and stupid man, and much tempted by the pleasures of the flesh.

How to make the girl cooperate? She was hardheaded and defiant, her spirit remained unbroken, and Shih Lung didn't dare beat her, for fear of causing scars and bruises. Yet if she were presented to Bogdo Khan bound and gagged, the great lama's vanity would be offended.

She must be presented to Bogdo Khan naked and submissive, in the most tempting way possible, to excite his lust. Shih Lung had not worked in the brothels of Shanghai for nothing. She knew exactly how to prepare the girl for inspection, with rouged lips and rouged nipples, artfully sprawled limbs and hips raised invitingly on silken cushions. There must be no ugly ropes to spoil the effect. Only a veil of silk gauze, to be snatched away at the proper moment.

Never mind. She had a plan.

Shih Lung felt very satisfied and pleased that she had sent someone to the Inn of the Green Parrot, to investigate the girl's story. It had given her a weapon.

She discounted the message left by the foreign devil, the girl's friend. For what engineer in Harbin could offer a ransom like that possessed by Bogdo Khan?

No. She would sell her to the lama, as his wife. He would pay a wonderful price.

When they reached the Mongolian border, Shih Lung felt certain she could bend the girl to her will. Luckily she possessed the means, she thought, hidden away in her saddlebag.

Yes, the Stone Dragon is very clever, Shih Lung thought. And soon she will be very, very wealthy.

Chapter 29

In his room at the Hotel Novy Mir, Nicholas stared thoughtfully into his closet.

He had a particular impression he wanted to make this evening, and a particular outcome he wanted to bring about. And everything, including his appearance, would work toward his purpose.

He reached out and moved the hangers along the pole, one by one, considering his choices.

The closet was full. Clothing had been his only extravagance. No, not an extravagance: looking your best was an investment. People took you at face value; first impressions always counted. And if you looked prosperous and self-confident, you created the right impression without saying a word.

The Japanese colonel, Kenji Matsuura, had been favorably disposed toward him from the beginning, Nicholas knew.

It would be useful to have an acquaintance at the Japanese Military Mission, he thought. Nicholas had plans for the future. According to the treaty which Japan had forced on China in 1915, the Japanese had many special privileges in Manchuria. They were entitled to develop mines and railways, engage in all kinds of trade and manufacturing. If Nicholas wanted to expand beyond warehouses and wool, he needed to establish himself with the Japanese.

The Tokyo government, he knew, referred to their commercial invasion of Manchuria as "peaceful penetration."

But the Japanese bankers and businessmen were extremely thorough and very shrewd, and they worked closely with the Japanese army.

So meeting Colonel Kenji Matsuura had been a good opportunity.

They'd met for the first time in the exclusive and elegant surroundings of the Railway Club.

"You seem to have made a large reputation in a very short time," the colonel had said smoothly. "You have only been in Harbin one month?"

"Two months, Colonel."

Matsuura had laughed, raising a cigarette to his mouth. "Yes, of course, two months. One forgets how quickly things happen in Manchuria. Welcome to Harbin, Mr. Federovsky. I predict you will enjoy a great success."

Nicholas had been careful, in that first conversation, to drop casual references to highly placed family friends at home in Russia; old acquaintances of his parents, titled wherever possible. The colonel was a snob. He was also susceptible to flattery, although he considered himself shrewd. But like many of the Japanese, he was touchy about racial slurs, and enjoyed being flattered by a European. It cost nothing to accommodate him, Nicholas thought.

Their lunch that day had been arranged by Hirsch's friend Herman Levy. Few Jews were invited to the Railway Club, but Levy was an exception.

He was not at all like Nachman Hirsch. Levy was a powerfully built, tight-lipped man with hard eyes and a shrewd, cold head for business. He'd made no overtures toward friendship with Nicholas beyond their business relationship, which suited them both.

Levy had succeeded in getting an excellent price for the stolen wool, using pathways he hadn't bothered to explain. The result had been well worth the percentage he had taken.

Even after the payment to Wang Tien-shan, for his help, Nicholas had found himself with enough profit to negotiate for the warehouses.

Now the Sung warehouses belonged to him. And they were proving to be fantastically profitable, far exceeding his hopes.

He spent most of his days on the waterfront, in a small upstairs office in one of the warehouses; in addition to the other warehouse employees, he'd had to hire a secretary, a meek young man from a refugee family, grateful for the employment.

Temporarily, though, Nicholas was keeping the books himself. There were too many transactions he preferred to keep confidential.

Levy was involved in the export trade, among other things. Little by little he was offering Nicholas opportunities to make investments.

Nicholas was keeping the import-export dealings separate from the warehouse concerns.

There was no reason, he thought, why you couldn't be involved in more than one thing at a time. He'd learned that in Kharkov. You just had to be willing to devote your time and attention to it.

But events in Harbin moved at an incredibly faster pace than they had at home.

He selected a blue-gray silk worsted suit from the closet, and laid it across the bed.

He could easily afford to move to the Grand Hotel. But he saw no reason to make a change yet. There were too many other interesting possibilities for available cash. He would live simply until it suited him to change his style.

When he was ready to move, he told himself, it would be a place of his own, in New Town.

When I get Daria back . . .

He remembered, with sudden bleak depression, the conversation earlier that afternoon with Brendan, at the Metropolitan Café.

The café had been crowded, as usual. Conversations in five or six languages blended and mixed. Thick blue smoke drifted in the air. Waiters snake-hipped between the tables with loaded trays high above their heads. Dishes clattered; voices called impatiently. "Waiter! Over here!"

Brendan was late. Nicholas wondered what was keeping him, as he folded back a page of his newspaper.

When the Irishman arrived, he looked regretful. He shook his head, taking a seat at the table. "Kolya, there's still no word of the Stone Dragon. Nobody's seen the woman for a long time. She seems to have disappeared."

"No rumors? Nothing?"

"One rumor—they say she's left for Mongolia."

"Mongolia!"

Brendan shrugged. "Take it for what it's worth."

"Why hasn't there been a ransom note," Nicholas muttered savagely. He flung the newspaper onto the table and put a hand over his eyes. "Two months . . ."

"Maybe the Stone Dragon doesn't have her. Maybe she's been sold out of the country. South, to Shanghai."

"No. I believe that Daria's here, above the border. I'm certain of it. I have an instinct about it." He dropped his hand and stared across the table. "Keep trying, Brendan. Keep asking questions. I must have information . . . even if it comes from Mongolia. Spend whatever you have to. Draw whatever money you need, I won't keep track. Sooner or later we'll hear something."

He wondered bleakly, as he buttoned his shirt in front of the mirror in the Hotel Novy Mir, if he could hold on to that determination.

Summer was ending. It didn't last long here in the north. Tonight he would need to wear a coat.

How long before he found her?

As long as it took. He couldn't give up hope.

He fitted amber-and-gold cuff links into his shirt. He realized he hadn't selected a necktie. The blue-and-gold silk, he decided. Just a bit flashy, but that would suit his purpose.

His conversation with Brendan at the Metropolitan Café had taken an unexpected turn.

"I have some other news that will interest you, Kolya."

"Oh? What's that?"

"See the little man with the shifty eyes? The one over at the bar?"

"Shall I look now?"

"Doesn't matter. He knows we're discussing him."

Nicholas twisted in his chair and stared openly. "Yes, I see him."

"He tells me a friend of yours is back in Harbin."

Nicholas felt his mind harden into an icy certainty of what that meant. "Dmitri Pavlovitch Chernov," he said softly, turning back to Brendan.

"Aye, the Mad Major. He's in Harbin right now." Bren-

346

dan sat back and grinned. "He's been having a little trouble lately. Seems his men deserted him up in Siberia, and refused to serve under him anymore. So he came back to Harbin with a new idea."

Nicholas waited, listening tensely.

"He decided to go into business," Brendan went on. "With some fellow officers." He leaned forward across the table. "I understand, Kolya, that they've brought in a big shipment of weapons to Harbin. The real thing. Colt rifles, Maxim machine guns—all in the original packing. Brand new. Worth a fortune to the right person."

"Such as Chang Tso-lin?"

"Any of the warlords, from here to Tientsin."

"Where is it, Brendan? Where are they keeping it?"

"Nobody knows."

Nicholas drummed his fingers on the table. "Call over that man," he said after a moment. "Let's talk to him."

In front of the mirror at the Novy Mir, he adjusted his necktie. He weighed the advisability of a diamond tie stud, and decided to wear it. Then he picked up his wristwatch from the top of the dresser and looked at it dubiously. Gold, on a black leather strap.

He still wasn't used to it. It seemed slightly effeminate to him, to wear a watch strapped around his wrist like a woman's bracelet. But the jeweler had assured him it was the latest style. He'd claimed all the young men were wearing their timepieces that way. Finally the jeweler had promised to reset the watch into a fob, if Nicholas didn't like it.

After a moment he buckled it around his wrist. He had to admit it was convenient, seeing the time by just turning your wrist, instead of fishing your watch out of your vest pocket. Maybe he'd get used to it, as the jeweler claimed.

The man had tried to talk him into a gold link bracelet instead of the leather strap, but that was going too far.

He knew Chernov's address, he thought grimly, putting on his suit jacket. The little man at the Metropolitan Café had given it readily. Chernov was living in a shabby neighborhood near the railroad station.

"Of course he's not there too often," the man had said slyly. Nicholas had bought him a glass of vodka, and he peered over the rim of the glass as he spoke.

"Do something for me," Nicholas said. He reached into his breast pocket and took out a business card and handed it across the table. "Give this to Dmitri Pavlovitch. Tell him to stay home tonight. By himself. Tell him that Kolya Federovsky would like to pay him a call."

He was almost ready, Nicholas thought, settling his shoulders inside the jacket. Brendan would be waiting for him in the lobby. The car and driver he'd hired would be outside at the curb.

He shrugged into his coat, dark gray cashmere with a velvet collar. Pearl gray homburg. Black pigskin gloves.

His shoes were black cowhide, handmade by an English bootery.

He was ready. He adjusted the hat brim in the mirror, picked up the gloves from the dresser top, and left the room.

He was putting on the gloves as he strode through the lobby. Brendan got up out of the chair he'd been sitting in.

"Think Chernov will recognize you?" he said with a chuckle.

"I have no doubt of it, Brendan. Let's go."

He didn't speak at all in the back seat of the car, sitting with his hand over his mouth, deep in thought. Brendan sat up front with the driver, making desultory conversation. A rifle lay at their feet, below the dashboard. It was necessary in this country, Nicholas knew, if you had any sense of self-preservation at all. Herman Levy traveled with two bodyguards, and his children were always guarded going back and forth to school. Anyone of wealth in Harbin did the same. You were a fool not to. Kidnapping was a way of life. Nicholas had bitter reason to know it. . . .

The car glided to a stop at the curb.

They had arrived.

They were on a street of red brick buildings, dirty and badly kept. One streetlight burned at the end of the road. A cat slunk along the pavement half a block away, then sprang into an alley, out of sight. The doorway of the building before them was crumbling stone. The hallway beyond the glass panel of the door was narrow, with dim yellow light.

Nicholas got out of the car and directed the driver to wait. Then he and Brendan entered the hallway.

There were no names beside the bell.

"Second floor," Brendan muttered. "Number three."

They climbed the stairs, past stained yellow marble walls.

The lightbulb on the first floor was burned out, and the hall was pitch black. But on the second floor a low-watt bulb was still casting sickly light.

Nicholas pressed his thumb against the bell of number three.

Nothing.

He pushed the bell again, letting his thumb stay pressed against it.

A thick-voiced growl came from inside. "What the hell do you want?"

"Open up, Dmitri."

"Kolya?"

"Yes. Open the door."

Silence. Then heavy footsteps thudded to the door. A chain grated. A lock clicked. The door was flung open, and Dmitri Chernov stood blinking in the doorway. His eyes were red-rimmed and bloodshot. He was breathing heavily, and each time he did, whiskey fumes floated into the hall. He wore a uniform jacket unbuttoned and hanging open over his bare chest.

He'd obviously just shaved, with an unsteady hand, because fresh razor nicks covered his jaw.

He threw back his head and burst into harsh laughter. "Oh my God. Is it you?"

"Of course. Why are you surprised? I told you I'd be here tonight."

"Yes, but I didn't . . . I never . . ." He stopped laughing, and his eyes narrowed, as he looked past Nicholas's shoulder at Brendan. "Who's that?"

"A friend of mine."

"You said you'd come alone."

"I never said that, Dmitri. I said I wanted you to be alone."

"He stays outside."

"Very well." Nicholas nodded to Brendan, very slightly, and Brendan immediately walked forward and pushed past Chernov into the flat. He began to stroll around, looking over the room. Then he disappeared through a doorway.

"Don't you trust me, Kolya?" Chernov smiled crookedly, leaning against the door.

"No. Why should I?"

Brendan came back into the hall. "All right. Nobody's there." He grinned. "Place could use a cleaning up, though."

"Wait here, Brendan."

"Aye. But leave the door unlocked, just in case. He's got a pistol on the table."

"If Dmitri had wanted to shoot me," Nicholas said pleasantly, turning to Chernov, "he could have done it once before." He smiled. "Isn't that so?" He walked through the doorway into the flat.

Brendan was right, he thought, looking around; the place was filthy. Dirty clothes were littered on the floor, stained whiskey glasses covered every surface, dust was everywhere. He smelled liquor and stale sweat.

He took off his hat and gloves and looked for somewhere to put them. Finally he set them down on a table that stood in the center of the room, sweeping off a place first with the flat of his hand.

"Don't you approve of my housekeeping arrangements?" Chernov closed the door with a soft click of the latch.

"The place is a pigsty."

Chernov shrugged. "I'm not here very often. Besides, I don't usually have such elegant visitors." Nicholas had unbuttoned his coat. Chernov came into the room and stared up and down. "You look very prosperous, Kolya," he said softly.

"Harbin is a city of opportunity."

"Quite a change from the last time we met."

"So it is." Nicholas pointedly refrained from commenting on Chernov's appearance.

"I suppose I've changed too."

"Somewhat."

"I've had a little turn of luck since the Inn of the Green Parrot. I'm thinking about giving up my military career. I'm getting tired of army life." He gestured at the table. "Sit down, I'll pour you a drink." Nicholas sat down at the table, crossing an ankle on his knee. Chernov spilled whiskey into two glass tumblers and shoved one over to Nicholas. "Water?"

"No, this will do."

"I hardly know what to say, Kolya. Except . . ." He raised his glass. "No grudges?"

Nicholas controlled a sudden surge of fury. Good Lord, was he insane? Yes, of course he was. Otherwise he would never have unlocked that door.

Your mistake, Dmitri Pavlovitch.

"Would I have come here, if I bore a grudge?" he said easily.

"You might. Looking for revenge."

"But you spared my life at the inn. You didn't have to do that." He smiled, picking up his glass. "And obviously things turned out for the best. I'm doing very well."

"So it appears." Chernov sat down. He faced Nicholas across the table, and stared with fascination at the diamond tie stud. "I must say, you look very attractive. But . . ." He smiled slowly. "Shall I speak my mind?"

"Go ahead."

He sat back and swallowed some whiskey. "I liked you even better, tied to that tree."

Nicholas forced himself to show no reaction.

"I'll wager anything you like," Chernov added, "that you're wearing silk underwear."

"Too bad you don't have Volchin and Grigorovitch here, to help you win your bet."

"Yes, too bad. But perhaps it's just as well. This time it's only the two of us." He paused. "How long can you stay?"

"That all depends."

"Why don't you plan to spend the night?" He made his voice casual, but his eyes were suddenly glittering. "Call off your bodyguard. Send him away. There's no need for protection, is there? Not anymore."

"I'm not so sure."

Chernov leaned forward. "Stay here, Kolya. Overnight. I'll do my best to entertain you, I promise."

So open, so soon, Dmitri? You must be very drunk.

"I've had a taste of your entertainment. Once was enough."

"Don't be a fool, you know what I mean. That was a necessary unpleasantness. But it's over now, it's in the past. We understand each other now."

"I'll have to think about it." Nicholas tapped his fingers against the side of the glass. "Why are you giving up the military, Dmitri? You're so well suited to it."

Chernov looked at him suspiciously, but he only cleared his throat. "I have a better opportunity. A chance to make some money."

"Turning businessman?"

"Maybe."

"Do you know anything about it?"

Chernov shrugged. "What is there to know?"

"Oh, more than you think. I'd hate to see you cheated, right in the beginning."

Chernov's eyes narrowed. "Why should you care?"

"Maybe you need a partner."

"You?"

"Why not?"

"I don't trust you, Kolya."

"I thought we understood each other."

"Not yet. Not yet." Chernov picked up the whiskey bottle and tilted it over his glass. A few drops trickled out. He cursed under his breath.

"All out?" Nicholas inquired.

"No, I have another bottle somewhere." He got up from the table and moved unsteadily to a row of cupboards over a grimy sink.

Nicholas glanced at the marble mantelpiece that faced him on the opposite wall. A photograph in a red plush frame stood next to a vase of dusty peacock feathers. A beautiful young woman wrapped in winter furs sat in a sleigh with snowflakes flying around her.

Chernov's wife? Sister? No, the clothes were too old-fashioned. Probably his mother.

Very touching.

Chernov came back with a fresh bottle. As he passed he laid a casual, comradely hand on Nicholas's shoulder. He let it rest just a fraction of a second too long before he removed it.

"Maybe we can talk about this partnership after all," he said, pulling the cork out of the bottle. "Maybe you're right. You seem to know what you're doing. Maybe I could use some advice."

Progress, Nicholas thought.

"Suppose I tell you what I already know, Dmitri."

Fresh suspicion flared in Chernov's eyes.

"You, and some others, have brought a shipment of weapons into Harbin. Colt rifles and Maxim machine guns. You're hiding them somewhere, until you can sell them." Nicholas paused. "Am I correct?"

Chernov's face was sullen. He poured whiskey into both glasses without answering.

"How much do you think you can make?" Nicholas asked.

"At least a hundred thousand rubles. Clear profit."

He may be right.

"Listen, Dmitri. If you hold out and put them up for auction, you can make more. Let all the warlords bid for them. The Japanese might be interested. You can push the price much higher."

"We can't wait that long."

"Why not?"

Sullen silence.

"Because you're afraid of being discovered," Nicholas said. "Because you don't have a safe hiding place. You need to get rid of them fast." He paused. "Isn't that so?"

No answer.

"I have warehouses, Dmitri," he said softly. "With excellent security. I supervise the security myself. I'll guarantee the safety of your weapons until you can sell them. At the price you want. You won't have to worry ever again, once the deal is made. You can tell the army to go to hell and live as you please." He looked around at the room. "And not in a place like this, either."

Chernov hesitated. Then he said, "What do you get out of it?"

"Profit, of course."

"What else?" He was suddenly tense.

Nicholas sat back and smiled. "A chance for a brand-new partnership. With no hard feelings."

Chernov let out his breath. "Can I trust you?"

"Decide for yourself."

"No. I can't trust you." He took a long swallow of whiskey. "You'll have to give me better proof." He glanced at Nicholas out of the corner of his eye.

"You have to prove to me," Nicholas said, "that you're

trustworthy. After all, I'm the one with the scars of the tashur on my back."

"I told you, that's forgotten."

"It's easy to say."

"Then what the hell did you come here for?" Chernov said roughly. "To show me what a big success you are? To make me eat dirt? Some day I'll be richer than you, Fedorovsky. I don't need your partnership."

"Fine." Nicholas rose and picked up his hat and gloves. "It's been an interesting talk. Thanks for the whiskey."

"Wait. Don't go."

"What more is there to say?"

Chernov's face suddenly contorted. He made a strange choking sound in his throat. "Listen, Kolya, I'm in trouble. I need help. I can't stay here alone, it drives me crazy. I need someone with me, until the morning. In daytime it's not so bad, but at night . . . oh God, if you knew what it was like—" He suddenly cradled his head in his arms on the table.

Entirely too practiced, Nicholas thought coldly. Too rehearsed. *Not convincing, Dmitri. How many times have you used that little speech? And I wonder how many times you've succeeded in getting what you wanted.*

But here, tonight, with Nicholas of all people. . . . He almost wanted to laugh, if a cold, controlled fury had not been consuming him.

But before he finished what he'd come to do, he thought, he would discover the location of those weapons.

He sat down again at the table. "Very well. But if I'm to help you, we'll have to speak frankly. There are things you must tell me."

Chernov raised his head. "What things?"

"Do you have a pencil and paper?" Nicholas reached into his jacket pocket. "Never mind, I have a notebook with me."

Chernov balked. He evaded. He changed the subject. The level in the whiskey bottle lowered, and his eyes grew hotter and more restless. He began to make suggestions more openly, in more specified terms, describing what activities they might engage in later on. Nicholas put him off and brought him back to the subject of the weapons.

"Goddamn you!" Chernov shouted suddenly. He sprang

354

to his feet. "Is that all you can think about? Money?" He leaned on the table with both hands, staring into Nicholas's face. "I should have finished what I started at the inn," he whispered.

"Why didn't you?"

He was breathing hard. "You know why."

Nicholas shoved the notebook and pencil at him. "Business first. Personal discussions later."

"Damn you!" Chernov suddenly seized the pencil. He pulled over the notebook. "At the railroad station," he muttered. "In the freight yards. Three freight cars, with the wheels off."

"Where? Which ones?" The railroad yards were crammed with out-of-service freight cars.

Chernov began to make slashing sketches in the notebook. "Here. Near the repair sheds."

"Are they guarded?"

"Don't be an ass. Of course they're guarded."

"How many men?"

"Twelve."

Four to a car. Not an unreasonable number. No, it was possible . . .

"Sit down, Dmitri," he said calmly, taking away the notebook and pencil and putting them back into his pocket. "Let's forget the partnership for a while. We can talk about it later."

"Are you finally being reasonable?" Chernov sat down slowly. "Or do you think you've gotten what you came for."

Nicholas felt a cold hard tension rise within him. How drunk was Chernov? How deep did his madness run? Soon he would find out.

"I'm amazed," he said. "I never intended to stay this long." He looked thoughtfully at his wristwatch. "And I am here against my better judgment. I don't understand it."

A flash of triumph sparked in Chernov's eyes. "Perhaps I do . . ."

Nicholas reached idly for the pistol that lay on the table by Chernov's hand. Chernov picked it up immediately, hot-eyed and tense. Nicholas withdrew his hand with an amiable shrug.

355

"I was just wondering if you still played roulette."

"Sometimes. When I'm drunk enough."

"You really are mad, you know, Dmitri."

"Is it mad to take a chance on ending your existence? Life has never been that sweet for me." His voice dropped. His chest began to rise and fall quickly. "But perhaps all that will change. After tonight."

"You're pinning a lot of hope on tonight."

"Yes. Because I have the feeling—" He suddenly seized the pistol, broke it between his hands and scattered the cartridges across the table. His eyes blazed. He snatched up a single cartridge, dropped it into the cylinder, closed it and spun it with his thumb. "Is this what you want? A game of chance?"

"No. I consider it a game for fools."

Chernov aimed the pistol across the table. "I did this once before, didn't I? Aimed a pistol at you. But I didn't shoot."

"Pull the trigger."

Chernov's hand shook. A mad light shone in his eyes. Then he leaned back with the gun in his lap. "Not this time either."

Silence fell. The sound of Chernov's breathing was harsh and heavy. Finally he whispered, "I want your word on something, Kolya."

"What's that?"

"I want you to agree that from now until the morning, you'll do anything I ask."

"At gunpoint?"

"Yes. Whatever I say, no matter how unreasonable it is." His eyes were still glittering crazily. "I know how stubborn you are. I don't want you raising objections."

"I doubt if I can agree to that."

"Consider it, Kolya. You'll discover that I can be very imaginative. Think about it carefully." He laughed. "After all . . . I have the gun."

Nicholas sat with his head bowed, hand against his mouth. Then he shook his head. "No."

"Why not?"

"Because there's something you must do first."

Chernov said nothing, only waited.

Nicholas rose to his feet. Chernov watched tensely as he

took off his coat, throwing it over the back of the chair. He deliberately loosened his tie. Then he walked over to Chernov's side of the table and spoke in a low hard voice. "Stand up."

Chernov sat panting for a long moment, staring up at Nicholas. Then he got to his feet. He was still clutching the pistol.

Nicholas smiled into his eyes, without amusement. Then he took Chernov by the lapels of his jacket, pulled him forward and kissed him full on the mouth.

Triumph and lust flamed in Chernov's eyes. He stepped back. "So it's time . . ." He moved forward to repeat the caress.

"Not yet." Nicholas held him off, speaking through his teeth. "Use the gun on yourself first, Dmitri. See if you win. Then you can have your way."

"I've always been a lucky gambler."

Nicholas shoved him in the chest, forcing him back into the chair. "Then test your luck," he said, keeping his hand on Chernov's bare chest. "Before we go on to other things."

Chernov threw back his head and laughed wildly. "What a fool you are, Kolya. Don't you know you can't win?"

"Prove it."

Chernov curled his lip. "I'll prove whatever you like. I've been thinking about this night for a long time. Ever since destiny gave you to me at the Inn of the Green Parrot."

With an arrogant smile he raised the pistol to his temple and pulled the trigger.

Click. Nothing.

He grinned up at Nicholas triumphantly. "I told you I was lucky. I'm about to get what I want. Nothing can stop me."

"Try it again."

"Do you want me to prove it to you twice, Kolya? Before I collect my bet?"

"Yes. Once more."

Chernov caught his breath. Then he said softly, "There's a long night ahead. I hope you are prepared." He raised the gun again smiling viciously, and pulled the trigger.

Brendan started, in the hallway. *Jesus, Mary and Joseph, that was a pistol shot! I knew I should have come inside . . . of all the damn fools . . .*

Frightened, he burst open the door. Then he stopped in relief. Nicholas was sitting at the table, calmly holding a match to a cigar. Not hurt. Chernov lay slumped in the opposite chair. One arm was dangling by his side. A pistol was clutched in his hand. His eyes were wide open, gazing sightlessly.

His brains were spattered in a dripping grayish-red mass all over the wall and the mantelpiece behind him.

Brendan stared again at Nicholas.

"He seems to have lost his gamble." Nicholas got to his feet with the cigar between his teeth. He picked up his coat, hat, and gloves. "We'd better leave, Brendan. Before somebody decides he heard a gunshot, and calls the police."

"Christ Almighty—"

They shut the door carefully behind them as they left.

Neither one of them said anything in the car going back. They rode in silence. The chauffeur was supposed to be trustworthy, but you never knew.

Nicholas waited until he and Brendan were standing on the sidewalk in front of the hotel and the car had pulled away before he spoke. They stood by the curb, unnoticed.

"Tomorrow night, Brendan, I want you to go to the railroad station. To the freight yards. I'll show you exactly where."

"Found the weapons, did you?"

"Yes. They've posted twelve guards."

Brendan pursed his lips thoughtfully.

"You'll have to take enough men with you to manage the twelve, and a truck to haul the crates, when they're loaded. Don't spare the expense. Hire as many as you need."

"You'll want to spread some money around for bribes, Kolya. So the railway guards will look the other way."

"Fine. Arrange for that too. I'll make space in the number four warehouse."

"Coming with us?"

"No. I'll leave it to you."

Brendan struck a match to light his cigarette and cupped it in his hand. "Right. I'll get busy first thing in the morning." He waved out the match and raised his head. "I'll open negotiations with Chang Tso-lin, if you like, when you're ready to deal. In the name of an old friendship."

"Yes, that will be helpful. But explain to him, Brendan, that he can't have it all his own way. We'll let him open the bidding." He paused. "Naturally my name is never mentioned."

"Naturally."

One hundred thousand rubles, Nicholas thought, staring down at the sidewalk. He was still in the grip of the cold tension that had been with him all evening. He wondered if he would sleep tonight. Probably not. A hundred thousand rubles. Chernov's figure. He would do better than that.

And this time, the profit would be all his.

The next day in his office he was on edge and restless. He had trouble concentrating. He kept wondering whether Brendan was having any problem hiring the men, and thinking about the freight yards and what was to happen that night.

He was distracted, in midmorning, by a message from Wang Tien-shan.

"Mr. Wang would like to see you at four o'clock, in his place of business in Fu Chia Tien," the secretary reported.

"Is he on the telephone?"

"No, he sent a messenger. The man's outside, waiting for an answer. He says it's very important."

Oh Lord, not today. Nicholas sighed. He couldn't refuse Wang Tien-shan, he thought wearily. "All right, tell Mr. Wang I'll be happy to see him at four o'clock. And have a car ready for me at quarter to four."

The secretary nodded and left.

This time, when Mr. Tsai opened the gate for Nicholas in Fu Chia Tien, he bowed ceremoniously. "Welcome, Honorable Visitor. Mr. Wang Tien-shan is expecting you. Please come in."

He led the way to a private room behind a beaded curtain at the back of the courtyard. It was furnished

359

with low couches and mahogany tables painted in dark red Ningpo varnish. Tea, wine, and moon cakes were set out on one of the tables.

Wang Tien-shan and two other men were already waiting for him. They stood up when he entered.

"Ah, Mr. Federovsky." Wang bowed, hands in sleeves. They were still on a last-name basis. They probably always would be, Nicholas thought. "Welcome once more to my humble establishment."

The two other men had a familiar look about them, Nicholas thought, as he returned the bow, though they were both Chinese, and he was certain he'd never seen them before. One of them wore spectacles, both had leather cases on the floor at their feet. But there was something about that air of alert competence, that impression of valuable information waiting to be imparted . . .

"These two gentlemen," Wang Tien-shan said, turning and gesturing, "are the lawyers for Madame Sung's estate. Let me introduce you."

Lawyers. Yes, of course, that was the familiar look. They had a worldwide family resemblance.

Wang was saying their names.

But Nicholas's mind was still coping dazedly with Wang Tien-shan's earlier phrase.

Madame Sung's estate?

What did that mean?

It could only have one meaning.

He sat down on one of the couches and passed a hand over his eyes. "Mr. Wang, I'm sorry, you must forgive me, but you used an expression I'm not sure I heard correctly. You referred to Madame Sung's estate."

One of the lawyers cleared his throat. Wang looked at Nicholas sympathetically.

"Of course, you hadn't heard. I must beg your forgiveness for the clumsy way of giving you the news." He gazed down at his lap. "It grieves me to tell you, Mr. Federovsky, that Sung Mei-ling has gone to join her ancestors."

Oh my God. What happened? Mei-ling!

Mr. Wang was explaining that she had chosen this path of her own free will, for reasons of her own, and it was to be hoped she had now attained the serenity and peace she so greatly longed for.

Nicholas's mind was a tumble of confused thoughts, regrets, and self-recriminations. She'd spoken of a journey —a far journey. Why hadn't he understood what she'd meant? What a fool he was, how blind! Why had he accepted her refusal to see him again? There must have been something he could have done, some way he could have stopped her . . . Nothing . . . nothing. Too late now. . . .

"We must accept her decision," Wang was saying gently, "and not torment ourselves with vain regrets. She would not have liked that."

"Yes, of course."

"May I offer you wine?"

"Thank you."

By the time they were ready to discuss their business, Nicholas had collected himself. He felt a sense of deep, calm sadness. He wondered why he was here, and what the lawyers had to say. Obviously Mei-ling had left him a remembrance. *You needn't have done that, Mei-ling . . .*

"You have been made a bequest by Sung Mei-ling," Wang said. "I will allow Mr. Han to explain it."

Nicholas nodded, cradling his wine glass.

"She was most generous," Mr. Han said crisply. He stooped and took some papers out of his case. "The Sung family, however, understands that everything is legal and in order, and they have agreed not to oppose Madame Sung's last wishes."

So the Sung family was angry at this bequest, Nicholas thought. He wondered what it was.

"This is the deed to the house in New Town," Mr. Han said. "It now belongs to you."

The house? Those pavilions, moon gates, and gardens, behind that high brick wall in New Town? He was speechless.

"The Sung family wishes you to understand, of course," Mr. Han said severely, "that none of the furnishings, rugs, antiques, or art objects are included in this bequest. Only the house and grounds."

"Of course . . ."

He heard the rest of the conversation in a daze. He must come to the lawyer's office in the next day or two to sign papers. Yes, yes. He would not be the legal owner of the house until all the papers had been filed properly.

"I believe, then, our business is concluded? May I have your business card, Mr. Federovsky?"

He stood up, since they were all standing, gave his business card to one of the lawyers, and received one in return. You were constantly exchanging cards here. He'd had his own printed in red, since that was considered a lucky color.

Finally when he had gathered his thoughts together he drew aside Wang Tien-shan in the courtyard.

"Mr. Wang, what's happened to Madame Sung's servants?"

"They are still in the house. They are in a state of confusion and grief, as you can imagine. They were most devoted to Sung Mei-ling."

"Yes. I know that. Would you do me a service, Mr. Wang? Tell them to remain. Tell them I'll pay their wages, as before, and that I wish them to stay."

"Certainly. They'll be happy to hear that."

"Tell them I'll come by to see them as soon as I can, as soon as my business permits. Right now I—"

Wang Tien-shan inclined his head. "I understand."

"Thank you, Mr. Wang."

When he was in the car returning to his office, the full irony of the situation washed over him.

That beautiful house in New Town, waiting to be furnished, to be filled with art objects, rugs, chests, statues. . . .

He could afford them now. Especially if he succeeded in taking those weapons from the freight cars and selling them at his price. If Brendan did his job tonight . . .

But when he moved into that house—when it was ready —who would be with him? Who would he share it with? A houseful of servants . . . and himself. Alone.

No, he couldn't—wouldn't—give up hope of finding Daria. All that bloody business with Chernov, from the Inn of the Green Parrot to last night, everything that had happened in Harbin—to what purpose? So that he could gain worldly goals, and achieve loneliness? No, he would never accept it. . . .

He hardened himself to keep on searching, no matter how long it took.

Chapter 30

Daria thought this village was the strangest, most exotic place she'd ever seen.

Not even in her schoolbooks, back in Saravenko, had there been descriptions of a scene like this.

She was seated on the ground, wearing a padded cotton jacket over her tunic and trousers, with Shih Lung and the bandits surrounding her, in a meadow just outside the village. They were somewhere on the Manchurian-Mongolian border. Above her, in the hard blue sky, gleaming with the sapphire of autumn, an eagle circled lazily. Below, a vast crowd of people spread in all directions, their clothing a swirl of brilliant colors against the grass.

They had come to witness the ceremonial feast that was about to take place.

Set on a knoll above them was a long wooden table heaped with fresh melons, peaches, grapes, and many varieties of cheese; silken cushions were scattered on the ground the length of the table, for the guests of honor.

Daria knew the principal guest was to be a nomad chieftain.

But the deepest excitement, she knew, would be reserved for the entrance of Bogdo Khan, the great lama; he was giving the feast.

Daria hadn't seen him yet. They'd been here for a week, staying in a Chinese inn, where she shared a k'ang with Shih Lung, in the best room available, the *shang fang* at the back of the courtyard. Daria thought a month had passed since her healing by the shaman. Winter was coming; it was almost the Chrysanthemum Moon. In another month it would snow. She was aware that Shih Lung was waiting for an audience with Bogdo Khan, but so far the Stone Dragon hadn't been able to arrange a meeting with the great lama. The bandit leader was growing irritable and impatient.

Here in the meadow, nothing had happened for a long time. Daria was curious to see Bogdo Khan, and wondered when he would appear. Would he resemble the other lamas she'd seen in the village, with their red silk robes and shaven heads?

She looked out at the horizon, feeling restless. A salt lake glittered in the distance. White cranes circled over it; she knew they were considered holy. Beyond the lake on a far hill, the circular shape of an *obo*—a shrine to the spirits—made a curved silhouette against the sky.

Black felt tents stretched as far as the horizon, with kneeling camels before them. Poles were set into huge wicker baskets of sand in front of every tent, to appease the spirits, with lengths of red-and-white calico waving from the crosspieces. The top of every pole was adorned with a tuft of dried grass.

One tent, set apart from the others, was pure white, triple the size of all the rest: the tent of Bogdo Khan.

Daria took a breath. She had learned that no tent must be pitched in the shade of a tree, because that was unlucky.

The tents were called yurts.

How strange this all was.

She'd read about Mongolia, of course, and she'd seen occasional Mongolian tribesmen in Chita, bowlegged and narrow-eyed, awkward when they were dismounted from their horses. And she had memories from her schoolbooks of nomads herding sheep and cattle across vast plains of waving grass, and camel caravans moving across the sands of the Gobi.

But nothing like this.

In the village, a place of low mud huts, the spirit of Genghis Khan seemed to walk the narrow streets. Every street had its storyteller, seated cross-legged on a rug on the ground, chanting his tales of the desert, and many of the tales were about the Great Khan.

". . . the loudness of his voice sounded like thunder in the mountains. The strength of his hands was like that of the paws of a bear. His hands could break a man in two as easily as an arrow . . ."

Prayer wheels stood at every street corner, glittering with gold leaf, protected by little sheds. Prayer flags fluttered from every rooftop. The wheels were always spinning, sending prayers to heaven, whirled by the pious.

The village streets were filled with the odors of burning camel dung and fermented mare's milk. They were crowded with lamas and tribesmen, and clamorous with the clang of hammers on metal, as the coppersmiths beat out their wares.

Daria shifted her position on the grass. Where was Bogdo Khan? Some of the guests were arriving for the feast in their long bright-colored sheepskin vests and baggy trousers, and were sitting down on the cushions. All around her, the Chinese bandits were chattering and laughing and gobbling dried watermelon seeds. She wondered again why Shih Lung had brought her here. Was it something to do with the lama? It had to be. Otherwise why was the Stone Dragon so anxious to meet him? The idea made her uneasy.

How long would they stay? There were so many unanswered questions in her mind. The festival would go on for weeks, she'd been told. The nomads had come from great distances to attend, and to be blessed by Bogdo Khan.

But now something was happening. She strained to see. People were chattering and murmuring and rising to their feet. Others were pulling them down again to keep them from blocking the view.

Bogdo Khan was making his long-delayed entrance.

He came in a stately walk, befitting a great lama. Lesser monks followed in a solemn procession. His robes were yellow silk, brilliant and gleaming with color. His head might have been shaved. Daria couldn't tell, because the orange felt helmet he wore covered his ears and the top of his head, rising to a high point adorned with peacock feathers, and falling in fringes to his shoulders.

His arm was crooked in front of him, and on it he carried a golden eagle, a big, fierce bird with predatory eyes, its claws gripping the leather gauntlet that protected Bogdo Khan's wrist.

The people exclaimed in admiration and amazement at the sight of the eagle. Other lamas and chieftains carried eagles, falcons, and hunting birds; falconry was a great sport here. But only on horseback, with a wooden crutch thrust into the saddle to support the weight of the bird.

Who but Bogdo Khan would carry an eagle on one arm, without even trembling?

The man was huge, Daria thought. He seemed gigantic. Perhaps it was the robe, the atmosphere of ceremony, his stately stride. But he towered over all the other monks and all the other celebrants, making them seem like children, with his great height and the breadth of his shoulders.

He sat down cross-legged on one of the silken cushions at the center of the table, with the guests of honor at his right and left. Someone ran up to take the eagle away. The feast began.

Beside Daria, Shih Lung was smoking a cigarette. Her eyes were narrowed, and an ugly grimace twisted her mouth. She was angry, Daria thought, because she hadn't spoken to the lama.

Maybe they would leave here and go back where they came from. Maybe Shih Lung would write to Nicholas.

Zora's prophecy was coming back to torment her again. A swift parting. The death of a blue-eyed man. *No. No. He is not dead.*

Shih Lung finally decided to converse, temporarily overcoming her bad humor.

"Do you see those wooden cups they're offering the guests of honor?" she said.

"Yes."

"They're made of zabia wood. It's a very precious wood, and has magic properties. It can make water boil, if the water's been poisoned."

But a more spectacular sight was arriving: huge wooden platters, each borne by two attendants, each platter holding an entire roasted sheep. The first pair of attendants was kneeling by Bogdo Khan, offering the platter. She could see that the four legs of the sheep had been cut off and were arranged around the rump. On top of the roasted carcass, the sheep's skull glared sightlessly at the lama.

Bogdo Khan had dipped his finger in the mutton fat and was making a holy mark on the skull.

Now they were cutting up the carcass, preparing to serve it, and the second platter was being offered to Bogdo Khan. Another skull, another mark.

Shih Lung hawked and spat. "This will go on for hours," she muttered. "We're wasting our time."

"Only wait," the old man called out from behind Daria. "There's to be a wrestling match afterward. The great lama himself will compete."

"What's the point? They say he always wins." But Shih Lung shrugged and remained where she was.

The feast continued. More courses, more ceremonies. Prayer flags fluttered in the crowd. Men twirled prayer wheels in their hands, or counted beads. Another wild eagle came to soar overhead; the sun sank lower in the sky. The *obo* shrine on the distant hill disappeared in shadows.

Men began to clear a space on the grass in front of the feast table. Bogo Khan stood up and so did the guest of honor on his left hand. Both of them began to fling off their clothes. Bogo Khan took off his helmet, revealing a shaved and gleaming head.

The wrestling match was about to begin.

Red-robed lamas were helping Bogdo Khan off with his yellow silk. Beneath it he was naked except for a small breechclout around his hips, which narrowed to a cord between his buttocks. He flexed his arms and shoulders, rippling the muscles, as the other monks began to spread mutton fat over his body.

His skin was completely smooth, except for the tuft of pubic hair that showed above the breechclout.

Shih Lung averted her face in disgust.

Bogo Khan's opponent, similarly stripped, was a well-built and muscular man, but it was obvious he was no match for the lama in height and weight.

The crowd grew hushed as the two men advanced toward each other on the grassy space. One of the monks on the sidelines raised his arm. Bogdo Khan suddenly jumped up into the air and slapped his thighs, uttering a wild cry. He came down in a crouch, elbows out.

"It's the eagle stance," the old man whispered in Daria's ear. "He'll flap his arms like an eagle."

Bodgo Khan's opponent was performing a similar ritual, crouched down with his elbows flapping. Then the two men stood up and fell upon one another, gripping each other by the neck.

For long moments they stood toe to toe, grunting and attempting to throw each other down by brute strength. Finally Bogdo Khan shoved his opponent away. He turned sideways, raised his leg and kicked the other man in the chest. The man staggered backwards. The lama was on him immediately, hooking a leg around his ankle so that he tripped. Then Bogdo Khan bore him down to the grass with his weight.

The man attempted to rise. Bogdo Khan, kneeling on top of him, locked his knees around the man's head, reached under his armpits and clasped his hands behind his opponent's back.

The man was pinned.

Bogdo Khan stood up, grinning, and allowed his opponent to rise.

As soon as the man had struggled to his feet, he shook his head to clear it. Then he circled quickly to the lama's rear and gripped Bogdo Khan in a headlock, one arm clenched tightly around his throat.

The lama, in a surge of massive muscles, shook himself free, like a dog shaking off water. Then he moved around swiftly to his opponent's back, gripped him by the neck and the crotch, heaved him up and held him high in the air.

This time, when he slammed his opponent to the ground, the man lay still.

"Is he dead?" Daria whispered.

"No, only stunned," Shih Lung said contemptuously. "I told you, Bogdo Khan always wins."

The lama was performing a kind of victory dance around the grassy square, slapping his thighs, then kneeling and slapping the ground. The crowd was shouting its approval. The fallen man was beginning to stir and moan.

Someone had come over to speak to Shih Lung, one of the red-robed monks. The man was whispering in her ear. The Stone Dragon stood up with a complacent smile and dusted off her clothes.

She gave orders to Yao, pointing to Daria. Yao took Daria's arm and hauled her to her feet.

Shih Lung was marching off with the monk.

Daria realized she was being taken back to the inn.

She began to feel anxious and nervous. Something was happening, but what?

Shih Lung walked confidently beside the red-robed monk across the meadow. She felt certain she was about to achieve her purpose.

Ai ya! The great Bogdo Khan was finally willing to see her! And now, she thought triumphantly, he would be in a very good mood. Because he had won his wrestling match and his vanity was flattered and pleased, he would listen to whatever she proposed with a favorable ear.

She told herself that after all, she had managed everything in exactly the right way. So far, so far . . .

She noted with satisfaction that the monk was taking her over the grass to the big white yurt of Bogdo Khan.

This was the only tent with a wooden vestibule. Because the great lama was also a magistrate and dispenser of justice, various instruments of punishment were hung by the door. Heavy leather ear-boxers. Finger-crushers. Several different sizes and styles of whips.

Signs of office: a warning to evil-doers.

And an ominous signal to a rebellious or disobedient wife, Shih Lung thought.

Once she was sold to the lama, the Stone Dragon told herself, the foreign devil would have a harder time of it. Bogdo Khan would never tolerate rebellion or sullen behavior. Punishment would be swift. Shih Lung amused herself with spiteful imaginings of the lama's wrath.

She knew the stories of Princess Norgidma, the lama's second wife. How the haughty princess had been laid across the great lama's knees in the courtyard of the monastery, with all the monks and villagers looking on, and how her flesh had been bared and then crimsoned by the strong hand of the lama, and how she had howled her pain and fury as the onlookers murmured their approval. Princess Norgidma had learned to be a dutiful and respectful wife, to the satisfaction of Bogdo Khan.

So would the foreign devil, Shih Lung thought maliciously. Once she'd been sold to the lama.

She prepared herself for the coming meeting.

Inside the tent, the lama was donning his silk robes, aided by two attendants. Shih Lung, ignored for the moment, had time to look around.

She observed the raised dais in the center of the floor, where an iron stove was sending smoke from burning camel dung through a hole in the roof. Woolen rugs were heaped on either side of the stove, for sitting or sleeping. All around the walls hung embroidered cloths of silk, cupboards holding red lacquered boxes, small mirrors, guns, powder horns, riding whips, and hobbles.

The lama was a man of many possessions.

Beneath her feet, Shih Lung noted Paotow carpets and Ningsia rugs.

Her greed began to rise.

Where, she wondered, were the snuff bottles?

Probably in one of the cupboards.

Bogdo Khan was reputed to have a fabulous collection of snuff bottles—green jade, translucent violet glass, golden amber—some of them two or three hundred years old. That was not very old by the standards of China, but for a nomad people like the Mongolians, it was a great age indeed. The snuff bottles were very rare.

Shih Lung knew the price she could get for them in the antique shops of Fu Chia Tien, in Harbin.

Let the other bandit chiefs bargain for weapons and money, she thought scornfully. I, the Stone Dragon, have more wit and cleverness.

Bogdo Khan was dressed. He had donned his orange helmet and was dismissing one of the attendants. The other was making tea. He was ready to speak to the Stone Dragon.

"I am having tea prepared," he said haughtily. "Will you take some with me?"

"Certainly, Bogdo Khan," Shih Lung said in his own language, an attempt to flatter and soothe his pride.

She took the guest seat on the left-hand side of the stove. Bogdo Khan chose to remain standing.

"What did you think of the festivities?" he inquired.

He was referring to the wrestling match, Shih Lung knew. "You are indeed a great fighter, as well as a great lama," she said respectfully. "No one can defeat you."

He inclined his head, agreeing with her.

The formalities were observed. They drank salted and buttered tea. He offered her snuff from a plain clay snuff bottle, which she accepted, and they followed the snuff-taking ritual.

Finally he gave her a severe glance, folding his arms.

"What gifts have you brought me?"

Shih Lung had brought a chestnut mare, which she had purchased in Tabool Ola, the Village of the Five Hills; a handsome brass tinderbox inlaid with copper; a set of silver pocket scales; and a generous supply of brick tea, the "coin of the desert," universal currency of the Gobi. She described the gifts to Bogdo Khan, who nodded his approval when she was done.

"Excellent gifts. They please me."

Shih Lung wondered if it was time to mention the woman. She studied him carefully out of the corner of her eye. Yes, this was a good moment, she decided. He was receptive.

"I have one other proposal for you, Bogdo Khan," she said softly.

He raised his eyebrows, willing to listen.

"I have taken captive a beautiful young woman from above the border, a foreign devil. A very rare prize. A girl who will dazzle you with the fairness of her form."

Bogdo Khan displayed only boredom. He shrugged his shoulders and turned aside. But he was interested, Shih Lung was certain of it. This indifference was a pose. She knew he was tired of his present wife.

"I've considered what to do with her," she went on, "and decided to bring her to you, Bogdo Khan. Before I

371

offered her for sale to anyone else. After all, you are the mightiest stallion of the desert, that is a well-known fact. So I thought you should have first sight of this beautiful mare."

"For what purpose? I have no need of a wife."

"Perhaps not. But it will cost you nothing to look her over. To see what a valuable property I have for sale."

"Look her over?" He sat down slowly on the right-hand side of the stove.

"Yes, Bogdo Khan. Here in the yurt. I'll present her to you unclothed, for your inspection. Then perhaps you'll change your mind. When you've had a chance to view her at your leisure."

He said nothing for a few moments. Then he waved a languid hand. "Well, perhaps. As you say, it will cost me nothing." He withdrew his snuff bottle from his robes and inhaled a pinch of snuff. "One wonders," he said dreamily, "if the girl might not be stolen from you."

"I've thought of that, great lama. I've brought fifty of my bandits with me, for protection. Just in case that should happen."

"One wonders," he said, in the same dreamy tone of voice, "if our own bandit leader, Dambin Janzang, might not come here and steal her away. After all, Dambin Janzang, with ten Mongol warriors, could easily defeat fifty sons of Han."

"Perhaps so, Bogdo Khan." Shih Lung made her voice very respectful and lowered her eyes. "But not even the bold and daring Dambin Janzang would disrupt a holy village with bloodshed and fighting, at a time of festival. Not even he would commit such a sacrilege."

"Hmm."

Bogdo Khan didn't like that, Shih Lung thought. Of course she had spoken the truth.

Finally, after pretending it was a matter of slight interest to him, Bogdo Khan agreed to inspect the woman. As a favor to Shih Lung.

"I must be alone with her for an hour," Shih Lung said. "Here, in the tent."

He objected to that, on form, but Shih Lung knew he'd agree. His curiosity was aroused; he wanted to see for himself what the woman looked like.

372

He rose to his feet, gathered his robes, and consented to give Shih Lung one hour before he returned. Then he stalked out.

When he had left her alone, Shih Lung sent a messenger to the inn: fetch the woman to me. And fetch my saddlebag—the one I had specially prepared.

Then she settled herself to wait.

When the girl appeared, shepherded by Yao, who was holding her roughly by the arm, she wore the familiar look of defiance on her face.

"Leave us," Shih Lung said sharply.

Yao flung down the saddlebag he was carrying and left the tent.

"Sit down," Shih Lung said to the girl.

"I'd rather stand."

"I have something to say to you. That's why I brought you here, to this tent. It's more private than the inn. Bogdo Khan very kindly lent us his yurt for an hour or two."

"What is it?" She was wary, suspicious, but fearful and trying to hide it.

"Will you sit?"

"No." The stubborn lift of the chin.

"Very well." Shih Lung paused, delaying the moment. Then she said abruptly, "I sent someone to the Inn of the Green Parrot, as you requested. Many weeks ago." That much was true.

The girl's face whitened. She said nothing, waiting.

"I thought it would be best not to tell you. But now I believe I was wrong. I'm tired of your whining about ransom notes to Harbin. You must hear the truth."

"What . . . truth?"

"Your lover is dead. The man you were traveling with was beaten to death by Cossacks, just outside the stockade of the inn."

For a minute Shih Lung thought the girl would faint, she went so white. She reached out a hand blindly.

"No . . . that's not true . . ."

"It is true."

She said nothing. Then she cried wildly, "I don't believe you! Why should I? You lie, all the time, and you're lying now!"

"It's not a lie."

"He isn't dead! He can't be!"

Shih Lung sighed wearily. "I see I must give you some proof." She rose and went over to the saddlebag and opened it up. When she turned, she was holding a crumpled piece of cloth. She brought it over to the girl and pressed it into her hand. "Do you recognize this?"

Daria stared down at it. A man's shirt, covered with dried bloodstains.

"Hao, the innkeeper, gave it to my messenger. The man was wearing it when he died." Shih Lung stared narrowly at the girl. "They buried him in a clean shirt," she added.

Daria turned over the shirt numbly. "Yes . . . yes . . . I recognize it." She hardly seemed to know what she was saying. Her fingers found something in the shirt pocket and she drew it out. It was a small empty wooden matchbox, with a crude drawing of a troika going over the snow. Her eyes filled with horror. "I bought these matches myself . . . in Khabarovsk . . . at one of those sidewalk stalls . . . when he was sick." She raised her head and gazed blindly at Shih Lung. "Zora was right!" she cried. "She was right! Oh God! What am I going to do?"

"Sit down. You must sit down."

Shih Lung led her over to the pile of rugs and forced her down. She prayed for tearless grief. Tears would redden the girl's eyes and make her look unattractive.

So far she was only staring sightlessly, white as parchment, and trembling from head to foot. Good. This was all working out very well.

Now the next step.

Shih Lung went over to her saddlebag again and found her opium kit, with all the necessary equipment. She brought it over to the girl and set it down at her feet.

"There's only one thing to do," she said in a brisk tone of voice. "You must forget your troubles for a little while, until your grief subsides."

"Go away," the girl whispered. "Leave me alone."

This would take persuasion, Shih Lung thought. She set her teeth angrily. Her fingers twitched, longing for her whip. There were ways to tame stubborn young women! But no, that wasn't possible. She'd have to leave that pleasure to Bogdo Khan, when he took possession of his bride. Right now she would have to use other methods. And right now the girl was weakened and overcome with anguish, just as she'd planned. The rest would go as planned too.

She set out the equipment for the opium pipe. She lit the lamp and cooked the opium, explaining all the while that it was the only way to heal grief and bring forgetfulness.

"You'll sleep," she said. "After you sleep, you'll feel stronger."

"Sleep." Daria's fingers curled around the pipestem. "How long will I sleep?"

"As long as you like. It will seem like years . . . centuries. You'll feel nothing, you'll only sink into a bottomless well of sleep."

"I don't know what to do . . . I can't think."

"Draw on the pipe. See if it helps."

"You're evil, Shih Lung. You want me to do something evil."

"Didn't I heal your illness with the shaman?"

"For your own reasons."

"What difference does it make?" Shih Lung spoke impatiently. "It helped you. And this will help too."

The girl bowed her head. "I feel so numb. I keep thinking of Cossacks . . . and blood . . . and beatings—"

"Stop thinking. Draw on the pipe."

Shih Lung began to feel angry and impatient. This was taking too long! She'd only asked for an hour, and she still had much to do!

Finally the girl tried to smoke the pipe. She coughed and choked, thrusting it away. Shih Lung put it back into her hands, explaining how to do it. Draw the smoke deep into your lungs, and hold it, then expel it slowly . . .

Daria was so unused to the drug, it took effect almost immediately. After a few puffs of the pipe, her head drooped and she began to fall asleep. Shih Lung forced her to inhale more smoke, supporting her with one arm around the girl's waist and holding the pipe to her mouth.

She must sleep long enough for Bogdo Khan to look his fill, Shih Lung thought. She'd promised the lama a thorough inspection, and the girl must be deeply unconscious.

At last she was sleeping heavily, overcome by the opium. Shih Lung was satisfied.

Moving quickly now, she pulled the clothes from Daria's limp, unresisting body and stretched her out naked on the pile of rugs beside the stove. The girl flung out an arm, muttering in her sleep. Would she wake up? No, she was in a sound, drugged sleep.

Shih Lung went back to the saddlebag. She found her pots of rouge, for the girl's lips, cheeks and nipples, the brush and black paint for her eyebrows, the comb for her hair, the length of transparent silk gauze to drape over her. The cushion for her hips? That could be found in the yurt. . . .

She went to work swiftly and efficiently, painting, rouging, combing, and arranging Daria's limbs in an artfully sprawled, invitingly lascivious posture. She wondered briefly if she should shave the girl's pubic hair. It would look more esthetic, she thought. But there wasn't time, and besides, it wasn't a Mongolian custom. They were barbarians.

When she was satisfied with her results, and had spread the girl's hair out on the rugs and slid the cushion beneath her hips, adding to the enticing attitude of her pose, she flung the silk gauze over Daria's body. Then she took a deep breath and sent for Bogdo Khan.

The great lama pretended indifference when he arrived. His face remained impassive, his eyes aloof. He barely glanced at the silken-covered figure on the rug. But that was all part of the bargaining game, Shih Lung knew. As she snatched away the gauze covering and he bent over the naked sleeping girl, she began to enumerate the attractions now revealed, pointing them out one by one, using a low seductive singsong—the texture of her skin, the fullness of her hips, the silkiness of her hair.

Bogdo Khan only grunted and waved a hand.

Turn her over.

Shih Lung stooped over the sleeping girl and coaxed her to turn over. She muttered but did as she was told.

Bogdo Khan objected that she was drugged with opium. Shih Lung brushed aside that objection, drawing his attention to the alluring curves now presented to him.

He made a lordly gesture, signaling her to step back and

cease her chattering. He would inspect the woman for himself.

Shih Lung stepped back, biting her lip. After a long and thoughtful stare, the lama was turning her over again on her back. He wasn't as gentle as Shih Lung. The girl suddenly opened her eyes and found herself gazing up into the slit-eyed, frowning face of Bogdo Khan in his orange helmet. She gasped and closed her eyes, crying out a name.

The name of the lover she believes dead, Shih Lung thought. She would wonder, later, if she dreamed all this. Shih Lung would tell her the lama had possessed her while she was sleeping; that would subdue her spirit.

Bogdo Khan was taking full advantage of his privilege. He was in no hurry to bring his inspection to an end. Snapping his fingers, he demanded another cushion to place beneath the first, to raise her higher; and Shih Lung hurried to provide it.

She told herself this was going well. He was pleased.

She began to think dreamily of what she would ask as a purchase price. Many of the snuff bottles, of course. Some of these valuable rugs and carpets. Certainly a large cash payment.

If he decided to make her his wife, Shih Lung thought, he would have to wait until after the festival. It would be at least two or three weeks. She would have to keep the girl locked in the shang fang. But she would be docile after this.

Once she belonged to the great lama, she would be beaten if she resisted him. But it matters nothing to me, Shih Lung thought, I'll have everything I want.

Bogdo Khan straightened up.

"I'll have to give this matter more consideration," he said pompously. "Before I can make a decision."

Shih Lung smiled to herself. He would buy her. There was no question in her mind that the matter was settled. She saw the proof of his desire displayed beneath his robe. Only the bargaining remained.

She bowed politely.

"Of course, great lama. I'll await your decision at the inn."

Chapter 31

His companion was looking extremely lovely, Nicholas thought. She was cool perfection, in her silver gown, with matched pearls around her throat and a tiny wrap of silver fox around her shoulders. She sat beside him in the back seat of the limousine, slim and aloof, lost in her own thoughts, as they moved through the nighttime streets of Pristan. In a poignant way, she reminded him of Sung Mei-ling. Perhaps, he thought, that was why he'd been attracted to her in the first place.

But Tanya Ivanovna, unlike Mei-ling, was honey and snow; a small straight nose, gleaming, honey-colored hair close to her shapely skull, translucent skin of palest white tinged with palest pink across her cheekbones.

Mei-ling had been ivory and jasmine.

He looked away, realizing with a bitter little twinge of regret that he always avoided reminders of Daria's dark gypsy beauty.

He reached for his cigarette case in the pocket of his dinner jacket. Outside the windows of the automobile, Harbin was rolling by in light and shadow, fleeting images. Couples walked close together beneath streetlamps. He heard the sound of laughter, saw the flare of a match, heard the tap-tap of women's heels against the pavement. Music floated out from the open door of a café. Gypsy strings, the throb of a woman's voice, husky with emotion —*I Do Not Speak to You,* in deep contralto. Daria had sung that once . . .

He must think of something else. Those guns in the warehouse. One week ago, Brendan had taken them out of the freight yards. By next week Nicholas would have them sold, faster than he'd expected. And then on to other things. He considered the Fushan coal mines of central Manchuria. The mines were being developed by Japanese business interests. But Herman Levy seemed to think there was an opportunity for outside investment. With Kenji Matsuura's help . . .

Power. While it lasted. Until someone set a match to the powder keg here in the East and blew up the world. Again. But by that time Nicholas would be ready. He wouldn't be caught in another explosion. Not this time.

Absently, he offered Tanya a cigarette.

"No, thank you."

Tanya looked at her companion out of the corner of her eye. She felt disturbed and frightened by the severe austerity of his beauty. She gazed from beneath her eyelashes at the somber classic features, the perfectly arched eyebrows, the symmetrical planes of jaw and cheekbones, thrown into relief by the half lighting of the automobile, the strong shapely throat set off by the white of his collar.

She distrusted handsome men. They made her uneasy. Especially when it was coupled with this unconscious male arrogance. She wished she hadn't come.

Her brother Paul, she thought, was good-looking. Not in this dark and elegant way; Paul was fair-haired, very blond, with a ruddy complexion and a husky build that would run to fat in a few years if he didn't stop drinking. But he had the same hint of swagger, that unspoken assumption of mastery that always made her shrink away.

Where was Paul now? Somewhere in Siberia, fighting with the White Guard. Thank God he was away. She dreaded seeing him again. She hated and feared her brother, and loved him too, since that unholy relationship had begun, two years ago in Moscow, when he'd come to her bed in drunken lust and warned her, with a hand over her mouth, to say nothing or she would regret it. Afterward, lying spent across her body, he'd wept in guilt

379

and misery. But it had continued. Ever since then, she'd feared the sight of him.

Why did I come tonight? she thought. Surely this man was nothing like Paul.

But she remembered how she'd felt the first time she'd seen Nicholas.

It had been last week, in Madame Vera's shop.

Little Masha, the seamstress who helped Madame Vera with alterations, had been peeking through the dressing room curtain.

"Tanya, come and see! He looks like a film star!"

Tanya, in her chemise, waiting for Madame Vera to select the next gown she would model, went to join Masha at the curtain.

"Who? The Japanese colonel?"

"No, of course not! The other man, the one in the coat with the black velvet collar. It's a very expensive coat, and he's wearing handmade boots, I can tell. He must be rich."

Tanya shrugged. "Probably."

Everyone who came to Madame Vera's shop was rich. Madame Vera was a shrewd businesswoman; her prices were extremely high.

This time it seemed to be the Japanese colonel who was doing the shopping, with his friend along to give him advice. Madame Vera herself was hovering around them, offering them chairs, cups of tea: make yourselves comfortable, gentlemen, Tanya will be out in a moment to show you a Paris original. . . .

So it was to be the smoke-blue chiffon, Tanya thought. It was her favorite gown in the shop. It was not an original, of course, only a copy, but it was a very good copy. She thought of Paris whenever she looked at it or tried it on—Paris, where she'd never been. Chestnut trees. Boulevards. The delicate loveliness of French perfume. Reminding you of the old days, in Moscow, the warmth and comfort, security and wealth, reminding you of a way of life that had come to an end in this filthy corner of the Orient. Did it still exist in Paris?

"Madame Vera's being very attentive," Masha said, still peering through the curtain. "She's even lighting his cigar. Oh, I wish it was me holding the match!"

"You spend too much time at the cinema, Masha. You're too romantic."

"Those blue eyes make me shiver," Masha said. "Tanya, if I looked like you—"

"Here comes Madame Vera. You'd better go back to your work."

Masha hastily dropped the curtain and returned to her seat, picking up her needle and thread as Madame Vera came into the dressing room in a cloud of attar of roses. In her right hand she held a cigarette in a long ivory holder.

"Tanya, darling," she said with a wave of her hand, "put on the smoke-blue chiffon."

"Yes, Madame Vera."

Tanya began to step into the gown. Madame Vera put out her cigarette and came to help her with the fastenings. She did up the hooks in the back with deft fingers, speaking in Tanya's ear as she worked.

"Tanya, dear, did you see the man outside in the velvet-collared coat?"

"Briefly, Madame Vera."

"Let me give you a bit of advice. Attract his attention. Look your prettiest. He's Harbin's newest millionaire, and a most attractive and interesting man. His name is Kolya Federovsky." She paused. "He'd be an excellent protector for you."

"I'm not interested in a protector."

"Don't be a fool. Of course you are. It's the only sensible course of action. Any girl as beautiful as you can do well for herself, if she's clever. And opportunities like this don't come very often. He's without a mistress, so I understand. His wife's been murdered by bandits, or kidnapped or some such thing. And he's certainly good-looking, and has wonderful manners."

What could she say, Tanya asked herself helplessly, adjusting the strap of the gown. That she didn't like good-looking, self-assured men? That they frightened her?

"Perhaps he won't be interested in me, Madame Vera."

"Nonsense. He's bound to be." Madame Vera patted a strand of Tanya's shining blonde hair. "Especially when he sees you in that gown. You look superb." She stepped back, surveying Tanya's lush form. "I'm saying this for your own good, my dear," she murmured. "I know your family situation."

Tanya sighed inwardly. Yes, probably she was. It would also be good for Madame Vera's business; but the shopowner was basically kindhearted, and thought she was giving good advice.

Madame Vera was right, Tanya admitted to herself. She couldn't afford to be proud and aloof; not with her whole family depending on her.

As she walked outside to model the smoke-blue gown, she tried to pretend she was alone in her own bedroom. She tried to ignore the two pairs of watching eyes. Walk. Turn. Pause. Walk again. Her posture was effortlessly perfect; it was part of her upbringing. She'd been born a countess. . . . Yes, you can forget where you are, that you do this for wages, that the old life is gone. . . . Pretend you're alone, not here at Madame Vera's. . . .

But suddenly her glance met the intensely blue gaze of the man in the velvet-collared coat.

Her heart sank. She felt herself begin to tremble. Unmistakable, that flare of interest, that speculative, quizzical expression on the handsome face. Madame Vera had been right, he would ask for her name.

And so here she was. In this limousine. Wearing Madame Vera's silver gown and silver fox wrap, lent to her for the evening. The pearls were her own, the only thing left.

Nicholas brought his mind back to the girl beside him. He was neglecting her, he realized. He'd promised himself not to do that.

Silver fox and pearls. No, she was made for sable and diamonds. But that was the old life in Moscow, where she's been a countess, and her father a high-ranking officer in His Majesty's Imperial Army. Now Tanya modeled clothes on the Kitaiskaya, and her father spent his days drinking himself into a stupor in the cafés of Harbin. Her brother was trying to get himself killed somewhere in Siberia, and Tanya supported the family.

Not an unusual story, in these times.

"What are you thinking about?" he asked.

"I was about to ask you the same thing."

"Only daydreaming. It's a bad habit of mine. I spend too much time alone."

"But you've engaged a private room." She flushed a little. "At the Caucasus Restaurant. You're still avoiding other people."

"Yes, so I am." He smiled. "But how can I make love to you if we're in public?"

The flush grew deeper, but her voice remained calm. She looked at her hands. "I wasn't aware those were your plans."

She was, of course, Nicholas thought. He'd made it perfectly clear. When a woman's escort engaged a private room at the Caucasus Restaurant, he expected more than dinner and champagne. Tanya understood that.

But if she had any serious objections or second thoughts, he told himself, he would naturally not insist. She'd had too much hardship in her short life to be burdened with an unwanted love affair.

"All my plans are subject to change," he said, "depending, of course, on you." He drew reflectively on his cigarette. "Have you tried their chicken Kiev? It's very good."

"Yes, perfection. I was there last month. Just prick the cutlet with your fork and all that lovely yellow butter spurts out."

He looked at her quizzically. "Were you in a private room last month?"

"No. I was with a group of other people." She smiled faintly. "I hope it pleases you to hear that."

"My dear Tanya, your life is your own."

"For what it's worth."

An expression of bitterness crossed Tanya's lovely features. She turned her head aside to gaze out of her window. She was unhappy, Nicholas thought. He sighed. There were so many unhappy people in this city. Lonely, despondent people, set adrift. What was the harm in trying to console one another? If such a thing were possible . . .

When they arrived at the restaurant, the doorman sprang to open the door and help Tanya to the sidewalk. His uniform was resplendent: peaked cap, braided epaulettes, smartly belted blouse, polished leather boots.

383

He inclined his head at Nicholas's tip. "Thank you, sir. It's a pleasure to see you here again."

Tanya watched with a curious smile on her face, adjusting the silver fox around her shoulders.

"Do you know," she said as he came up to her, "that my Uncle Konstantin works as a doorman at the Paramount Café?"

He took her arm. "And if it weren't for extremely good luck, I myself might be driving a taxi on the Kitaiskaya."

"I can't imagine such a thing."

But it was true, Nicholas thought somberly as they entered the restaurant. It was impossible to predict the twists and turns of fate. You could make all your plans, formulate all your resolutions, try to think ahead, and then one wrong move—one misjudgment or one evil star—and it was all snatched away.

Yakov, the headwaiter, was advancing toward them with his menus under his arm.

"Welcome, my dear Mr. Federovsky." He lowered his voice. "Your room is ready, upstairs."

"Thank you, Yakov."

Here downstairs, the room was long and narrow, discreetly lit. Beaded curtains hid some of the tables, and on others could be seen the glint of heavy silver and the gleam of sparkling crystal. The waiters all wore sashed blouses with high embroidered collars. They moved quietly back and forth carrying trays with covered dishes. The air was redolent with the odors of perfume, cigars, and rich food. Most of the tables were occupied. The rooms upstairs had to be engaged well in advance; there were only four.

On the upper floor, Yakov opened the door to the private room.

Two armchairs upholstered in striped silk stood on either side of a fireplace that faced the door. Logs were set for a fire. Against one wall stood a davenport covered with a length of patterned Persian silk.

Tanya walked into the room. To the right, an open window let in a cool autumn breeze. Curtains fluttered. The branches of a flowering plum tree tapped against the windowsill. She glanced at the davenport, and glanced away.

Golden sconces in the wall cast a subdued, gentle light. A table stood in front of the fireplace, set for dinner with a linen cloth, crystal and silverware, a tiny vase holding a rosebud, and a pair of silver candlesticks.

Yakov stood by Nicholas in the doorway. "Does it meet with your approval?"

"Yes, excellent."

"Shall I light the fire?"

"No, that won't be necessary. Bring the sherry right away . . . the oysters in an hour."

"Very good."

Yakov withdrew, shutting the door behind him.

Tanya turned restlessly in the middle of the floor, before finally dropping into one of the armchairs. Nicholas walked over to the mantelpiece and leaned one elbow against it. He was silent for a moment. Then he asked, "Are you ill at ease with me, Tanya?"

Pinkness rose into her cheeks. She lowered her eyes. "Yes, a little. You have a . . . a reputation, you know."

"What sort of reputation?"

"It's hard to explain. People are afraid of you, I think."

"I can't imagine why." He smiled ruefully. "Right now I feel tongue-tied, seeing you sitting there looking so lovely and unapproachable. I'm longing for the waiter to arrive. At least I'll know what to say to him."

In spite of herself, Tanya laughed. "I can't believe that." She relaxed a little.

The waiter arrived with the sherry, served it, and left again. Tanya began to seem happier, and a sparkle came into her eyes. The tension eased, and the conversation grew light and inconsequential. Nicholas shut out of his mind all his thoughts of business and concentrated on amusing and entertaining his guest. Time passed; the oysters arrived, then the chilled vichysoisse, the poached river trout in sauce Mornay, the salad, the chicken Kiev. When it was time for the tiny raspberries with powdered sugar, the bowl of fruit, the tray of cheese, and the chilled champagne, Tanya was animated and pink-cheeked.

She sat back and sighed. "I can't eat another thing. I mustn't gain weight, you know. I'll lose my livelihood if I put on an extra ounce."

"No one gains weight by drinking champagne."

"That's not true. But never mind, I'll have another glass. It reminds me of Paris."

"Have you been there?"

"No. Only in my dreams."

"Perhaps you'll go some day."

She grew wistful; a faraway look came into her eyes. "I wish I had dreams like other girls. Of falling in love and getting married . . . a home, and children."

"Don't you?"

"No. My dreams are very different."

"Tell me about them."

She didn't answer at first. Then she said softly, "I dream about escaping, Nicholas. Escaping from the East. From the cold winters, and the bandits, and the warlords, and the opium shops, and being poor, and living where we're living, and being stared at by Japanese officers in the dress shop on the Kitaiskaya. I dream about going to Paris. I have relatives there—an aunt and an uncle. They have a flat near the Bois de Boulogne. My aunt knows many people; she could find me a position as a model for a couturier. I'm sure she could." She laughed and brushed back a strand of hair. "But I'm boring you."

"Not at all."

"Perhaps I mean I'm boring myself."

"Don't do that. You mustn't be bored." He rose from the table and went over to the open window. "None of us should be bored. There's no excuse for that, in Harbin." He looked out at the branches of the tree tapping against the windowsill; the tree was small, barely reaching the window. He reached out and snapped off a twig. "The flowering plum tree," he said, looking down at it. "*La me hua.* do you know what the Chinese say about it?"

"No."

"The colder the winds blow in the winter, the more profusely the plum tree blooms and the sweeter its fragance."

"Last winter was freezing cold. I think the chill of last winter will stay in my soul forever."

"Yes, the plum tree must have been very lovely last spring." He tossed the twig out the window. Then he turned to face her with his arms folded across his chest. When he spoke, his voice was casual, but his eyes were serious. "Shall I make love to you, Tanya?"

386

"If you like."

"Don't you care?"

"Not very much."

"What do you care about? Only Paris?"

"I don't know." She turned her profile to him, gazing at the logs in the fireplace. "I used to think I cared about loving God, when I was young. Once I cared about my brother. Then I thought I cared about staying alive, just being warm, living through the winter . . . when we were running from the Bolsheviks, and afraid, and starving, and freezing to death, and our old life was gone, destroyed, a lovely dream that vanished. Now, in Manchuria, I can't seem to care about anything. It's all over. I'm twenty-three, and my life is over. Can you believe such a thing?"

"No, Tanya, I can't believe it."

"I think it's true."

"I think we must prove it's a lie . . . just for tonight. Just for an hour or two. Perhaps we'll prove it to one another. That we're both still living, and not just walking shells."

He walked over to where she was sitting and held out his hand. After a moment, looking up wide-eyed into his face, she took his hand and stood up.

"Don't expect too much," she whispered.

He led her to the davenport without replying.

She sat down slowly. "You see, I . . . I can't fall in love with anyone. Not even you. Although if I were different . . . it would be very easy to fall in love with you. But there's a kind of emptiness inside me—"

"Don't apologize." He was removing his cuff links. "Or explain. I won't ask any more of you than you can give." He sat down beside her and drew her close, putting his lips against her hair. "Because I'm not free either. My soul isn't entirely my own. We're both wounded, I think. But for a little while, we can try to forget . . ."

The tree was still tapping against the windowsill half an hour later, as it started to rain. Little wet gusts of raindrops blew in through the open window, spattered the carpet, and made gleaming little drops of moisture on Tanya's silver dress, flung across the chair, and on Nicholas's cuff links, scattered on the table beside the bud vase. Neither of them noticed.

Time passed.

Tanya sighed. She lay back against the cushions of the davenport; her bare breasts were white marble tipped with pink. She reached up and touched his face. "I'm not afraid of you anymore."

"You should never have been afraid of me."

"Now I wonder why I was."

He raised himself on his elbow. "Would you like me to close the window? It's raining."

"No. I like the rain."

But the winter was coming, he thought. Another long, cold winter. The rain would change to snow. And then?

One evil star. One twist of fate. . . .

No, don't think about it. Keep on believing you'll find her.

Chapter 32

Brendan propped his feet up comfortably on Nicholas's desk in the office at the number three warehouse. He helped himself to a cigar from the humidor on the desk and passed it under his nose, sniffing appreciatively.

"I ask myself, Kolya," he said, "why the hell you stay in this rotten little place on the waterfront." He put the cigar into his mouth and bit off the end, spitting it accurately into the wastebasket. "Now last month, before you got hold of those rifles and machine guns, I'd say you were saving money. But since you closed the deal . . ." He grinned. "How much did you make?"

"Enough."

"Aye, I'll wager you did." He struck a match and held it to the cigar. "I understand you're seeing a girl from Madame Vera's."

"Yes."

"They say she's a very pretty girl."

Nicholas sighed. "It doesn't mean very much, Brendan. To either of us." He sat back in his chair and tapped his fingers on the desk. His face was somber. He wore black and gray: a black wool suit and vest, perfectly tailored, a pale gray shirt, a black-and-silver necktie. The deep red fire of the ruby ring on his right hand and the intense blue of his eyes, were the only touches of color. He looked withdrawn, remote, and very handsome. He stared off into the distance. "If it will make you any happier to hear it,

I'm moving my office very soon. I've just rented office space in Pristan."

"And when are you moving yourself? Out of the hotel?"

"Next week. The house in New Town is partly furnished, enough to be livable." He glanced at Brendan. "There's a small gatehouse that you can use for yourself, if you like. Hire your own guards, name your own wages. I need someone to look after security."

"Why not." Brendan settled back and recrossed his ankles on the desk. "I don't mind staying in Harbin for a while." He thought for a moment. "Since you're getting yourself a new office, Kolya, what are you doing about a new secretary?"

"Nothing. What's wrong with Eugene? He works hard. Sometimes he even gets here as early as I do."

"Too bad. I was thinking of someone a little . . . well . . ."

Nicholas smiled faintly. "What's her name?"

"Well, since you ask, it's Olga. Pretty little thing. Down on her luck. Refugee family, lost all their money, fallen on hard times, that sort of thing."

"Can she use a typewriter?"

Brendan looked slightly startled. "I never thought to ask."

Nicholas sighed. "All right, send her to see Eugene. Maybe he can put her to work filing."

"Ah now, you've a kind heart. Ye'll be remembered in heaven for that."

Nicholas reached into his pocket for a cigarette. "Is that why you came here today? A job for Olga?"

"No, Kolya. As a matter of fact, I didn't." Brendan took his feet down from the desk, and leaned forward, tapping the cigar ash into the ashtray. "I have some information for you. I was saving it, thinking of how to tell you."

Nicholas tensed. "What is it?"

"Now don't get your hopes up; it isn't certain."

"*Tell me.*"

"All right." Brendan stared at the floor for a moment. "You know I passed the word all through the Nahaloika district of the city that I was looking for information about a kidnapped girl, and willing to pay for it."

Nicholas nodded.

390

"Well, last night I got some results. I met a horse dealer who just got back from the Mongolian border. Last week he went through a festival village near the town of Solun, before loading his ponies onto a freight train in Tsitsihar."

"Go on."

"A great lama named Bogdo Khan is in the festival village to conduct the rituals." Brendan paused. "And so is Shih Lung. With fifty of her bandits."

Nicholas leaned forward. He clenched his hand into a fist. His voice tightened. "Who else?"

"The Stone Dragon has a girl with her, Kolya. A foreign devil."

A short, tense silence fell.

"What does the girl look like?"

"The man wasn't sure. Young, he thought, and possibly dark-haired. He hadn't seen her. Shih Lung is keeping the girl hidden, locked up in the Chinese inn."

Nicholas sat back again. His hand went to his mouth, stroking his mustache. "It must be," he whispered. "It must be Daria." His eyes flared with hope.

"If it is, Kolya, we'd better move fast. The man said that in two weeks she's to be married to Bogdo Khan."

"Married!" Nicholas dropped his hand and stared at Brendan in leaping anger. "To the lama?"

"Aye, so the man said."

"I thought those Buddhist monks were celibate!"

"In theory. Maybe in Tibet they are. But in Mongolia they don't honor the theory very well."

Nicholas stared into space. His jaw set. "To hell with him, then. If it's Daria—and it is, I'm sure it is—then we'll go and get her back—"

"Fine. It's worth a try—the chances are good it's Daria." Brendan drew thoughtfully on his cigar, exhaling a cloud of smoke. "We should pay a visit to the governor of the province before we go to the village. Get some kind of official paper preventing the ceremony. All you need is your marriage certificate, to prove she's your wife and can't marry Bogdo Khan. There won't be much Shih Lung can do about it, not in a festival village. If she tries any gunplay, the tribesmen will tear her apart—including those bandits of hers."

"We can't do it that way, Brendan."

"It's the only sensible way, Kolya. Nice and legal. You've got the Stone Dragon where you want her, in Bogdo Khan's jurisdiction. I told you, he's a lama, he's got prestige and authority, he'll keep her under control. But he can't fight a legal paper from the governor."

"There's a small problem."

"What's that?"

"I have no marriage certificate." Nicholas closed his fist again on top of the desk. "We were never married. She's not my legal wife."

It was Brendan's turn to fall silent. "Oh Christ," he said finally. "Then you have no legal claim at all."

"No."

"There isn't any relationship you can point to—guardian, relative, anything?"

"No."

"Jesus. We'll have to think about this."

"There isn't anything to think about." Nicholas's face was hard. "We'll hire enough men to take over the village, and go and get her back."

"Not so easy. You won't be in Harbin, remember. You'll be out on the Mongolian border, and you'll be dealing with a holy man, surrounded by his people. Nomads, villagers, tribal chieftains—they come from all over the desert, and they believe in Bogdo Khan. Start any trouble, Kolya, and you're liable to start a war. Nobody would come out of it alive." Brendan stubbed out his cigar in the ashtray. "And if they did—hell, I'm willing to take a chance, but do you want to risk Daria's life?" He lifted his gaze to Nicholas's face. "You've been clever up to now, Kolya. Use your brains. Think of something better."

"Maybe you're right." Nicholas sank into reflection. "Is there any way to steal her ourselves? Without gunplay?"

"Long odds. We'll stick out like snow on the desert. White men in a Mongol-Manchurian village? They'll double, triple the guard. Shih Lung is nobody's fool."

"Damn it! There has to be a way, without risking Daria's life. I haven't waited this long to lose her now. Not by taking foolish chances . . ." He was silent again. "We know about Shih Lung," he said, half to himself. "If she wanted to negotiate, she would have written to me long ago. So we'll have to think about Bogdo Khan." He raised his glance. "What do you know about him, Brendan?"

"I told you, he's a great lama. Big giant of a man, famous wrestling champion, head of his monastery, wealthy, powerful—"

Nicholas cut him off. "Wrestling champion?"

"Aye, he's very proud of that. They say he's never been beaten. Wrestling is a popular sport in Mongolia."

"That's a possibility. I did some wrestling, years ago."

"Forget it, Kolya." Brendan waved a hand in the air. "From what I understand, the man's enormous. He must have you outweighed by fifty pounds."

"Then he'd probably accept a challenge."

"Why not?" Brendan laughed shortly. "He'd wipe you all over the grass. The Chinks and Mongolians don't get too many chances to disgrace a white man. He'd accept in a minute."

"Fine. I'll put in my claim for Daria publicly, and if he disputes it, let him fight me for her. If I win, I can take her away without bloodshed. Without risk."

"Except the risk of breaking your back." Brendan made a disgusted face. "How the hell do you think you can win? You're not talking about skill now, Kolya. You're not talking about a chess game. You're talking about a wrestling match. Pure brute strength. It's no scientific sport, not the way the Mongolians fight."

"What rules do they follow?"

"Whatever you like. Catch-as-catch-can. Kneeing, kicking, arm-twisting, eye-gouging—the only thing you can't do is use your fists." Brendan frowned. "Hell, Kolya, you're not serious about this, are you?"

"Brendan, listen. There's a Japanese system of wrestling that uses skill. I've heard of it. A way to defeat a bigger, heavier opponent." Nicholas bit his lip.

"Judo?"

"Yes, that's it."

"How much judo do you think you can learn, in the time you've got? We have two weeks. Once Daria's married to the lama . . ."

Nicholas stared at Brendan with blazing eyes. "Married to him! Never! I won't let that happen. Before I do—" He stood up suddenly and paced around the room, dark-faced and furious. Then he opened the door to the office. "Eugene," he said to the secretary, "get me Colonel Matsuura, at the Japanese Military Mission. Let me know when he's on the telephone." He closed the door partway and went back to his desk. He dropped down into the chair. "How far is the village, Brendan?" he said in a low voice.

"Three hundred kilometers. Maybe a little more."

"What's the nearest railroad stop?"

"Tsitsihar. But it's about two hundred kilometers to the north."

"Stupid to go by rail then. We'll need our own transportation. One week to make preparations, one week to get there . . ." He sat silently brooding. "How are the roads?"

"You know what they say in China about a road."

"Yes, I know. Good for ten years, and bad for ten thousand. Is that the situation?"

"Just about."

"Then we'll need a truck. Do you know where you can get one? If not, I'll put Eugene to work."

"No, I think I know of a Dodge truck that's available. I can see about it this afternoon. But—"

"Make sure it's in good condition. Pay cash, so you can put it into a garage this week for an overhaul. It has to be ready in a week."

"Kolya, do you think you can learn enough judo in a week—"

"Leave that to me." Nicholas made a steeple of his fingers. "We'll need to take plenty of fuel, and plenty of water and supplies. Spare parts. We'll have to do the repairs ourselves."

"Aye, and pray you don't break an axle or smash a gearbox."

"That's the chance we'll have to take. Hire a couple of boys to come along, Brendan, for odd jobs. We'll do the driving ourselves, I don't trust anyone else."

"There won't be room for them, with all the supplies you'll need."

"They can fit themselves in somewhere, on top of the boxes." Nicholas brooded for a moment. "Daria will sit up front with us on the way back," he said, very low.

Brendan sighed. "Do you really think this lunatic idea will work?"

"It has to. Or else, as you say, we'll start a war."

Eugene appeared in the doorway. "Colonel Matsuura is on the line, sir."

Nicholas pulled over the tall black telephone and lifted off the receiver, settling himself back in the chair. "Kenji? How are you, my dear fellow? Busy as usual, I suppose. I won't waste your time. I have a very odd request to make of you, Kenji, and I hope you're in a mood to indulge me . . ." He waved to Brendan, who had gotten up and was leaving the office, then returned to his conversation.

When he replaced the receiver on the hook, he'd made arrangements to meet Matsuura that night at seven o'clock in the Japanese barracks.

Then he sat for a moment, organizing his thoughts.

The Japanese sergeant was speaking in English. His name was Sergeant Kano.

"The Randori system of judo," he intoned, "means free exercise. We practice it under conditions of actual contest, as you see." He waved behind him at the big empty floor covered with mats. They were in the gymnasium of the Japanese barracks. Kenji Matsuura, looking cool and amused, attired in his khaki uniform smartly belted in black leather, stood beside Nicholas, who had changed into the clothes he'd been given: a loose white tunic with a sash around the waist and knee-length white cotton trousers. Sergeant Kano, the judo instructor, a tall brawny man with hard hands and a weather-beaten face, wore similar clothes. They were both barefoot.

Two and three at a time, off-duty Japanese soldiers were arriving in the gymnasium to watch the lesson. They ranged themselves around the wall, leaning back with their arms folded, preparing, like Matsuura, to be amused. The European man was a novice in the art of judo, so they'd been told. This demonstration promised to be entertaining.

"The Randori system," Sergeant Kano went on, raising his voice slightly for the benefit of the audience, "involves throwing, choking, holding down, and bending or twisting the opponent's arms or legs." Obviously quite a few of the onlookers understood English, for they were paying attention. Kano directed his remarks to Nicholas. "Suppose we estimate a man's strength in units of ten. Let's say yours is ten units, and mine is seven."

Many of the watching soldiers grinned.

Nicholas set his jaw and steeled himself for some public humiliation. He was here to learn, he told himself, not to look like a hero in the Japanese barracks. If they wanted to watch, it was none of his concern. He would pay no attention.

"Shall we move to the mat?" Sergeant Kano said, bowing politely.

"Certainly."

"This is a rather strange whim of yours, Kolya," Matsuura said softly into Nicholas's ear. "I hope you realize the game is rather rough."

"It's all right, Kenji. I'm ready." Nicholas went to join Kano on the mat.

The instructor stood in the center of the mat and held out his arms. "Push against me, please. Use all your force."

Nicholas took hold of his arms and shoved him backwards.

Kano suddenly wasn't there. He'd leaned backward with the shove, not resisting, and Nicholas found himself slightly off balance. Kano pulled him easily to one side, and tripped him with his right foot. Nicholas stumbled to one knee.

"As you see, if I leave you unresisted, withdrawing my body just as much as you push, at the same time keeping my balance, you lean forward and lose your balance. Your strength becomes three instead of ten." Kano smiled slightly, stepping away. "Of course, if I had greater strength than you, I would have shoved back. But first I would have left you unresisted. It economizes energy."

Nicholas, who had gotten to his feet, nodded grimly.

"Judo means the soft or gentle art. We take advantage of the opponent's loss of equilibrium. I'll demonstrate further."

Matsuura, who was lighting a cigarette, stood near the mat, observing the lesson. A small smile curved his lips.

"Step forward on your right leg, please," Kano said.

Nicholas stepped forward.

"Wait until your opponent's foot is touching the ground,"

Kano went on. "Then push it, near the Achilles tendon."
Kano acted as he spoke, with sudden lightning speed. Push.
Heave. Throw. Over his shoulder.

Nicholas found himself lying full-length on the mat.

What happened?

He sat up and shook his head.

Kano was kneeling beside him, explaining what he'd
done. The onlookers were grinning openly now. "I waited
until the weight of your body was being transferred to
your front leg. Then a slight tap was enough to throw you."
He paused. "Shall we go on?" he inquired politely.

Nicholas stood up. His face was grim. "Yes, let's go on."

"Attempt to hit me, please. With your right arm. Use the
flat of your hand."

Nicholas did as he asked.

Kano, with his left arm, grabbed Nicholas's sleeve near
the elbow and pulled it forward. He brought up his right
arm against Nicholas's throat. Then he used his left hand
to shove Nicholas from behind, at the base of the spine.
Finally, when Nicholas was off balance, he brought up
his left hand to choke him.

It was easy. It was effective. But you had to be fast.

"Show me that again," Nicholas said, stepping back.
He'd forgotten the onlookers, who were grinning and
chuckling with amusement. To hell with them. "Teach me
that choking move."

"Certainly," Sergeant Kano said. "Shall we try it once
more?"

One week. He had one week.

"Suppose your opponent tries to hoist your body, intending to make you fall. He grips you from behind—like this,
with both arms—leave him unresisted. While so doing,
pull him this way, and throw your body on the ground.
Now you can throw him very easily. Excellent, we're
making progress . . ."

Four more days.

"Randori seeks to train not only the body but the mind
and will. It teaches decision and prompt action. Strive for
mental composure. Develop the attitude of readiness to
meet any emergency."

Three days left.

"Randori is competition between two persons, using all the resources at their command. Become aware, if possible, of the strong and weak points of your opponent. Learn his mental and physical characteristics. Know everything, in short, that can help you devise a means to beat him."

Two more days.

"Employ only as much of your force as you absolutely need for the purpose in question. Don't overexert. Don't underexert. Don't fail because you go too far. Economize your energy."

Tomorrow, Nicholas thought, they would leave for the border because there was no more time.

Chapter 33

"Brendan, what do they wear in these Mongolian wrestling matches?"

The Dodge truck was jolting over a dirt road, deeply rutted and narrowing every moment. The road ran uphill, with scarred, burned-over pastureland stretching on either side as far as the horizon. There hadn't been a village for the past six hours. Nicholas, at the wheel, had shifted to low gear, fighting the road and the hill, his eyes slitted against the rising smoke from the cigarette between his lips. They'd been traveling for five days. The two Chinese boys in the back of the truck, sitting on the boxes of supplies, were forced to hold on with both hands. The truck stank of petrol, which had splashed over the sides from the jolts and bumps. Brendan and Nicholas nervously doused matches in their fingers after lighting cigarettes.

"Depends." Brendan flexed his shoulders, relaxing after his long stretch at the wheel. Like Nicholas, he wore khaki trousers and a khaki shirt, short-sleeved and open at the throat. "I've seen them in tunics and trousers, and I've seen them stripped to breechclouts. You won't know till you get there."

"After we reach the village, see if you can find out for me. Not that it will make a big difference. But any advance information might be helpful."

"Oh Christ. There goes the road."

They'd come to the top of the hill. The track had disappeared. Empty prairie lay ahead, covered with long brown grass, dry as tinder. Beneath the grass, the ground undulated in a series of rolling dips and rises. In the far distance, purple smudges marked the foothills of the Khingan Mountains. To their right a pair of cranes rose up from an unseen water hole, soaring off into a hard blue sky.

"Brace yourself," Nicholas muttered.

He swung the truck onto the featureless grass, choosing a path at random.

The jolting grew fiercer.

Nicholas cursed under his breath. They'd bumped to a stop at the bottom of a particularly steep hill, masked by the grass. Brendan only smiled and closed his eyes.

"Patience, patience."

"Thanks for the advice. You sound like the judo instructor. Maximum efficiency in use of mind and body." He raced the motor experimentally. The wheels spun. The truck stayed where it was. He crushed out his cigarette, carefully shredding it to pieces in his fingers, before he went back to the wheel.

One of the Chinese boys stood up and pointed to the left, uttering a cry.

"What's the matter with him?" Brendan sat up straight and looked around. "I don't see anyth—"

Two figures had risen from the grass. They were peasants in cone-shaped straw hats and padded blue jackets. They gaped at the truck for a moment before turning and running hard in the opposite direction.

"What the hell! Kolya, we'd better get out of here—and I mean fast."

An ominous crackling noise was rising from the grass. Wisps of black smoke were drifting into the air. Licking little tongues of flame were starting to appear, writhing through the grass like crimson snakes.

"They're burning the grass. They do it all the time, to make new growth. Goddamn it, one touch of flame on this truck, and we go up like a charge of dynamite."

"Shut up, Brendan. I can see for myself."

Nicholas's voice was hard and controlled, but he was starting to sweat. He pressed on the accelerator.

The motor coughed. The wheels spun.

The crackling noise was getting louder. They could feel

the heat from the flames and smell the acrid odor of the smoke. It was drifting over the grass straight toward them, blown by the wind.

The two Chinese boys sat rigid on the boxes. At any moment they would leap for safety.

The motor coughed and groaned. The wheels bit into the ground. The vehicle bucked. Once more. Try again. Now. They were moving. They were down . . . grinding up . . . out. . . !

Nicholas swung the wheel away from the flames in a wide circle around the brush fire. The truck bumped over the grass. The two boys gripped the boxes against the jolting. Brendan let out his breath.

"Jesus, Mary, and Joseph, that was too close. Too fucking close. I don't fancy going up like a torch."

"Neither do I. I intend to reach that village by the day after tomorrow."

And hope I'm not too late, he added silently.

"This is opium country," Brendan said. It was the next day. He waved out the window from his seat at the wheel. Poppy fields stretched in all directions, covered with nodding flowers, not the red poppies of Europe, but the silky-white blossoms of the Orient. The poppy season had ended; this was the last bloom before the frost. "The Chinese rent this land from the Mongols, to grow the opium," Brendan went on. "Then they make big money smuggling it into town." He struck a match on his thumbnail. "By winter, they'll have the money all spent. Then they'll turn bandit and take to the hills."

"How far are we from the village?"

"Not far. We should reach it by noon tomorrow."

"Good. I'm anxious to meet Bogdo Khan."

By the next morning they were on the village road. Traffic began to gather in front of them. A group of girls passed on foot, their clothes jingling with silver ornaments, round oiled-paper flasks dangling from their shoulders. Six Mongols on ponyback, herded a group of shaggy camels that plodded steadily on huge dusty hooves. A Mongolian family with all their possessions loaded onto the backs of three gray mules stopped to gape at them. One narrow-eyed Chinese horseman with a shaved head stared at the truck for long moments before wheeling his mount and galloping for the village.

Nicholas leaned impatiently on the horn.

They'd come to a halt. A flock of sheep milled in front of them, baaing and shoving in disorganized confusion. The shepherd was taking his time about moving them to the side of the road.

"Nobody's in a hurry around here, as you can see," Brendan murmured. "They've got all day."

Nicholas pressed the horn again. "That's how long we may be here, before he gets those damned sheep out of the road."

"They never saw a motor vehicle before. They want to take a good look."

Nicholas laughed ruefully. One of the animals was thrusting a woolly black-nosed face against the door of the truck with a mournful bleat. "You may be right."

Finally the last ewe and lamb were crossing the road. The shepherd grinned and waved his staff, which was decorated with red silk ribbons, as the truck crawled ahead.

"Did you see that character with the shaved head?" Brendan remarked when they were moving again. "I didn't much like the looks of him."

"Hunghutze?"

"Aye, it well could be."

"We've been spotted, then." Nicholas set his jaw. Then he slowed his speed. They were entering the main road of the village. Prayer wheels were spinning like tops at every crossing, flashing in a blur of gold leaf. Red-robed lamas with shaven heads moved like crimson birds along the road. The wails and prayers of the faithful mingled with the bray of mules, the clack of prayer beads and the clang of metalsmiths' hammers. The truck slowed down again to a crawl, behind a molasses-slow tide of traffic.

Nicholas pulled up the brake, bringing the truck to a halt. He leaned back. "Meet me at the Chinese inn, Brendan. I think I'll find the place on foot."

"Right. Maybe I'll see what I can find out about the lama."

"Fine. I'll do the same at the inn."

Brendan slid over to the driver's seat as Nicholas got out

onto the road. In the exotic crowd of Mongols, Manchus, and Chinese, he stood out like a beacon, drawing curious stares. Who was this tall blue-eyed white man with the arrogant lift to his chin?

He began to shoulder his way through the crowd, leaving the truck behind.

He found the Chinese inn on the outskirts of the village, behind a mud stockade. He strode through the courtyard and into the main room, feeling eerily reminded as he did so, of the Inn of the Green Parrot. But this room contained an ancient billiard table, which was pushed against the wall. He saw the man with the shaved head whom they'd seen on the road, playing billiards with a companion. The second man wore a row of tin medals on his chest.

The innkeeper, a short fat man with very red lips, came up to Nicholas and began his greeting. The usual bowing, the usual welcome to his humble establishment . . . Nicholas decided to behave in the way he was expected to behave.

"Give me your best room," he said carelessly, interrupting the greeting. "Sweep the floor before you show it to me. Make sure the k'angs are clean, and don't pass off any filthy blankets. Understand?"

The innkeeper paused. "Certainly," he murmured, lowering his eyes.

"There are two of us. My companion is on his way. Also we have two boys, who can sleep out here."

"I understand." The innkeeper raised his head with an ingratiating smile. "You're fortunate. The shang fang is available—our best room, at the back of the courtyard. It's just been vacated."

Nicholas nodded, uninterested in the innkeeper's problems. "Bring me over a bottle of whiskey and a clean glass," he said. "I'll be at the table."

"Yes, right away."

Nicholas threw himself down at the table.

Why was the shang fang available, in a crowded village like this?

The innkeeper brought over the whiskey and the glass himself, and set them down in front of Nicholas.

"Sit down," Nicholas said, waving at the opposite chair. "Let's talk for a few minutes."

"Of course." The innkeeper sat down warily. The man with the shaved head was busy with his billiard game, and the innkeeper, glancing at him out of the corner of his eye, relaxed a little.

"I wonder why your best room is vacant," Nicholas said, pouring himself some whiskey. "Now that I think it over. Why should that be?"

"It only became vacant this morning," the innkeeper replied. "Only about an hour ago." He drew himself up proudly. "The famous bandit Shih Lung was staying here. And also the destined bride of Bogdo Khan. Both of them, here at my inn."

"Is that so." Nicholas shrugged his shoulders. "I wonder why they'd move out of such a fine establishment."

The innkeeper missed the sarcasm. He seemed pleased with the compliment. "They've moved to a yurt belonging to the great lama," he said complacently. "Tomorrow is the wedding ceremony. They must prepare the bride."

"I see. The great lama. Where is the great man? I'd like to have a look at him."

"Today he's conducting a ritual at the obo on the hill— the shrine. His procession should be returning very soon."

"Mmm." Nicholas swallowed some whiskey. "I understand his bride is a foreign devil. Is that true?"

"Yes, true."

"Pretty? Yellow hair?"

"No, dark hair. Dark eyes."

"Not English then."

"No, she is Russian." The innkeeper lowered his voice. "Do you see the two men playing billiards? They found her. They and some others. Not far from a Chinese inn like my own."

"What was the name of the inn, do you remember?" Nicholas spoke carelessly, making circles on the table with the bottom of his glass.

"Some bird or other. A falcon, a skylark . . ."

"Could it have been a green parrot?"

"Yes, perhaps. Not so fine a place as this, though."

"I'm sure it isn't." Nicholas sat back and made an impatient gesture with his right hand. "All right, leave me alone now. I'm tired of talking. See to that room."

By the time he heard Brendan sounding the horn of the

truck, beyond the courtyard, he'd had two large whiskeys. He got up and went to the door, telling the innkeeper he'd be back in an hour, with his companion: have something for us to eat, when we get back. Something decent! Yes, yes . . .

He climbed into the truck beside Brendan. The two boys jumped off and entered the courtyard. Nicholas leaned back and closed his eyes. "The girl is Daria."

"Are you sure?"

"Yes, I'm sure." He sighed. "They're keeping her in a yurt, but which one? There are hundreds of those damned tents out there."

Brendan frowned. "Tomorrow, I understand, they'll take her to Bogdo Khan's yurt. It's the big white tent near the open space, right off the east road."

"Damn it, Brendan, if we could get word to her some way, let her know we're here. Tell her not to lose hope . . ."

"One more day, Kolya. By tomorrow, if all goes well—"

"Let's find the lama. His procession should be coming back from the shrine just about now. Let's get this over with."

Brendan turned the key in the ignition.

The procession was winding its way over the prairie, making its way back from the shrine, to the area of the tents. Red and yellow robes made splashes of color against the vast stretches of brown grass, as the lamas moved like a silken river toward the yurts. Brendan and Nicholas, in the truck, watched from the top of a little rise.

"How close can you get, Brendan?"

"I can stop in front of Bogdo Khan's yurt. The road passes right by it. We can walk from there, and come face to face with the lama. He's the one in yellow, at the head of the procession."

Nicholas stared out at the figure in yellow. "Good Lord. Is he as big as he looks?"

"Aye, that he is. I warned you, Kolya."

"Maybe he's overconfident."

"Aye. And maybe you should have brought a slingshot." He started the truck.

They found a place on the road near the yurt of Bogdo Khan to leave the truck, and then made their way over the grass until they had come to within a few yards of the moving procession. Nicholas walked forward. holding up his hand.

"Are you the great Bogdo Khan?"

The procession halted. The lama frowned, drawing himself up to his full height.

"Who wishes to know?"

He spoke Russian with a heavy accent. His yellow robes fluttered in the breeze. The fringes of his orange helmet stirred on his shoulders. His face was dark. A prayer flag carried by one of the monks flapped in the stillness. Dozens of pairs of narrow black eyes stared silently at Nicholas across the grass.

"I wish to challenge the lama for his bride."

Into the sudden silence came the flap-flap of the prayer flag and the whinny of a distant pony. Brendan stood a few feet behind Nicholas, watchful and quiet. The breeze whispered over the grass.

Bogdo Khan stood absolutely still. Then he spoke in a low guttural tone.

"Get out of the way. You're interrupting a procession."

Nicholas didn't move. "The woman is mine, Bogdo Khan. There won't be a wedding tomorrow."

Seconds passed. Then the lama moved forward in a slow and stately walk. The other monks remained in their procession. When Bogdo Khan was face to face with Nicholas, he folded his arms across his massive chest. In his orange helmet, he was almost a full head taller.

"What is the meaning of this sacrilege?"

Nicholas stood his ground. "You can't marry the Russian woman. She's already my promised wife."

"Worthless words. I reject them."

"I challenge you, then, in the hearing of your followers, to defend your claim. The woman belongs to me."

"Defend my claim?" The lama's face darkened in anger.

"Yes, in any way you like."

The lama threw his head back and laughed. His laughter made a harsh booming sound in the quiet grass. "Get out of my way," he said when the laughter was done.

"Are you afraid to accept my challenge, Bogdo Khan?" Nicholas paused. The breeze rustled Bogdo Khan's silk robes. "Are you afraid you'll lose your bride on the field of battle?"

"I fear nothing. Least of all you."

Bogdo Khan turned slowly to the monks who were standing behind him. He raised his arm. "Hear me, O believers in the Living God! I will deal with this intruder tomorrow, two hours past dawn! We will hold a contest on the meadow by the festival field! We will continue until one of us," he turned back to Nicholas, "is defeated and cannot continue. " He folded his arms across his chest and narrowed his eyes. "Do you agree?"

Nicholas bowed. "I agree, Bogdo Khan. The winner will take the woman for his bride."

"I, myself, will marry her at noon tomorrow. Now remove yourself from my path."

Nicholas stepped aside, and Bogdo Khan continued his stately procession toward the yurt.

Brendan sighed heavily. "You've got your wish."

Later that night, in the back of the courtyard in the Chinese inn, Nicholas lay across the k'ang with his arm over his eyes. Brendan sat on the other k'ang, pouring himself a whiskey.

"Sure you won't join me, Kolya?"

"No. I'm better off not eating or drinking until after the fight."

"Suit yourself." Brendan swallowed from the glass. "Nervous?"

"I keep telling myself I'm confident. But I don't think I'm convincing myself."

"Can't say I blame you."

"For God's sake, Brendan, you're supposed to be on my side."

"Right." Brendan sat forward. "You'll fight stripped, did I mention that?"

"No." So much for tugging your opponent's sleeve, Nicholas thought. It would be bare flesh, and slippery at that.

"He'll be smooth as a baby's ass," Brendan said, echoing his thoughts. "Care to shave your body hair?"

"No."

"I didn't think you would." He took another swallow of the whiskey. "I'll get you some oil, anyway."

"Mmm." Nicholas brooded for a moment. "How long are the rounds?"

"That appears to be a flexible matter. Depending on whether or not Bogdo Khan is doing well."

"Keep track, Brendan. Keep it honest. Let them see you're holding a watch and checking the time."

"What would you say to four minutes a round?"

"Is that the best we can do?"

"No Marquis of Queensbury rules here. It's not a boxing match."

"All right, I'll have to settle." Nicholas glanced over. "Did you find out any Mongolian insults for me?"

Brendan nodded, and poured more whiskey into his glass. "Aye. Here's what you'll say if you need to insult him . . ."

Outside the village, in the tent encampment on the meadow, Shih Lung was awake.

She stood outside the doorway of the black felt yurt she was sharing with Daria, who was in an exhausted and grief-stricken sleep within, ignorant of the new developments. Shih Lung was furiously angry. She stared at Yao unbelievingly, her fists clenched.

"He accepted the challenge of the yang kweitze?"

"Yes, so everyone says."

"Bogdo Khan will hold a wrestling match tomorrow? Against the foreign devil? With the woman as the prize?" Her voice rose with every enraged question. "It can't be!"

"But it's so, Shih Lung. Two hours after dawn. All the people are coming to watch."

"And suppose he loses?" Her voice dropped to a sibilant hiss. Her eyes blazed with rage. "What becomes of my payment? My ransom?"

"He won't lose. Bogdo Khan never loses."

"If he should lose tomorrow and rob me of my prize—after all my plans—I will slaughter them all. That huge turtle's egg, Bogdo Khan, the arrogant yang kweitze with his clever challenges—and the woman too. All of them. I swear it."

"He can't lose, Shih Lung. Don't think of it." Yao put a consoling hand on the Stone Dragon's arm. She shook it off angrily. She hated to be touched. She turned her back on Yao and folded her arms across her chest, closing her eyes, willing the match to be a great victory for Bogdo Khan and a disgrace and humiliation for the yang kweitze. If not . . . if not . . .

She ground her teeth silently, fighting her scarlet rage. Morning would tell the story.

She arrived with her bandits on the grassy space by the festival field well before the time of the match. She wanted an unobstructed view. It was a clear cool morning, with a hint of frost. Already the field was crowded with onlookers, many of them nomad chieftains with hard eyes and grim faces, fingering their daggers. More were arriving every minute, on foot and on horseback. Vendors were moving through the crowd selling hot spiced food and cups of fermented mare's milk.

Shih Lung, her rifle slung over her shoulder, pushed arrogantly through the crowd for a ringside place. Angry mutters and narrow-eyed stares followed her. She was unpopular with these people. They tolerated her for the sake of Bogdo Khan. But fists clenched as she pushed her way past, and the silver daggers, called *utgas,* were half drawn from their scabbards.

Shih Lung ignored them. When she got to the edge of the grass, she saw that the foreign devil was already here. Blue-eyed and handsome in the foreign way, and well-built, but not the size of the giant lama. Few men were. She prayed that he would be clumsy, and make a fool of himself. Was he clever? It didn't matter, for Bogdo Khan was too strong for him. Cleverness would be of no help in a wrestling match.

She willed it to be so.

The foreign devil was wearing a khaki shirt and trousers. He was seated on a small wooden chair on one side of the field. Bogdo Khan's chair, on the opposite side, was still empty. The companion of the foreign devil, a bald-headed man with a fringe of gray-red hair over his ears, was purchasing a cup of mare's milk for his friend. They were in earnest conversation.

The sun rose higher, glittering on the salt lake in the near distance. An eagle came to soar overhead. The scent of cool grass drifted up from the ground, mingled with the odor of sweat and dirty sheepskin. Shih Lung stirred restlessly, seated cross-legged on the grass.

Perhaps Bogdo Khan has changed his mind, she thought. They were bringing the woman to the big white yurt and dressing her for the wedding; Shih Lung knew that. She began to feel happier. Let the foreign devil sit there until he rots. The lama would not appear. Everything would go as planned. There would not be a wrestling match after all. Only a wedding.

But no, Bogdo Khan was approaching. It was almost two hours past dawn, and the lama was arriving for the match. Ripples of comment washed through the crowd and murmurs of anticipation rose from all the onlookers as the lama stalked into view followed by three red-robed companions.

Bogdo Khan raised his arms and spoke to the people. He began to walk around the grass, explaining the purpose of the contest. This foreign devil claims my bride! Then let him win her—if he can! It will be a fair match! The victor will claim the glory and the prize!

Shih Lung stifled her fury. It was *her* prize, not theirs! They were fools! They were idiots! How dared they create this contest without asking Shih Lung? The Stone Dragon had captured the woman—and she would be paid! One way or another!

Both men were stripping off their clothes.

Shih Lung swallowed her revulsion at the sight of Bogdo Khan in his breechclout. It was disgusting. To be forced to look at all that nakedness.

But at least his loins were covered, after a fashion. The foreign devil was even worse. He wore white silk underpants, not as brief as the lama's loincloth, but more immodest, for the silk material concealed nothing, revealed all.

She made her features impassive, hiding her revulsion. Both contestants were being smeared with oil by their companions. It was almost time for the match to begin. The bald-headed man was holding up a watch and gesturing elaborately. Bogdo Khan's seconds nodded with impatience. Certainly. Four minutes a round.

Bogdo Khan, crouched on his chair, expanded his chest

and smiled with confidence. Two monks were setting up a huge brass gong by the edge of the field.

Brendan leaned over the chair where Nicholas was sitting. "How do you feel, Kolya? Are you ready?"

Nicholas nodded. "I think so." He glanced up. "But that gloomy face of yours is no help."

"Jesus Christ and all the saints, I thought I was smiling." Brendan chewed his lip. "Stay away from him until you figure him out, Kolya. He'll try to take you by the neck in the first few seconds. He likes to do that. And whatever you do, don't let him grab you from behind. That's his favorite trick."

"I'll do my best."

Bonggg . . .

"That's it," Brendan whispered. "Round one."

He stepped back, holding the watch conspicuously in the palm of his hand.

Nicholas and Bogdo Khan approached each other warily in the center of the grass. They began to circle to the right, both in a semicrouch, the lama on the outside. Bogdo Khan made the first move, lashing out his foot in a kick to the groin. Nicholas moved quickly to avoid it, but not quickly enough; the blow landed heavily on his thigh.

The crowd let out a long *ooh*.

All right, Kolya, Brendan thought. *Let that be a lesson to you. He's not as clumsy as he looks.*

Nicholas's face was set and intent. The lama wore a faint, contemptuous smile. He suddenly stopped circling, straightened up and put his hands on his hips, as if to say, Approach me! I dare you! I invite your attack!

He was obviously hoping to try his throat grip, Brendan thought.

Watch out, Kolya. This may be a trap. Be careful.

But Nicholas sprang forward, accepting the challenge, and seized the lama's wrist. Bogdo Khan flexed his huge biceps, exerting casual strength against the attack. Nicholas held his wrist in both hands and threw all his weight down against it, pushing in the same direction as the lama's exertion. Bogdo Khan's expression of contempt changed to surprise. He was suddenly falling to one side, borne down by the full weight of Nicholas's body against his

411

arm. That weight, added to his own momentum, was carrying him to the grass.

He made a thudding noise when he hit the ground, landing on his back.

Nicholas dropped with him, swiftly pressing his right knee into Bogdo Khan's stomach.

Christ! Brendan thought. The bleeding bastard should have been helpless, with a knee in his stomach. It should have been all over very fast.

But Bogdo Khan was incredibly strong. He let out his breath in a whoosh, heaved himself up, and threw off the knee.

Nicholas sprang away, panting.

The lama was up. He was no longer smiling. This time, as he circled, he looked ferocious. Snarling, he leaped on Nicholas from behind, too quickly to be avoided. He hoisted Nicholas up in both arms and threw him face down on the grass, then fell heavily on top of him. Both men grunted at the impact.

The crowd was standing now, trying to see what was happening.

The lama was keeping Nicholas on his stomach. He grabbed Nicholas's foot, placing it under his own armpit.

Get out of there, Kolya! In one more second, he'll break your toe!

Nicholas obviously realized the danger himself. In a desperate surge of adrenalin-charged effort he was wrenching his foot away, rolling over twice on the grass and rising to one knee.

The lama stalked forward, curling his lip.

Nicholas stood up and backed away, warily studying his opponent. He was visibly tired. His breath was coming fast.

Brendan suddenly looked at his watch. *Four minutes! Goddamnit, Four minutes!*

"Time!" he yelled. "The round is over!"

One of the monks, who had been watching wide-eyed, blinked and picked up the hammer. He struck the gong.

Not one second too soon.

"You're not doing so bad," Brendan muttered as Nicholas sat panting on the chair. "You've got him worried."

"He doesn't look very worried to me."

"Ah, well. It takes time to feel out a man's style."

"One more round like that—"

"Have confidence. That's what you keep telling me."

"Right. Know your opponent."

"Just get your breath back, Kolya."

Because he was going to need it. Christ Almighty, that was plain enough.

Among the spectators, Shih Lung was tensely watching everything that transpired. Seated on the edge of the grass, she darted her eyes from Brendan to Nicholas and back again. She was wondering, in a rage, if she had made a mistake. Was this foreign devil a penniless engineer? If so, how had he managed to come here to the Mongolian border, with a motor vehicle and three helpers?

The idea that she had misjudged him was enraging. It was intolerable. Suppose he were really wealthy, she asked herself, and able to pay a high ransom for the woman. What would that mean to herself, Shih Lung? It would mean that she had been stupid, shortsighted, a miserable ignorant coolie. It would mean she was still Ah Ting.

No, that was not possible. Her plan must succeed. This spawn of a turtle, this yang kweitze, must be defeated by Bogdo Khan. There was no other possibility.

Scarlet tongues of unreason licked around the edges of her mind.

Bonggg . . .

The opponents came out onto the grass for the second round. Bogdo Khan crouched for a moment, slapping his thighs. Then he stood up straight, with an arrogant smile. He turned his back on Nicholas and strolled casually in the opposite direction, hands on hips.

The gesture was clear: you're beneath my contempt; I can finish you whenever I like.

The crowd laughed. Bogdo Khan waved and grinned, acknowledging their support.

Nicholas stood still in the middle of the grass and folded his arms over his chest. He spoke in Mongolian.

"Only the whelp of a yellow dog," he said clearly, "turns his back on a fight."

Bogdo Khan whirled around. He crouched. He snarled, deep in his throat. Then he stalked toward Nicholas, shooting out the flat of his hand, aiming for the windpipe.

The blow never landed. Nicholas caught his arm and pulled it forward. The lama should have fallen, hurled down by his own momentum. But this time he was saved by the oily surface of his skin. Nicholas's hand slipped, and he had to spring back from the lama's renewed fury.

Bogdo Khan came at him in a lunge, head lowered. Nicholas sidestepped, and hooked a leg around the lama's ankle. Bogdo Khan fell heavily on his face, then rolled onto his back.

Nicholas knelt quickly and turned Bogdo Khan over on his stomach.

The lama was still too strong, Brendan thought. Bogdo Khan was tireless. He had the strength of a bull. He was pulling Nicholas into a headlock.

For long seconds they grunted and struggled on the grass.

Bogdo Khan was up. Then Nicholas. Both men were panting, sweat-streaked, covered with dust and oil. You couldn't tell who was the Mongol, and who the European.

Bogdo Khan lunged forward. Nicholas fell full-length on the ground, evading the attack. As he did so, he hooked his right leg around Bogdo Khan's left ankle. The lama struggled wildly to keep his balance.

Anybody else, Brendan thought, would be down by now. Anybody else . . .

Bonggg.

The round was over.

"I can't last much longer, Brendan."

"You're doing fine."

"No, I have to finish him in the next round."

"He's barely touched you."

"Then why do I feel as if I've been run over by an ox-cart?" Nicholas was taking long ragged breaths, sitting in the chair. "It's now or never."

"Save your breath."

"Listen, Brendan. He'll try that rear hoist again. It worked well for him in the first round, I'm sure he'll try it again."

"Aye. He'll pick you up by the neck and the crotch—"

"I'll be ready. I hope."

Bonggg . . .

* * *

Shih Lung sat like a statue on the grass, listening to the reverberation of the gong. Her muscles had turned to stone: she was the Stone Dragon. Only her thoughts lived.

The turtle's egg still fights. Bogdo Khan should have disposed of him long ago. Instead he begins the third round.

They will pay. They will both pay.

Nicholas's face was a mask of sweat and determination. Beneath the dirt and oil, his skin was pale. His jaw was clenched as he stalked onto the grass.

Bogdo Khan moved straight to the attack, hoping for a quick finish, seeing his opponent's exhaustion. He grabbed Nicholas's wrist. Nicholas moved his arm so that his whole strength counteracted the handgrip. It cost him an effort. But it was worth it. Bogdo Khan, grinding his teeth, grimacing fiercely, was forced to give way.

The lama leaped back, grunting with fury, then leaped. This time from the rear. The back hoist again, propelled by the full strength of his massive body. When he landed, he would have Nicholas in a steel-muscled embrace, and nothing would break it.

He landed.

Nicholas clutched Bogdo Khan's right arm, locking it under his own, and heaved the lama across his back in a blindingly swift surge of movement. Bogdo Khan was still under the propulsion of his own leap. He was flying over Nicholas's shoulder. He was hitting the ground. *Thud.* The earth shook. The lama lay flat on his back, stretched out full-length. Motionless. Eyes closed.

Nicholas knelt beside him, preparing to complete the action. *Place your hand against your opponent's chin and push his neck sharply to the left . . . if he moves, he'll dislocate his neck . . .*

But it wasn't necessary. Clearly, the fight was over. Nicholas, still kneeling, bowed his head.

Brendan let out his breath in a long whistle of relief. Jesus, Mary, and Joseph!

Then he noticed something. The crowd was very quiet, staring at the fallen figure of the lama. But a woman was standing at the edge of the grass, her face twisted in a hideous snarl. She looked like an enraged animal. And she

415

was holding a rifle. She was putting it to her shoulder.

"Kolya! For God's sake, get out of the way!"

Nicholas looked up, startled. He saw the woman and threw himself to one side just as the rifle cracked.

Bogdo Khan stirred on the grass. He sat up. Blood was suddenly gushing from his mouth. His face wore an expression of amazement. He spat blood. Another gout of blood was spouting from his chest. He looked down at himself in surprise. Then he toppled to one side, slowly, like a giant, blood-spattered doll.

"*Yang kweitze!*" the woman yelled. "Foreign devil! You're too late!"

Nicholas stared at her.

"Hear me! You'll never take the woman! Do you understand? You've come too late!" She laughed crazily. "Because it's your turn to die! Like Bogdo Khan!"

She raised the rifle to her shoulder.

Nicholas backed away, moving to the left, his face white beneath the dust. Shih Lung moved with him, following him with the rifle.

Brendan had withdrawn the pistol from his belt. He extended his arm, taking careful aim. *One shot. Don't miss . . .*

But the crowd had suddenly realized what had happened to Bogdo Khan. A huge animal roar was going up. People were rising to their feet. Hundreds of throats were suddenly growling in outrage and fury. Then they were yelling. A war cry was echoing over the grass. Shih Lung's rifle was suddenly knocked from her hands. She was pulled down by dozens of pairs of hands. She screamed in fear. Fists began to rise and fall. Booted feet began to pound. Daggers flashed. The Stone Dragon's scream turned into an agonized screech. The shouts of the mob grew louder. They were fighting to get at her.

The shrieking grew steady and rhythmic, like a machine. Over and over. Earsplitting. Hideous. Then it stopped. It gurgled away into silence. The fists and feet continued to rise and fall in savage vengeance. Silver *utgas* made points against the sky, red with blood. The woman must be dead, Brendan thought. She must be a pulp. *Holy Christ.*

He thrust his pistol back into the waistband of his trousers. Then he broke into a run toward the place on the grass where Nicholas was standing.

"Kolya, we've got to get out of here. This is a mob. We may be next."

Nicholas nodded tensely. "Get the truck. Are the boys on it?"

"Aye."

"Bring it around to the east road, near Bogdo Khan's tent. I'll find Daria. She's there, I'm sure of it."

"Move fast. I'll keep the motor running."

They took off, running in different directions, Brendan up to the road, Nicholas toward the big white yurt of Bogdo Khan.

Nicholas forgot his exhaustion, his aching muscles and straining lungs. He saw only the white tent facing him at the top of a rise.

Guards? No, they were all running for the grass, trying to reach Bogdo Khan. It was too late, he was dead. But they didn't know that yet. They would find out. But God willing, he and Daria would be well away, when they did.

Pray that she's here . . .

Doorway. Wooden vestibule. Inner door. And here, inside. . . .

He stopped in the doorway to catch his breath. Sweat made streaks of grime down his naked body. He stared, panting and wild-eyed, at the figure of the girl sitting by the iron stove.

Is that Daria?

She wore a long, barbarically colored striped robe, beneath a floor-length red felt vest covered with silver and gilt embroidery. Silver ornaments hung from her ears and her wrists and around her throat. Her hair was oiled and arranged in an elaborate coiffure of swirls and loops. She was staring at the floor, in an attitude of utter dejection.

"Daria."

She looked up. Beneath the rouge in her cheeks, she went absolutely white. She swayed. She reached out her arms. Her lips moved, but no sound came out.

He sprang forward before she toppled over, and caught her in his arms.

"It can't be," she said brokenly. "It can't be . . . you're not real . . ."

"Yes, darling, I'm real. I'm here. I've come to bring you home . . ."

He realized he would have to carry her. She was trembling too hard to walk, and there was no time to lose.

He picked her up in his arms and strode to the door. *Pray Brendan has the truck outside. Pray that mob is still down on the grass, thinking of the hunghutze, and not of us.*

Outside on the road, the truck roared to a stop in a cloud of dust. Nicholas stood barefoot and naked in the dirt, holding Daria, in her wedding clothes, close against him.

"For God's sake, Kolya, hurry up! They're on their way!"

He threw her up into the front seat, next to Brendan, who had the motor running. Then he climbed in himself and slammed the door.

"All right," he said, leaning back and closing his eyes. "All right, Brendan. Get us the hell out of here."

Chapter 34

The railroad station in Harbin was crowded, as usual.
Japanese officers wearing clanking samurai swords at their
hips paused in frowning conversation with White Russian
colonels and generals whose uniforms dripped with braid
at the epaulettes, whose boots were polished to a mirror
gleam, and whose gloved hands stroked silky mustaches as
they talked. Rickshaw coolies darted in and out of the
crowds crying for customers, and lined up by their vehicles
in the cobblestone square outside the station with their fur
caps pulled down to their eyebrows and their earflaps hugging their cheeks. Newsboys hawked papers: the *Voice of
Russia,* the *Daily Mail.*

Inside the terminal, the luggage coolies struggled with
heavy loads. Passengers queued at the ticket windows making their requests in Chinese, Russian, English, Japanese.
When is the next departure for Vladivostok? Tsitsihar? Port
Arthur? Can I make connections for Shanghai? Vendors
roamed the floor calling their wares; sweets, tobacco, snuff,
dried melon seeds.

The northbound train of the South Manchuria Railway
was just arriving from the port of Dairen, in South Manchuria. It was pulling up to one of the long open platforms.
Overhead, the sky was the sullen gray-white of early winter.
A passenger swung himself off the metal steps and onto the
platform before the train had come to a complete stop.
He was temporarily hidden from sight by hissing white
clouds of steam. Then he walked out of the steam and into

419

the terminal, a luggage porter scurrying ahead of him laden with bags. The man carried himself with an air of military arrogance, although he wore civilian clothes. His name was Saburo Nishimoto. He was a captain in the Japanese Imperial Army, although he was preferring, at the moment, to keep that fact unknown to the general public.

When he had reached the cobblestone square in front of the terminal, he ignored the clamoring rickshaw coolies and paused instead by the side of a newsboy selling the daily Russian-language paper, the *Voice of Russia*. The boy proffered a paper, gabbling the headlines. The world war was ending in Europe. They were about to sign an armistice. The civil war continued in Siberia. Read it for yourself! Nishimoto only frowned.

"What is that?" he demanded abruptly, speaking passable Russian, pointing to a sheet of paper lying across the cobblestones.

"Nothing, barin. Just some trash."

"I would like to inspect it myself." Nishimoto's tone was chilly. He was obviously not going to stoop and pick it up himself. With a shrug the boy did so, and offered it to him. Nishimoto stuffed the paper into his overcoat pocket and walked away. The boy muttered some words under his breath, advising the owner of the departing back to commit incest with his mother. He'd been hoping for a tip. Then his face brightened. He'd caught sight of a well-known Harbin personality: the Black Lily, with her Girls of All Nations, who had just entered the square in an open automobile with little flags fluttering from its hood. The car began to drive in wide circles around and around the square, advertising the House of All Nations, while the girls, wrapped in furs, waved and smiled from the back seat. The Black Lily herself sat regally among them in a black karakul coat and Cossack hat. She was as handsome as any of her Girls of All Nations, the newsboy thought to himself with a grin. He waved back.

Another automobile entered the square, unnoticed by the newsboy. This one, long and black, flew a tiny Japanese flag from its hood. The car pulled up in front of Captain Nishimoto, who immediately snapped his fingers for the luggage coolie to bring up his bags.

The back door of the automobile opened, and the smooth, urbane tones of Colonel Kenji Matsuura came from the plush interior.

"Welcome to Harbin, Nishimoto-san."

"Thank you, Colonel."

Captain Nishimoto climbed into the automobile. When he was settled in the back seat beside Matsuura and the chauffeur had driven them out of the square and into the stream of traffic, the two men exchanged polite greetings. The colonel inquired about friends and acquaintances in Tokyo and asked if the captain had had a pleasant journey from Japan. He had not. The steamer crossing had been rough, and he had missed his train connection in Dairen and been forced to spend the night in a hotel. However, now that he was in Harbin, he intended to lose no time familiarizing himself with the city.

Matsuura commented, with a soft laugh, on the fact that Captain Nishimoto was supposed to be a civilian photographic expert, attached to the Military Mission. Nishimoto responded with a cold, perfunctory smile.

Colonel Matsuura lit a cigarette. "Next week," he said delicately, exhaling smoke, "perhaps you would like to accompany me to a wedding reception. A personal friend of mine, Kolya Federovsky, is to be married. He is a White Russian, from a very good family. The gathering should be an interesting one. You'll meet some influential people."

"Yes, that would be a valuable experience."

Matsuura, who was having some difficulty keeping the conversation going with this unpleasant companion, seized on the topic of the wedding. He expanded on the ordeal of the bride-to-be, who had been kidnapped by Chinese bandits. The problem of bandits was a severe one in Manchuria, as the captain would discover.

"Was the woman held for ransom?"

"One isn't sure. The story is rather vague."

Nishimoto frowned. "Perhaps she wasn't really kidnapped at all. Perhaps that was just a contrived story, to cover up some other activity."

Matsuura raised his eyebrows in cool surprise. "You're very suspicious, Nishimoto-san."

"It's my job to be suspicious," the captain replied stiffly.

Matsuura sighed and gazed out of the window.

Captain Nishimoto pulled a sheet of paper from his overcoat pocket. "I discovered this lying on the ground in front of the railroad terminal," he said, curling his lip. "It's a Bolshevik propaganda rag called the *New East*. It seems to be filled with lies about our Imperial government."

"Ah. You read Russian." Matsuura looked back from the window.

"Certainly. It's one reason why I was sent to Harbin."

"Yes, that newspaper began to appear on the streets a few weeks ago. It's done on a hand printing press." Matsuura shrugged. "It's the usual hysteria, calling for an end to Japanese influence in Manchuria. Now that the agitators have murdered their Czar in Russia, they're trying to start trouble in China. But the rag will accomplish nothing."

"Nevertheless." Nishimoto pressed his lips together. He gazed down at the paper. "Who is this man who signs himself the Gadfly?"

"We don't know yet," Matsuura said carelessly.

"Where is his printing press?"

"We don't know that either."

"I will make it my business to find out," Captain Nishimoto said coldly, returning the sheet of paper to his pocket.

In another part of the city, the section called Nahaloika, a district of brothels, opium dens and dimly lit taverns, the man who was known as the Gadfly sat in a wooden chair beside his printing press, in the basement of a red brick building. He tilted the chair back on its legs and gazed thoughtfully at the printing press in front of him. It was too early in the day to begin operations, he thought, and besides, his comrade hadn't arrived yet. To work the press efficiently required two people. It was an old Albion machine.

He told himself that he should be writing his lead article for next week's edition of the *New East*. He knew just what he wanted to say. But instead he picked up the newspaper that was lying on his lap, yesterday's copy of the Harbin *Voice of Russia*. He opened it to the social announcements and folded back the pages. Then he studied

422

the brief announcement in the center of the column, which he already knew by heart. Miss Daria Petrovna was to marry Mr. Nicholas Sergeievitch Federovsky, next week in St. Gregory's Chapel. It would be a private ceremony. A small wedding reception would be held later, at Federovsky's home in New Town.

The Gadfly was not invited, he thought bitterly. In a sudden, abrupt motion, he flung the paper onto the floor. Then he spoke aloud, in a hoarse mutter. "First Federovsky's mistress, and now his wife." He looked down unseeingly at the newspaper lying on the floor. "But you'll answer to me," he whispered aloud. He threw his head back and closed his eyes, returning the chair to an upright position with a thump of its wooden legs. "One day soon," he muttered, running a hand over his cheek. "Yes, I promise you that. One day soon."

The house of yellow brick in New Town, late that same evening, was peaceful and quiet. Brendan O'Reilly had settled down for the night with a bottle of whiskey by his elbow, in the small gatehouse near the road, listening with one ear for intruders beyond the wall. The servants in the kitchen off the rear courtyard had finished their tasks and were seated around the table chattering to one another with soft singsong voices. Mr. Chen, the head manservant, was smoking his pipe.

In the south pavilion, facing the willow garden, a rose silk dressing room adjoined a spacious bedroom. Daria sat in the dressing room on a bench in front of the dressing table and stared at herself in the mirror with anxious dark eyes. She touched the robe she wore over her nightgown: ivory satin with lace embroidery, deeply cut over her breasts. How lovely it was. She took a deep breath. It was hers, she told herself. She couldn't quite believe it. The closet in her bedroom was full of clothes, hers as well, including the brand-new blue velvet wedding dress with its matching coat trimmed with white ermine. And this beautiful house, filled with rugs and porcelains, moon gates and pavilions, chests and silk screens—all of it would belong to her, next week, when she became Madame Federovska. Already the servants called her Tai Tai. Mistress of the house.

She felt bewildered. Everything had happened too fast, she told herself. Events had moved too quickly, in the three short weeks since Nicholas had found her in the Mongol village.

He was wealthy, she thought. She pushed back her hair with both hands, still staring at herself in the mirror. His wealth bewildered her. Nicholas was not just an engineer from Kharkov. He was someone else. He was a stranger, an unknown stranger, with mysterious dealings that she didn't understand. Would she ever get used to this new life? She wondered if she would always, in her heart, be just Daria Petrovna, a girl from the village of Saravenko. She found herself longing for the lost days on the *Kwan Yin*. That river steamer, she thought, leaning forward with both elbows on the table. Those days on the river. Gone; they seemed so long ago.

Finally she rose from the bench, smoothed her robe, and walked out into the bedroom, thinking it was time to go to bed. The room was empty, quiet. The coverlet was turned down on the wide teakwood bed. The white porcelain lamp on the bedside table cast soft light from beneath its silk shade, leaving the corners of the room in shadow. Then she felt a cool breeze on her arms and shivered. She realized that the terrace door was open, leading to the willow garden.

But she wasn't alone, she saw with a start. Nicholas was here. He was standing on the terrace, profile turned, one foot resting on a stone lion-dog, one arm lying across his knee. In his hand he held a burning cigarette. He hadn't heard her come to the doorway. How beautiful he was, she thought, with the planes of his face shadowed by moonlight. But even now the aura of mastery surrounded him. He was beautiful and frightening, stern and far away. She stood quietly, hands folded, not wanting to move.

But she knew she would. She gazed down, remembering the rediscovered ecstasy of being loved, her own body arched in helpless passion beneath the lean strong length of his, and she felt weak and trembling, and knew that in the next second she would go forward into his arms. She had no choice.

"Daria?" he said, turning his head and seeing her. "I didn't realize you were there."

He moved to enter the bedroom, but she stopped him. "No, don't come in. I'll come out to you."

"It's chilly on the terrace."

"I don't mind. Just for a moment."

She walked out to the terrace to join him, her satin robe flowing behind her as she moved. Nicholas cast away his cigarette. He reached out and took her by the arms when she approached. His eyes were grave.

"Daria . . . Daryushka. Why are you so worried and unhappy?"

She felt a hot lump rising into her throat. Should she explain it to him? Her fear and uncertainty? Should she tell him about this house, and how it overpowered her? And himself . . . and this new identity of his . . .

"It's the wedding reception," she said finally. "The idea of meeting all those strange people frightens me a little." She rested her head against his shoulder. "I wish we could call it off."

"But that's not possible. We've discussed it before." He gathered her close. "You'll grow accustomed to this new life, Daryushka. It will only take time."

Wordlessly she raised her face for his kiss. As the familiar flame of excitement leaped up in the center of herself at the touch of his lips and she felt the empty place inside her again yearning to be filled, she yielded, blotting out the memory of her fears.

In another part of the city, the man called the Gadfly had already gone to bed. But he couldn't sleep. He turned over restlessly in bed, then reached for a cigarette on the table, lit it and stared at the ceiling, exhaling smoke. He resolved once more that his day of settlement would come soon. On that day, he told himself grimly, he would call in all his debts.

Chapter 35

St. Gregory's Chapel crowned the top of a high hill. Far below, at the foot of the hill, the frozen Sungari gleamed like polished pewter in the afternoon light. The church was a small, graceful building of weathered pink brick, with ornately carved wooden doors and a gold onion dome that caught the lowering sun in a blaze of fire. It was four o'clock.

Inside, the brick alcoves and vaults of the church were dimly lit, and fragrant with the smell of incense. The interior space was empty; there were no pews. The domed ceiling was richly decorated, with the figure of Christ in the center, surrounded by all the orders of angels—seraphim, cherubim, angels and archangels. Beyond them was a border of wide blue sky with the twelve signs of the zodiac, then the seasons of the earth, embellished with birds and trees, rivers and valleys. Icons of the saints hung all around the walls, lighting up the dimness with glowing color. St. Michael. St. George. St. Gregory. The Holy Virgin.

At the altar, Daria stood beside Nicholas with a lighted candle in her hand, listening to the words of the priest. She felt the strange weight of her betrothal ring on her finger, as she tilted her candlestick to a slant, so that the wax could drip down slowly. She saw in bemusement that the wax flowers on the candle were melting.

"This servant of God, Nicholas, is betrothed to this servant of God, Daria . . ."

The priest wore a robe of heavy cloth-of-silver, embroidered with a great golden cross. Nicholas, beside her, looked grave and handsome in black cashmere and white silk, standing tall and straight-shouldered with his lighted candle. She found herself thinking of her grandfather, Alexey Alexeyevitch. She wished he were here.

The candle flames suddenly leaped up golden against the dimness, flickering wildly as a draft swept through the chapel. Then they steadied again, and somehow the dimness seemed brighter. Daria bowed her head to receive the blessing of the priest, feeling his hand warm and heavy on her hair.

"God eternal, who joineth together them that were separated . . ."

Joining together those who were separated, she thought. She wondered if that were possible. She cast her eyes down and imagined she could hear drops of wax falling. Incense moved on the air.

Now they must answer the ritual questions. Had they a true desire to enter into matrimony? Had they promised themselves to others? Yes. No. Her own voice sounded small and faint in her own ears. She had not promised herself to any other.

The priest was holding out a shallow silver cup. She must drink. Red wine mixed with water tasted warm and sweet on her tongue. Then the priest was saying the final prayer, and taking the candlesticks from their hands, and she turned to Nicholas and raised her face to receive his kiss. How blue his eyes were. How warm his lips. She closed her eyes. She was Madame Federovska now, and everything would be different.

As Daria and Nicholas left St. Gregory's Chapel in New Town, the establishment called the House of All Nations in Nahaloika was preparing for the evening's business. Inside the red brick building, at the top of the long staircase above the entrance hall floored with black-and-white tiles, the Black Lily was emerging from her private office. She was saying good-bye to a visitor. The man stood erect and aloof beside her, wearing an expression of cold distaste.

"Are you sure you won't stay for a while, Nishimoto-san?" the Black Lily asked. She tilted her head to one side and put one hand on her hip, regarding her visitor with amused dark eyes. She knew very well that Captain Nishimoto would refuse her invitation. He was wearing formal clothes, and obviously had somewhere else to go.

He made his excuses without even a show of politeness. He was annoyed by the conversation that had just taken place and wasn't bothering to conceal it.

"I'm sorry I couldn't be of more use to you," she added. "But I've never been a military spy, and I don't intend to start now. I'm afraid I can't help you."

"I have not asked you to spy," Nishimoto said coldly. "Merely provide me with information from time to time. I've offered to pay you well. I believed you were a businesswoman." He cleared his throat. "And since you're a Jewess into the bargain . . ." He let the sentence trail off with a meaningful shrug of his shoulders.

"I must love money." She completed the sentence for him.

"Yes. Exactly."

"I imagine you have a dossier on me already, Mr. Nishimoto." The Black Lily was aware of his military rank, but she was observing the fiction of his civilian status.

"You were born," Nishimoto said frostily, "in a small village south of Kiev in the Russian Ukraine. Your real name is Anna Cohen. You are a widow. Your married name is Levinsky." He looked around the hallway with a faint sneer. Girls in pink silk underwear darted in and out of doorways, giggling with laughter. "This establishment," he went on, "was financed by your lover, who is a businessman of Harbin. We know his name."

"And?" The Black Lily gazed at him inquiringly, waiting for him to go on. Amusement glinted in the depths of her heavy-lidded dark eyes. She was a full-bodied handsome woman in her middle thirties, dressed in black velvet with garnets around her throat. She tossed back her head. "What more do you know, Nishimoto-san? Tell me the details."

"If there is more to know, I will discover it, I can assure you." Nishimoto clicked his heels and bowed from the waist. "And now, if you will excuse me, I have an engagement." He turned with rude abruptness and began to march down the stairs toward the front door.

The Black Lily watched him go with narrowed eyes. When the door had closed behind him, she cursed under her breath. Then she called for Sasha, her majordomo. She would be gone for a short time; would he please look after things in her absence? She would be away no more than half an hour.

Then she made her way to the depths of the basement, climbing down a steep flight of wooden stairs, crossing the concrete floor, holding up the hem of her gown as she passed the coalbin and the furnace. When she came to a heavy padlocked wooden door, she unlocked it and entered the room beyond.

Inside, the room was small, square, and low-ceilinged. The dim lightbulb hanging from the ceiling illuminated an Albion printing press, well-kept and in good running order. Stacks of clean paper were piled on a table beside it, waiting to be fed into the machine. Two straight-backed wooden chairs stood by the table. In one of them sat the man called the Gadfly.

He folded his arms across his chest and gazed steadily at the Black Lily as she entered. "Well?" he asked. "All clear?"

"Yes, he's gone." She shut the door behind her, uttering an uncomplimentary remark about Captain Nishimoto.

"He didn't stay to enjoy the hospitality?"

"No, thank God. He's the type who enjoys using his fists on a lady. I've seen his kind before." She shrugged. "He thinks he knows all about me. But I don't think he knows about Kalman."

Kalman Rappaport was her sister's son. He, along with another young man, Josef Martov, had been murdered in Harbin five months ago; both young men had been burned alive in a boiler at the Harbin railroad station. The Japanese were said to be responsible. Both young men had been dedicated Bolsheviks.

In memory of her nephew, the Black Lily provided shelter for the Gadfly and his printing press in her basement. It was an uneasy alliance, since neither of them totally approved of the other. But so far it had worked.

"Be careful," the Black Lily said, biting her lips. "Wait for the music and noise upstairs before you start operating the machine."

"I'm not a fool. I know that much."

"Well, from now on be doubly careful. Nishimoto's not a fool either."

"Nervous, Lily?" the Gadfly inquired mildly.

"Yes, of course! Why wouldn't I be?"

He laughed. "Tell me something," he said, uncrossing his arms. "To change the subject for a minute. What do you know about a man named Kolya Federovsky?"

"Why?"

"I'm curious."

"He never comes here, if that's what you mean," the Black Lily said, shrugging her shoulders.

"No, I wouldn't think so."

"Then why are you asking?"

"Personal reasons."

She frowned. "I've heard quite a few stories," she said slowly. "I have a friend who owns a dress shop . . . Madame Vera. There's a girl who works for her—well, besides that, Kolya Federovsky has acquired a notorious reputation in Harbin, in a very short time."

"Good." The Gadfly kicked the second wooden chair with the toe of his boot. His lips tightened. "Sit down for a minute," he said, knitting his eyebrows, "and tell me what you know."

Captain Nishimoto was passing the gatehouse near the road and entering the inner courtyard, on his way to the drawing room in the central pavilion, where the wedding reception was being held for Kolya Federovsky and his bride. He found himself disliking the gatekeeper, a wiry bald-headed man with cold blue eyes. He detested the arrogance of the white man in the Orient, he told himself with gritted teeth as he crossed the courtyard. Some day Europeans would learn respect for the descendants of the Sun Goddess. But that day was still to come.

As he entered the drawing room, he noted the elegant furnishings, the mahogany sofa and chairs covered in white silk, the black laquered chests inlaid with gold against the walls, the cloisonné vases on the tables, the pale gold four-paneled screen in one corner of the room depicting clouds, dragons, and the seasons of the Moon Year. Underfoot, the blue-and-ivory Chinese rugs were woven in elaborate patterns of birds, animals, leaves, flowers, and willow trees.

He observed the host in conversation with a certain Jew of Harbin named Herman Levy, but Levy was considered cooperative by the Imperial government, and Federovsky himself was already known to Nishimoto. He dismissed both men from his mind for the moment.

The room was crowded and the air was warm, scented with perfume and cigar smoke. Nishimoto paid no attention. He was not here for enjoyment's sake. As he helped himself to a glass of champagne from a passing tray, he caught sight of the bride, in blue velvet, looking flushed and somewhat ill at ease, at the center of a group of people. She was very young, he thought, sipping his champagne. But an unknown personality. He made up his mind to have a conversation with her.

Then he was being greeted by his host, and then Colonel Kenji Matsuura was at his side. His opportunity to speak to Madame Federovska would come very soon, he thought.

Conversation swirled around the room in little snatches. The armistice in Europe. The coming peace conference, to be held in Paris. The recovery of Lenin, in Russia, from the shooting attack on him last August. Harbin gossip. The plight of the Russian refugees, who were suffering a typhus epidemic. The outrageous conduct of Semonov's mistress, Masha Saraban, who was flaunting her diamonds and furs in all the cabarets and restaurants of the city. The status of the Chinese Eastern Railway, still in the hands of the White regime. Bandits, always bandits. And that new propaganda paper, the *New East,* have you seen that damnable rag floating around the streets?

Nishimoto frowned to hear the paper mentioned. Unfinished business, he thought. Then he noticed Madame Federovska standing alone by the mantelpiece beneath a green jade carving of the Three Monkeys. She looked slightly lost and forlorn, despite the pink flush on her cheeks, and seemed to be trying to get her husband's attention. Nishimoto strolled over to her side, edging smoothly past groups of people as he did so. He reached the mantelpiece and paused.

"Madame Federovska?"

"Yes."

"Allow me to introduce myself." He bowed from the waist. "Saburo Nishimoto, of the Japanese Military Mission." He congratulated her on the occasion of her wedding, and explained his civilian status as a photographic expert, newly arrived in Harbin from Japan. She obviously believed him, and attempted to discuss photography. He dismissed that topic impatiently. Others did the necessary photographing for him. He only examined the results. Not that she needed to know that. He changed the subject.

"I would prefer to hear about your interesting experience," he remarked with an ingratiating smile.

"What experience is that, Mr. Nishimoto?"

"Your period of captivity as a prisoner of Chinese bandits."

She looked a little startled. "Do you know about that?"

"Certainly."

"But I hardly think you'd care to hear the story. It's— it's not very pleasant."

"Nevertheless, Madame Federovska. I would like to hear it."

She blushed. "I'm doing my best to forget all about it, Mr. Nishimoto. Especially on a day like this."

"I am your guest, am I not?"

"Yes, of course."

"Very well, then." He paused as she stood hesitating. He prompted her. "Begin," he said, "by explaining the circumstances of your capture."

She stared at him, wondering why he was being so insistent. He felt amused, enjoying her discomfort. "In detail," he added smoothly.

"The details are very blurred in my mind, Mr. Nishimoto, as you can imagine—"

"Not at all. I'm sure they are very vivid in your mind." His tone became slightly coaxing, yet somehow threatening at the same time. "Think back, Madame Federovska," he said softly. "Recreate the occasion. I'm sure you're able to do so."

For the first time a spark of anger flashed in her eyes. She was beginning to feel baited, he realized, and starting to rebel. It was a familiar pattern for Captain Nishimoto. He had conducted many interrogations in the course of his career. He waited, smiling inwardly, but keeping his features smooth and impassive.

At that unfortunate moment, his host interrupted.

"May I borrow my wife for a moment, Mr. Nishimoto? A small domestic crisis seems to have arisen. I'm sure you understand."

"Yes, of course."

Nishimoto stepped back. He noted with annoyance the expression of relief on the girl's face as she took her husband's arm and moved away. He would remember this petty defeat. He always did.

Daria turned to Nicholas when they were alone, and stared up into his face. "Who is that man?" she burst out. "He's very discourteous."

"A friend of Kenji Matsuura's." Nicholas made a wry face. "I'm sorry he trapped you like that, Daryushka. I only invited him as a favor to Matsuura. But he's an unpleasant person, with a nasty job."

"Photography? It seems so innocent."

"It would be, if it were photography. But he's in the business of collecting information. And they say he does it very well, although his methods aren't very subtle."

"Information?" Her expression grew curious. "I don't suppose he can do anything about what he finds out, can he?"

"Not officially. But the Japanese can do as they please with Chang Tso-lin. The Old Marshal is on their payroll. The Japanese can get away with almost anything in this city. Interrogations, executions. They've done it before."

Daria looked indignant. "If that's his job, no wonder he questions people so rudely." She took a deep breath. "I hope I never have to see him again."

"You won't. Not in this house." Nicholas paused. "Are you having such an unpleasant time, Daria?" he asked gently.

"Oh, no. I'm only a little tired, that's all."

"Ah, well. This is a strain for you, I know. But it will all be over soon, and everyone will leave, and then we can be alone." He tipped up her chin.

She cast her eyes down, hoping he wouldn't guess how fervently she was waiting for that moment. How often, she wondered, would she have to play the self-confident and

Chapter 36

"I will speak to you frankly, Kolya," said Kenji Matsuura, sitting back in his swivel chair behind his desk in his office at the Japanese Military Mission. He made a steeple of his fingers. "We intend to ask for Shantung, at the peace conference. We feel we have a perfect right to do so."

"The German concessions in Shantung." Nicholas looked thoughtful. "Don't you suppose the Chinese will object?" He smiled. "They were on the winning side too, as I recall."

"The Chinese government is a disorganized muddle," Matsuura said scornfully. "Who will listen to their objections?" He swiveled in the chair, reached up behind him to the wall, and pulled down a large colored map of China. Both men stared at it, considering. The German concessions in Shantung Province were outlined in green.

This was a new year: January, 1919. The peace conference was beginning in Paris, to draft a treaty that would officially end the world war. The Japanese intended to take a fair share of the spoils.

Perhaps more than a fair share, Nicholas thought.

"Look, Kolya," Matsuura said after a moment. He pointed to the map. "Here in the north. Peking-Tientsin. Suiyuan and Charhar provinces. Do you know what they represent?"

Nicholas smiled, leaning back and folding his arms. "Iron ore."

"Yes. Enormous iron ore deposits. Unused—lying idle." Matsuura's eyes shone as he turned from the map. "How valuable they would be to the right people! But to have control of that area—" He broke off abruptly.

Nicholas finished his thought. "You would have to control all of China north of the Yellow River."

"Yes," Matsuura breathed. "Just so."

He fell silent. Nicholas finally stirred.

"Great plans, Kenji. Dreams of empire."

"Oh, well." Matsuura carelessly snapped the map up into place on the wall. "Everything in its time, of course." He waved his hand languidly. "Right now we're interested in Shantung." He smiled. "Did you know that General Togawa is planning to leave for Paris, to attend the conference? He's a relative of someone very important." Matsuura mentioned the name of a highly placed director of the Mitsui Company. Nicholas looked impressed.

"Would you like to meet the general?" Matsuura asked. "He'll be in Harbin for a few days, on his way to Europe."

"Very much."

"I'll arrange it. He's an excellent man to know." Matsuura glanced at his watch. It was almost time for lunch.

At that moment Daria was on her way in the limousine to Madame Vera's dress shop on the Bolshoi Prospekt. She hadn't told Nicholas where she was going. Madame Vera's had been recommended to her by a milliner, last week, and Daria thought she would take her own initiative.

She looked out of the automobile window at the noontime traffic on the Kitaiskaya as she smoothed a loose thread on her glove. Today was sunny. That was unusual in Harbin in January. In winter this was such a gray city. The only color to be seen was in the blue-and-gold onion domes of the churches, and in the red-lined cloak of an officer striding down the Kitaiskaya, and the scarlet cockade on his hat. But so much else was gray, she thought. The brooding winter sky, the dull pewter-gray of the river, the cotton uniforms of the warlord's soldiers, the women's faces beneath their rouge as they walked the chilly pavements of the city. . . . She might be one of those women, she thought with a stab of pity and guilt. If she hadn't been lucky. She was sitting here in this luxurious limousine, warm and safe. But it could have been so different.

They had turned into the Bolshoi Prospekt, and were approaching Madame Vera's. Daria sighed to herself. She hoped they wouldn't make a fuss over her, as they did at the milliner's: yes, Madame Federovska; no, Madame Federovska . . . an honor and a pleasure to serve you . . . such a charming customer . . . everything looks so well on you. She always wished they wouldn't do it, it made her uncomfortable.

The automobile pulled up at the curb, and she opened the door herself and got out without waiting for the chauffeur. Then she told herself she mustn't do that, she must wait, but it was too late this time. She dismissed the chauffeur. She would ask Madame Vera to call her a taxi when her errand was over. She started for the store entrance.

A young boy accosted her by the door. Would she like to buy a newspaper? No—but—she began to fish in her purse for a coin.

The boy cleared his throat. "I have a message for you, lady."

"Oh? What is that?" She waited, smiling down at him.

His face became solemn. "I believe you are Madame Federovska," he said in a formal tone of voice.

She was startled, then alert. Her palm closed over the coin. Was this some sort of trick? A kidnapper's ruse? A shop assistant in Madame Vera's was beckoning to her through the window from inside the shop. People were passing by on the sidewalk. Surely nothing could happen on this busy street. But she felt her body grow tense and her face stiffen.

"The message is from the Gadfly," the boy went on. "He would like you to meet him at the Ukrainian Café."

"The Gadfly?"

"Yes, lady."

"You've made a mistake."

"No, he's waiting for you at the Ukrainian Café."

"You have the wrong person." She turned away.

"No, lady! You are the right person!"

"I've never heard of the Gadfly. You made an error."

The boy ran around to block her path. "He said to give you this!" He held out a small folded piece of paper.

Daria hesitated. She looked at the boy carefully. He

was an ordinary, ragged child of the streets, like the young girls who sold paper flowers outside the cafés and restaurants of the city. After a moment she took the paper from his hand. He watched her face as she unfolded it and read it. Her cheeks grew pale; she crumpled the paper in her hand. "Where did you get this?" she said, half whispering. "Who gave it to you?"

"I told you, the Gadfly."

"Who is he?"

"You'll meet him for yourself."

"What sort of trick are you playing?" Daria whispered.

"No trick, lady. It's a true message."

After standing irresolute for long seconds, she took a breath. "Where is the Ukrainian Café?" she asked.

"Not far. We can go there in a taxi, if—" He paused, studying her expression. "If you can pay for it." He glanced at her fur hat and fur-trimmed coat. "Otherwise we can walk."

She bit her lip. Then she shook her head. "No. Wait here while I make a telephone call. Someone must accompany me."

"That's not possible, lady. You must come by yourself."

"No, that's not possible either."

This time she determinedly turned her back on him and pushed open the door of Madame Vera's and entered the shop. But she couldn't prevent herself from looking through the window when she was standing within. The boy was waiting on the sidewalk.

She took a deep breath and turned her face away from the window. Here inside, a woman was approaching across a pearl-gray carpet. Daria caught the scent of attar of of roses.

"Good afternoon, my dear lady," the woman said, coming closer. "I am Madame Vera. How may I help you?"

"I was thinking of an evening dress," Daria said faintly. "My name is Madame Federovska. I was recommended to you by the milliner, Petra Natalya."

"Yes, of course." Madame Vera's eyes narrowed. She paused. A curious expression moved across her face as she glanced at Daria. But she only said, after a moment, "Violet, I believe. Something in violet would be marvelous with such dark eyes."

Daria saw a flowered curtain move in the wall to her right. A girl emerged from a dressing room in a pale yellow silk gown. The girl was slender and delicate, with exquisite bones, a lovely face, and shining fair hair. She moved across the carpet in a graceful glide.

"What a beautiful girl," Daria exclaimed.

"She's only a model," Madame Vera said brusquely. She took Daria's arm. "Come with me, Madame Federovska. I will show you the violet chiffon myself."

"Just a moment please, Madame Vera."

Daria disengaged her arm and turned to the window. She had to look outside just once more.

The sidewalk was empty.

Panic swept over her. She had to find out what the boy had meant. She knew that now. She had to discover the meaning of that note.

She turned and made hurried, confused excuses to Madame Vera. She promised to return to the shop this afternoon, or tomorrow, certainly very soon. But she'd just remembered a very important engagement, and she must leave at once.

Then she rushed out onto the street.

"Here I am, lady."

The boy was leaning against a round poster pole by the curb. A program of Tchaikovsky music would be performed at the Palm Court of the Grand Hotel, she read, during the last week in January. The boy grinned, straightening up. "I waited for you."

She tightened her lips. "So I see."

"Shall we walk," he inquired, "or shall we take a taxi?"

We'll get this over with quickly, she thought. "A taxi," she said firmly. "And we'll do it at once. If it's a trick," she added, giving him a stern glance, "you and your friends will pay dearly. Remember that."

"It's no trick," he said solemnly, shaking his head. Then he darted out into the street to hail a taxi.

They didn't speak during the ride across the city. The boy was absorbed in the unaccustomed luxury of the automobile. Daria was nervous and tense. She kept folding and unfolding the piece of paper with the note, wearing the creases ragged.

They had come to a working-class district near the

waterfront. Small red brick buildings, newly built and raw-looking in the winter sunlight, alternated with grocery stores, a livery stable, and a ramshackle wooden brewery. Piles of dirty snow heaped the gutters. Here was the Ukrainian Café, on the right-hand side of the street. Just a storefront with a black-painted window. She wondered again if this was a trick. But this note—

The boy was struggling with mingled feelings, satisfaction at accomplishing his errand, and regret at leaving the warm interior of the taxi. His emotions showed clearly on his face as he hopped to the sidewalk.

"Inside at the back table, lady, you'll find the Gadfly."

"Aren't you coming with me?"

"No, I have to go back to work!"

Before she could say anything else, the boy was running up the street, waving his hand. As she stared, he turned the corner and disappeared from sight. Daria sighed, turning away. The taxi driver was waiting to be paid. She could climb back inside, she thought, and direct him to take her home. Or she could go back to Madame Vera's. But she had come this far, she might as well see it through.

She entered the café. The air was steamy and close. She smelled boiling cabbage, beer, cigarette smoke, and frying onions. Wooden tables covered with mended cotton table-cloths crowded the room. All of them were occupied. Men in workingmen's caps and shabby jackets were eating, talking, and smoking. The language was Russian. One tired-looking blonde waitress was trying to serve lunch.

This was a mistake, she thought again. I don't know anyone here. I shouldn't have come.

But she scanned the back of the room, just to make sure. She felt several pairs of eyes staring at her as she stood by the door, and felt self-conscious in her fur-trimmed coat, French leather gloves, expensive high boots, and fur hat tilted over one eye. She didn't belong here. That was obvious.

One pair of eyes, at the back of the room, was staring, not at her clothes, but at her face. This man was sitting alone at a table. He was the only customer sitting by himself. He was young, but there were lines around his mouth and a weary expression in his eyes. Both hands were thrust into the pockets of his sheepskin jacket as he sat slouching in the chair. A livid purple-red scar curved like a crescent moon across one side of his face, from the temple to the jaw.

Daria stretched out one hand in bewilderment. "Lev," she said, speaking to herself, whispering out loud. "What's happened to you? Your face! Oh no . . . Lev Omansky!"

It was already past lunchtime. Colonel Matsuura crushed out a cigarette in the ashtray on his desk.

"Shall we try the Railway Club?" he asked, stretching in his chair.

"At this hour, Kenji, it will be very crowded."

"But I'm hungry. Let's take our chances."

Matsuura rose from the chair. As he stood up behind the desk, he knocked a sheet of paper to the floor. Nicholas bent and picked it up. "What's this, Kenji?" he asked with a smile. "The *New East*?"

Matsuura made a face, taking the paper from Nicholas's hand. "It's Saburo Nishimoto's favorite project. He intends to find the Gadfly. He's surveying all the Bolshevik gathering places in the city."

"Does he really think it's important?"

"Somehow these people have gotten wind of General Togawa's visit to Harbin. They're threatening to make an example of him. China for the Chinese and so forth." Matsuura tossed the paper back on the desk. "It's all nonsense, of course, but Saburo takes it seriously."

"He takes everything seriously," Nicholas murmured.

"I suppose that's his function." Matsuura shrugged disdainfully as they left the office. "Come, let's go to lunch."

Chapter 37

Daria stared down once more at the crumpled piece of paper in her hand. The words blurred in front of her eyes. "I have news of your grandfather, Alexey Alexeyevitch." She understood them now.

She raised her head. Lev was still gazing at her from the back table. She was almost afraid to walk forward. But there was so much she had to ask. So much she had to say. What had happened to his face? Oh, Lev! It had been so long, she thought, since Saravenko and Chita Station!

The kitchen door opened in a blast of steam, clattering crockery, and clashing silverware. The waitress edged past her with a tray of hot dishes. Daria moved forward automatically, avoiding the waitress. She began to make her way to the back of the room.

When she approached the table, she searched for words to say to Lev. A greeting. A way to begin. But Lev spoke first.

"Do you remember me, Madame Federovska?" He emphasized her name with chilly irony as he leaned back in his chair, lifting his gaze to her face. She was startled by the cold hostility she saw in his eyes.

"Lev! Lev Omansky! Of course I remember you!"

"Good. It's been so long, I thought you might have forgotten." He waved across the table. "Take a seat."

She realized with a stab of embarrassment that she'd been waiting for him to rise. She sat down quickly. She'd grown accustomed to Nicholas's courteous manners. But

442

she was not in the Railway Club or the Palm Court, she reminded herself. She was in the Ukrainian Café. Women weren't given any special courtesies here.

"Lev, I don't know what to say." She pressed her hands together in her lap. "I never expected . . . I didn't think . . ." She stopped, hating herself for stammering. Lev said nothing. He obviously didn't intend to help her. She took a breath and began again. "Are you really the Gadfly, Lev?" she asked quietly.

He still didn't answer. She felt herself flushing and dropped her eyes.

"Take your hat off," he said abruptly.

After a moment she took off her hat and shook out her hair. Another silence fell.

Finally she broke the silence. "I left word at Cousin Victor's address," she said desperately, putting her hat on the next seat. "He moved away. He wasn't there anymore. I couldn't locate him, but I told the girl who lived there where I could be reached. Is that how you found me?"

"No."

"Then I suppose it's a kind of lucky chance you did find me. Because we promised to meet in Harbin, didn't we? That night I left Chita Station. How sad it would be if somehow we missed one another . . ."

Oh, God. First she was stammering, and now she was babbling. *Help me, Lev. Say something.*

"Didn't it occur to you," he said coldly, when some seconds had passed, "that your wedding announcement would be in the papers?"

"Oh! Oh, yes . . . I'd forgotten about that."

"I'm surprised. I didn't think that was the sort of thing people forgot."

"I didn't mean I'd forgotten my wedding, I only meant—"

"Yes, I understand what you meant."

She felt suddenly close to tears. Why was she on the defensive, she asked herself. This was growing more difficult every moment. It wasn't the way she'd pictured this meeting at all. She told him so. She'd thought this would be a happy reunion, she told him. She'd believed they would remember old times when they met in Harbin.

"Did you?" He smiled grimly. "How often?"

443

"What do you mean?"

"How often did you think about our meeting in Harbin?" He stared at her coldly. "How many times?"

"I don't know——"

"Did you picture it in your mind? Was it something you looked forward to?"

She didn't answer.

"Can you count how many times, Daria?"

"No, not exactly."

"Once? Twice?"

"I don't know."

"As many as four?"

She realized, finally, what lay behind his sarcasm. She looked down at her lap, feeling ashamed that she hadn't realized before.

"I'm sorry, Lev," she said quietly. "If I could have written to you, I would have explained about my—my marriage, and how it happened."

"The usual way, I suppose," he said pleasantly. "Unless you've discovered some strange new variation."

She flushed. There was no answer to that.

He drummed his fingers on the table. Finally he said, "What would you like for lunch?"

"I'm not very hungry."

"We may be here for a while, so you might as well order something."

"Tea, then."

"With pastry? The viroshki isn't bad."

She nodded agreement.

He summoned the waitress and ordered tea and viroshki. Then he leaned forward and stared down at the tablecloth, picking at a mended patch in the cotton. "All right, Daria. Ask your question. Get it over with."

"What question?"

"What happened to my face."

She looked away. "I wasn't going to ask that, Lev."

"But you were wondering."

"Yes, a little. But the scar isn't very noticeable."

"Oh my God, don't lie. I know what it looks like. I'm not sensitive."

She wanted to cry all over again. This was so hopeless,

444

she thought. She couldn't think of anything to say. Finally she whispered, "You needn't tell me. I understand how it must have happened . . . in Siberia."

"Ah, yes. The war in Siberia."

She hesitated. "Are you going back?"

"I don't know." He rubbed his cheek. "Probably not. I may just stay here and write a newspaper."

"Then you are the Gadfly."

"For the time being." He shrugged. "The war will have to get along without me for a while." A shadow crossed his eyes; he stared down at the tablecloth again. "I wasn't much use to them by the time I left," he said in a low voice.

"I can't picture it, Lev," Daria whispered. "I can't imagine what it was like."

"Can't you?" He raised his head and gave her an angry look. "I thought you crossed Siberia on the railroad."

"I did."

"Well, picture railroad tracks. Picture walking along them on foot, in the snow. Not in deep winter, in October. But it's cold, and there's snow on the ground. And there's somebody with you. A man named Fyodor. Just a big good-natured peasant, with a fat belly and a rumbling laugh . . . not a soldier, just a muzhik. Can you picture that?"

She nodded.

"Oh Christ, what's the use." He sat back and lapsed into another angry silence.

The waitress arrived with glasses of tea, slices of lemon, and the dish of cheese pastry. She set them on the table and left again. Lev moodily dumped sugar in his tea. Square little lumps of sugar, one, two three. The memories were running again, he thought. That moving picture in his head was running, displaying certain episodes over and over again, whether he wanted to remember them or not. He had no way to stop them. No way at all. Daria was sitting unhappily in her chair, crumbling a piece of pastry in her fingers. She was different from the way she used to be, he thought. The same, yet different. It was the sameness that troubled him. He wished she were completely changed, it would make everything easier. But in spite of the fashionable clothes, the expensive furs, the becoming new hairdo, she was still Daria, and her eyes were still huge pools of dark compassion.

"Listen," he said finally, unable to stop himself from speaking, "I'll tell you about it, if you want to hear."

She nodded.

"About Fyodor."

"All right."

"He didn't really want to fight, you know."

The moving picture was running in his head. But he heard sounds and voices too, unlike a cinema. He heard Fyodor's voice. They'd been tramping alongside the railway tracks that day, on their way to a small railway depot. They'd already covered twenty versts on foot in the two days since they'd left the partisan camp. "I'll explain how I came to be a partisan, Lyova," Fyodor had said, chuckling to himself.

"Fine," he'd answered.

"Here's how it happened, my friend. We were making illegal vodka in our village—samogonk—and keeping it a secret from the tax collectors. We asked ourselves why we should fill the pockets of those greedy bastards."

Lev had nodded, with a grin.

"Not that we had anything against the Czar—the little father—we were just looking out for our own interests. So we took to the woods with our still. Then we heard that the Czar had abdicated, and Kerensky was the head of the government. What the hell, we stayed hidden in the trees. Next thing you know we were fighting the Cossacks, and Kerensky was out, and the Bolsheviks were in, and we were a partisan band—a fighting unit. We were just protecting our vodka still, Lyova." He laughed again.

Lev began to check over the supply of long-handled grenades hooked to his belt. They'd be the key to the success of this mission, he thought. He and Fyodor had to reach the depot and take cover before the enemy troop train arrived at the station. Then it would be all over in two or three minutes. So much had to go right, he thought. Including the condition of these hand grenades. Could you trust them? They were German-made "potato mashers," but so many were defective. You could blow yourself to

446

hell if you primed one for action and something went wrong.

He'd been fool enough to volunteer for this. So had Fyodor. Like Vanya, he thought, volunteering to locate the Czech field guns. He wondered what had happened to Vanya. Was the old coal miner still alive?

"Lyova, there it is."

"Where?"

"Beyond the grove of birch trees. See the rooftop?"

"Yes, I see it."

A peaked log roof with a chimney was just visible between the slender white forms of the birch trees. It must be in a hollow of ground, Lev thought, all you could see was the roof. But it was the depot, no doubt of it. He tensed. Did he see smoke coming out of the chimney? The depot should have been deserted. But he was sure he saw a wisp of smoke against the sky, barely visible against the gray-white clouds.

"We'll approach separately, Fyodor," he said. "I think I see something coming out of the chimney."

"Look at the cottage next to the depot," Fyodor muttered. "That's where the smoke is coming from."

"We'll search the cottage first."

They unstrapped their rifles from their shoulders, holding them hip-high and ready, and separated as they approached the area of the station. Cautiously, warily, one on either side, they went forward a few steps at a time, boots silent on the frostbitten brown grass.

Semaphore signals. Telegraph pole. Concrete platform. Water tower. Log store on the left. Depot in the center. Red brick cottage on the right. Yes, Fyodor was right, the smoke was coming from the cottage. If there was a fire inside, it was dying embers. He hoped. The place looked deserted. But you never knew, you couldn't be sure . . .

In one swift movement he kicked open the door of the cottage and sprang over the threshold, sweeping his rifle from side to side with narrowed eyes and bunched-up muscles.

Empty.

He let out his breath and relaxed, then waved to Fyodor to join him.

"Somebody was here pretty recently, Lyova!" Fyodor's tone was jovial, as he stood on the threshold. "Look at that —they were cooking potatoes!"

A skillet of cooked potatoes was cooling on the iron stove that stood against the back wall.

"Whoever it was left in a hurry."

"In that case," Fyodor said, swaggering over to the stove, "I'll help myself to a meal. How about you?"

Lev grinned with relief, lowering his rifle. "Why not. I could use some hot food."

They'd been eating black bread and cheese for two days. Now the potatoes were delicious. The best he'd ever tasted. He laid aside the skillet when it was empty and wiped his mouth with the back of his hand.

"Shall we go over the procedure with the grenades, Fedya?"

They would aim for the boiler on the engine, he thought. Hoping to block the tracks. The armored cars, in the lead, would be carrying the machine gunners and the riflemen. That would be dangerous. They'd be firing from the windows. Behind the broneviks would be the freight cars, the forty-and-eights carrying Cossack cavalrymen and their mounts. That wasn't so much to worry about. The Cossacks would need time to quiet their horses, lead them outside, and mount up for pursuit.

He and Fedya would be away by then. Into the forest. If everything went well.

Lev sighed. "Suppose I take the position by the water tower."

"Fine."

"You'll stand inside the depot door." He thought for a moment, staring down at the floor, rubbing the scar on his cheek in a nervous habit he'd developed. "We'll have to show ourselves in plain sight, just before we toss the grenades. There's no help for that, Fedya."

"Don't worry about it, son." The usual joking tone was absent from Fyodor's voice. He put a hand on Lev's shoulder. "I'm prepared," he said gruffly. "So are you. There's nothing more we can do now until the train pulls in."

Lev brought himself back with an effort to the Ukrainian Café, and Daria. Had he been talking all this time? Daria's glass of tea was almost empty.

"I must be boring the hell out of you," he muttered, swallowing some of his own tea. It was lukewarm.

"No, I'm not bored."

What the hell was she supposed to say? he asked himself. Was she going to tell him to keep his mouth shut, because she didn't want to hear it? Well, neither did he. That was too damn bad. He'd started this story, he would finish. The memory was running fast now in his head. He saw himself pressed up against the water tower, Fyodor waiting inside the depot door. He was hearing the rumble of the approaching train along the tracks. The bitter metallic taste of fear was in his mouth. His hands were sweating. He wiped them along the side of his trousers, telling himself he needed dry hands. He told himself to think about what he had to do. He knew the procedure. He was ready.

Here it comes.

Engine first, pulling the armored cars. Right. Slowing down for the station, and the bend in the track. Gunports clicking open in the roof of the bronevik; they were being cautious. Ugly round snouts of gun barrels poking out, like sniffing animals. Ignore them. Unhook the first grenade. Now. Step away from the tower. Step back. Weight on your rear foot. Grasp the handle. Throw overhand, in a slow arc . . .

Oh Christ, the noise . . . steel splinters flying up all over the place, coming at your eyes . . . *Duck.* Unhook another grenade. HE MUSTN'T WASTE TIME. HE DIDN'T HAVE MUCH TIME.

They were firing now, with rifles and handguns, out of the train window. Hard rattle of small-arms fire. Was he hit? Didn't know. Didn't have time to check. Another boom . . . another grenade. His or Fedya's? It didn't matter. The boiler was leaking steam in a dozen places. They'd crippled the train. They'd done what they came for . . . *Let's go.*

"Fedya, let's go! Never mind the last one! Get rid of it!"

Too late. Fyodor was stumbling backward, struck in the chest by a pistol bullet. He was falling up against the wall of the depot. He was still holding his last grenade by the handle; the lever was pulled.

Too late, too late, it was all over, don't listen, don't

look at that mangled heap of flesh and blood in front of the depot that used to be Fedya, just run for the trees . . .

He set down his glass of tea on the table and put his head in his hands. He felt sick. He felt like crying. He was afraid he would start shaking, and he didn't want to do that.

"Lev." Daria was reaching her hand across the table. "Lev, stop. Don't talk about this anymore."

"You sound like Captain Mikhailovitch." He glanced up, grinning wryly. Calm again. He hoped. " 'Spend some time in Harbin,' the captain said, 'and pull yourself together. They need somebody to run a printing press.' " And so, he'd taken the train from Vladivostok, jamming himself onto one of those crowded teplushkas that were packed with refugees.

"So you became the Gadfly."

"More or less."

The tables at the Ukrainian Café were emptying now. Only one man sat at the neighboring table, a fat man with mournful eyes who was absorbed in his bowl of kasha and his glass of lemon tea. He was drinking it noisily through a lump of sugar held between his teeth. My grandfather used to do that, Lev thought absently.

Funny, Daria was asking now about her grandfather.

"You said in your note that you have news about Alexey Alexeyevitch. Was that true, Lev?"

He didn't answer.

"I never got any response to my letters. It worried me."

"You had reason to worry, Daria." He waited for her to steel herself before he continued. Then he explained about Saravenko. How the village had been razed by Semenov and his Cossacks two months after she'd left. How it was burned to the ground. How the villagers had died defending their izbas and their land. But that he believed Alexey Alexeyevitch had died a brave man. "I'm sure he was glad he sent you away, Daria," he muttered finally. "I'm sure he'd like to know you were safe in Harbin."

She nodded, unable to speak.

Oh, hell. He might as well say something cheerful. It wouldn't cost anything. He made an effort, and reminded her of the night they had met in Saravenko. "Do you remember when the Cossacks came in and your grandfather was teaching me the alphabet?"

She suddenly smiled through her unshed tears. "Oh, Lev! When you were pretending to be Ivan the Simple! And you had that terrible vacant look on your face! How could I forget it?"

To his amazement, and hers, they both burst out laughing.

Somehow it was easier after that. Easier and harder. Because he still had to do what he'd planned to do, and what his comrades expected him to do, and what he'd almost sabotaged with his own unruly emotions. He had a request to make. He would make it in the name of an old friendship. They were talking naturally now, with the tension and hostility gone, almost as if they were the old Lev and Daria. But he knew it wasn't so.

"Daria, have you seen the *New East*?"

"Once or twice. I never guessed you were the Gadfly." She picked up a fresh glass of tea, which the waitress had just brought, and took a sip. "Why do you keep writing about the Japanese in China?"

"Because once we defeat the counterrevolution at home, there'll be a new struggle in China. Sun Yat-sen may be losing his battle in Canton, but the fight isn't over. The Japanese have to be driven out of China, and so do all the other capitalist nations." His face turned grim; he rubbed his cheek. "And besides, I have a special grudge against the Japanese."

She looked slightly embarrassed and glanced away. He knew that her husband was particularly friendly with Colonel Matsuura, at the Japanese Military Mission. It would have been tactful not to mention it, he thought, but he brought it up anyway. She tried to change the subject.

"I have a special reason for talking about this, Daria. You see, you can help me."

"In what way?"

"Something very simple. Just find out for me what General Togawa's movements will be when he's in Harbin."

"I don't even know General Togawa."

"Your husband will know."

"Lev—I can't do that!"

"It's extremely simple. We just want to give him a list

451

of demands, before he goes to the peace conference. Just for the record. But they're keeping his itinerary a secret. They're afraid of God knows what." He was lying about the list of demands, there was no such thing. But she couldn't know that.

"Lev, it's disloyal. It's like spying."

"Our friendship goes back to the time before you left Saravenko," he said steadily. "Don't you owe me a little loyalty?"

"That's not fair."

No, it wasn't fair. But he was asking it anyway.

Daria paused. "Lev," she said finally, "suppose I introduce you to Nicholas, and you can ask him yourself."

He began to laugh. "That's a wonderful idea. It's perfect. Let me think about it for a while."

She sighed. "I suppose you're right, it wouldn't work."

Her small, vivid face was clouded with unhappiness and worry. She disliked refusing him, that was clear. She was torn. Appeal to her sympathy long enough and hard enough, he thought, and perhaps she would change her mind. Then he began to hate himself. He asked himself angrily what was wrong with him. Wasn't this what he'd planned all along? To use her connection with Federovsky to get the information they needed about the Japanese? And after Togawa left, she might still be a valuable source of information. Anything could happen.

"Lev, it's time for me to go. I've stayed too long. I've already missed a meeting of the Refugee Relief Committee, and I was only asked to join a little while ago."

"Oh, the relief committee. Of course. Naturally. That must be very important work."

"Don't be sarcastic again! Not when we've just found an old friendship."

He said nothing. Then he asked, "Is this the end of it? Or can we meet some other time?"

She struggled for an answer.

"I don't see what harm it can do," he remarked, "to have tea together every now and then. And I think it might do me some good. This has cheered me up—this talk we've had."

It was a shameless bid for sympathy, and he knew it would succeed.

"Perhaps we can," she said uncertainly. "Some time soon."

Before they left the restaurant, he'd made her commit herself to another meeting, four days in the future. She would use the excuse of the Refugee Relief Committee. He told himself that he would have to be satisfied with that much progress. And stifle his feeling of self-disgust at using her this way.

When they were outside in the doorway of the café, they paused to look for a taxi. Absorbed in their own thoughts and emotions, neither of them noticed the man with the camera in his hands, who held himself out of sight in the shadow of a doorway across the street. When the camera clicked, it was much too far away for either of them to hear it.

Chapter 38

In the drawing room of the house of the yellow brick the three green jade monkeys were wreathed in drifting clouds of cigar smoke. They saw no evil, heard no evil, and spoke no evil, perched quietly on the mantelpiece. Below them, Nicholas and Brendan sat in white silk-covered chairs finishing glasses of whiskey.

"Are you aware, Brendan," Nicholas said somberly, "that last month my wife was twenty-one years old?"

"Ah, well, Kolya, that's about the size of it." Since his host showed no signs of doing so, Brendan poured more whiskey into Nicholas's glass, and then into his own. It was a gray February dusk; Daria was still dressing in her bedroom. He grinned. "Feeling your age, are you?"

Nicholas sighed and crossed one ankle over his knee. The gleam on his shoes caught the lamplight. He was dressed for the evening in black dinner clothes, with diamond cuff links in his shirt. "I suppose I am. I think it's time to simplify my life."

"In other words," Brendan said, "you're wondering how to say good-bye to Tanya."

Nicholas took a sip of his whiskey. He'd already done so.

He had seen Tanya yesterday after she left Madame Vera's dress shop. He'd called for her in the limousine, and as he'd waited for her, he'd remembered what she had said once, in a private room at the Caucasus Restaurant.

"I dream about escaping, Nicholas. Escaping from the

East. From the cold winters, and the bandits, and the warlords, and the opium shops, and being poor, and living where we're living, and being stared at by Japanese officers in the dress shop on the Kitaiskaya . . . I dream about going to Paris."

Yes, she would be happier there, he'd thought.

When she was beside him in the back seat of the automobile, looking exquisite and far away and faintly sad, as she always did, and they were driving through the city streets, he made his offer.

Tanya's eyes widened in disbelief. Then she shook her exquisite fair head. A look of anguish crossed her face. "I couldn't, Kolya. I couldn't go to Paris. Not even if you gave me the passage money."

"Why not?"

"Who would look after my family?"

"You could, once you were established. You could send them money."

"But until then . . ." She stared into space. Then she lowered her eyes. "No, it's useless, they wouldn't be able to get along."

He took her hand in his. "It's quite simple, Tanya. I'll send you enough to look after your family until you're settled. They need never know. Then you can pay me back, when you can afford it."

"Oh my God, Kolya, that isn't why . . . I didn't mean . . ."

"Dear girl, I know that. Of course I know. Don't cry. I'm not handing over my life savings. I won't suffer; it will please me. And I'm not paying you. It's a loan, from one friend to another."

She was weeping softly in his arms.

It was little enough to do, he thought, stroking her hair. If it would make her happy. If only all dreams could be so easily fulfilled. . . .

But Brendan was speaking to him in the drawing room of the house of yellow brick. "So you think your life will be less complicated from now on, do you?" He chuckled.

"I'm not referring to the social obligations, Brendan." Nicholas smiled wryly. "Those go on forever. . . ."

Tonight there was the banquet at the Grand Hotel for the Refugee Relief Committee. Tomorrow there would be the dinner with General Togawa. That was very confidential. The location was a closely kept secret, since the Japanese were still on edge about a Bolshevik attack on the general, which had been threatened for weeks.

"Where will I be driving you tomorrow night, Kolya?"

"The Railway Club, Brendan."

After that, Nicholas would take a taxi to the Caucasus Restaurant, where the dinner would take place. Not even Brendan knew that. The only person he had trusted with the information was Daria, in case she needed to reach him.

He was deliberately ignoring the warning he'd received two days ago from Kenji Matsuura.

"Nishimoto has been making strange remarks about your wife, Kolya," Matsuura had said. "Dropping hints, you might say."

"What sort of hints?"

"One isn't sure. He seems to suspect Madame Federovska of Bolshevik sympathies."

"Ridiculous. On what basis? He's only met her once."

"He implies she's been seen at a notorious revolutionary café."

Nicholas remained angrily silent.

"You might mention it to her," Matsuura remarked. "It was probably completely innocent. She might have stopped there for tea, not knowing what sort of place it was." He shrugged. "But Nishimoto distrusts everyone and everything."

It would be despicable to suspect Daria, Nicholas thought now, remembering that conversation. To entertain suspicions about your own wife was a completely dishonorable action. He must put those thoughts out of his mind. And he would.

Two hours later, in Nahaloika, in the basement of the House of All Nations, the printing press was clattering noisily. Its sounds was masked by the loud thumping of band music coming from the Don Cossack Lounge on the floor directly above.

Lev felt reasonably sure they couldn't be heard. He wielded his roller of ink across the type keys, then nodded to his partner, David Solomovitch, to pull the bar handle across the machine. It was an automatic process by now.

David pulled the handle and forced down the platen, making an inked impression on the blank sheet of paper lying beneath it. Lev picked up the wet paper and laid it on the table.

It was a slow procedure, he thought, but not very difficult. The machine was light, and easy to repair and clean. They'd taken it apart completely two nights ago and put it together again, and now it was working well.

"For God's sake, Lev, you're supposed to be watching the ink. Look at that page." David nodded impatiently at the last sheet of paper. The black ink was dark on one side, light on the other, in a strange shadowed effect.

"Sorry." It wasn't so automatic after all, Lev thought. He hadn't really been paying attention.

"What's the matter with you lately?" David asked.

"Let's go on. I want to finish this job."

"I mean it, Lev." David released his grip on the handle of the machine and reached for a cigarette in his shirt pocket. "People are beginning to talk about you," he said soberly. "I don't like what they're saying. I think you should know."

"What are they saying?" Lev asked tightly.

"That you never got the information you were supposed to get from the Federovska woman. That we had to find out for ourselves about Togawa and the Caucasus Restaurant."

"That's no crime."

"They're wondering if you have a personal interest in the woman."

"Suppose I do."

"Consider it, Lev. She's the wife of a counterrevolutionary opportunist. And she's a friend of yours. What does that make you?"

"On the principle of guilt by association," Lev said grimly, "that makes me a counterrevolutionary opportunist." He paused. "Is that what they're saying?"

"Not quite. But close."

Lev said nothing for a moment. Then he shrugged. "I'm considering going back to Moscow with the others, day after tomorrow. Maybe that would solve the whole problem."

"And maybe it's running away."

Lev didn't answer.

"Be careful, Lev," David said in a low voice. "You may be asked to pay a visit to twenty-two Lubianka Street, when you get back to Moscow. It won't be so easy, explaining yourself to Djerzinsky."

"I'll explain it to you," Lev said in a sudden passionate outburst, "and then we'll get back to work." He took a deep breath. "About Daria—Madame Federovska. She made a mistake. She understands that now. She's ready to join the revolutionary struggle and come back to Russia with me." He looked steadily at David. "Does that explain what I've been doing for the past couple of weeks?"

"It might."

"Then let's get back to the printing press. All right?" He picked up his roller, and David, with a shrug, let the conversation lapse and laid a sheet of paper on the machine, centering it for the platen. They began to work silently. This time it went fast.

When another two hours had gone by, Lev thought he had had enough. He put down the roller. He wanted to walk, he thought, and get out into the cold air. He needed to think. Besides, the music had grown too quiet upstairs. He said so to David, who agreed. They began to tidy up the room and collect the printed sheets of paper and put them in order.

When they had said good night to one another, outside on the pavement beneath the awning of the House of All Nations, they took different directions. Lev wanted to be alone. He turned up the collar of his jacket against the chill of the night air as he began to walk. He put his hands into his trouser pockets. In his right-hand pocket he felt the comforting weight of his revolver, smooth steel against his hand. The gun was fully loaded. When you walked in Nahaloika late at night, you felt better with a weapon. He'd grown used to carrying it with him.

For a long time he didn't think about anything. He took streets at random, turning corners aimlessly and keeping up a fast rhythmic pace. No one accosted him. He was walking too quickly to be stopped by the girls who loitered under the streetlamps, shivering in their thin woolen coats. He found himself, after a while, in Pristan.

The dark alleys and shadowy half-deserted streets of

Nahaloika gave way here to lights, music, people, and laughter. Restaurants were serving late diners. Cabarets were coming alive. Droshkies clopped-clopped along hard-packed snow in the middle of the road. Sometimes a taxi or a limousine went by with a whoosh of tires. Children still wandered the pavement selling paper flowers, their faces pinched and pale in the yellow glare of the street-lights.

He thought he would be glad to return to Moscow.

But would Daria come with him? He had no reason to think so. She was still loyal to her husband. She'd refused to pass on any information. His words to David Solomo-vitch had been sheer bravado. He was confused and at the same time disgusted with himself, wondering why he still hesitated to use his former friendship.

He saw that he was passing by the steps of the Grand Hotel. Some sort of affair had just ended; limousines were waiting by the curb. He slowed his pace to stare at the closest one, a black and gleaming automobile with a uni-formed chauffeur in the front seat and an armed bodyguard leaning against the hood.

This was typical of Harbin, he thought with disgust. The car belonged, no doubt, to some bastard of a war profiteer, feeding off other people's misery.

He stopped in anger to light a cigarette, glancing under his eyelashes at the bodyguard, who was lounging against the hood with his arms folded, studying Lev with an im-passive arrogance.

Go ahead and look, you son of a bitch, Lev thought tensely. He found himself fingering the gun in his pocket. Then he reminded himself that the man was only trying to make a living. He was just an employee. He wasn't the en-emy. Lev took a long breath, removing his hand from his pocket. No, he thought, the guilty man was the one who paid the bodyguard's salary.

He took a deep drag on his cigarette. The bodyguard was gazing up the steps now. Lev followed his glance. A couple was coming out of the Grand Hotel and descending the stairs. On their way they stopped to talk to someone who was smiling and speaking with an effusive waving of arms.

So glad you could come and so forth and so on, Lev

thought cynically. Good night, your excellency. He flicked his cigarette into the gutter and began to walk on. Then he stopped. He realized he'd recognized the woman.

Then he told himself he must be mistaken.

He looked at the steps again. The couple was proceeding down to the limousine. The young woman was wearing violet chiffon beneath an ankle-length gray sable coat. Amethysts sparkled in her ears. She looked impossibly remote and lovely. Yes, it was Daria. The man with her wore an opera cape over his evening clothes, with a scarlet silk lining that flared as he walked. He was dark-haired, handsome, and lithely graceful. Diamond studs flashed in his shirt.

Lev cast his gaze down, clenching his jaw. The notorious Kolya Federovsky. He'd pictured Daria's husband as a paunchy middle-aged businessman, in spite of what he'd been told. The reality was slightly sickening.

They were entering the back seat of the limousine. The door slammed. As he watched, the automobile pulled away from the curb, then turned a corner and disappeared.

Lev turned away. Tomorrow night, he thought in anger and confusion, when he saw Daria, he would tell her the truth about her husband. Federovsky would be at the Caucasus Restaurant with General Togawa, so he and Daria would have time to talk. She would learn the ugly facts about her husband. She would hear the stories Lev had suppressed up to now as sordid gossip.

And after that, he would ask her to come to Moscow. He had nothing to lose. Not now.

Chapter 39

"My dear Mr. Federovsky," said a smooth voice from the doorway, "may I have a word with you before you leave? I realize it's quite late. I won't keep you long."

Nicholas glanced up from his desk in his Pristan office and laid aside the paper he was holding. It was a list of new freight charges on the Chinese Eastern Railway. The rates were outrageously high, since all the freight cars were allocated to military use these days, with the war continuing in Siberia. If you wanted to ship nonmilitary goods, such as raw wool, you took what was available, *sub rosa,* and paid the price.

He did much the same thing in his own warehouses. Still, it was infuriating to be forced against the wall in order to have your pocket picked. Something would have to be done about it, he thought.

Now, however, Saburo Nishimoto wanted to have a word with him. The captain stood in the doorway with an inquiring and falsely polite smile on his face. Eugene hovered nervously behind his shoulder.

"Certainly, Mr. Nishimoto." Nicholas spoke pleasantly to conceal his irritation. "Please come in. Be seated." He smiled. "Although I'm sure you know that General Togawa doesn't like to be kept waiting."

"Ah, yes. Tonight you dine with the general. I will stay only a moment." Nishimoto sauntered into the office, but ignored the invitation to be seated. Eugene disappeared from the doorway.

"I envy you your pleasant evening," Nishimoto remarked, standing by Nicholas's desk. "I myself have an unwelcome task ahead of me. Tonight I must interrogate a Bolshevik agitator who calls himself the Gadfly. I'm afraid it will be a bloody business. A very unpleasant prospect." The grim anticipation in Nishimoto's eyes belied his words.

"Then you have him in custody, Mr. Nishimoto."

"Oh, not yet. But I will have, very soon." Nishimoto glanced at his watch. "In approximately one hour, I believe."

"And how can I help you?"

"Simply take a look at this photograph. Tell me if you recognize the young man. We are almost certain he is the Gadfly, but a further identification can't hurt."

"What makes you think I can identify him?" Nicholas said coldly. He barely glanced at the photograph Nishimoto had laid on the desk.

"It is, you might say . . . intuition, Mr. Federovsky."

A tense, short silence suddenly fell. Nicholas refrained from looking again at the photograph. It showed a young man and a young woman standing in front of a shabby café. It had been taken from across the street, and the faces were blurry. The bottom half of the young woman's figure was obscured by a passing horsecart. But Nicholas had needed only one glance to see that it was Daria. He recognized the coat and hat she was wearing, and the angle of her head, and the line of her cheek. The young man was a stranger.

He repressed his rising fury and the angry questions that were boiling to the surface of his mind. He would deal with Daria himself, later tonight, he told himself tautly, when the Togawa dinner was over. Now he wanted only to to get rid of Nishimoto.

Obviously the man had one purpose in showing him the photograph: to display Madame Federovska's treachery, and observe Nicholas's reaction.

"It's impossible to tell anything from that picture," he said calmly. "The faces are blurred. Whoever took it should have been standing closer."

"I suppose you are right." Nishimoto shrugged. "But after all, one can't ask them to pose." He tucked the photograph away in his breast pocket. "Fortunately we have an informant in an establishment of pleasure called the House of All Nations in Nahaloika. A young woman who is half-Japanese. She has been persuaded to see that her patriotic duty to her Emperor takes precedence over any misplaced loyalty to her employer."

"I understand." Nicholas stood up and cleared his throat. "I have no wish to rush you, Mr. Nishimoto," he said deliberately, "but time grows short, and I have an engagement."

"Of course." Nishimoto bowed from the waist, clicking his heels. "Convey my respectful regards to General Togawa when you see him. My apologies for detaining you so long."

"Not at all."

Nishimoto sauntered out as casually as he had entered. Nicholas stood tensely silent for a moment, thinking about the photograph, before telling himself that he owed Daria a chance to explain before he jumped to any conclusions.

By the time he entered the Caucasus Restaurant, one hour later, he had succeeded in putting Nishimoto out of his mind. Daria had already gone out for the evening when he'd arrived home to change his clothes. But she would be back in the house of yellow brick by the time this dinner was over. And then they would have time to talk. There was an innocent explanation, he told himself.

The dinner with Togawa was to be held upstairs in a private room, although not the same room where he'd dined with Tanya Ivanovna. Two husky Japanese soldiers stood guard outside the door; they were taking no chances on an attack. He passed the sentries and entered the room. The furnishings were ornate. This room had red velvet curtains and gilt moldings, and a crystal chandelier hanging from the ceiling. Burning logs snapped in the fireplace. A long linen-covered table in the center of the floor was set for dinner. The management of the Caucasus Restaurant, in honor of their Japanese guests, had provided bottles of saki wine, which stood at intervals along the table.

General Togawa and his party were already present. Kenji Matsuura, Nicholas observed, was not his usual urbane self. In the presence of the general he seemed to be ill at ease, mopping his face frequently with a handkerchief. The general was a small man with an arrogant expression and round gold-rimmed spectacles that caught the light whenever he turned his head.

Nicholas accepted a glass of warm saki and settled himself for the predinner conversation.

In the working-class district of the city near the waterfront, the black-painted windows of the Ukrainian Café shielded the interior from inquisitive eyes on the pavement. Inside, the odor of cooking filled the air, and every time the door to the kitchen opened and closed, the clatter of dishes drowned out the voices of the patrons.

Lev and Daria, at a table in the rear, were unaware of their surroundings. Plates of hot borscht stood cooling on the table in front of them, untouched. She was staring at him, white-faced.

"Lev, if you're going back to Moscow tomorrow, why have you told me all these ugly stories?"

"Because they're true. At least in substance, if not in detail."

"But that filthy gossip about Chernov—"

"You don't believe your husband was the lover of the Mad Major? It's what everyone believes. That he seduced Chernov in order to find out the location of some stolen weapons in the railway freightyard, and then goaded him into a drunken game of Russian roulette, until Chernov blew his brains out."

"Oh my God, Lev."

"Ask anyone at the Metropolitan Café. They were alone together in Chernov's flat the night he died. That's common knowledge."

"It doesn't matter. I won't believe it."

"Do you enjoy the comfort of that elegant house you're living in?" Lev went on relentlessly. "It belonged to a Chinese widow named Sung Mei-ling. She was your husband's mistress. He made love to her in order to get control of her warehouses. After that he threw her over and she committed suicide in despair. Then he bought her house, before anyone else knew it was available."

"No!"

"Two suicides." He paused grimly. "Both of them very profitable for your husband."

She shook her head in helpless denial.

"I've already explained to you about the girl in Madame Vera's dress shop." Lev flung himself back and stared moodily down at the table. "That's still going on."

"If that's true . . . I think it hurts most of all."

She remembered the beautiful fair-haired girl in the yellow silk gown, and closed her eyes.

"Daria, it's *all* true." As she remained silent, he leaned forward, narrowing his eyes. His voice grew husky. "Don't stay with a man like that, Daria. He's betrayed you before, and he'll keep doing it. Again and again."

She said nothing.

"Why don't you understand the truth?"

"What is the truth?"

"That you can leave him."

"No."

"Don't you see it?"

"Even if I left Nicholas . . . even if I wanted to . . . where would I go?"

"Come back to Moscow with me."

"Lev!"

"Why not? Back to Russia, where you belong. Where a whole other life is waiting for you, full of new challenges and new opportunities. Away from a world of trickery and crime."

"It's not like that. You don't understand."

"I understand that you're living in a house with bloodstained walls, a house that belonged to one of your husband's mistresses. Doesn't that sicken you? If not, think of the girl in the dress shop."

"I am thinking of her," she said. Once more the vision of the exquisite girl in Madame Vera's dress shop came back to her mind. She pressed her hands together in her lap, lowering her head. "I once said," she whispered, half to herself, "that I wouldn't care if Nicholas made love to every girl between here and Shanghai." But she'd been young and ignorant then, she thought. She hadn't known how much it would hurt.

She looked up at last and realized that Lev wasn't listening. He was staring past her at the front of the café. An intent, narrow-eyed expression crossed his face. She started to turn her head, to see what he was looking at.

"Don't turn your head," he said abruptly. "Just sit still. Don't look until I tell you."

"What's wrong?"

"I think we have some unwelcome visitors." He pretended to drink some soup. "All right, look now. But be very casual."

She glanced out of the corner of her eye at the front tables near the door. Two Japanese men sat at one table, looking out of place in their neat business suits. A lone customer sat at another table, sipping a glass of beer. He was also Japanese.

Daria gasped and looked away. "Lev, I know that man."

"Which one?"

"The one sitting by himself. His name is Nishimoto. He's in charge of espionage at the Japanese Military Mission. But he pretends to be a photography expert."

"Does he know you?"

"Yes, we met at my wedding reception."

"Then I don't suppose you want to meet him again." Lev tightened his lips. "And I don't particularly care to speak to the Japanese either." He rubbed his cheek. "I've had a taste of their interrogation methods. I wonder . . ." After a moment he looked at her steadily. "Daria, we'd better leave."

"Yes, you're right." She hesitated. "Past the door?"

"No, through the kitchen. But not yet."

He called over the waitress, who was passing by with a tray, and spoke to her in a low voice as she bent over the table. She straightened up and nodded. Then she moved away.

"She's going to drop the tray of dishes," Lev said to Daria. "When she does, people will come running out of the kitchen. It's a signal for a commotion. As soon as it happens, we'll duck into the kitchen, then out the back way."

"Is there an entrance to the street?"

"Not through the yard, it's fenced. But we can go through the watchmaker's shop next door." He paused. "This may be unnecessary, but I don't think so. Not with your friend Nishimoto on the scene."

She nodded tensely.

"So we'll do all we can to get rid of them, all right?"

"Yes, all right."

A muffled shriek suddenly sounded, accompanied by a great crash of silverware, the clang of a metal tray, and the smashing of crockery. The waitress had dropped her tray. She wrung her hands, moaning loudly.

"What the hell?" The cook, red-faced and sweating, stood in the kitchen door, shouting abuse while his helpers peered over his shoulder.

Lev stood up and grabbed Daria by the wrist. "Now!"

She just had time to glimpse Nishimoto and his two companions springing to their feet before she and Lev were hurrying through the kitchen door and into the kitchen.

"This way."

The back door stood next to an ancient, corroded sink. The door was latched, and the metal was rusty. Lev struggled with it briefly, cursing under his breath. Daria imagined she heard footsteps behind her. She whirled, to see the cook standing over her, and smelled his pungent sweat.

"Go ahead. I'll latch it again when you're out," he muttered.

The door was open. They went through it into the backyard; it slammed behind them. She saw heaps of dirty snow piled by the wall, and overflowing cans of garbage illuminated by the light from the kitchen window. A cat slunk away and huddled by the board fence, snarling, its eyes burning green in the darkness.

Lev was crossing the yard to another building. He was knocking softly on a door. She hurried to join him.

"Perhaps he's gone to bed," she whispered.

"No, he's an old man. He'll be working late, he always does."

She glanced over her shoulder. "Will they follow us into the yard?"

"I don't know. We'll try to lose them on the street."

"If he opens the door."

Just then it opened. A slight old man with white hair stood in a crack of light, peering into the yard. "Who's there?"

"We need a short cut, Dedushka. May we use your shop?"

"Ah. Yes, come in."

He stood aside. They brushed past him into the hallway, breathing hard. She inhaled dust and the odor of mice. The door shut behind them. She began to feel safer.

"Wait a few moments," the old man said. "Give yourself time to catch your breath."

"We don't have time. Someone may be following us."

"I don't hear anything."

They all listened. She could hear nothing but the meow of the cat in the yard and the ticking of clocks.

"Come this way," the old man said.

He led them through the passageway and into the shop, turning off a light as he went. The long, narrow shop was lit only by the light of a streetlamp falling through the window. The street outside looked deserted. Daria shivered, wishing there were people out there. Little ticking noises surrounded her, clocks and watches on the shadowy shelves on either side. She put her hand out and touched a wooden counter. She could hear Lev breathing beside her.

"We won't gain anything by waiting," he said in a low voice. "No matter what they've decided to do."

"Do you suppose they've given up?"

"They won't give up that easily."

"But why haven't they followed us?"

"We'll soon find out." He took her hand and drew her to the front door. The old man watched them in the shadows. Lev whispered his thanks, and the watchmaker nodded silently. Then Lev opened the door and they slipped out onto the street.

"Which way?" she asked, looking to either side. The street seemed innocent and empty, the packed snow gleaming yellow under the streetlamps, the livery stable padlocked and deserted halfway up the block. The Ukrainian Café itself appeared quiet behind its black windows.

"To the left. Once we turn that corner, we'll find pedestrians."

But they'd only taken a few steps when Lev pulled her back into the doorway. An automobile was gliding slowly around the corner and moving down the center of the road.

"Citroën," Lev whispered.

The automobile was a seven-passenger French-made sedan, a Citroën. Three men sat in the front seat. Daria felt a chill in the pit of her stomach as she realized they were looking for her. The pursuit was suddenly terribly real. The automobile was like a hunting animal. Moving slowly. Slowly. Crawling along the road, headlights questing.

She shrank back into the doorway. Finally the car went past and turned the far corner.

"They'll circle around again," Lev whispered. "We can't go left."

"Can we go back to the Ukrainian Café?"

"They'll be expecting that. Somebody will be watching the place. Come on. We'll have to try to lose them on the waterfront."

Turning right, they began to run, trying to cover as much ground as they could while they were out of sight of the automobile.

They reached the end of the block and turned right again. Run, she told herself. Strange sounds; unhuman. Chittering of rats under the splintery piers stretching into the icebound river. This was the waterfront. And smells. Barrels of dried tobacco. Kegs of uncured dogskin. *My God, what a stench. Keep running.* How loud their footsteps sounded on these empty warehouse-lined streets. But there was no Citroën.

They stopped for breath in the doorway of a warehouse that loomed huge and silent above them. On one side was the frozen river, on the other side the snowy street.

"Have we lost them?" she whispered, panting.

"I don't know." Lev was breathing hard. "Damn. This is no place to be trapped. I don't see any taxis, I don't see anything."

Just then they heard the purr of a motor.

Maybe it was a taxi, she thought desperately. The sound grew closer. Then they saw the automobile.

It was the Citroën.

Headlights struck her full in the face. She threw up her arm. She heard a strange crack-thud noise. *Pinggg.*

"Run!" Lev yelled.

She began to run—into a narrow alley, too small for a car, hearing only the pounding of her own feet, the

469

whistling of her own breath, the laboring of her own lungs. She couldn't even tell if Lev was behind her. Someone else was running. She heard many feet. Not the automobile, she thought. Nishimoto and the others had left the car and were pursuing on foot. Another of those dull thudding noises. She knew it was a bullet. Someone was shooting. Were they shooting at her? A voice yelled stop. That wasn't Lev. She didn't stop. Out of the alley, into a road.

Clop-clop, clop-clop, clop-clop . . . a new noise. Someone's hand gripped her upper arm in a fierce and hurting clasp. Her knees turned to water, then she realized it was Lev.

"Daria, there's a droshky. Climb in."

She nodded, not looking back, and ran for the droshky in the middle of the road. Lev was already grabbing the reins of the gaunt, bony horse, halting the carriage.

"What do you think you're doing!" The isvostchik, a red-faced man in a fur hat and long fur coat, was standing up and yelling at them indignantly. Daria hurled herself into the carriage, gasping for breath.

"Get that horse moving, comrade, we can pay." Lev had leaped up beside her.

After a moment the isvostchik grunted. "Where are you going?"

"Try the Street of the Georgians."

"No, not there," Daria whispered urgently, clutching his arm. Nicholas was at the Caucasus Restaurant on the Street of the Georgians. "Anywhere else."

"Anywhere," Lev said through his teeth. "Just hurry."

The driver turned in his seat and whipped up the horse. *Clop-clop, clop-clop.* Daria began to catch her breath. Were they being followed? They would know soon enough. She flung herself back in the jolting droshky, listening to her heart beat.

In the private room upstairs at the Causasus Restaurant, the dinner was coming to an end. The logs in the fireplace were hissing softly. The men lingered over the ritual brandy and cigars. General Togawa had been displeased with the food. The soup had tasted extremely peculiar. The roast lamb was too bland; he preferred more salt in his food.

The gravy was too thick and too floury. And the dessert —sweet meringue! Impossible. Inedible.

He shoved aside the dessert plate and accepted a cigar from his aide. As he relaxed in his chair, he began to look more amiable.

He started a conversation, for the first time, with his Russian guest.

"So, Mr. Federovsky," he remarked, "you are a newcomer to Manchuria."

"Like many others, General."

"Yes, yes. But not all are so successful."

"I've been particularly fortunate."

The general smiled skeptically. "Colonel Matsuura tells me you are very clever."

"It's kind of him to say so."

"Indeed." The general narrowed his eyes, waving his cigar. "Tell me, Mr. Federovsky. Where is it you do your banking?"

"The Russo-Asiatic Bank, General."

"*So deska.* Is that so? I have some advice for you, if you would like to hear it."

"Certainly."

"We are about to open many branches of the Bank of Chosen, throughout Manchuria. There will be a branch in Harbin, as well as Mukden, Dairen, Port Arthur. Those who deal with the Bank of Chosen from now on will be in a favorable position with our government."

"That's very interesting, General Togawa." Nicholas smiled. "I'm sure it's good advice."

"I see you understand me." The general put the cigar into his mouth. His spectacles glittered in the firelight. He belched softly, then frowned. "And now let us discuss the development of the Fushan mines. Of course they will be developed with Japanese capital. But perhaps there's room for an outsider. Those who cooperate with the Imperial Army will have many advantages in Manchuria."

A log fell apart in a shower of sparks in the fireplace. Kenji Matsuura mopped his face with his handkerchief; the room was very warm. Time passed.

The isvostchik twisted on his seat in the moving droshky and turned his head to glare at his two young passengers.

He reined his bony horse; the carriage stopped. "Do you know where we are?" he demanded, waving his hand at the dark snowy street that lay ahead. "We're on the fringe of Nahaloika." He drew his eyebrows together in a scowl. "That's not for Ilya Maximovitch," he muttered, and tugged his fur hat lower on his forehead. "Not at this hour of night."

"Very well, Ilya Maximovitch," Lev said sardonically. Daria saw that he was fingering something in his pocket. "We'll part company here and now, if that's how you want it."

"Pay me before you go, my fine young friend."

Daria climbed down to the pavement as Lev searched for coins to pay the driver. She had never been in Nahaloika, she thought, peering ahead. It was the underworld district of the city. The streets looked narrow and cold, and she thought the cobblestone alleys had a sinister appearance, gleaming wetly under the streetlamps. She thought she saw a face peering from behind a grimy curtain at a second-story window. It was a yellow face like a skull . . . oh God, she must be imagining it, because now she didn't see anything at all. She wrapped her coat around herself and shivered.

"I would like to go home," she said faintly to Lev, when he joined her.

"We'll find you a taxi." He took her arm. "But the streets aren't safe. Not here. We'll telephone from inside."

"Where?" She looked around her at the looming buildings.

"I know of a cabaret a few doors from here, it's called the Blue Heaven. We'll go there."

They began to walk quickly, side by side, heels tapping against the cobblestones. A door opened and closed just below street level to her left, and she heard a burst of music and saw a smoky interior, crowded tables, and a wooden stage.

"Here," Lev said, stopping. "The Blue Heaven."

He drew her down a short flight of steps to the door that had just closed. He pushed it open again and gestured her inside. She went in hesitantly, then stood blinking in the atmosphere of noise, smoke, and sweat mingled with the reek of cheap perfume. The light coming from a blue

472

lightbulb in the ceiling cast a sickly glow over the patrons. The room seemed to be filled with women in silk dresses with rouge on their cheeks, beaded mascara on their lashes, and dark smudges beneath their eyes. The men with them were gaunt and shabbily dressed, laughing feverishly in hollow voices, holding cigarettes in nicotine-stained fingers. The blue light made them all look like corpses. It seemed like a glimpse of hell, she thought dazedly. How odd. The place was called the Blue Heaven.

She put out her hand to steady herself and drew it back quickly when it touched something wet and cold; a galvanized iron bin packed with ice. It was the *zakuska* tray, offering pickled beets, hard-boiled eggs, black bread, and pickled onions. All the food had a bluish tint.

"Sit down at the front," Lev said into her ear. "There's a table empty by the stage. I'll join you in a minute."

She nodded and moved into the room. When she found the empty table, she sat down. She was overdressed in her coat and hat and gloves, but she didn't care.

The cabaret was just starting. An emaciated woman in a low-cut velvet gown stalked onto the stage. A gold crucifix gleamed beween her skinny breasts. One spotlight picked out her face as faint applause pattered through the room. The music began, a violin and accordion, and the woman extended her arms and began to sing, pleadingly, stridently, begging the audience to like her. The song was *Landushi, Lilies of the Valley*, but she was singing it too fast, Daria thought. It didn't matter. The woman needed applause, approval, and she moved her bony hips in a desperate plea for attention, back and forth, around and around. The song ended abruptly, too abruptly, and she stopped at once and went limp, like a puppet abandoned by the puppet-master. The applause was light and scattered. The woman looked as if she were about to cry.

Then a young man with feverishly glittering eyes rose from one of the tables. He wore a muffler wound around his throat to disguise the fact that he had no collar. He unpinned a wilted rose from the lapel of his overcoat and threw it onto the stage. "Bravo," he said hoarsely.

The woman stooped and picked up the flower, smiling gratefully, showing uneven teeth. The music began again.

Daria thought she had stepped into a nightmare. She

shuddered and glanced at the door, wondering what had happened to Lev. Then her hand flew to her mouth; her eyes widened. Fear stabbed through her.

No! It couldn't be!

Nishimoto and his two companions were standing in the entrance, surveying the room.

She couldn't stay where she was, she thought desperately, averting her face. She had to move. But she felt paralyzed. Agonizing seconds went by, and she still couldn't move.

A noise cracked, over the song and the music. Glass shattered. Sound exploded. The room plunged into darkness. The woman on the stage shrieked, and so did someone else, as bits of broken glass showered down from the ceiling and onto the floor and the tables. The lightbulb, Daria thought. She put her hand up to her cheek, feeling wet sticky blood. She'd been cut.

Somebody yelled, "Get under the tables, they're shooting!"

"This man is hit," screamed somebody else. Then another shriek: "Oh my God, I think this man is dead!"

Lev? she wondered wildly. She put herself into motion and threw herself to the floor.

She remained there in the dark for what seemed like centuries, listening to wailing moans and the scuffling of feet, wondering what had happened to Lev. Then she almost fainted with relief at hearing his voice beside her.

"Onto the stage. There's a side exit."

They crawled together over broken glass in the darkness, which was fitfully illuminated now by the spotlight playing over the room, then onto the wooden stage. She stood upright, hands extended, stumbled, groped, bumped into the wall, finally felt cold air slap her face and knew they'd found the door. They went through it into the alley. She took a long gasping breath, feeling her knees shake.

"There are only two of them now," Lev said grimly, standing against the brick wall.

"Then it was you who was shooting." The icy air hit her face, stinging her where she was cut.

He nodded. "There's no time to talk now. Let's get out of this dead end."

They began to edge cautiously along the wall of the

alley until they reached the street. Then they stopped. Nishimoto and his aide were standing on the pavement, intent on watching the front entrance of the cabaret. The second man suddenly turned and saw them. He raised his arm and shouted, pointing his finger.

"Across the street!" Lev pushed her in the small of the back. She dashed into the road, narrowly avoiding the hooves of a droshky horse, stumbled on a patch of ice, found her balance, kept running, and heard another shot. Then a confusion of sounds: the horse whinnying, a man's deep-throated scream, the droshky driver roaring curses. Hooves stamped, followed by another stream of curses. She turned once to see what had happened, and glimpsed a man's figure lying in the road beneath the frantically rearing horse, before she felt Lev's hand close over her wrist, pulling her. "Don't stop! Keep running!"

She was pounding beside him down the dark street, into the waiting maze of Nahaloika.

Across the city, on the Street of the Georgians, a startling event was taking place.

The quiet room at the Caucasus Restaurant had become a place of sickening, retching horror.

General Togawa's gold-rimmed spectacles lay shattered on the floor beside the table, one lens ground into powder by a heedless foot. No one was bothering about the spectacles. Three men knelt around the figure of the general himself, who lay doubled up on the floor vomiting violently. Whenever a spasm of retching stopped, he screamed for water. Every time he drank, he threw it up again. The sour smell of vomit filled the air.

The general began to clutch his stomach, yelling in Japanese. His fingers scratched and tore at the cloth of his shirt, trying to get at the skin, trying to tear out the burning agony inside. The quiet snap of burning logs in the fireplace made an ironic contrast to his writhing figure.

Nicholas watched him grimly, standing apart, a dead cigar in his fingers. Poison, he thought. The one thing the Japanese hadn't anticipated. Arsenic? Arsenic was supposed to be tasteless, and the general had complained about the taste of the soup. Whatever it was, the waiter must have known. Yes, it was the waiter. He'd be long gone by now.

The general's face had taken on the hideous dark blue color of cyanosis. His voice was growing feeble, and his features looked strangely sunken. Yes, this was arsenic poisoning, Nicholas thought. One of the men stooping over him began to feel for the general's pulse in his wrist. All the faces bending over the fallen man were ashen and glistening with sweat.

Hopeless, Nicholas thought. They must have given him enough to kill an ox.

"Kolya, he's dying." Kenji Matsuura was standing by his elbow. His voice was a hoarse whisper. "No doctor, no hospital can help now."

"I'm afraid you're right." Nicholas put the dead cigar into his mouth, not looking at Matsuura.

"We have to think about ourselves."

Nicholas whirled to face the colonel. There was a desperate glint in Kenji's eyes.

"Don't you see?" Matsuura whispered. "We have to do something about Saburo Nishimoto."

The dying man had stopped struggling. He lay stretched out on the floor, sunken-faced. He was groaning rhythmically, inhumanly, like a machine.

"Kolya, listen." Matsuura stepped closer to Nicholas. His voice became an urgent hiss. "Who knew about this meeting place tonight? Think back."

"What are you implying?"

"I'm not implying. I'm asking you directly—did you tell your wife about the Caucasus Restaurant?"

Nicholas didn't answer. Of course he had.

"Nishimoto suspects her, I told you that. If he implicates Madame Federovska in the general's death, he will implicate you—*and I am your friend.*"

The general's groans were growing weaker. Another even more sickening odor was added to that of sour vomit. It signaled the end, Nicholas thought. A matter of minutes now. He stood silent, biting down on the dead cigar, remembering the unknown young man standing beside Daria in the photograph Nishimoto had shown him. Who was it, he asked himself. Was it a lover—had Daria betrayed him? If so . . .

"I will deal with my wife," he said finally, his voice sounding strangled in his own ears. "There'll be time enough to think about Nishimoto tomorrow."

In a Nahaloika alley, Lev spoke tautly to Daria. They stood pressed closely together against a brick wall, listening for footsteps along the pavement beyond the end of the alley. The air was cold, damp, still, without any wind. One streetlamp spilled light over the cobblestones of the street, leaving the alley in shadows. "It's only Nishimoto now," Lev said between his teeth. "If we can lose him, we'll be free."

"Will we, Lev? He saw me with you tonight. He'll tell my husband. I should have told Nicholas before, about meeting you." She bit her lip.

"We'll talk about it at the railroad station tomorrow."

"I haven't said I'll come," she began. But Lev's hand was over her mouth and he was hissing, "Be quiet, I—hear something."

Were those footsteps coming along the cobblestones? She was so weary and filled with worry; her body ached with running and her ears strained to hear footsteps, gunshots. Suppose Nishimoto found them—what would he do, what was an interrogation like? It would be worse than this pursuit, much worse . . . She leaned tiredly against Lev, who put his arm around her.

A drunk went reeling by along the pavement and then disappeared from sight, heel taps echoing in the darkness.

"I have one bullet left," Lev muttered. "I'm saving it for our Japanese friend. But I don't intend to waste it on a wild shot."

"Maybe he's given up."

"There's a Japanese belief called Bushido, the Way of the Samurai. If Nishimoto follows the code of Bushido, I don't think he'll give up."

She felt the tenseness of his body against her. She spoke just to say something. "How did you think of the name the Gadfly?"

"I found it in a book, an English novel."

They both listened for sounds. There was nothing.

"I'll lend it to you some day."

"I don't read English very well."

A thin, distant shout came from somewhere across the street, then a window slammed.

"It's translated," Lev said. She glanced up and saw his shadowy face. She couldn't read his expression. "You can have a *nom de guerre* too, if you like," he said in a low voice. "We'll call you Gemma. That's the name of the girl in the book."

She felt a sudden ache of pity and regret and anguish, and looked away, wondering what would become of all this. What was she doing in this alley with Lev? Why was she here instead of home . . . with Nicholas? *He has a mistress.* Hurt rose up in her again.

Lev's body stiffened. Someone else was walking along the street beyond the alley. They both listened, standing very still.

This time the footsteps were hard and deliberate, click-click-click. Nishimoto, she thought. He hadn't given up. He was still coming.

Lev withdrew the gun from his pocket.

A shadow flattened itself against the wall of the alley. Daria felt her heart hammering in her throat.

"If you are the Gadfly, why don't you shoot?" called a voice. She recognized it. She'd heard it in her own drawing room.

"My gun is empty," Lev called back.

"I wish to speak with you, Gadfly. Come out here."

"You'll have to stand in the light, so I can see you."

Nishimoto laughed harshly. Instead of answering, he fired his gun. The bullet pinged against the brick wall. "My gun is not empty!" he called. "Remember that!" He sprang forward into the shadows, moving too quickly to form a target. Lev pulled Daria deeper into the alley. She wondered where they were going; a blank wall was behind them. Nishimoto would be on them any minute.

No. Lev pushed a door open in the wall; she hadn't even seen it. A sweet, terrible odor rushed out at her. Lev shoved her through the doorway, leaped through himself, and slammed home the bolt, then stood listening. They were in semidarkness. A fist began to pound from outside. She wondered if the door would withstand a bullet. Perhaps Nishimoto was saving his bullets too.

"We do not bolt that door," said a soft voice behind

478

them. They both turned. A tall, thin Chinese man in a scarlet dragon robe was regarding them calmly with slitted eyes. His hands were in the sleeves of his robe. Behind him, on either side, stretched two narrow rooms, dimly lit, furnished with tiers of wooden shelves with wooden headrests. Unmoving figures lay on the shelves, surrounded by clouds of drifting smoke.

She recognized the odor. It was opium.

"That door is for customers who are acquainted with this house," the Chinese man said. He inclined his head. "The House of a Thousand Dreams," he added, breathing the name. He allowed a faint smile to cross his lips. "The door is never locked."

"It is now," Lev said grimly. The pounding continued from outside. "At least until we leave."

"Then leave quickly."

"Is there a front door?"

"Certainly."

The pounding had stopped. Either Nishimoto was still in the alley, Daria thought, or he was going around to the front entrance. There was no way to tell.

"We can't take a chance on opening this door," Lev said, reading her mind. "He might be out there waiting. I think I'll let him come inside. We'll settle it right here."

"I wish no trouble," the Chinese man said.

"Your customers won't know the difference," Lev replied cynically. "They're already in dreamland." He pulled some paper money from his pocket. "To cover any disturbance you might have."

The money changed hands almost invisibly, disappearing into the scarlet sleeves.

"The front entrance is at the end of the passageway," the Chinese man said with a courteous bow. He melted into the shadows of the adjoining room.

"Daria." Lev took her by the arms. "He'll be here in a second. I need one clear shot. It has to count. The minute he opens the door."

Suppose Lev missed, she thought, but didn't dare to say it. She couldn't think about any future beyond this minute. She raised her face, gazing anxiously into his eyes, and he bent his head and kissed her. It was a strange, sweet, passionate kiss, born of the dangers of the night. Time

479

stopped, whirled, shivered in an opium dream. Then Lev released her and shoved her into one of the opium-filled, smoky rooms off the passage. For a wild moment, inhaling the opium smell, she thought of Shih Lung and the Village of the Stone Dragon.

Then she heard, simultaneously, the opening of a door, the sound of a cry, and the crack of a gun. No, it was more than one gunshot. It was two. Three. Oh God, she couldn't tell, everything was so confused. She heard the thud of a body, but now it was silent again, horribly silent, and the figures all around her in their opium trance still hadn't moved. They lay quietly on their wooden shelves, dreaming.

Seconds crawled, stretched into years.

Lev came to the door, and Daria felt her body go weak. "As soon as we drag Nishimoto's body into the alley," he said hoarsely, "we can get out of here. I'll find a way to get you home."

She stared at him.

"Then you can think about tomorrow."

Tomorrow! There would be a tomorrow. This was over. It was really over.

She buried her face in her hands.

She sat in the taxi, at last, on her way to the house of yellow brick, slumped against the seat, too tired to think. She wondered wearily what time it was. Very late. Perhaps close to dawn.

Brendan opened the gate for her and paid the taxi driver. She noticed that he was fully dressed, although unshaven, but she dismissed it. She could think only of her own bedroom.

She passed through the quiet, sleeping house to the south pavilion in a kind of trance. But she stopped on the threshold of her bedroom.

The light was burning by her bedside. Nicholas sat in the chair beside the table, staring at her with eyes that were blazing blue ice. He was still in his dinner clothes.

"I think we'd better have a talk, Daria. Now." He clenched his jaw, cleared his throat. "Suppose you start," he said, "by telling me where you've been."

Chapter 40

She couldn't answer. Words and phrases tumbled over themselves in her mind, but she couldn't frame a sentence. Where should she begin, she asked herself, transfixed by blazing blue eyes, what should she speak of first? Lev was the Gadfly. Was that the first thing to say?

Nicholas was staring at her. "What happened to your cheek?" he said at last. "You've been cut."

She put her hand up to the dried blood. She'd forgotten all about it. She felt herself swaying on her feet. She felt weary, confused, unable to answer any questions. Suppose she said she was cut by a lightbulb, she asked herself half-hysterically, what would that mean? "Nicholas, I'd like to go to bed."

"Yes, it's rather late." His voice was coldly ironic. He glanced at the little crystal clock on the bedside table. It was four o'clock. "Still, since you've appeared so unexpectedly in the middle of the night with rumpled clothes and blood on your cheek, I think we have matters to discuss."

"Can't we speak of it in the morning?"

"No, Daria. We cannot."

He was the Man of Ice. He was someone out of an old nightmare of hers, a terrifying figure from the Siberian boxcar, and she felt a shocking and unexpected surge of anger. Nishimoto was dead, she thought. But she was still being tormented. By Nicholas. But he was not the tender lover of the *Kwan Yin*. He was someone she barely knew.

A man who told her he loved her yet lay in the arms of a golden-haired girl. Defiance rose up in her. She had a shivering foreboding of disaster, but she plunged ahead, lifting her chin.

"What would you like to know?" she asked. "Where I've been?"

"We can begin with that explanation."

"I have been with Lev Omansky."

She saw that the name meant nothing to him.

"An old friend," she added. "I mentioned him once before, a long time ago. You've probably forgotten."

"Then you lied about where you were going. It was not a committee meeting, after all."

What did it matter, she thought savagely. *He* had lied. Whenever he spent time with the girl from Madame Vera's dress shop, he was lying. Now all the stories Lev had told her came back to her in a flood of memory, and she clenched her teeth, trying to subdue her anger.

"Can't we talk about it tomorrow," she said in a low mutter.

"No. We will talk about it now."

She set her mouth and didn't answer. A long, terrible silence came over the room. The crystal clock ticked. She heard her own breathing.

"Very well," Nicholas said finally, crossing one ankle on his knee. "Suppose I ask you something else. What do you know about the fate of General Togawa?"

"Nothing. I don't know what you're talking about."

"Is Lev Omansky your Bolshevik friend from Siberia?"

"Yes."

"Then I suppose you mentioned to him that we were meeting at the Caucasus Restaurant tonight."

"No, I didn't."

"Why should I believe you?" he asked pleasantly.

"We had other things to talk about," she burst out, unable to help herself.

Nicholas's face darkened. "I see." He seemed to struggle with himself for a moment before he remarked, "Matters of a personal nature, no doubt."

"Yes!"

His face was chiseled from marble. He was terrible and

beautiful and frightening, the Man of Ice, and she almost hated him. She was tired, so tired. "We talked about you," she cried. "And how you got this house, and everything in it!"

"How did I get this house?"

She ignored the question and asked one of her own. "Who is Sung Mei-ling?"

It was Nicholas's turn to remain silent. Only his eyes were alive, blue fire.

"And the girl from Madame Vera's dress shop," Daria whispered, "who is she?"

"You've learned a great deal from your Bolshevik friend," Nicholas said tightly. "All the techniques of argument. How to score points in debate. Is that what you're doing? Trying to win a contest?"

"No."

They stared at one another, locked in icy cages of anger and withdrawal.

"Did you betray the meeting place tonight, Daria?"

"I told you, I did not!"

"I've been betrayed before, you know, it's not a new experience."

Her bosom rose and fell with her breath.

"Some day I must tell you all about Céline; it might amuse you."

She couldn't bear the tone of his voice. Or the mention of Céline.

"You're hateful," she whispered. "You're cold and hateful, and I don't want to talk any longer."

"You prefer conversation with your old friend, Lev Omansky."

"Yes! Yes, I do! At least he's human!" She was saying things she didn't mean, but she couldn't help it.

"Then why did you come home at all?"

Tick-tock, tick-tock. The clock went on, marking off the seconds.

"I don't know." Her voice had become almost inaudible. She struggled to speak through the choking lump in her throat. She put both hands to her face. "Lev asked me to come back with him to Moscow," she said clearly, after a great effort. "Perhaps I will."

483

She averted her face, not wanting to look at him. She sensed that he had risen to his feet. She sensed his rage. His voice came to her from a long distance away.

"How long have you been meeting your lover?"

She'd never thought she would hear Nicholas speaking to her that way. She felt a strange sinking sensation in the pit of her stomach.

"He's not my lover," she said dully.

"How would you describe him, then?"

"He writes a newspaper. He calls himself the Gadfly."

"I see. And you expect me to believe that you told him nothing about General Togawa?"

"Yes, I expect you to believe that."

"And that you've been having an innocent conversation until four o'clock in the morning?"

"It was innocent on our part."

"And that all your secret meetings have been for the sake of an old friendship?"

"Yes." She lowered her gaze. "Everything I told you is true."

He walked to her side. "Then you've been incredibly, abysmally stupid."

She did hate him. He was standing very close now. She wanted to reach out and push him away. "I don't care if you believe me or not." She moved forward and tried to brush past him. "I'm very tired."

"I imagine you are."

Damn you, she thought. All the events of the night were washing over her in a blurred rush of memory. She couldn't think straight.

"Nicholas, I'd like to go to bed."

"In that case, dear Daria," he said icily, "we will go to bed."

He couldn't mean that. Not in anger and dislike, not this way. She made another attempt to go by him, and he took her by the arm. She felt the touch of his hand burning through her sleeve, and felt weak and faint. Incredibly, she wanted him. She wanted his touch. She wanted the hard, exciting length of him pressing against her body, possessing her. She wanted Nicholas. She hated herself. She raised her head. "Please don't touch me," she said in a clear frosty voice that she hardly recognized as her own.

"I don't want you to touch me. Not tonight, perhaps not ever."

Oh, my God. What had she said. Whose were those words?

His face darkened. "Is that how you really feel?" The tone of his voice stabbed her deep inside in some buried, hurting place.

"Yes, it's how I feel. Please let me go."

No. No. She didn't mean it.

"Certainly." Nicholas released her arm, stepped back, and made an ironic half bow. "You are free."

"Thank you." She inclined her head.

"To do whatever you like."

She nodded again.

"You have my permission to leave for Moscow," he said, "any time you please."

"Tomorrow at noon," she replied at once, in that cold, small voice that belonged to someone else.

"If that's your choice."

"Yes. It is." She stared at him defiantly. "Noon, from the railroad station."

"Fine. I'll put the car at your disposal."

She only nodded.

"I don't suppose we'll see each other in the morning."

"Probably not."

"You may write to me when you arrive in Moscow. We may have some matters to settle."

"I suppose we will."

He tightened his jaw. "I'll arrange to leave you some money before you go."

"That's not necessary, I don't need any money. Lev will look after me."

There was no way out of this nightmare trap. It was going on and on. Like a sudden tidal wave it was sweeping her away.

"Of course," he said stiffly. "I should have realized that your friend would look after you. I apologize for my offer."

She had never seen that expression in his eyes before. It was as though her own pain were reflected in his face. She desperately wanted to cry. She saw him very clearly, every detail, every feature—the tired, hurt look, the lines around his mouth, the dark unshaven stubble on his jaw; he wasn't a man of ice at all, he was flesh and blood, and she had never loved him so fiercely. But it was hopeless. She wanted to hurl herself into his arms and be comforted, held, loved. Instead there was this frozen desert between them. No way to cross it.

Nicholas! What was happening!

She wanted to cry out to him, wanted to tell him she'd lied, she didn't mean anything she'd said, but it was too late. He was already crossing the threshold and leaving the bedroom, angry, cold, withdrawn, turning his back on her, and suddenly she was alone.

Chapter 41

Nicholas sat back wearily in the chair in Kenji Matsuura's office. He wondered again what had happened, what had gone wrong. He'd been alone before, and so he would be again. It was useless to fight your destiny, he told himself. It was hopeless to battle fate. But the house of yellow brick was very empty. He hadn't seen Daria at all. She was probably on her way to the railroad station, he thought, with the car and chauffeur.

Let her go, he told himself. She had betrayed him, as Céline had done. Let her go.

"I apologize for the implication that Madame Federovska was involved in last night's affair," Matsuura was saying. He had regained most of his lost confidence, since Nicholas had seen him at the Caucasus Restaurant last night. Now his eyes shone with relief and satisfaction. "We have found the waiter who was responsible. Before he died, he told us what we needed to know."

"I see."

"Your wife had nothing to do with it, Kolya."

So Daria had told him the truth after all, Nicholas thought wearily. But it didn't really make any difference. There were other betrayals, too many to forgive.

"Will Nishimoto believe that, Kenji?" he asked.

"That's another worry which is removed." Matsuura sat back in his swivel chair and sighed with relief. "Nishimoto is dead. He was murdered in Nahaloika, outside an opium den. His body was found this morning in an alley."

487

"How unfortunate," Nicholas said drily.

"Yes, unfortunate for Nishimoto-san. But for you and me, Kolya, it's rather fortuitous." He waved his hand in the air. "So you see, our problems are over.'"

"So it would seem."

Nicholas was only making perfunctory answers to Matsuura. He was still thinking about Daria.

If she'd told him the truth about Togawa, perhaps she'd been telling the truth about other things as well. "He is not my lover," she'd said. "Everything I told you is true."

Perhaps he'd been hasty and harsh.

It was still possible to stop her, he thought. Even if she boarded the train and left Harbin, he could send a telegram to the next station. Tsitsihar, perhaps. He could have her taken off the train and called back to Harbin.

But would she come? He wondered if she would. The cold words that had passed between them last night still echoed in his mind. She wanted to leave him. She wanted to run away, back to Moscow.

But in a quarrel, people said things they didn't mean.

Maybe he'd been a fool.

Maybe it wasn't too late.

The house of yellow brick was very empty.

He brought his mind back to Matsuura. Something the colonel was saying was suddenly setting off a warning bell in his mind. He began to pay attention.

"We're taking our own steps to avenge Togawa's death, Kolya," Matsuura was saying. "We learned from the waiter last night that a group of Bolsheviks is returning to Moscow, on the noon train." He leaned back, making the swivel chair squeak protestingly under his weight. "Or so they believe."

"What do you mean?"

"I think I can assure you that the particular car they are traveling in will never leave the station." Matsuura smiled.

Nicholas stared at him, feeling the blood drain from his face. "Make yourself clearer, Kenji."

Matsuura pulled out his watch and consulted it, then returned it to his pocket with an air of grim satisfaction. "It's now eleven forty-five," he said. "In exactly fifteen minutes, there will be a rather ugly incident at the railroad station." He gazed at Nicholas with a sudden fanaticism in his eyes. "These terrorists will learn what it means, Kolya," he said softly, "to defy the Imperial Japanese Government."

Nicholas sprang to his feet, barely avoiding knocking over the chair.

The noon train.

That was the train Daria was boarding.

She was going to Moscow with the Bolsheviks . . .

Lord, no. This couldn't happen.

It might be too late after all.

"I have to go, Kenji. At once." He was making sudden excuses to Matsuura and leaving the office. Then he was waiting for the lift. He was pacing, for interminable seconds. It was taking too long, he'd use the stairs. Two flights, at a run. Ground floor now, past the desks, the typewriters, the uniformed lieutenant staring after him . . .

Out onto the street. Look for a taxi. *Where the hell is a taxi?*

He was suddenly living in a nightmare of delay and frustration and fear, afraid he would be too late, trying not to believe this was real, knowing it was all too real, wondering how much time he had left.

A taxi stopped and he yanked open the door and sprang into the back seat. "How fast can you get to the railroad station?"

"The traffic is bad today, gospodin."

"I need to make the noon train."

"You didn't leave yourself much time."

"I know that. But hurry."

"I'll do my best."

They moved out into the road. Traffic clogged the way, and Nicholas hunched forward, willing them to move faster, faster.

The railroad station was the usual murmuring confusion of crowds, vendors, rickshaw men, foreigners, military uniforms, grit, soot, and noise.

On the open platform, under the sky, Lev stood peering inside the terminal building, searching the crowd. He was looking for Daria. Suddenly he felt a sense of leaping triumph as he saw a figure hurrying toward him through the crowd. Daria, he thought. She was wearing a green velour coat with a black karakul collar and cuffs, and a matching fur hat, and she carried a black karakul muff in her hand. Beneath the brim of her hat, her face was anxious and pale and worried and very lovely, marred only by the scratch on her cheek. Her huge dark eyes were searching all the faces as she went by. She would see him any minute.

So she'd come after all, he thought, drawing a breath. And just in time—he looked up at the big wall clock—because it was ten minutes to twelve. But there was still enough time to board the train.

He stepped forward to call her. Just at that moment she saw him, and their eyes met.

Everything was about to happen just as he'd hoped, he thought in quiet jubilation, signaling to her with his hand. Somehow, it was all turning out as he dreamed. He stopped worrying about twenty-two Lubianka Street. Yes, there were problems needing to be solved, he knew that, there would be obstacles, setbacks, stubborn difficulties ahead, but he felt strong and happy and confident, now that Daria was moving toward him. Capable of solving any kind of problem. With enough time, he thought, and with enough courage and faith . . .

Then his eyes widened. He stared in sudden, shocking recognition at another face in the crowd. He forgot about Daria, who had almost reached him. He forgot about the second hand sweeping around the big wall clock. Everything receded except the hated, remembered face that was suddenly standing out in the crowd of faces like blood against the snow.

He was remembering a bronevik in Siberia, and a flashing bayonet. He was hearing the sound of a tortured scream. He was recalling words: "Use my rank when you speak to me, pig." He was looking into the face of his tormentor, Lieutenant Haneda.

He'd never hoped for this marvelous, incredible luck, he thought, feeling his body turn icy and his heart start to pound. Haneda. Here in the station. He began to shoulder his way past knots of people, not bothering to apologize, not saying anything, ignoring angry comments, not even hearing them, his eyes fixed on his goal, the strutting, arrogant figure in the Japanese uniform.

Alone at that, he thought. Better and better. Perfect. He

had a surprise for the lieutenant, he thought. His fingers closed around the gun in his pocket.

"Lev, what's wrong? We don't have much time. I'm sorry I'm late."

Daria. Yes, Daria. Go over to the second car from the end, Daria, it's standing on the platform, meet me there, meet me on board. I'll be there in just a moment— He was speaking automatically, still keeping his eyes fixed on Haneda, who had paused to buy cigarettes from a vendor.

"I have things to explain, Lev." ·

Not now, Daria. Meet me on board. He put her aside gently with a hand on her arm, directing her toward the platform. The train was being announced, he realized, time was running out. She moved hesitantly toward the platform. As he saw her go he was reassured. He quickened his step.

"Good morning, Lieutenant Haneda. Remember me?"

The man's eyes narrowed in instant recognition as he turned and saw Lev and looked at the scar on Lev's cheek.

"I have a gun in my pocket, Lieutenant. It's almost at your belly. So just do as I say."

Haneda's lip curled in a smile. He stepped back. "You will not do anything foolhardy and reckless in the railroad station."

"Oh won't I?" Lev walked up very close and spoke in a low quick voice, detailing the death of Nishimoto-san in a Nahaloika alley. As he spoke he began to shove Haneda toward the open platform, nudging him with the barrel of the gun still hidden in his pocket.

Haneda tried to maintain his air of contempt. "Just what do you think you're accomplishing?" he demanded. But his arrogance was starting to crumble.

"We're going to get on board the train, because it's almost twelve o'clock. And then we're going to have a discussion. The two of us. Don't stop, Lieutenant. Keep on walking."

They had reached the train. Haneda looked down the platform, and as he saw the second car from the end, beads of perspiration broke out on his upper lip. He turned to Lev.

"You're acting in a ridiculous and stupid manner," he said, breathing hard.

"I told you to keep on going."

"What's the purpose of this?" They were nearing the second car from the last.

"Stop delaying. You know the purpose. If you do as I say, you may live a little while longer. So don't argue. Just get on board."

They had reached the metal steps. Lev put his foot on the first step and gestured with the gun for Haneda to mount. Haneda stepped back, shaking his head. His muscles were suddenly bunched in visible tension. His eyes were glazed with terror.

He was preparing to run, Lev thought incredulously. It was hard to believe that Haneda would be that stupid. He removed the gun from his pocket, clicking off the safety catch.

Haneda broke into a run, pelting down the platform at full speed with his back turned.

Lev extended his arm and fired. Once. Twice. Someone shouted. A soldier, a policeman, the stationmaster, somebody. Never mind, it was one second to noon, too late to halt the train . . .

Haneda had pitched forward on his face against the concrete, arms outstretched, a crimson stain spreading between his shoulder blades.

Lev slowly lowered his arm. He'd wanted it another way, he thought grimly, feeling the hot metal of the gun against his palm. But Haneda was too much of a coward to face the consequences of his own actions, and so—

Booommm . . .

Lev staggered, trying to keep his balance. The steps had buckled under his feet. Pieces of metal were flying from nowhere, straight at his face. He threw up his arm, trying to shield his eyes. He fell backward. Hot black smoke was suddenly pouring from the windows of the car. People were screaming, somewhere inside. Shrieking. Beneath his body he felt another tremor, heard another explosion, felt the heat of flames. He struggled to breathe against choking fumes, tried to raise himself up, gain his feet, get away, out of this hell, but something fell across his body, crushing his ribs. Inside him, something was torn. He sensed it. The object pinning him down was heavy and sharp. Very heavy. Piercing. Stabbing. He felt pain. Incredible pain.

Get it off. Lift it away from me. What was happening? What was happening to him?

Blessed art Thou O Lord our God, King of the Universe . . .

A woman's voice was screaming. He thought he heard his own name. Daria? Was that Daria? Where was she? Inside that flaming car? Get her out of there . . .

He tried to sit up, but something heavy and hurting was holding him down. He fell back against the searing-hot metal of the steps, thumping his head. But it didn't hurt, suddenly. Nothing did. Not even the torn thing inside him. There was no pain now. None at all. It had gone away. Daria was calling him. Where was she? He tried to see, widening his eyes as far as he could, but everything was getting strangely dark. Why couldn't he see. God, why was it so dark? And he was cold. Very cold. Get a blanket, he thought, I have to keep warm. Turn on the lights, he couldn't see.

Who turned the lights off? Help me. Help me.

No, he didn't need help. He was fine. He was slipping into cool hazy darkness. Everything was blurring out. As in a dream.

He was very very calm and comfortable, even though he was so cold. If only he could see, he thought blurrily, everything would be all right. *Don't worry, Mama, I'll come home to Kiev. Very soon.*

Then slowly, quietly, easily—chillingly—he thought nothing.

Nicholas's taxi was crawling along a traffic-clogged road.

In a surge of fear and frustration he leaped out of the automobile in the middle of the street and slammed the door behind him. He shoved money through the window at the driver. He was still two blocks from the station. But it was already noon. He cursed the traffic, the crowds, the clock, everything that stood in his way, but it was useless, there was no way he could stop time, this was all useless. But he had to try; maybe there was still a chance. Horns were honking. Voices were shouting after him indignantly. Two blocks stretched to two thousand. Two minutes slid by like twin flashes of lightning. His thoughts raced. Maybe Matsuura was mistaken, maybe the plan had gone wrong, maybe this was all foolish panic. *Oh, Lord. Let that be so.*

He reached the railroad station. Knots of people were gathered by the entrance, shouting, gesturing, waving their arms. Uniforms were everywhere. Policemen, soldiers of the warlord, Japanese officers, men with guns who were using the butts like clubs to clear a path inside. Too late, he thought. Icy certainty closed over his mind as he slowed his step. Something had happened. Matsuura's prediction had been hideously accurate.

Two men ran past him carrying a stretcher.

He had to find her, he thought despairingly. Whatever the truth, he had to know it.

He tried not to hear the mocking laughter of fate that was sounding in his head.

He began to push his way into the station, past the shouting, arm-waving policemen who were trying to keep people out. *Damn you. Let me by. Out of my way.* Once or twice he muttered something aloud, but kept shouldering his way forward, until unexpectedly he broke through the last barrier and found himself inside.

He was standing amid pandemonium. Screams, shouting, weeping, smoke pouring out of the platform end of the terminal; madness. But he had to find her. And bring her home. One way or another, he would take Daria home.

He began to make his way toward the platform. This time no one opposed him. All the footsteps were running in the opposite direction, away from the burning, smoking railway car at the end of the platform.

He kept going until he came to the outdoors, where he found himself coughing in clouds of greasy smoke blown by the wind. Shards of broken glass were crunching under his feet. He took out his handkerchief and covered his nose and mouth, steeling himself to start his grisly search. There, he told himself, in that smoking wreckage, there he must begin. He blinked, his eyes tearing in the smoke. He had to find her before anyone else did. He didn't know exactly why. But it was very important. Extremely important. It was everything. All that was left.

A few stumbling figures were appearing out of the smoke. One of them . . . He lowered the handkerchief. No. No. He was imagining it because of his hope. A small figure in a green velour coat was coming toward him, emerging more clearly as a stray gust of wind blew aside the clouds of smoke. Yes, it was so. It was Daria.

She walked into his arms. Trembling, tearstained, grimy, soot-covered, her coat ripped, her stockings torn, her face white, but safe. Alive. He bowed his head.

"Nicholas, he's dead," she whispered against his shoulder.

"Come inside, Daryushka. Out of the smoke."

He led her into the terminal, and over by the wall. The brazen clang of bells was sounding from outside, as fire engines started to arrive. Running feet pounded past them; hoarse voices shouted orders. Daria raised her face.

"Zora was right," she whispered. "Do you remember the gypsy woman?"

"Yes."

"She read my fortune once. She said she saw a swift parting and the death of a blue-eyed man. I thought it was you, Nicholas. But it wasn't." Her voice was trembling. "It was Lev. He's dead. I saw him . . . lying on the steps . . . with a piece of steel across his body—"

"But you're safe. You're not hurt."

"No."

"Then we must thank God." He folded her against him. "This morning I thought . . . I was afraid . . . that you were running away from me." He looked down at her. "Were you, Daryushka? Were you running away from me?"

"No." She hid her face again. "I was just coming to say good-bye to Lev. I could never do that—I could never run away from you. In spite of what I said last night. Because you are my destiny. I know that now. I think I always knew it, from the moment I saw you in the boxcar at Chita Station." She took a long ragged breath. "No matter what we say or do, Nicholas." She tried to smile, gazing up at him. "You see, I realize now that you're not perfect. I'm not looking through a pink haze anymore. I see you as you are."

"And do you still love me?"

"Yes. I will always love you." She stepped back. Tears were standing in her eyes. "What will happen to us, Nicholas? I'm frightened. Who destroyed the train?" She brushed back a strand of hair from her cheek and blinked back her tears. "I hear people say there'll be another war."

"Yes, I believe there will."

"Between China and Japan."

"Some day."

"What will become of us?"

Someone in uniform pushed past them roughly, and Nicholas put a protective arm around her, drawing her close. "I don't know, Daryushka. I can't predict the future. All we can do is love one another, as well and completely as we can, and hope each night that we will see another sunrise in the morning." He studied her gravely, searching her face. "Is that enough?"

"Yes." She sighed, leaning against him. "Oh yes, Nicholas, that will be enough."

Still holding her close, he began to lead her out of the terminal, through the grime, smoke, and shards of broken glass, into the daylight.